Three tycoons – hot-blooded,
passionate, they just
need…wives!

the Greek

TYCOONS' TAKEOVER

Three glamorous, intense novels by
three fabulous writers: Jane Porter,
Anne McAllister and Chantelle Shaw

the Greek

TYCOONS' TAKEOVER

JANE PORTER
ANNE McALLISTER
CHANTELLE SHAW

All the characters in this book have no existence outside the imagination of the author, and have no relation whatsoever to anyone bearing the same name or names. They are not even distantly inspired by any individual known or unknown to the author, and all the incidents are pure invention.

THE GREEK TYCOONS' TAKEOVER
© Harlequin Enterprises II B.V./S.à.r.l. 2010

At the Greek Boss's Bidding, The Antonides Marriage Deal and *The Greek Boss's Bride* were first published in Great Britain by Harlequin Mills & Boon Limited in separate, single volumes.

At the Greek Boss's Bidding © Jane Porter 2007
The Antonides Marriage Deal © Barbara Schenck 2006
The Greek Boss's Bride © Chantelle Shaw 2006

ISBN: 978 0 263 87395 5

010-0610

Harlequin Mills & Boon policy is to use papers that are natural, renewable and recyclable products and made from wood grown in sustainable forests. The logging and manufacturing processes conform to the legal environmental regulations of the country of origin.

Printed and bound in Spain
by Litografia Rosés S.A., Barcelona

At the Greek Boss's Bidding

JANE PORTER

Jane Porter grew up on a diet of Mills & Boon®
romances, reading late at night under the covers so
her mother wouldn't see! She wrote her first book at
age eight and spent many of her school and college
years living abroad, immersing herself in other
cultures and continuing to read voraciously. Now
Jane has settled down in rugged Seattle, Washington,
with her two gorgeous sons. Jane loves to hear from
her readers. You can write to her at PO Box 524,
Bellevue, WA 98009, USA. Or visit her website at
www.janeporter.com

**Don't miss Jane Porter's exciting new novella,
which will be out in November 2010
from M&B™.**

For two of my favourite heroes,
my brothers Dr Thomas W Porter and
Robert George Porter

PROLOGUE

THE helicopter slammed against the rocky incline of the mountain thick with drifts of snow.

Glass shattered, metal crunched and red flames shot from the engine, turning what Kristian Koumantaros knew was glacial white into a shimmering dance of fire and ice.

Unable to see, he struggled with his seatbelt. The helicopter tilted, sliding a few feet. Fire burned everywhere as the heat surged, surrounding him. Kristian tugged his seatbelt again. The clip was jammed.

The smoke seared his lungs, blistering each breath.

Life and death, he thought woozily. Life and death came down to this. And life-and-death decisions were often no different than any other decisions. You did what you had to do and the consequences be damned.

Kristian had done what he had to do and the consequences damned him.

As the roar of the fire grew louder, the helicopter shifted again, the snow giving way.

My God. Kristian threw his arms out, and yet there was nothing to grab, and they were sent tumbling down the mountain face. Another avalanche, he thought, deafened by the endless roar—

And then nothing.

CHAPTER ONE

"*OHI.* No." The deep rough voice could be none other than Kristian Koumantaros himself. "Not interested. Tell her to go away."

Standing in the hall outside the library, Elizabeth Hatchet drew a deep breath, strengthening her resolve. This was not going to be easy, but then nothing about Kristian Koumantaros's case had been easy. Not the accident, not the rehab, not the location of his estate.

It had taken her two days to get here from London—a flight from London to Athens, an endless drive from Athens to Sparta, and finally a bone-jarring cart and donkey trip halfway up the ridiculously inaccessible mountain.

Why anybody, much less a man who couldn't walk and couldn't see, would want to live in a former monastery built on a rocky crag on a slope of Taygetos, the highest mountain in the Peloponnese, was beyond her. But now that she was here, she wasn't going to go away.

"*Kyrios.*" Another voice sounded from within the library and Elizabeth recognized the voice as the Greek servant who'd met her at the door. "She's traveled a long way—"

"I've had it with the bloody help from First Class Rehab. First Class, my ass."

Elizabeth closed her eyes and exhaled slowly, counting to ten as she did so.

She'd been told by her Athens staff that it was a long trip to the former monastery.

She'd been warned that reaching rugged Taygetos, with its severe landscape but breathtaking vistas, was nearly as exhausting as caring for Mr. Koumantaros.

Her staff had counseled that traveling up this spectacular mountain with its ancient Byzantine ruins would seem at turns mythical as well as impossible, but Elizabeth, climbing into the donkey cart, had thought she'd been prepared. She'd thought she knew what she was getting into.

Just like she'd thought she knew what she was getting into when she agreed to provide Mr. Koumantaros's home health care after he was released from the French hospital.

In both cases she had been wrong.

The painfully slow, bumpy ride had left her woozy, with a queasy stomach and a pounding headache.

Attempting to rehabilitate Mr. Koumantaros had made her suffer far worse. Quite bluntly, he'd nearly bankrupted her company.

Elizabeth tensed at the sound of glass breaking, followed by a string of select and exceptionally colorful Greek curses.

"*Kyrios,* it's just a glass. It can be replaced."

"I hate this, Pano. Hate everything about this—"

"I know, *kyrios.*" Pano's voice dropped low, and Elizabeth couldn't hear much of what was said, but apparently it had the effect of calming Mr. Koumantaros.

Elizabeth wasn't soothed.

Kristian Koumantaros might be fabulously wealthy and able to afford an eccentric and reclusive lifestyle in the Peloponnese, but that didn't excuse his behavior. And his behavior was nothing short of self-absorbed and self-destructive.

She was here because Kristian Koumantaros couldn't keep a nurse, and he couldn't keep a nurse because he couldn't keep his temper.

The voices in the library were growing louder again. Elizabeth, fluent in Greek, listened as they discussed her.

Mr. Koumantaros didn't want her here.

Pano, the elderly butler, was attempting to convince that Mr. Koumantaros it wouldn't be polite to send the nurse away without seeing her.

Mr. Koumantaros said he didn't care about being polite.

Elizabeth's mouth curved wryly as the butler urged Mr. Koumantaros to at least offer her some refreshment.

Her wry smile disappeared as she heard Mr. Koumantaros answer that as most nurses from First Class Rehab were large women Ms. Hatchet could probably benefit from passing on an afternoon snack.

"Kyrios," Pano persisted, "she's brought a suitcase. Luggage. Ms. Hatchet intends to stay."

"Stay?" Koumantaros roared.

"Yes, *kyrios.*" The elderly Greek's tone couldn't have been any more apologetic, but his words had the effect of sending Kristian into another litany of curses.

"For God's sake, Pano, leave the damn glass alone and dispense with her. Throw her a bone. Get her a donkey. I don't care. Just do it. *Now.*"

"But she's traveled from London—"

"I don't care if she flew from the moon. She had no business coming here. I left a message two weeks ago with the service. That woman knows perfectly well I've fired them. I didn't ask her to come. And it's not my problem she wasted her time."

Speaking of which, Elizabeth thought, rubbing at the back of her neck to ease the pinch of pain, she *was* wasting time standing here. It was time to introduce herself, get the meeting underway.

Shoulders squared, Elizabeth took a deep breath and pushed the tall door open. As she entered the room, her low heels made a faint clicking sound on the hardwood floor.

"Good afternoon, Mr. Koumantaros," she said. Her narrowed gaze flashed across the shuttered windows, cluttered coffee table, newspapers stacked computer-high on a corner desk. Had to be a month's newspapers piled there, unread.

"You're trespassing, and cavesdropping." Kristian jerked upright in his wheelchair, his deep voice vibrating with fury.

She barely glanced his way, heading instead for the small table filled with prescription bottles. "You were shouting, Mr. Koumantaros. I didn't need to eavesdrop. And I'd be trespassing if your care weren't my responsibility, but it is, so you're going to have to deal with me."

At the table, Elizabeth picked up one of the medicine bottles to check the label, and then the others. It was an old habit, an automatic habit. The first thing a medical professional needed to know was what, if anything, the patient was taking.

Kristian's hunched figure in the wheelchair shuddered as he tried to follow the sound of her movements, his eyes shielded by a white gauze bandage wrapped around his head, the white gauze a brilliant contrast to his thick onyx hair. "Your services have already been terminated," he said tersely.

"You've been overruled," Elizabeth answered, returning the bottles to the table to study him. The bandages swathing his eyes exposed the hard, carved contours of his face. He had chiseled cheekbones, a firm chin and strong jaw shadowed with a rough black beard. From the look of it, he hadn't shaved since the last nurse had been sent packing.

"By whom?" he demanded, leaning crookedly in his chair.

"Your physicians."

"My physicians?"

"Yes, indeed. We're in daily contact with them, Mr. Koumantaros, and these past several months have made them question your mental soundness."

"You must be joking."

"Not at all. There is a discussion that perhaps you'd be better cared for in a facility—"

"Get out!" he demanded, pointing at the door. "Get out now."

Elizabeth didn't move. Instead she cocked her head, coolly examining him. He looked impossibly unkempt, nothing like the sophisticated powerful tycoon he'd reportedly been, with castles and estates scattered all over the world and a gorgeous mistress tucked enticingly in each.

"They fear for you, Mr. Koumantaros," she added quietly, "and so do I. You need help."

"That's absurd. If my doctors were so concerned, they'd be here. And you…you don't know me. You can't drop in here and make assessments based on two minutes of observation."

"I can, because I've managed your case from day one, when you were released from the hospital. No one knows more about you and your day-to-day care than I do. And if you'd always been this despondent we'd see it as a personality issue, but your despair is new—"

"There's no despair. I'm just tired."

"Then let's address that, shall we?" Elizabeth flipped open her leather portfolio and scribbled some notes. One couldn't be too careful these days. She had to protect the agency, not to mention her staff. She'd learned early to document everything. "It's tragic you're still in your present condition— tragic to isolate yourself here on Taygetos when there are people waiting for you in Athens, people wanting you to come home."

"I live here permanently now."

She glanced up at him. "You've no intention of returning?"

"I spent years renovating this monastery, updating and converting it into a modern home to meet my needs."

"That was before you were injured. It's not practical for you to live here now. You can't fly—"

"Don't tell me what I can't do."

She swallowed, tried again. "It's not easy for your friends or family to see you. You're absolutely secluded here—"

"As I wish to be."

"But how can you fully recover when you're so alone in what is undoubtedly one of the most remote places in Greece?"

He averted his head, giving her a glimpse of a very strong, very proud profile. "This is my home," he repeated stubbornly, his tone colder, flintier.

"And what of your company? The businesses? Have you given those up along with your friends and family?"

"If this is your bedside manner—"

"Oh, it is," she assured him unapologetically. "Mr. Koumantaros, I'm not here to coddle you. Nor to say pretty things and try to make you laugh. I'm here to get you on your feet again."

"It's not going to happen."

"Because you like being helpless, or because you're afraid of pain?"

For a moment he said nothing, his face growing paler against the white gauze bandaging his head. Finally he found his voice. "How dare you?" he demanded. "How dare you waltz into my home—?"

"It wasn't exactly a waltz, Mr. Koumantaros. It took me

two days to get here and that included planes, taxis, buses and asses." She smiled thinly. This was the last place she'd wanted to come, and the last person she wanted to nurse. "It's been nearly a year since your accident," she continued. "There's no medical reason for you to be as helpless as you are."

"Get out."

"I can't. Not only have I've nowhere to go—as you must know, it's too dark to take a donkey back down the mountain."

"No, I don't know. I'm blind. I've no idea what time of day it is."

Heat surged to her cheeks. Heat and shame and disgust. Not for her, but him. If he expected her to feel sorry for him, he had another thing coming, and if he hoped to intimidate her, he was wrong again. He could shout and break things, but she wasn't about to cower like a frightened puppy dog. Just because he was a famous Greek with a billion-dollar company didn't mean he deserved her respect. Respect was earned, not automatically given.

"It's almost four o'clock, Mr. Koumantaros. Half of the mountain is already steeped in shadows. I couldn't go home tonight even if I wanted to. Your doctors have authorized me to stay, so I must. It's either that or you go to a rehab facility in Athens. *Your* choice."

"Not much of a choice."

"No, it's not." Elizabeth picked up one of the prescription bottles and popped off the plastic cap to see the number of tablets inside. Three remained from a count of thirty. The prescription had only been refilled a week ago. "Still not sleeping, Mr. Koumantaros?"

"I *can't.*"

"Still in a lot of pain, then?" She pressed the notebook to her chest, stared at him over the portfolio's edge. Probably addicted to his painkillers now. Happened more often than not. One more battle ahead.

Kristian Koumantaros shifted in his wheelchair. The bandages that hid his eyes revealed the sharp twist of his lips. "As if you care."

She didn't even blink. His self-pity didn't trigger sympathy. Self-pity was a typical stage in the healing process—an early stage, one of the first. And the fact that Kristian Koumantaros hadn't moved beyond it meant he had a long, long way to go.

"I do care," she answered flatly. Elizabeth didn't bother to add that she also cared about the future of her company, First Class Rehab, and that providing for Kristian Koumantaros's medical needs had nearly ruined her four-year-old company. "I do care, but I won't be like the others—going soft on you, accepting your excuses, allowing you to get away with murder."

"And what do you know of murder, Miss Holier-Than-Thou?" He wrenched his wheelchair forward, the hard rubber tires crunching glass shards.

"Careful, Mr. Koumantaros! You'll pop a tire."

"*Good.* Pop the goddamn tires. I hate this chair. I hate not seeing. I despise living like this." He swore violently, but at least he'd stopped rolling forward and was sitting still while the butler hurriedly finished sweeping up the glass with a small broom and dustpan.

As Kristian sat, his enormous shoulders turned inward, his dark head hung low.

Despair.

The word whispered to her, summing up what she saw, what she felt. His black mood wasn't merely anger. It was bigger than that, darker than that. His black mood was fed by despair.

He was, she thought, feeling the smallest prick of sympathy, a ruin of a great man.

As swiftly as the sympathy came, she pushed it aside, replacing tenderness with resolve. He'd get well. There was no reason he couldn't.

Elizabeth signaled to Pano that she wanted a word alone with his employer and, nodding, he left them, exiting the library with his dustpan of broken glass.

"Now, then, Mr. Koumantaros," she said as the library doors closed, "we need to get you back on your rehab program. But we can't do that if you insist on intimidating your nurses."

"They were all completely useless, incompetent—"

"All six?" she interrupted, taking a seat on the nearest armchair arm.

He'd gone through the roster of home healthcare specialists in record fashion. In fact, they'd run out of possible candidates. There was no one else to send. And yet Mr. Koumantaros couldn't be left alone. He required more than a butler. He still needed around-the-clock medical care.

"One nurse wasn't so bad. Well, in some ways," he said grudgingly, tapping the metal rim of his wheelchair with his finger tips. "The young one. Calista. And believe me, if she was the best it should show you how bad the others were. But that's another story—"

"Miss Aravantinos isn't coming back." Elizabeth felt her temper rise. Of course he'd request the one nurse he'd broken into bits. The poor girl, barely out of nursing school, had been putty in Kristian Koumantaros's hands. Literally. For a man with life-threatening injuries he'd been incredibly adept at seduction.

His dark head tipped sideways. "Was that her last name?"

"You behaved in a most unscrupulous manner. You're thirty—what?" She quickly flipped through his chart, found his age. "Nearly thirty-six. And she was barely twenty-three. She quit, you know. Left our Athens office. She felt terribly demoralized."

"I never asked Calista to fall in love with me."

"*Love?*" she choked. "Love didn't have anything to do with it. You seduced her. Out of boredom. And spite."

"You've got me all wrong, Nurse Cratchett—" He paused, a corner of his mouth smirking. "You *are* English, are you not?"

"I speak English, yes," she answered curtly.

"Well, Cratchett, you have me wrong. You see, I'm a lover, not a fighter."

Blood surged to Elizabeth's cheeks. "That's quite enough."

"I've never forced myself on a woman." His voice dropped, the pitch growing deeper, rougher. "If anything, our dear delightful Calista forced herself on me."

"Mr. Koumantaros." Acutely uncomfortable, she gripped her pen tightly, growing warm, warmer. She hated his mocking smile and resented his tone. She could see why Calista had thrown the towel in. How was a young girl to cope with him?

"She romanticized me," he continued, in the same infuriatingly smug vein. "She wanted to know what an invalid was capable of, I suppose. And she discovered that although I can't walk, I can still—"

"*Mr. Koumantaros!*" Elizabeth jumped to her feet, suddenly oppressed by the warm, dark room. It was late afternoon, and the day had been cloudless, blissfully sunny. She couldn't fathom why the windows and shutters were all closed, keeping the fresh mountain air out. "I do not wish to hear the details."

"But you need them." Kristian pushed his wheelchair toward her, blue cotton sleeves rolled back on his forearms, corded tendons tight beneath his skin. He'd once had a very deep tan, but the tan had long ago faded. His olive skin was pale, testament to his long months indoors. "You're misinformed if you think I took advantage of Calista. Calista got what Calista wanted."

She averted her head and ground her teeth together. "She was a wonderful, promising young nurse."

"I don't know about wonderful, but I'll give you naïve. And since she quit, I think you've deliberately assigned me nurses from hell."

"We do not employ nurses from hell. All of our nurses are professional, efficient, compassionate—"

"And stink to high heaven."

"Excuse me?" Elizabeth drew back, affronted. "That's a crude accusation."

"Crude, but true. And I didn't want them in my home, and I refused to have them touching me."

So that was it. He didn't want a real nurse. He wanted something from late-night T.V.—big hair, big breasts, and a short, tight skirt.

Elizabeth took a deep breath, fighting to hang on to her professional composure. She was beginning to see how he wore his nurses down, brow-beating and tormenting until they begged for a reprieve. *Anyone but Mr. Koumantaros. Any job but that!*

Well, she wasn't about to let Mr. Koumantaros break her. He couldn't get a rise out of her because she wouldn't let him. "Did Calista smell bad?"

"No, Calista smelled like heaven."

For a moment she could have sworn Kristian was smiling, and the fact that he could smile over ruining a young nurse's career infuriated her.

He rolled another foot closer. "But then after Calista fled you sent only old, fat, frumpy nurses to torture me, punish-

ing me for what was really Calista's fault. And don't tell me
they weren't old and fat and frumpy, because I might be blind
but I'm not stupid."

Elizabeth's blood pressure shot up again. "I assigned
mature nurses, but they were well-trained and certainly
prepared for the rigors of the job."

"One smelled like a tobacco shop. One of fish. I'm quite
certain another could have been a battleship—"

"You're being insulting."

"I'm being honest. You replaced Calista with prison guards."

Elizabeth's anger spiked, and then her lips twitched.
Kristian Koumantaros was actually right.

After poor Calista's disgrace, Elizabeth had intentionally
assigned Mr. Koumantaros only the older, less responsive
nurses, realizing that he required special care. Very special care.

She smiled faintly, amused despite herself. He might not
be walking, and he might not have his vision, but his brain
worked just fine.

Still smiling, she studied him dispassionately, aware of his
injuries, his months of painful rehabilitation, his prognosis. He
was lucky to have escaped such a serious accident with his life.
The trauma to his head had been so extensive he'd been expected
to suffer severe brain damage. Happily, his mental faculties
were intact. His motor skills could be repaired, but his eyesight
was questionable. Sometimes the brain healed itself. Sometimes
it didn't. Only time and continued therapy would tell.

"Well, that's all in the past now," she said, forcing a
note of cheer into her voice. "The battleaxe nurses are
gone. I am here—"

"And you are probably worse than all of them."

"Indeed, I am. They whisper behind my back that I'm
every patient's worst nightmare."

"So I can call you Nurse Cratchett, then?"

"If you'd like. Or you can call me by my name, which is Nurse Hatchet. But they're so similar, I'll answer either way."

He sat in silence, his jaw set, his expression increasingly wary. Elizabeth felt the edges of her mouth lift, curl. He couldn't browbeat or intimidate her. She knew what Greek tycoons were. She'd once been married to one.

"It's time to move on," she added briskly. "And the first place we start is with your meals. I know it's late, Mr. Koumantaros, but have you eaten lunch yet?"

"I'm not hungry."

Elizabeth closed her portfolio and slipped the pen into the leather case. "You need to eat. Your body needs the nutrition. I'll see about a light meal." She moved toward the door, unwilling to waste time arguing.

Kristian shoved his wheelchair forward, inadvertently slamming into the edge of the couch. His frustration was written in every line of his face. "I don't want food—"

"Of course not. Why eat when you're addicted to pain pills?" She flashed a tight, strained smile he couldn't see. "Now, if you'll excuse me, I'll see to your meal."

The vaulted stone kitchen was in the tower, or *pyrgos,* and there the butler, cook and senior housekeeper had gathered beneath one of the medieval arches. They were in such deep conversation that they didn't hear Elizabeth enter.

Once they realized she was there, all three fell silent and turned to face her with varying degrees of hostility.

Elizabeth wasn't surprised. For one, unlike the other nurses, she wasn't Greek. Two, despite being foreign, she spoke Greek fluently. And three, she wasn't showing proper deference to their employer, a very wealthy, powerful Greek man.

"Hello," Elizabeth said, attempting to ignore the icy

welcome. "I thought I'd see if I could help with Mr. Koumantaros's lunch."

Everyone continued to gape at her until Pano, the butler, cleared his throat. "Mr. Koumantaros doesn't eat lunch."

"Does he take a late breakfast, then?" Elizabeth asked.

"No, just coffee."

"Then when does he eat his first meal?"

"Not until evening."

"I see." Elizabeth's brow furrowed as she studied the three staffers, wondering how long they'd been employed by Kristian Koumantaros and how they coped with his black moods and display of temper. "Does he eat well then?"

"Sometimes," the short, stocky cook answered, wiping her hands across the starched white fabric of her apron. "And sometimes he just pecks. He used to have an excellent appetite—fish, *moussaka, dolmades,* cheese, meat, vegetables—but that was before the accident."

Elizabeth nodded, glad to see at least one of them had been with him a while. That was good. Loyalty was always a plus, but misplaced loyalty could also be a hindrance to Kristian recovering. "We'll have to improve his appetite," she said. "Starting with a light meal right now. Perhaps a *horiatiki salata,*" she said, suggesting what most Europeans and Americans thought of as a Greek salad—feta cheese and onion, tomato and cucumber, drizzled with olive oil and a few drops of homemade wine vinegar.

"There must be someplace outside—a sunny terrace— where he can enjoy his meal. Mr. Koumantaros needs the sun and fresh air—"

"Excuse me, ma'am," Pano interrupted, "but the sun bothers Mr. Koumantaros's eyes."

"It's because Mr. Koumantaros has spent too much time

sitting in the dark. The light will do him good. Sunlight stim-ulates the pituitary gland, helps alleviate depression and promotes healing. But, seeing as he's been inside so much, we can transition today by having lunch in the shade. I assume part of the terrace is covered?"

"Yes, ma'am," the cook answered. "But Mr. Koumantaros won't go."

"Oh, he will." Elizabeth swallowed, summoning all her de-termination. She knew Kristian would eventually go. But it'd be a struggle.

Sitting in the library, Kristian heard the English nurse's foot-steps disappear as she went in search of the kitchen, and after a number of long minutes heard her footsteps return.

So she was coming back. Wonderful.

He tipped his head, looking up at nothing, since everything was and had been dark since the crash, fourteen months and eleven days ago.

The door opened, and he knew from the way the handle turned and the lightness of the step that it was her. "You're wrong about something else," he said abruptly as she entered the library. "The accident wasn't a year ago. It was almost a year and a half ago. It happened late February."

She'd stopped walking and he felt her there, beyond his sight, beyond his reach, standing, staring, *waiting*. It galled him, this lack of knowing, seeing. He'd achieved what he'd achieved by utilizing his eyes, his mind, his gut. He trusted his eyes and his gut, and now, without those, he didn't know what was true, or real.

Like Calista, for example.

"That's even worse," his new nightmare nurse shot back. "You should be back at work by now. You've a corporation to run, people dependent on you. You're doing no one any good hiding away here in your villa."

"I can't run my company if I can't walk or see—"

"But you *can* walk, and there might be a chance you could see—"

"A less than five percent chance." He laughed bitterly. "You know, before the last round of surgeries I had a thirty-five percent chance of seeing, but they botched those—"

"They weren't botched. They were just highly experimental."

"Yes, and that experimental treatment reduced my chances of seeing again to nil."

"Not nil."

"Five percent. There's not much difference. Especially when they say that even if the operation were a success I'd still never be able to drive, or fly, or sail. That there's too much trauma for me to do what I used to do."

"And your answer is to sit here shrouded in bandages and darkness and feel sorry for yourself?" she said tartly, her voice growing closer.

Kristian shifted in his chair, and felt an active and growing dislike for Cratchett. She was standing off to his right, and her smug, superior attitude rubbed him the wrong way. "Your company's services have been terminated."

"They haven't—"

"I may be blind, but you're apparently deaf. First Class Rehab has received its last—*final*—check. There is no more coming from me. There will be no more payments for services rendered."

He heard her exhale—a soft, quick breath that was so uniquely feminine that he drew back, momentarily startled.

And in that half-second he felt betrayed.

She was the one not listening. She was the one forcing herself on him. And yet—and yet she was a woman. And he was—or had been—a gentleman, and gentlemen were supposed to have manners. Gentlemen were supposed to be above reproach.

Growling, he leaned back in his chair, gripped the rims on the wheels and glared at where he imagined her to be standing.

He shouldn't feel bad for speaking bluntly. His brow furrowed even more deeply. It was her fault. She'd come here, barging in with a righteous high-handed, bossy attitude that turned his stomach.

The accident hadn't been yesterday. He'd lived like this long enough to know what he was dealing with. He didn't need her telling him this and that, as though he couldn't figure it out for himself.

No, she—Nurse Hatchet-Cratchett, his nurse number seven—had the same bloody mentality as the first six. In their eyes the wheelchair rendered him incompetent, unable to think for himself.

"I'm not paying you any longer," he repeated firmly, determined to get this over and done with. "You've had your last payment. You and your company are finished here."

And then she made that sound again—that little sound which had made him draw back. But this time he recognized the sound for what it was.

A laugh.

She was laughing at him.

Laughing and walking around the side of his chair so he had to crane his head to try to follow her.

He felt her hands settle on the back of his chair. She must have bent down, or perhaps she wasn't very tall, because her voice came surprisingly close to his ear.

"But *you* aren't paying me any longer. Our services have been retained and we are authorized to continue providing your care. Only now, instead of you paying for your care, the financial arrangements are being handled by a private source."

He went cold—cold and heavy. Even his legs, with their only limited sensation. *"What?"*

"It's true," she continued, beginning to push his chair and moving him forward. "I'm not the only one who thinks its high time you recovered." She continued pushing him despite his attempt to resist. "You're going to get well," she added, her voice whispering sweetly in his ear. "Whether you want to or not."

CHAPTER TWO

KRISTIAN clamped down on the wheel-rims, holding them tight to stop their progress. "Who is paying for my care?"

Elizabeth hated played games, and she didn't believe it was right to keep anyone in the dark, but she'd signed a confidentiality agreement and she had to honor it. "I'm sorry, Mr. Koumantaros. I'm not at liberty to say."

Her answer only antagonized him further. Kristian threw his head back and his powerful shoulders squared. His hands gripped the rims so tightly his knuckles shone white. "I won't have someone else assuming responsibility for my care, much less for what is surely questionable care."

Elizabeth cringed at the criticism. The criticism—slander?—was personal. It was her company. She personally interviewed, hired and trained each nurse that worked for First Class Rehab. Not that he knew. And not that she wanted him to know right now.

No, what mattered now was getting Mr. Koumantaros on a schedule, creating a predictable routine with regular periods of nourishment, exercise and rest. And to do that she really needed him to have his lunch.

"We can talk more over lunch," Elizabeth replied, beginning to roll him back out onto the terrace once more. But, just like before, Kristian clamped his hands down and gripped the wheel-rims hard, preventing him from going forward.

"I don't like being pushed."

Elizabeth stepped away and stared down at him, seeing for the first time the dark pink scar that snaked from beneath the sleeve of his sky-blue Egyptian cotton shirt, running from elbow to wrist. A multiple fracture, she thought, recalling just how many bones had broken. By all indications he should have died. But he hadn't. He'd survived. And after all that she wasn't about to let him give up now and wither away inside this shuttered villa.

"I didn't think you could get yourself around," she said, hanging on to her patience by a thread.

"I can push myself short distances."

"That's not quite the same thing as walking, is it?" she said exasperatedly. If he could do more…if he could walk…why didn't he? *Ornio,* she thought, using the Greek word for ornery. The previous nurses hadn't exaggerated a bit. Kristian was as obstinate as a mule.

He snorted. "Is that your idea of encouragement?"

Her lips compressed. Kristian also knew how to play both sides. One minute he was the aggressor, the next the victim. Worse, he was succeeding in baiting her, getting to her, and no one ever—*ever*—got under her skin. Not anymore. "It's a statement of fact, Mr. Koumantaros. You're still in the chair because your muscles have atrophied since the accident. But initially the doctors expected you to walk again." *They thought you'd want to.*

"It didn't work out."

"Because it hurt too much?"

"The therapy wasn't working."

"You gave up." She reached for the handles on the back of his chair and gave a hard push. "Now, how about that lunch?"

He wouldn't release the rims. "How about you tell me who is covering your services, and then we'll have lunch?"

Part of her admired his bargaining skill and tactics. He was clearly a leader, and accustomed to being in control. But she was a leader, too, and she was just as comfortable giving direction. "I can't tell you." Her jaw firmed. "Not until you're walking."

He craned to see her, even though he couldn't see anything. "So you *can* tell me."

"Once you're walking."

"Why not until then?"

She shrugged. "It's the terms of the contract."

"But you know this person?"

"We spoke on the phone."

He grew still, his expression changing as well, as though he were thinking, turning inward. "How long until I walk?"

"It depends entirely on you. Your hamstrings and hip muscles have unfortunately tightened, shortening up, but it's not irreparable, Mr. Koumantaros. It just requires diligent physical therapy."

"But even with *diligent* therapy I'll always need a walker."

She heard his bitterness but didn't comment on it. It wouldn't serve anything at this point. "A walker or a cane. But isn't that better than a wheelchair? Wouldn't you enjoy being independent again?"

"But it'll never be the same, never as it was—"

"People are confronted by change every day, Mr. Koumantaros."

"Do not patronize me." His voice deepened, roughened, revealing blistering fury.

"I'm not trying to. I'm trying to understand. And if this is because others died and you—"

"Not one more word," he growled. "Not one."

"Mr. Koumantaros, you are no less of a man because others died and you didn't."

"Then you do not know me. You do not know who I am, or who I was before. Because the best part of me—the good in me—died that day on the mountain. The good in me perished while I was saving someone I didn't even like."

He laughed harshly, the laugh tinged with self-loathing. "I'm not a hero. I'm a monster." And, reaching up, with a savage yank he ripped the bandages from his head. Rearing back in his wheelchair, Kristian threw his head into sunlight. "Do you see the monster now?"

Elizabeth sucked in her breath as the warm Mediterranean light touched the hard planes of his face.

A jagged scar ran the length of the right side of his face, ending precariously close to his right eye. The skin was still a tender pink, although one day it would pale, lightening until it nearly matched his skin tone—as long as he stayed out of the sun.

But the scar wasn't why she stared. And the scar wasn't what caused her chest to seize up, squeezing with a terrible, breathless tenderness.

Kristian Koumantaros was beautiful. Beyond beautiful. Even with the scar snaking like a fork of lightning over his cheekbone, running from the corner of his mouth to the edge of his eye.

"God gave me a face to match my heart. Finally the outside and inside look the same," he gritted, hands convulsing in his lap.

"You're wrong." Elizabeth could hardly breathe. His words gave her so much pain, so much sorrow, she felt tears sting her eyes. "If God gave you a face to match your heart, your heart is beautiful, too. Because a scar doesn't ruin a face, and a scar doesn't ruin a heart. It just shows that you've lived—" she took a rough breath "—and loved."

He said nothing and she pressed on. "Besides, I think the scar suits you. You were too good-looking before."

For a split second he said nothing, and then he laughed, a fierce guttural laugh that was more animal-like than human. "Finally. Someone to tell me the truth."

Elizabeth ignored the pain pricking her insides, the stab of more pain in her chest. Something about him, something about this—the scarred face, the shattered life, the fury, the fire, the intelligence and passion—touched her. Hurt her. It was not that anyone should suffer, but somehow on Kristian the suffering became bigger, larger than life, a thing in and of itself.

"You're an attractive man even with the scar," she said, still kneeling next to his chair.

"It's a hideous scar. It runs the length of my face. I can feel it."

"You're quite vain, then, Mr. Koumantaros?"

His head swung around and the expression on his face, matched by the cloudiness in his deep blue eyes, stole her breath. *He didn't suit the chair.*

Or the chair didn't suit him. He was too big, too strong, too much of everything. And it was wrong, his body, his life, his personality contained by it. Confined to it.

"No man wants to feel like Frankenstein," Kristian said with another rough laugh.

She knew then that it wasn't his face that made him feel so broken, but his heart and mind. Those memories of his that haunted him, the flashes of the past that made him relive the accident over and over. She knew because she'd once been the same. She, too, had relived an accident in endless detail, stopping the mental camera constantly, freezing the lens at the first burst of flame and the final ball of fire. But that was her story, not his, and she couldn't allow her own experiences and emotions to cloud her judgment now.

She had to regain some control, retreat as quickly as possible to professional detachment. She wasn't here for him; she was here for a job. She wasn't his love interest. He had one in Athens, waiting for him to recover. It was this lover of his who'd insisted he walk, he function, he see, and that was why she was here. To help him recover. To help him return to her.

"You're far from Frankenstein," she said crisply, covering her suddenly ambivalent emotions. She rose to her feet, smoothed her straight skirt and adjusted her blouse. "But, since you require flattery, let me give it to you. The scar suits you. Gives your face character. Makes you look less like a model or a movie star and more like a man."

"A man," he repeated with a bitter laugh.

"Yes, a man. And with some luck and hard work, soon we'll have you acting like a man, too."

Chaotic emotions rushed across his face. Surprise, then confusion, and as she watched the confusion shifted into anger. She'd caught him off guard and hurt him. She could see she'd hurt him.

Swallowing the twinge of guilt, she felt it on the tip of her tongue to apologize, as she hadn't meant to hurt his feelings so much as provoke him into taking action.

But even as she attempted to put a proper apology together, she sensed anything she said, particularly anything sympathetic, would only antagonize him more. He was living in his own hell.

More gently she added, "You've skied the most inaccessible mountain faces in the world, piloted helicopters in blizzards, rescued a half-dozen—"

"Enough."

"You can do anything," she persisted. His suffering was so obvious it was criminal. She'd become a nurse to help those wounded, not to inflict fresh wounds, but sometimes patients were so overwhelmed by physical pain and mental misery that they self-destructed.

Brilliant men—daring, risk-taking, gifted men—were particularly vulnerable, and she'd learned the hard way that these same men self-destructed if they had no outlet for their anger, no place for their pain.

Elizabeth vowed to find the outlet for Kristian, vowed she'd channel his fury somehow, turning pain into positives.

And so, before he could speak, before he could give voice to any of his anger, or contradict her again, she mentioned the pretty table setting before them, adding that the cook and butler had done a superb job preparing their late lunch.

"Your staff have outdone themselves, Mr. Koumantaros. They've set a beautiful table on your terrace. Can you feel that breeze? You can smell the scent of pine in the warm air."

"I don't smell it."

"Then come here, where I'm standing. It really is lovely. You can get a whiff of the herbs in your garden, too. Rosemary, and lemongrass."

But he didn't roll forward. He rolled backward, retreating back toward the shadows. "It's too bright. The light makes my head hurt."

"Even if I replace the bandages?"

"Even with the bandages." His voice grew harsh, pained. "And I don't want lunch. I already told you that but you don't listen. You won't listen. No one does."

"We could move lunch inside—"

"*I don't want lunch.*" And with a hard push he disappeared into the cooler library, where he promptly bumped into a side-table and sent it crashing, which led to him cursing and another bang of furniture.

Tensing, Elizabeth fought the natural inclination to hurry and help him. She wanted to rush to his side, but knew that doing so would only prolong his helpless state. She couldn't become an enabler, couldn't allow him to continue as he'd done—retreating from life, retreating from living, retreating into the dark shadows of his mind.

Instead, with nerves of steel, she left him as he was, muttering and cursing and banging into the table he'd overturned, and headed slowly across the terrace to the pretty lunch table, with its cheerful blue and white linens and cluster of meadow flowers in the middle.

And while she briefly appreciated the pretty linens and fresh flowers, she forgot both just as quickly, her thoughts focused on one thing and only one—Kristian Koumantaros.

It had cost her to speak to him so bluntly. She'd never been this confrontational—she'd never needed to be until now—but, frankly, she didn't know what else to do with him at this point. Her agency had tried everything—they'd sent every capable nurse, attempted every course of therapy—all to no avail.

As Elizabeth gratefully took a seat at the table, she knew her exhaustion wasn't just caused by Kristian's obstinance, but by Kristian himself.

Kristian had gotten beneath her skin.

And it's not his savage beauty, she told herself sternly. It couldn't be. She wasn't so superficial as to be moved by the violence in his face and frame—although he had an undeniably handsome face. So what was it? Why did she feel horrifyingly close to tears?

Ignoring the nervous flutter in her middle, she unfolded her linen serviette and spread it across her lap.

Pano appeared, a bottle of bubbling mineral water in his hand. "Water, ma'am?"

"Please, Pano. Thank you."

"And is Mr. Koumantaros joining you?"

She glanced toward the library doors, which had just been shut. She felt a weight on her heart, and the weight seemed to swell and grow. "No, Pano, not today. Not after all."

He filled her glass. "Shall I take him a plate?"

Elizabeth shot another glance toward the closed and shuttered library doors. She hesitated but a moment. "No. We'll try again tonight at dinner."

"So nothing if he asks?" The butler sounded positively pained.

"I know it seems hard, but I must somehow reach him. I must make him respond. He can't hide here forever. He's too young, and there are too many people that love him and miss him."

Pano seemed to understand this. His bald head inclined and, with a polite, "Your luncheon will be served immediately," he disappeared, after leaving the mineral water bottle on the table within her reach.

One of the villa's younger staff served the lunch— *souvlaki,* with sliced cucumbers and warm fresh pitta. It wasn't the meal she'd requested, and Elizabeth suspected it was intentional, the cook's own rebellion, but at least a meal had been prepared.

Elizabeth didn't eat immediately, choosing to give Kristian time in case he changed his mind. Brushing a buzzing fly away, she waited five minutes, and then another five more, reflecting that she hadn't gotten off to the best start here. It had been bumpy in more ways than one. But she could only press on, persevere. Everything would work out. Kristian Koumantaros would walk again, and eventually return to Athens, where he'd resume responsibility for the huge corporation he owned and had once single-handedly run. She'd go home to England and be rid of Greece and Greek tycoons.

After fifteen minutes Elizabeth gave up the vigil. Kristian wasn't coming. Finally she ate, concentrating on savoring the excellent meal and doing her best to avoid thinking about the next confrontation with her mulish patient.

Lunch finished, Elizabeth wiped her mouth on her serviette and pushed away from the table. Time to check on Kristian.

In the darkened library, Kristian lifted his head as she entered the room. "Have a nice lunch?" he asked in terse Greek.

She winced at the bitterness in his voice. "Yes, thank you. You have an excellent cook."

"Did you enjoy the view?"

"It is spectacular," she agreed, although she'd actually spent most of the time thinking about him instead of the view. She hadn't felt this involved with any case in years. But then, she hadn't nursed anyone directly in years, either.

After her stint in nursing school, and then three years working at a regional hospital, she'd gone back to school and earned her Masters in Business Administration, with an emphasis on Hospital and Medical Administration. After graduating she had immediately found work. So much work she had realized she'd be better off working for herself than anyone else—which was how her small, exclusive First Class Rehab had been born.

But Kristian Koumantaros's case was special. Kristian Koumantaros hadn't improved in her company's care. He'd worsened.

And to Elizabeth it was completely unacceptable.

Locating her notebook on the side-table, where she'd left it earlier, she took a seat on the couch. "Mr. Koumantaros, I know you don't want a nurse, but you still need one. In fact, you need several."

"Why not prescribe a fleet?" he asked sarcastically.

"I think I shall." She flipped open her brown leather port-folio and, scanning her previous notes, began to scribble again. "A live-in nursing assistant to help with bathing, personal hygiene. Male, preferably. Someone strong to lift you in and out of your chair since you're not disposed to walk."

"I can't walk, Mrs.—"

"*Ms.* Hatchet," she supplied, before crisply continuing, "And you could walk if you had worked with your last four physical therapists. They all tried, Mr. Koumantaros, but you were more interested in terrifying them than in making progress."

Elizabeth wrote another couple of notes, then clicked her pen closed. "You also require an occupational therapist, as you desperately need someone to adapt your lifestyle. If you've no intention of getting better, your house and habits will need to change. Ramps, a second lift, a properly outfitted bathroom, rails and grabs in the pool—"

"No," he thundered, face darkening. "No bars, no rails, and no goddamn grabs in this house."

She clicked her pen open again. "Perhaps its time we called in a psychiatrist—someone to evaluate your depression and recommend a course of therapy. Pills, perhaps, or sessions of counseling."

"I will never talk—"

"You are now," she said cheerfully, scribbling yet another note to herself, glancing at Kristian Koumantaros from beneath her lashes. His jaw was thick, and rage was stiffening his spine, improving his posture, curling his hands into fists.

Good, she thought, with a defiant tap of her pen. He hadn't given up on living, just given up on healing. There was something she—and her agency—could still do.

She watched him for a long dispassionate moment.

"Talking—counseling—will help alleviate your depression, and it's depression that's keeping you from recovering."

"I'm not depressed."

"Then someone to treat your rage. You *are* raging, Mr. Koumantaros. Are you aware of your tone?"

"*My* tone?" He threw himself back in his chair, hands flailing against the rims of the wheels, furious skin against steel. "*My* tone? You come into my house and lecture me about my tone? Who the hell do you think you are?"

The raw savagery in his voice cut her more than his words, and for a moment the library spun. Elizabeth held her breath, silent, stunned.

"You think you're so good." Kristian's voice sounded from behind her, mocking her. "So righteous, so sure of everything. But would you be so sure of yourself if the rug was pulled from beneath *your* feet? Would you be so callous then?"

Of course he didn't know the rug *had* been pulled from beneath her feet. No one got through life unscathed. But her personal tragedies had toughened her, and she thought of the old wounds as scar tissue…something that was just part of her.

Even so, Elizabeth felt a moment of gratitude that Kristian couldn't see her, or the conflicting emotions flickering over her face. Hers wasn't a recent loss, hers was seven years ago, and yet if she wasn't careful to keep up the defenses the loss still felt as though it had happened yesterday.

As the silence stretched Kristian laughed low, harshly. "I got you on that one." His laughter deepened, and then abruptly ended. "Hard to sit in judgment until you've walked a mile in someone else's shoes."

Through the open doors Elizabeth could hear the warble of a bird, and she wondered if it was the dark green bird, the one with the lemon-yellow breast, she'd seen while eating on the patio terrace.

"I'm not as callous as you think," she said, her voice cool enough to contradict her words. "But I'm here to help you, and I'll do whatever I must to see you move into the next step of recovery."

"And why should I want to recover?" His head angled, and his expression was ferocious. "And don't give me some sickly-sweet answer about finding my true love and having a family and all that nonsense."

Elizabeth's lips curved in a faint, hard smile. No, she'd never dangle love as a motivational tool, because even that could be taken away. "I wasn't. You should know by now that's not my style."

"So tell me? Give it to me straight? Why should I bother to get better?"

Why bother? Why bother, indeed? Elizabeth felt her heart race—part anger, part sympathy. "Because you're still alive, that's why."

"That's it?" Kristian laughed bitterly. "Sorry, that's not much incentive."

"Too bad," she answered, thinking she *was* sorry about his accident, but he wasn't dead.

Maybe he couldn't walk easily or see clearly, but he was still intact and he had his life, his heart, his body, his mind. Maybe he wasn't exactly as he had been before the injury, but that didn't make him less of a man...not unless he let it. And he was allowing it.

Pressing the tip of her finger against her mouth, she fought to hold back all the angry things she longed to say, knowing she wasn't here to judge. He was just a patient, and her job was to provide medical care, not morality lessons. But, even acknowledging that it wasn't her place to criticize, she felt her tension grow.

Despite her best efforts, she resented his poor-me attitude, was irritated that he was so busy looking at the small picture he was missing the big one. Life was so precious. Life was a gift, not a right, and he still possessed the gift.

He could love and be loved. Fall in love, make love, shower someone with affection—hugs, kisses, tender touches. There was no reason he couldn't make someone feel cherished, important, unforgettable. No reason other than that he didn't want to, that he'd rather feel sorry for himself than reach out to another.

"Because, for whatever reason, Mr. Koumantaros, you're still here with us, still alive. Don't look a gift horse in the mouth. Live. Live fully, wisely. And if you can't do it for yourself, then do it for those who didn't escape the avalanche that day with you." She took a deep breath. "Do it for Cosima. Do it for Andreas."

CHAPTER THREE

COSIMA and Andreas. Kristian was surprised his English Nurse Cratchett knew their names, as it was Cosima and Andreas who haunted him. And for very different reasons.

Kristian shifted restlessly in bed. His legs ached at the moment. Sometimes the pain was worse than others, and it was intense tonight. Nothing made him comfortable.

The accident. A winter holiday with friends and family in the French Alps.

He'd been in a coma for weeks after the accident, and when he'd come out of it he'd been immobilized for another couple weeks to give his spine a chance to heal. He'd been told he was lucky there was no lasting paralysis, told he was lucky to have survived such a horrific accident.

But for Kristian the horror continued. And it wasn't even his eyes he missed, or his strength. It was Andreas, Andreas— not just his big brother, but his best friend.

And while he and Andreas had always been about the extreme—extreme skiing, extreme diving, extreme parasailing—Andreas, the eldest, had been the straight arrow, as good as the sun, while Kristian had played the bad boy and rebel.

Put them together—fair-haired Andreas and devilish Kristian—and they'd been unstoppable. They'd had too much damn fun. Not that they hadn't worked—they'd worked hard—but they had played even harder.

It had helped that they were both tall, strong, physical. They'd practically grown up on skis, and Kristian couldn't even remember a time when he and Andreas hadn't participated in some ridiculous, reckless thrill-seeking adventure. Their father, Stavros, had been an avid sportsman, and their stunning French mother hadn't been just beautiful, she'd once represented France in the Winter Olympics. Sport had been the family passion.

Of course there had been dangers, but their father had taught them to read mountains, study weather reports, discuss snow conditions with avalanche experts. They'd coupled their love of adventure with intelligent risk-taking. And, so armed, they had embraced life.

And why shouldn't they have? They'd been part of a famous, wealthy, powerful family. Money and opportunity had never been an issue.

But money and opportunity didn't protect one from tragedy. It didn't insure against heartbreak or loss.

Andreas was the reason Kristian needed the pills. Andreas was the reason he couldn't sleep.

Why hadn't he saved his brother first? Why had he waited?

Kristian stirred yet again, his legs alive and on fire. The doctors said it was nerves and tissue healing, but the pain was maddening. Felt like licks of lightning everywhere.

Kristian searched the top of his bedside table for medicine but found nothing. His nurse must have taken the pain meds he always kept there.

If only he could sleep.

If he could just relax maybe the pain would go away. But he wasn't relaxing, and he needed something—anything—to take his mind off the accident and what had happened that day on Le Meije.

There had been ten of them who had set off together for a final run. They'd been heli-skiing all week, and it had been their next to last day. Conditions had looked good, the ski guides had given the okay, and the helicopter had taken off. Less than two hours later, only three of their group survived.

Cosima had lived, but not Andreas.

Kristian had saved Cosima instead of his brother, and that was the decision that tormented him.

Kristian had never even liked Cosima—not even at their first meeting. From the very beginning she'd struck him as a shallow party girl who lived for the social scene, and nothing she'd said or done during the next two years had convinced him otherwise. Of course Andreas had never seen that side in her. He'd only seen her beauty, her style, and her fun—and maybe she was beautiful, stylish, but Andreas could have done better.

Driven to find relief, Kristian searched the table-top again, before painfully rolling over onto his stomach to reach into the small drawers, in case the bottles had been put there. Nothing.

Then he remembered the bottle tucked between the mattresses, and was just reaching for it when his bedroom door opened and he heard the click of a light switch on the wall.

"You're still awake." It was dear old Cratchett, on her night rounds.

"Missing the hospital routine?" he drawled, slowly rolling onto his back and dragging himself into a sitting position.

Elizabeth approached the bed. "I haven't worked in a hospital in years. My company specializes in private home healthcare."

He listened to her footsteps, trying to imagine her age. He'd played this game with all the nurses. Since he couldn't see, he created his own visual images. And, listening to Elizabeth Hatchet's voice and footsteps, he began to create a mental picture of her.

Age? Thirty-something. Maybe close to forty.

Brunette, redhead, black-haired or blonde?

She leaned over the bed and he felt her warmth even as he caught a whiff of a light fresh scent—the same crisp, slightly sweet fragrance he'd smelled earlier. Not exactly citrus, and not hay—possibly grass? Fresh green grass. With sunshine. But also rain.

"Can't sleep?" she asked, and her voice sounded tantalizingly near.

"I never sleep."

"In pain?"

"My legs are on fire."

"You need to use them, exercise them. It'd improve circulation and eventually alleviate most of the pain symptoms you're experiencing."

For a woman with such a brusque bedside manner she had a lovely voice. The tone and pitch reminded him of the string section of the orchestra. Not a cello or bass, but a violin. Warm, sweet, evocative.

"You sound so sure of yourself," he said, hearing her move again, sensing her closeness.

"This is my job. It's what I do," she said. "And tell me, Mr. Koumantaros, what do *you* do—besides throw yourself down impossibly vertical slopes?"

"You don't approve of extreme skiing?"

Elizabeth felt her chest grow tight. Extreme skiing. Jumping off mountains. Dodging avalanches. It was ridiculous—ridiculous to tempt fate like that.

Impatiently she tugged the sheets and coverlet straight at the foot of the bed, before smoothing the covers with a jerk on the sheet at its edge.

"I don't approve of risking life for sport," she answered. "No."

"But sport is exercise—and isn't that what you're telling me I must do?"

She looked down at him, knowing he was attempting to bait her once again. He wasn't wearing a shirt, and his chest was big, his shoulders immense. She realized that this was all just a game to him, like his love of sport.

He wanted to push her—had pushed her nurses, pushed all of them. Trying to distract them from doing their job was a form of entertainment for him, a diversion to keep him from facing the consequences of his horrific accident.

"Mr. Koumantaros, there are plenty of exercises that don't risk life or limb—or cost an exorbitant amount of money."

"Is it the sport or the money you object to, Nurse?"

"Both," she answered firmly.

"How refreshing. An Englishwoman with an opinion on everything."

Once again she didn't rise to the bait. She knew he must be disappointed, too. Maybe he'd been able to torment his other nurses, but he wouldn't succeed in torturing her.

She had a job to do, and she'd do it, and then she'd go home and life would continue—far more smoothly once she had Kristian Koumantaros out of it.

"Your pillows," she said, her voice as starchy as the white blouse tucked into cream slacks. Her only bit of ornamentation was the slender gold belt at her waist.

She'd thought she'd given him ample warning that she was about to lean over and adjust his pillows, but as she reached across him he suddenly reached up toward her and his hand became entangled in her hair.

She quickly stepped back, flustered. She'd heard all about Kristian's playboy antics, knew his reputation was that of a lady's man, but she was dumbfounded that he'd still try to pull that on her. "Without being able to see, you didn't realize I was there," she said coolly, wanting to avoid all allegations of improper conduct. "In the future I will ask you to move before I adjust your pillows or covers."

"It was just your hair," he said mildly. "It brushed my face. I was merely moving it out of the way."

"I'll make sure to wear it pulled back tomorrow."

"Your hair is very long."

She didn't want to get into the personal arena. She already felt exceedingly uncomfortable being back in Greece, and so isolated here on Taygetos, at a former monastery. Kristian Koumantaros couldn't have found a more remote place to live if he'd tried.

"I would have thought your hair was all short and frizzy," he continued, "or up tight in a bun. You sound like a woman who'd wear her hair scraped back and tightly pinned up."

He was still trying to goad her, still trying to get a reaction. "I do like buns, yes. They're professional."

"And you're so *very* professional," he mocked.

She stiffened, her face paling. An icy lump hit her stomach.

Her former husband, another Greek playboy, had put her through two years of hell before they were finally legally separated, and it had taken her nearly five years to recover. One Greek playboy had already broken her heart. She refused to let another break her spirit.

Elizabeth squared her shoulders, lifted her head. "Since there's nothing else, Mr. Koumantaros, I'll say goodnight."

And before he could speak she'd exited the room and firmly shut the door behind her.

But Elizabeth's control snapped the moment she reached the hall. Swiftly, she put a hand out to brace herself against the wall.

She couldn't do this.

Couldn't stay here, live like this, be tormented like this.

She despised spoiled, pampered Greeks—particularly wealthy tycoons with far too much time on their hands.

After her divorce she'd vowed she'd never return to Greece, but here she was. Not just in Greece, but trapped on a mountain peak in a medieval monastery with Kristian Koumantaros, a man so rich, so powerful, he made Arab sheikhs look poor.

Elizabeth exhaled hard, breathing out in a desperate, painful rush.

She couldn't let tomorrow be a repeat of today, either. She was losing control of Koumantaros and the situation already.

This couldn't continue. Her patient didn't respect her, wasn't even listening to her, and he felt entirely too comfortable mocking her.

Elizabeth gave her head a slight dazed shake. How was this happening? She was supposed to be in charge.

Tomorrow, she told herself fiercely, returning to the bedroom the housekeeper had given her. Tomorrow she'd prove to him she was the one in charge, the one running the show.

She could do this. She had to.

The day had been warm, and although it was now night, her bedroom retained the heat. Like the other tower rooms, its plaster ceiling was high, at least ten or eleven feet, and decorated with elaborate painted friezes.

She crossed to open her windows and allow the evening breeze in. Her three arched windows overlooked the gardens, now bathed in moonlight, and then the mountain valley beyond.

It was beautiful here, uncommonly beautiful, with the ancient monastery tucked among rocks, cliffs and chestnut trees. But also incredibly dangerous. Kristian Koumantaros was a man used to dominating his world. She needed him to work with her, cooperate with her, or he could destroy her business and reputation completely.

At the antique marble bureau, Elizabeth twisted her long hair and then reached for one of her hair combs to fasten the knot on top of her head.

As she slid the comb in, she glanced up into the ornate silver filigree mirror over the bureau. Glimpsing her reflection—fair, light eyes, an oval face with a surprisingly strong chin—she grimaced. Back when she'd done more with herself, back when she'd had a luxurious lifestyle, she'd been a paler blonde, more like champagne, softer, prettier. But she'd given up the expensive highlights along with the New York and London stylists. She didn't own a single couture item anymore, nor any high-end real estate. The lifestyle she'd once known—taken for granted, assumed to be as much a part of her birthright as her name—was gone.

Over.

Forgotten.

But, turning back suddenly to the mirror, she saw the flicker in her eyes and knew she hadn't forgotten.

Medicine—nursing—offered her an escape, provided structure, a regimented routine and a satisfying amount of control. While medicine in and of itself wasn't safe, medicine coupled with business administration became something far more predictable. Far more manageable. Which was exactly what she prayed Kristian would be tomorrow.

* * *

The next morning Elizabeth woke early, ready to get to work, but even at seven the monastery-turned-villa was still dark except for a few lights in the kitchen.

Heartened that the villa was coming to life, Elizabeth dressed in a pale blue shirt and matching blue tailored skirt—her idea of a nursing uniform—before heading to find breakfast, which seemed to surprise the cook, throwing her into a state of anxiety and confusion.

Elizabeth managed to convince her that all she really needed was a cup of coffee and a bite to eat. The cook obliged with both, and over Greek coffee—undrinkable—and a *tiropita,* or cheese pie, Elizabeth visited with Pano.

She learned that Kristian usually slept in and then had coffee in his bed, before making his way to the library where he spent each day.

"What does he do all day?" she asked, breaking the pie into smaller bites. Pano hesitated, and then finally shrugged.

"He does nothing?" Elizabeth guessed.

Pano shifted his shoulders. "It is difficult for him."

"I understand in the beginning he did the physical therapy. But then something happened?"

"It was the eye surgery—the attempt to repair the retinas." Pano sighed heavily, and the same girl who'd served Elizabeth lunch yesterday came forward with fresh hot coffee. "He'd had some sight until then—not much, but enough that he could see light and shadows, shapes—but something went wrong in the repeated surgeries and he is now as you see him. Blind."

Elizabeth knew that losing the rest of his sight would have been a terrible blow. "I read in his chart that there is still a slight chance he could regain some sight with another treatment. It'd be minimal, I realize."

Elderly Pano shrugged.

"Why doesn't he do it?" she persisted.

"I think…" His wrinkled face wrinkled further. "He's afraid. It's his last hope."

Elizabeth said nothing, and Pano lifted his hands to try to make her understand.

"As long as he postpones the surgery, he can hope that one day he might see again. But once he has the surgery, and it doesn't work—" the old man snapped his fingers "—then there is nothing else for him to hope for."

And that Elizabeth actually understood.

But as the hours passed, and the morning turned to noon, Elizabeth grew increasingly less sympathetic.

What kind of life was this? To just sleep all day?

She peeked into his room just before twelve and he was still out, sprawled half-naked between white sheets, his dark hair tousled.

Elizabeth went in search of Pano once more, to enquire into Kristian's sleeping habits.

"Is it usual for Kirios Koumantaros to sleep this late?" she asked.

"It's not late. Not for him. He can sleep 'til one or two in the afternoon."

Unable to hide her incredulity, she demanded, "Did his other nurses allow this?"

Pano's bald head shone in the light as he bent over the big table and finished straightening the mail and papers piled there. "His other nurses couldn't control him. He is a man. He does as he wants to do."

"No. Not when his medical care costs thousands and thousands of pounds each week."

Mail sorted and newspapers straightened, Pano looked up at her. "You don't tell a grown man what to do."

She made a rough sound. "Yes, you do. If what he's doing is destructive."

Pano didn't answer, and after a glance at the tall library clock—it was now five minutes until one—she turned around and headed straight for Kristian's bedroom. What she found there, on his bedside table, explained his long, deep sleep.

He'd taken sleeping pills. She didn't know how many, and she didn't know when they'd been taken, but the bottle hadn't been there earlier in the evening when she'd checked on him.

She'd collected the bottles from the small table in the library and put them in her room, under lock and key, so for him to have had access to this bottle meant he had a secret stash of his own to medicate himself as he pleased.

But still, he couldn't get the prescriptions filled if Pano or another staff member weren't aiding him. Someone—and she suspected Pano again—was making it too easy for Kristian to be dependent.

Elizabeth spoke Kristian's name to wake him. No response. She said his name again. "Mr. Koumantaros, it's gone noon—time to wake up."

Nothing.

"Mr. Koumantaros." She stepped closer to the bed, stood over him and said, more loudly, "It's gone noon, Mr. Koumantaros. Time to get up. You can't sleep all day."

Kristian wasn't moving. He wasn't dead, either. She could see that much. He was breathing, and there was eye movement beneath his closed lids, but he certainly wasn't interested in waking up.

She cleared her throat and practically shouted, "Kristian Koumantaros—it's time to get up."

Kristian heard the woman. How could he not? She sounded as if she had a bullhorn. But he didn't want to wake.

He wanted to sleep.

He needed to keep sleeping, craved the deep dreamless sleep that would mercifully make all dark and quiet and peaceful.

But the voice didn't stop. It just grew louder. And louder.

Now there was a tug on the covers, and in the next moment they were stripped back, leaving him bare.

"Go away," he growled.

"It's gone noon, Mr. Koumantaros. Time to get up. Your first physical therapy session is in less than an hour."

And that was when he remembered. He wasn't dealing with just any old nurse, but nurse number seven. Elizabeth Hatchet. The latest nurse, an English nurse of all things, sent to make his life miserable.

He rolled over onto his stomach. "You're not allowed to wake me up."

"Yes, I am. It's gone noon and you can't sleep the day away."

"Why not? I was up most of the night."

"Your first physical therapy session begins soon."

"You're mad."

"Not mad, not even angry. Just ready to get you back into treatment, following a proper exercise program."

"No."

Elizabeth didn't bother to argue. There was no point. One way or another he would resume physical therapy. "Pano is on his way with breakfast. I told him you could eat in the dining room, like a civilized man, but he insisted he serve you in bed."

"Good man," Kristian said under his breath.

Elizabeth let this pass, too. "But this is your last morning being served in bed. You're neither an invalid nor a prince. You can eat at a table like the rest of us."

She rolled his wheelchair closer to the bed. "Your chair is here, in case you need it, and I'll be just a moment while I gather a few things." And with that she took the medicine bottle from the table and headed for the bathroom adjoining his bedroom. In the bathroom she quickly opened drawers and cupboard doors, before returning to his room with another two bottles in her hands.

"What are you doing?" Kristian asked, sitting up and listening to her open and close the drawers in his dresser.

"Looking for the rest of your secret stash."

"Secret stash of what?"

"You know perfectly well."

"If I knew, I wouldn't be asking."

She found another pill bottle at the back of his top drawer, right behind his belts. "Just how much stuff are you taking?"

"I take very little—"

"Then why do you have enough prescriptions and bottles to fill a pharmacy?"

It was his turn to fall silent, and she snorted as she finished checking his room. She found nothing else. Not in the armchair in the corner, or the drawer of the nightstand, nor between the mattresses of his bed. Good. Maybe she'd found the last of it. She certainly hoped so.

"Now what?" he asked, as Elizabeth scooped up the bottles and marched through the master bedroom's French doors outside to the pool.

"Just finishing the job," she said, leaving the French doors open and heading across the sunlit patio to the pool and fountain.

"Those are mine," he shouted furiously.

"Not anymore," she called back.

"I can't sleep without them—"

"You could if you got regular fresh air and exercise." Elizabeth was walking quickly, but not so fast that she couldn't hear Kristian make the awkward transfer from his bed into his wheelchair.

"Parakalo," he demanded. "Please. Wait a blasted moment."

She did. Only because it was the first time she'd heard him use the word *please*. As she paused, she heard Kristian hit the open door with a loud bang, before backing up and banging his way forward again, this time managing to get through. Just as clumsily he pushed across the pale stone deck, his chair tires humming on the deck.

"I waited," she said, walking again, "but I'm not giving them back. They're poison. They're absolutely toxic for you."

Kristian was gaining on her and, reaching the fountain, she popped the caps off the bottles and turned toward him.

His black hair was wild, and the scar on his cheek like face paint from an ancient tribe. He might very well have been one of the warring Greeks.

"Everything you put in your body," she said, trying to slow the racing of her heart, as well as the sickening feeling that she was once again losing control, "and everything you do to your body is my responsibility."

And with that she emptied the bottles into the fountain, the splash of pills loud enough to catch Kristian's attention.

"You did it," he said.

"I did," she agreed.

A line formed between his eyebrows and his cheekbones grew more pronounced. "I declare war, then," he said, and the edge of his mouth lifted, tilted in a dark smile. "War. War against your company, and war against you." His voice dropped, deepened. "I'm fairly certain that very soon, Ms. Hatchet, you will deeply regret ever coming here."

CHAPTER FOUR

ELIZABETH'S heart thumped hard. So hard she thought it would burst from her chest.

It was a threat. Not just a small threat, but one meant to send her to her knees.

For a moment she didn't know what to think, or do, and as her heart raced she felt overwhelmed by fear and dread. And then she found her backbone, and knew she couldn't let a man—much less a man like Kristian—intimidate her. She wasn't a timid little church mouse, nor a country bumpkin. She'd come from a family every bit as powerful as the Koumantaros family—not that she talked about her past, or wanted anyone to know about it.

"Am I supposed to be afraid, Mr. Koumantaros?" she asked, capping the bottles and dropping them in her skirt pocket. "You must realize you're not a very threatening adversary."

Drawing on her courage, she continued coolly, "You can hardly walk, and you can't see, and you depend on everyone else to take care of you. So, really, why should I be frightened? What's the worst you can do? Call me names?"

He leaned back in his wheelchair, his black hair a striking contrast to the pale stone wall behind him. "I don't know whether to admire your moxie or pity your naïveté."

The day hadn't started well, she thought with a deep sigh, and it was just getting worse. Everything with him was a battle. If he only focused half his considerable intelligence and energy on healing instead of baiting nurses he'd be walking by now, instead of sitting like a wounded caveman in his wheelchair.

"Pity?" she scoffed. "Don't pity me. You're the one that hasn't worked in a year. You're the one that needs your personal and business affairs managed by others."

"You take so many liberties."

"They're not liberties; they're truths. If you were half the man your friends say you are, you wouldn't still be hiding away and licking your wounds."

"Licking my wounds?" he repeated slowly.

"I know eight people died that day in France, and I know one of them was your brother. I know you tried to rescue him, and I know you were hurt going back for him. But you will not bring him back by killing yourself—" She broke off as he reached out and grasped her wrist with his hand.

Elizabeth tried to pull back, but he didn't let her go. "No personal contact, Mr. Koumantaros," she rebuked sternly, tugging at her hand. "There are strict guidelines for patient-nurse relationships."

He laughed as though she'd just told a joke. But he also swiftly released her. "I don't think your highly trained Calista got that memo."

She glanced down at her wrist, which suddenly burned, checking for marks. There were none. And yet her skin felt hot, tender, and she rubbed it nervously. "It's not a memo. It's an ethics standard. Every nurse knows there are lines that cannot be crossed. There are no gray areas on this one. It's very black and white."

"You might want to explain that one to Calista, because she *begged* me to make love to her. But then she also asked me for money—confusing for a patient, I can assure you."

The sun shone directly overhead, and the heat coming off the stone terrace was intense, and yet Elizabeth froze. "What do you mean, she asked you for money?"

"Surely the UK has its fair share of blackmail?"

"You're trying to shift responsibility and the blame," she said, glancing around quickly, suppressing panic. Panic because if Calista *had* attempted to blackmail Mr. Koumantaros, one of Greece's most illustrious sons…oh…bad. Very, very bad. It was so bad she couldn't even finish the thought.

Expression veiled, Kristian shrugged and rested his hands on the rims of his wheelchair tires. "But as you say, Cratchett, she was twenty-three—very young. Maybe she didn't realize it wasn't ethical to seduce a patient and then demand hush money." He paused. "Maybe she didn't realize that blackmailing me while being employed by First Class Rehab meant that First Class Rehab would be held liable."

Elizabeth's legs wobbled. She'd dealt with a lot of problems in the past year, had sorted out everything from poor budgeting to soaring travel costs, but she hadn't seen this one coming.

"And you *are* First Class Rehab, aren't you, Ms. Hatchet? It is your company?"

She couldn't speak. Her mouth dried. Her heart pounded. She was suddenly too afraid to make a sound.

"I did some research, Ms. Hatchet."

She very much wished there was a chair close by, something she could sit down on, but all the furniture had been exiled to one end of the terrace, to give Mr. Koumantaros more room to maneuver his wheelchair.

"Calista left here months ago," she whispered, plucking

back a bit of hair as the breeze kicked in. "Why didn't you come to me then? Why did you wait so long to tell me?"

His mouth slanted, his black lashes dropped, concealing his intensely blue eyes. "I decided I'd wait and see if the level of care improved. It did not—"

"You refused to cooperate!" she exclaimed, her voice rising.

"I'm thirty-six, a world traveler, head of an international corporation and not used to being dependent on anyone—much less young women. Furthermore, I'd just lost my brother, four of my best friends, a cousin, his girlfriend, and her best friend." His voice vibrated with fury. "It was a lot to deal with."

"Which is why we were trying to help you—"

"By sending me a twenty-three-year-old former exotic dancer?"

"She wasn't."

"She was. She had also posed topless in numerous magazines—not that I ever saw them; she just bragged about them, and about how men loved her breasts. They were natural, you see."

Elizabeth was shaking. This was bad—very bad—and getting worse. "Mr. Koumantaros—" she pleaded.

But he didn't stop. "You say you personally hire and train every nurse? You say you do background reports and conduct all the interviews?"

"In the beginning, yes, I did it all. And I still interview all of the UK applicants."

"But *you* don't personally screen every candidate? You don't do the background checks yourself anymore, either. Do you?"

The tension whipped through her, tightening every muscle and nerve. "No."

He paused, as though considering her. "Your agency literature says you do."

Sickened, Elizabeth bit her lip, feeling trapped, cornered. She'd never worked harder than she had in the past year. She'd never accomplished so much, or fought so many battles, either. "We've grown a great deal in the past year. Doubled in size. I've been stretched—"

"Now listen to who has all the excuses."

Blood surged to her cheeks, making her face unbearably warm. She supposed she deserved that. "I've offices in seven cities, including Athens, and I employ hundreds of women throughout Europe. I'd vouch for nearly every one of them."

"Nearly?" he mocked. "So much for First Class Rehab's guarantee of first-class care and service."

Elizabeth didn't know which way to turn. "I'd be happy to rewrite our company mission statement."

"I'm sure you will be." His mouth curved slowly. "Once you've finished providing me with the quality care I so desperately need." His smile stretched. "As well as deserve."

She crossed her arms over her chest, shaken and more than a little afraid. "Does that mean you'll be working with me this afternoon on your physical therapy?" she asked, finding it so hard to ask the question that her voice was but a whisper.

"No, it means *you* will be working with *me*." He began rolling forward, slowly pushing himself back to the tower rooms. "I imagine it's one now, which means lunch will be served in an hour. I'll meet you for lunch, and we can discuss my thoughts on my therapy then."

Elizabeth spent the next hour in a state of nervous shock. She couldn't absorb anything from the conversation she'd had with Kristian on the patio. Couldn't believe everything she'd thought, everything she knew, was just possibly wrong.

She'd flown Calista into London for her final interview. It

had been an all-expenses paid trip, too, and Calista had impressed Elizabeth immediately as a warm, energetic, dedicated nurse. A true professional. There was no way she could be, or ever have been, an exotic dancer. Nor a topless model. Impossible.

Furthermore, Calista wouldn't *dream* of seducing a man like Kristian Koumantaros. She was a good Greek girl, a young woman raised in Piraeus, the port of Athens, with her grandmother and a spinster great-aunt. Calista had solid family values.

And not much money.

Elizabeth closed her eyes, shook her head once, not wanting to believe the worst.

Then don't, she told herself, opening her eyes and heading for her room, to splash cold water on her face. Don't believe the worst. Look for the best in people. Always.

And yet as she walked through the cool arched passages of the tower to her own room a little voice whispered, *Isn't that why you married a man like Nico? Because you only wanted to believe the best in him?*

Forty-five minutes later, Elizabeth returned downstairs, walking outside to the terrace where she'd had a late lunch yesterday. She discovered Kristian was already there, enjoying his coffee.

Elizabeth, remembering her own morning coffee, grimaced inwardly. She'd always thought that Greek coffee—or what was really Turkish coffee—tasted like sludge. Nico had loved the stuff, and had made fun of her preference for *café au lait* and cappuccino, but she'd grown up with a coffee house on every corner in New York, and a latte or a mocha was infinitely preferable to thick black mud.

At her footsteps Kristian lifted his head and looked up in her direction. Her breath caught in her throat.

Kristian had shaved. His thick black hair had been trimmed and combed, and as he turned his attention on her the blue of his eyes was shocking. Intense. Maybe even more intense without sight, as he was forced to focus, to really listen.

His blue eyes were such a sharp contrast to his black hair and hard, masculine features that she felt an odd shiver race through her—a shiver of awareness, appreciation—and it bewildered her, just as nearly everything about this man threw her off balance. For a moment she felt what Calista must have felt, confronted by a man like this.

"Hello." Elizabeth sat down, suddenly shy. "You look nice," she added, her voice coming out strangely husky.

"A good shave goes a long way."

It wasn't just the shave, she thought, lifting her napkin from the table and spreading it across her lap. It was the alert expression on Kristian's face, the sense that he was there, mentally, physically, clearly paying attention.

"I am very sorry about the communication problems," she said, desperately wanting to start over, get things off on a better foot. "I understand you are very frustrated, and I want you to know I am eager to make everything better—"

"I know," he interrupted quietly.

"You do?"

"You're afraid I'll destroy your company." One black eyebrow quirked. "And it would be easy to do, too. Within a month you'd be gone."

There wasn't a cloud in the sky, and yet the day suddenly grew darker, as though the sun itself had dimmed. "Mr. Koumantaros—"

"Seeing as we're going to be working so closely together, isn't it time we were on a first-name basis?" he suggested.

She eyed him warily. He was reminding her of a wild

animal at the moment—dangerous and unpredictable. "That might be difficult."

"And why is that?"

She wondered if she should be honest, wondered if now was the time to flatter him, win him over with insincere compliments, and then decided against it. She'd always been truthful, and she'd remain so now. "The name Kristian doesn't suit you at all. It implies Christ-like, and you're far from that."

She had expected him to respond with anger. Instead he smiled faintly, the top of his finger tapping against the rim of his cup. "My mother once said she'd given us the wrong names. My older brother Andreas should have had my name, and she felt I would have been better with his. Andreas—or Andrew—in Greek means—"

"Strong," she finished for him. "Manly. Courageous."

Kristian's head lifted as though he could see her. She knew he could not, and she felt a prick of pain for him. Vision was so important. She relied on her eyes for everything.

"I've noticed you're fluent in Greek," he said thoughtfully. "That's unusual, considering your background."

He didn't know her background. He didn't know anything about her. But now wasn't the time to be correcting him. In an effort to make peace, she was willing to be conciliatory. "So, you are the strong one and your brother was the saint?"

Kristian shrugged. "He's dead, and I'm alive."

And, even though she wanted peace, she couldn't help thinking that Kristian really was no saint. He'd been a thorn in her side from the beginning, and she was anxious to be rid of him. "You said earlier that you were willing to start your therapy, but you want to be in charge of your rehabilitation program?"

He nodded. "That's right. You are here to help me accomplish my goals."

"Great. I'm anxious to help you meet your goals." She crossed her legs and settled her hands in her lap. "So, what do you want me to do?"

"Whatever it is I need done."

Elizabeth's mouth opened, then closed. "That's rather vague," she said, when she finally found her voice.

"Oh, don't worry. It won't be vague. I'll be completely in control. I'll tell you what time we start our day, what time we finish, and what we do in between."

"What about the actual exercises? The stretching, the strengthening—"

"I'll take care of that."

He would devise his own course of treatment? He would manage his rehabilitation program?

Her head spun. She couldn't think her way clear. This was all too ridiculous. But then finally, fortunately, logic returned. "Mr. Koumantaros, you might be an excellent executive, and able to make millions of dollars, but that doesn't mean you know the basics of physical therapy—"

"Nurse Hatchet, I haven't walked because I haven't wanted to walk. It's as simple as that."

"Is it?"

"Yes."

My God, he was arrogant—and overly confident. "And you want to walk now?"

"Yes."

Weakly she leaned back in her chair and stared at him. Kristian was changing before her eyes. Metamorphosing.

Pano and the housekeeper appeared with their lunch, but Kristian paid them no heed. "You were the one who told me I need to move forward, Cratchett, and you're absolutely right. It's time I moved forward and got back on my feet."

She watched the myriad of small plates set before them. *Mezedhes*—lots of delicious dips, ranging from eggplant purée to cucumber, yoghurt and garlic, cheese. There were also plates of steaming *keftedhes, dolmadhes, tsiros.* And it all smelled amazing. Elizabeth might not love Greek coffee, but she loved Greek food. Only right now it would be impossible to eat a bite of anything.

"And when do you intend to start your…program?" she asked.

"Today. Immediately after lunch." He sat still while Pano moved the plates around for him, and quietly explained where the plates were and what each dish was.

When Pano and the housekeeper had left, Kristian continued. "I want to be walking soon. I need to be walking this time next week if I hope to travel to Athens in a month's time."

"Walking next *week?*" she choked, unable to take it all in. She couldn't believe the change in him. Couldn't believe the swift turn of events, either. From waking him, to the pills being dumped into the fountain, to the revelation about Calista—everything was different.

Everything, she repeated silently, but especially him. And just looking at him from across the table she saw he seemed so much bigger. Taller. More imposing.

"A week," he insisted.

"Kristian, it's good to have goals. But please be realistic. It's highly unlikely you'll be able to walk unaided in the next couple of weeks, but with hard work you might manage short distances with your walker—"

"If I go to Athens there can be no walker."

"But—"

"It's a matter of culture and respect, Ms. Hatchet. You're not Greek; you don't understand—"

"I *do* understand. That's why I'm here. But give yourself time to meet your goals. Two or three months is far more realistic."

With a rough push of his wheelchair, he rolled back a short distance from the table. "Enough!"

Slowly he placed one foot on the ground, and then the other, and then, leaning forward, put his hands on the table. For a moment it seemed as though nothing was happening, and then, little by little, he began to push up, utilizing his triceps, biceps and shoulders to give himself leverage.

His face paled and perspiration beaded his brow. Thick jet-black hair fell forward as, jaw set, he continued to press up until he was fully upright.

As soon as he was straight he threw his head back in an almost primal act of conquest. *"There."* The word rumbled from him.

He'd proved her wrong.

It had cost him to stand unassisted, too. She could see from his pallor and the lines etched at his mouth that he was hurting, but he didn't utter a word of complaint.

She couldn't help looking at him with fresh respect. What he had done had not been easy. It had taken him long, grueling minutes to concentrate, to work muscles that hadn't been utilized in far too long. But he had succeeded. He'd stood by himself.

And he'd done it as an act of protest and defiance.

He'd done it as something to prove.

"That's a start," she said crisply, hiding her awe. He wasn't just any man. He was a force to be reckoned with. "It's impressive. But you know it's just going to get harder from here."

Kristian shifted his weight, steadied himself, and removed one hand from the table so that he already stood taller.

Silent emotion flickered across his beautiful scarred face. "Good," he said. "I'm ready."

Reaching back for his wheelchair, he nearly stumbled, and Elizabeth jumped to her feet even as Pano rushed forward from the shadows.

Kristian angrily waved both off. *"Ohi!"* he snapped, strain evident in the deep lines shaping his mouth. "No."

"Kyrios," Pano pleaded, pained to see Kristian struggle so.

But Kristian rattled off a rebuke in furious Greek. "I can do it," he insisted, after taking a breath. "I *must* do it."

Pano reluctantly dropped back, and Elizabeth slowly sat down again, torn between admiration and exasperation. While she admired the fact that Kristian would not allow anyone to help him be reseated, she also knew that if he went at his entire therapy like this he'd soon be exhausted, frustrated, and possibly injured worse.

He needed to build his strength gradually, with a systematic and scientific approach.

But Kristian had a different plan—which he outlined after lunch.

Standing—walking—was merely an issue of mind over matter, he said, and her job wasn't to provide obstacles, tell him no, or even offer advice. Her job was to be there when he wanted something, and that was it.

"I'm a handmaid?" she asked, trying to hide her indignation. After four years earning a nursing degree, and then another two years earning a Masters in Business Administration? "You could hire anyone to come and play handmaid. I'm a little over-qualified and rather expensive—"

"I know," he said grimly. "Your agency charged an exorbitant amount for my care—little good did it do me."

"You chose not to improve."

"Your agency's methods were useless."

"I protest."

"You may protest all you like, but it doesn't change the facts. Under your agency's care, not only did I fail to recover, but I was harassed as well as blackmailed. The bottom line, Kyria Hatchet, is that not only did you milk the system—and me— for hundreds and thousands of euros, but you also dared to show up here, uninvited, unwanted, and force yourself on me."

Sick at heart, she rose. "I'll leave, then. Let's just forget this—pretend it never happened—"

"What about the doctors, Nurse? What about those specialists who insisted you come here or I go to their facility in Athens? Was that true, or another of your lies?"

"Lies?"

"I know why you're here—"

"To get you better!"

"You have exactly ten seconds to give me the full name and contact number of the person now responsible for paying my medical bills or I shall begin dismantling your company within the hour. All it will take is one phone call to my office in Athens and your life as you know it will be forever changed."

"Kristian—"

"Nine seconds."

"Kris—"

"Eight."

"I promised—"

"Seven."

"A deal is—"

"Six."

Livid tears scalded her eyes. "It's because she cares. It's because she loves you—"

"Four."

"She wants you back. Home. Close to her."

"Two."

Elizabeth balled her hands into fists. *"Please."*

"One."

"Cosima." She pressed one fist to her chest, to slow the panicked beating of her heart. "Cosima hired me. She's desperate. She just wants you home."

CHAPTER FIVE

COSIMA?

Kristian's jaw hardened and his voice turned flinty. How could Cosima possibly pay for his care? She might be Andreas's former fiancée and Athens's most popular socialite, but she had more financial problems than anyone he knew.

"Cosima hired you?" he repeated, thinking maybe he'd heard wrong. "She was the one that contacted you in London?"

"Yes. But I promised her—*promised*—I wouldn't tell you."

"Why?"

"She said you'd be very upset if you knew, she said you were so proud—" Elizabeth broke off, the threat of tears evident in her voice. "She said she had to do something to show you how much she believed in you."

Cosima believed in him?

Kristian silently, mockingly, repeated Elizabeth's words. Or maybe it was that Cosima felt indebted to him. Maybe she felt as guilt-ridden as he did. Because, after all, she lived and Andreas had died, and it was Kristian who'd made the decision. It was Kristian who'd played God that day.

No wonder he had nightmares. No wonder he had nightmares during the day.

He couldn't accept the decision he'd made. Nor could he accept that it was a decision that couldn't be changed.

Kristian, wealthy and powerful beyond measure, couldn't buy or secure the one thing he wanted most: his brother's life.

But Elizabeth knew nothing of Kristian's loathing, and anger, and pressed on. "Now that you know," she continued, "the contract isn't valid. I can't remain—"

"Of course you can," he interrupted shortly. "She doesn't have to know that I know. There's no point in wrecking her little plan."

His words were greeted by silence, and for a moment he thought maybe Elizabeth had left, going God knew where, but then he heard the faintest shuffle, and an even softer sigh.

"She just wants what is best for you," Elizabeth said wearily. "Please don't be angry with her. She seems like such a kind person."

It was in that moment that Kristian learned something very important about Elizabeth Hatchet.

Elizabeth Hatchet might have honest intentions, but she was a lousy judge of character.

It was on the tip of his tongue to ask if Elizabeth was aware that Cosima and Calista had gone to school together. To ask her if she knew that both women had shared a flat for more than a year, and had gone into modeling together, too.

He could tell her that Calista and Cosima had been the best of friends until their lives had gone in very different directions.

Cosima had met Andreas Koumantaros and become girlfriend and then fiancée to one of Greece's most wealthy men.

Calista, unable to find a rich enough boyfriend, or enough modeling jobs to pay her rent, had turned to exotic dancing and questionable modeling gigs.

The two seemed to have had nothing more in common after

a couple years. Cosima had traveled the world as the pampered bride-to-be, and Calista had struggled to make ends meet.

And then tragedy had struck and evened the score.

Andreas had died in the avalanche, Cosima had survived but lost her lifestyle, and Calista, who had still been struggling along, had thought she'd found a sugar-daddy of her own.

Albeit a handicapped one.

The corner of his mouth curved crookedly, the tilt of his lips hiding the depth of his anger as well as his derision. Calista hadn't been the first to imagine he'd be an easy conquest. A dozen women from all over Europe had flocked to his side during his hospital stay. They'd brought flowers, gifts, seductive promises. *I love you. I'll be here for you. I'll never leave you.*

It would have been one thing if any of them had genuinely cared for him. Instead they'd all been opportunists, thinking a life with an invalid wouldn't be so bad if the invalid was a Greek tycoon.

Again Kristian felt the whip of anger. Did women think that just because he couldn't see he'd lost his mind?

That his inability to travel unaided across the room meant he'd enjoy the company of a shallow, self-absorbed, materialistic woman? He hadn't enjoyed shallow and self-absorbed women before. Why would he now?

"You've met Cosima, then," he said flatly.

"We've only spoken on the phone, but her concern—and she *is* concerned—touched me," Elizabeth added anxiously, trying to fill the silence. "She obviously has a good heart, and it wouldn't be fair to punish her for trying to help you."

Kristian ran his hand over his jaw. "No, you're right. And you said, she seems most anxious to see me on my feet."

"Yes. Yes—and she's just so worried about you. She

was in tears on the phone. I think she's afraid you're shutting her out—"

"Really?" This did intrigue him. Was Cosima possibly imagining some kind of future for the two of them? The idea was as grotesque as it was laughable.

"She said you've become too reclusive here."

"This is my home."

"But she's concerned you're overly depressed and far too despondent."

"Were those her actual words?" he asked, struggling to keep the sarcasm from his voice.

"Yes, as a matter of fact. I have it in my notes, if you want to see—"

"No. I believe you." His brows flattened, his curiosity colored by disbelief. Cosima wasn't sentimental. She wasn't particularly emotional or sensitive, either. So why would she be so anxious to have him return to Athens? "And so," he added, wanting to hear more about Cosima's concern, "you were sent here to rescue me."

"Not rescue, just motivate you. Get you on your feet."

"And look!" he said grandly, gesturing with his hands. "Today I stood. Tomorrow I climb Mount Everest."

"Not Everest," Elizabeth corrected, sounding genuinely bemused. "Just walk in time for your wedding."

Wedding?

Wedding?

Kristian had heard it all now. He didn't know whether to roar with amusement or anguish. His wedding. To Cosima, his late brother's lover, he presumed. My God, this was like an ancient Greek comedy—a bold work conceived of by Aristophanes. One full of bawdy mirth but founded on tragedy.

And as he sat there, trying to take it all in, Cosima and Calista's scheming reminded him of the two Greek sisters: Penia, goddess of poverty, and Amakhania, goddess of helplessness. Goddesses known for tormenting with their evil and greed.

But now that he knew, he wouldn't be tormented any longer.

No, he'd write a little Greek play of his own. And if all went well his good Nurse Cratchett could even help him by playing a leading role.

"Let's not tell her I know," Kristian said. "Let's work hard, and we'll surprise her with my progress."

"So where do we start?" Elizabeth asked. "What do we do first?"

He nearly smiled at her enthusiasm. She sounded so pleased with him already. "*I've* already hired a physical therapist from Sparta," he answered, making it clear that this was not a joint decision, but his and his alone. "The therapist arrives tomorrow."

"And until then?"

"I'll probably relax, nap. Swim."

"Swim?" she asked. "You're swimming?"

Her surprise made his lip curl. She really thought he was in dreadful shape, didn't she? "I have been for the past two weeks."

"Ever since your last nurse left?" she said quietly.

He didn't answer. He didn't need to.

"Maybe you could show me the pool?" she asked.

For a moment he almost felt sorry for her. She was trying so hard to do what she thought was the right thing, but her idea of right wasn't necessarily what he wanted or needed. "Of course. If you'll come with me."

Together they traveled across the stone courtyard with its trellis-covered patio, where they'd just enjoyed lunch, with

Kristian pushing his own wheelchair and Elizabeth walking next to him.

They headed toward the fountain and then passed it, moving from the stone patio to the garden, with its gravel path.

"The gardens are beautiful," Elizabeth said, walking slowly enough for Kristian to push his chair at a comfortable pace.

His tires sank into the gravel, and he wrestled a moment with his chair until he found traction again and pushed faster, to keep from sinking back into the crushed stones. "You'd do better with a stone path here, wouldn't you?" she asked, glancing down at his arms, impressed by his strength.

Warm color darkened his cheekbones. "It was suggested months ago that I change it, but I knew I wouldn't be in a wheelchair forever so I left it."

"So you planned on getting out of your wheelchair?"

His head lifted, and he shot her a look as though he could see, his brow furrowing, lines deepening between his eyes. He resented her question, and his resentment brought home yet again just who he was, and what he'd accomplished in his lifetime.

Watching him struggle through the gravel, it crossed her mind that maybe he hadn't remained in the wheelchair because he was lazy, but because without sight he felt exposed. Maybe for him the wheelchair wasn't transportation so much as a suit of armor, a form of protection.

"Are we almost to the hedge?" he asked, pausing a moment to try and get his bearings.

"Yes, it's just in front of us."

"The pool, then, is to the left."

Elizabeth turned toward her left and was momentarily dazzled by the sun's reflection off brilliant blue water. The long lap pool sparkled in its emerald-green setting, making it appear even more jewel-like than it already was.

"It's a new pool?" she guessed, from the young landscaping and the gorgeous artisan tilework.

"I wish I could say it was my only extravagance, but I've been renovating the monastery for nearly a decade now. It's been a labor of love."

They'd reached a low stone wall that bordered the pool, and Elizabeth moved forward to open the pretty gate. "But why Taygetos? Why a ruined monastery? You don't have family from here, do you?"

"No, but I love the mountains—this is where I feel at home," he said, lifting a hand to his face as if to block the sun. "My mother was French, raised in a small town at the base of the Alps. I've grown up hiking, skiing, rock-climbing. These are the things my father taught us to do, things my mother enjoyed, and it just feels right living here."

Elizabeth saw how he kept trying to shield his eyes with his hand. "Is the sun bothering you?"

"I usually wear bandages, or dark glasses."

"You've that much light sensitivity?"

"It's painful," he admitted.

She didn't want him in pain, but the tenderness and sensitivity gave her hope that maybe, one day, he might get at least a little of his vision back. "Shall I call Pano to get your glasses?"

"It's not necessary. We won't be here long."

"But it's lovely out," she said wistfully, gazing around the pool area and admiring the tiny purplish campanula flowers that were growing up and over the stone walls. The tiny violet-hued blossoms were such a pretty contrast to the rugged rock. "Let me get them. That way you can relax a little, be more comfortable."

"No, just find me a little shade—or perhaps position me away from the sun."

"There's some shade on the other side of the pool, near the rock wall." She hesitated. "Shall I push you?"

"I can do it myself."

But somehow in the struggle, as Elizabeth pushed forward and Kristian grappled for control, the front castors of his chair ran off the stone edge and over the side, and once the front casters went forward, the rest of the chair followed.

He hit the pool with a big splash.

It all happened in slow motion.

Just before he hit the water Elizabeth could see herself grabbing at his chair, hanging tight to the handles and trying to pull him back, but she was unable to get enough leverage to stop the momentum. In the end she let go, knowing she couldn't stop him and afraid she'd fall on him and hurt him worse.

Heart pounding, Elizabeth dropped to her knees, horrified that her patient and his wheelchair had just tumbled in.

How could she have let this happen? How could she have been so reckless?

Elizabeth was close to jumping in when Kristian surfaced. His chair, though, was another matter. While Kristian was swimming toward the side of the pool, his chair was slowly, steadily, sinking to the bottom.

"Kristian—I'm sorry, I'm sorry," she apologized repeatedly as she knelt on the pool deck. She'd never felt less professional in her entire life. An accident like this was pure carelessness. He knew it, and so did she.

"I cut the corner too close. I should have been paying closer attention. I'm so sorry."

He swam toward her.

Leaning forward, she extended her hand as far as it would

go. "You're almost at the wall. My hand's right in front of it. You've almost got it," she encouraged as he reached for her.

His fingers curled around hers. Relief surged through her. He was fine. "I've got you," she said.

"Are you sure?" he asked, hand tightening on hers. "Or do I have you?"

And, with a hard tug, he pulled her off her knees and into the pool.

Elizabeth landed hard on her stomach, splashing water wildly.

He'd pulled her in. Deliberately. She couldn't believe it. So much for poor, helpless Kristian Koumantaros.

He was far from helpless. And he'd fooled her three times now.

Spluttering to the surface, she looked around for Kristian and spotted him leaning casually against the wall.

"That was mean," she said, swimming toward him, her wet clothes hampering her movements.

He laughed softly and ran a hand through his hair, pushing the inky black strands back from his face. "I thought you'd find it refreshing."

She squeezed water from her own hair. "I didn't want you to fall in. I'd never want that to happen."

"Your concern for my wellbeing is most touching. You know, Cratchett, I was worried you might be like my other nurses, but I have to tell you, you're worse."

She swallowed hard. She deserved that. "I'm sorry," she said, knowing a responsible nurse would never have permitted such a thing to happen. Indeed, if any of her nurses had allowed a patient in their care to fall into a pool she'd have fired the nurse on the spot. "It's been a while since I actually did any in-home care. As you know, I'm the head administrator for the company now."

"Skills a little rusty?" he said.

"Mmmm." Using the ladder, she climbed out and sat down on the deck, to pluck at her shirt and tug her soggy shoes off.

"So why are *you* here and not another nurse?"

Wringing water from her skirt, she sighed. Defeated. "The agency's close to bankruptcy. I couldn't afford to send another nurse. It was me or nothing."

"But my insurance has paid you, and I've paid you."

Elizabeth watched the water trickle from her skirt to the stone pavers. "There were expenses not covered, and those costs were difficult to manage, and eventually they ate into the profits until we were barely breaking even." She didn't bother to tell him that Calista had needed counseling and compensation after leaving Kristian's employment. And covering Calista's bills had cost her dearly, too.

"I think I better get your chair," she said, not wanting to think about things she found very difficult to control.

"I do need it," he agreed. "Are you a strong swimmer?"

"I can swim."

"You're not inspiring much confidence, Cratchett."

She smiled despite herself. "It'll be okay." And it would be. She wasn't going to panic about holding her breath or swimming deep under water. She'd just go down and grab the chair, and haul it back up.

He sighed, pushed back wet hair from his face. "You're scared."

"No."

"You're not a very good swimmer."

She made a little exasperated sound. "I can swim laps. Pretty well. It's just in deep water I get…nervous."

"Claustrophobic?"

"Oh, it's silly, but—" She broke off, not wanting to tell him.

She didn't need him making fun of her. It was a genuine fear, and there wasn't a lot she could do about it.

"But what?"

"I had an accident when I was little." He said nothing, and she knew he was still waiting for the details. "I was playing a diving game with a girl I'd met. We'd toss coins and then go pick them up. Well, in this hotel pool there was a huge drain at the bottom, and somehow—" She broke off, feeling a little sick from the retelling. "There was a lot of suction, and somehow the strings on my swimsuit got tangled, stuck. I couldn't get them out and couldn't get my suit off."

Kristian didn't speak, and Elizabeth tried to smile. "They got me out, of course. Obviously. Here I am. But…" She felt a painful flutter inside, a memory of panic and what it had been like. Her shoulders lifted, fell. "I was scared."

"How old were you?"

"Six."

"You must have been a good swimmer to be playing diving games in the deep end at six."

She laughed a little. "I think as a little girl I was a bit on the wild side. My nanny—" She broke off, rephrased. "Anyway, after that I didn't want to swim anymore. Especially not in big pools. And since then I've pretty much stuck to the shallow end. Kind of boring, but safe."

Elizabeth could feel Kristian's scrutiny even though he couldn't see her. He was trying to understand her, to reconcile what he'd thought he knew with this.

"I'll make you a deal," he said at last.

Her eyes narrowed. So far his deals had been terrible. "What kind of deal?"

"I'll go get my own chair if you don't look while I strip. I can't dive down in my clothes."

Elizabeth pulled her knees up to her chest and tried not to laugh. "You're afraid I'll see you naked?"

"I'm trying to protect you. You're a nurse without a lot of field experience lately. I'm afraid my...nudity...might overwhelm you."

She grinned against her wet kneecap. "Fine."

One black eyebrow arched. "Fine, what? Fine, you'll look at me? Or fine, you'll politely avert your gaze?"

"Fine. I'll politely avert my gaze."

"Endaxi," he said, still in the pool. "Okay." And then he began peeling his clothes off one by one.

And although Elizabeth had made a promise not to look, the sound of wet cotton inching its way off wet skin was too tempting.

She did watch, and as the clothes came off she discovered he had a rather amazing body, despite the accident and horrific injuries. His torso was still powerful, thick with honed muscle, while from her vantage point on the deck his legs looked long and well shaped.

Clothes gone, he disappeared beneath the surface, swimming toward the bottom with strong, powerful strokes. Even though he couldn't see, he was heading in the right direction. It took him a moment to find the chair's exact location, but once he found it he took hold of the back and immediately began to swim up with it.

Incredible.

As Kristian surfaced with the chair, Pano and one of the housemaids came running through the small wrought-iron gate with a huge stack of towels.

"Kyrios," Pano called, "are you all right?"

"I'm fine." Kristian answered, dragging the chair to the side of the pool.

Pano was there to take the chair. He tipped it sideways and water streamed from the spokes and castors. He tipped it the other way and more water spurted from open screwholes, and then he passed the chair to the maid, who began vigorously toweling the wheelchair dry.

In the meantime Kristian placed his hands on the stone deck and hauled himself up and out, using only his shoulders, biceps and triceps. He was far stronger than he let on, and far more capable of taking care of himself than she'd thought.

He didn't need anyone pushing him.

He probably didn't need anyone taking care of him.

If everyone just stepped back and left him alone, she suspected that soon he'd manage just fine.

And, speaking of fine, Elizabeth couldn't tear her eyes from Kristian's broad muscular back, lean waist, and tight hard buttocks as he shifted his weight around. His body was almost perfectly proportioned, every muscle shaped and honed. He didn't look ill, or like a patient. He looked like a man, an incredibly physical, virile man.

Once his thighs had cleared the water he did a quick turn and sat down. Pano swiftly draped a towel over Kristian's shoulders and threw another one over his lap, but not before Elizabeth had seen as much of Kristian's front as she had seen of his back.

And his front was even more impressive. His shoulders broad and thick, his chest shaped into two hard planes of muscle, his belly flat, lean, and his...

His...

She shouldn't be staring at his lap, it was completely unprofessional, but he was very, very big there, too.

She felt blood surge to her cheeks, and she battled shyness, shame and interest.

His body was so beautiful, and his size, that symbol of masculinity—wow. Ridiculously impressive. And Elizabeth wasn't easily impressed.

No wonder Kristian was so comfortable naked. Even after a year plus in a wheelchair he was still every inch a man.

"I thought we had a deal," Kristian murmured, dragging the towel over his head and then his chest.

"We did. We do." Flushing crimson, Elizabeth jumped to her feet and twisted her damp skirt yet again. "Maybe I should go get some dry clothes."

"A good idea," Kristian said, leaning back on his hands, face lifted. He was smiling a little, a smile that indicated he knew she'd been looking at him, knew she'd been fascinated by his anatomy. "I wouldn't want you to catch a chill."

"No."

His lips curled, and the sunlight played over the carved planes of his face, lingering on the jagged scar, and she felt her heart leap at the savage violence done to his Greek beauty. "I'll see you at dinner, then."

See her at dinner.

He couldn't see her, of course, but he'd meet her, and her heart did another peculiar flutter. "Dinner tonight?"

"I thought I was to eat all my meals with you," he answered lazily. "Something about you needing to socialize me. Make me civil again."

Her heart was drumming a mile a minute. "Right." She forced a tight, pained smile. "I'll look forward to that…then."

Elizabeth turned so quickly that she stubbed her toe. With a hop and a whimper she set off at a run for the sanctuary of her room, lecturing herself the entire way. *Do not get personally involved, do not get personally involved, no matter what you do, do not get personally involved.*

But as she reached her tower bedroom and began to strip her wet clothes off she almost cried with vexation.

She already was involved.

CHAPTER SIX

OUTSIDE in the garden, as Kristian struggled to make his way back to the villa, water dripped from the chair and his cushion sagged, waterlogged.

Thank God he was almost done with this wheelchair.

Falling into the pool today had been infuriating and insightful. He hated how helpless he'd felt as he went blindly tumbling in. He'd hated the shock and surprise as he'd thrashed in his clothes in the water. But at the same time his unexpected fall had had unexpected results.

For one, Elizabeth had dropped some of her brittle guard, and he'd discovered she was far less icy then he'd thought. She was in many ways quite gentle, and her fear about the deep end had struck home with him. As a boy he'd been thrown from a horse, and he hadn't ridden again for years.

Getting back into the wet wheelchair had been another lesson. As he'd been transferred in, he'd realized the chair had served its purpose. He didn't want it anymore—didn't want to be confined or contained. He craved freedom, and knew that for the first time since his accident he was truly ready for whatever therapy was required to allow him to walk and run again.

Water still dripping, he cautiously rolled his way from grass patio, and from patio toward the wing where his room was.

But as he rolled down the loggia he couldn't seem to find his bedroom door. He began to second-guess himself, and soon thought he'd gone the wrong way.

Pano, who'd been following several paces behind, couldn't keep silent any longer. "*Kyrie,* your room is just here." And, without waiting for Kristian to find it himself, the butler steered the wheelchair around the corner and over the door's threshold.

Kristian felt a tinge of annoyance at the help. He'd wanted to do it alone, felt an increasing need to do more for himself, but Pano, a good loyal employee of the past fifteen years, couldn't bear for Kristian to struggle.

"How did you end up in the pool?" Pano asked, closing the outside door.

Kristian shrugged and tugged the wet towel from around his shoulders. "Ms. Hatchet was pushing me toward the shade and misjudged the distance to the pool's edge."

"*Despinis* pushed you into the pool?" Pano cried, horrified.

"It was an accident."

"How could she push you into the pool?"

"It was a tight corner."

"How can that happen? How is that proper?" The butler muttered to himself as he opened and closed drawers, retrieving dry clothes for his master. "I knew she wasn't a proper nurse—knew she couldn't do the job. I *knew* it."

Kristian checked his smile. Pano was a traditional Greek, from the old school of hearth and home. "And how is she not a proper nurse?"

"If you could see—"

"But I can't. So you must tell me."

"First, she doesn't act like one, and second, she doesn't *look* like one."

"Why not? Is she too old, too heavy, what?"

"*Ohi*," Pano groaned. "No. She's not too old, or too fat, or anything like that. It's the opposite. She's too small. She's delicate. Like a little bird in a tiny cage. And if you want a little blonde bird for a nurse, fine. But if you need a big, sturdy woman to lift and carry…" Pano sighed, shrugging expressively. "Then Despinis Elizabeth is not for you."

So she was blonde, Kristian thought after Pano had left him alone to dress.

And Elizabeth Hatchet was neither old nor unattractive. Rather she was fine-boned, slender, a lady.

Kristian tried to picture her, this ladylike nurse of his, who hadn't actually nursed in years, who proclaimed Cosima kind, and as a child had stayed at hotels with a nanny to look after her.

But it was impossible to visualize her. He'd dated plenty of fair English and American girls, Scandinavians and Dutch, but he would have wagered a thousand euros Elizabeth was brunette.

But wasn't that like her? So full of surprises. For example her voice—melodic, like that of a violin—and her fragrance—not floral, not exotic spice, but fresh, clean, grass or melon. And then last night, when she'd leaned close to his bed to adjust his pillows, he'd been surprised she wore her hair down. Something about her brisk manner had made him assume she was the classic all-business, no-nonsense executive.

Apparently he was wrong.

Apparently his Cratchett was blonde, slender, delicate, *pretty*. Not even close to a battleaxe.

In trying to form a new impression of her, he wondered at er age, and her height, as well as the shade of her hair. Was e a pale, silvery blonde? Or a golden blonde with streaks arm amber and honey?

ut it wasn't just her age or appearance that intrigued him. s her story, too, of a six-year-old who'd once been a daring swimmer now afraid to leave the shallow end, as well as the haunting image of a child trapped, swimsuit ties tangled, in that pool's powerful drain.

In her bedroom, after several lovely long hours devoted to nothing but reading and taking a delicious and much needed nap, Elizabeth was dressing for dinner as well as having a crisis of conscience.

She didn't know what she was doing here. Kristian didn't need a nurse, and he certainly didn't need the round-the-clock supervision her agency and staff had been providing.

How could she stay here? How could she take Cosima's money? It was not as if Kristian was even letting her do anything. He wanted to be in control—which was fine with her if he could truly motivate himself. He really would be better off with a sports trainer and an occupational therapist to help him adapt to his loss of sight rather than someone trained to deal with concussions, wounds, injuries and infections.

And, to compound her worry, she didn't have the foggiest idea how to dress for dinner.

She, who'd grown up in five-star hotels all over the world, was suffering a mild panic attack because she couldn't figure out what to wear for a late evening meal, at an old monastery, in the middle of the Taygetos.

One by one Elizabeth pulled out things from her wardrobe and discarded them. A swingy pleated navy skirt. Too school-girl. A straight brown gabardine skirt that nearly reached her ankles. She'd once thought it smart, but now she found i boring. A gray plaid skirt with a narrow velvet trim. Sl sighed, thinking they were all so serious and practical.

But wasn't that what she was supposed to be? Seric Practical?

This isn't a holiday, she reminded herself sternly, retrieving the gray plaid skirt and pairing it with a pewter silk blouse. Dressing, she wrinkled her nose at her reflection. Ugh. So *not* pretty.

But why did she even care what she was wearing?

And that was when she felt a little wobble in her middle—butterflies, worry, guilt.

She was acting as if she was dressing for a dinner date instead of dinner with a patient. And that was wrong. Her being here, feeling this way, was wrong.

She was here for business. Medicine.

And yet as she remembered Kristian's smile by the pool, and his cool, mocking, "I thought we had a deal," she felt the wobble inside her again. And this time the wobble was followed by an expectant shiver.

She was nervous.

And excited.

And both emotions were equally inappropriate. Kristian was in her care. She'd been hired by his girlfriend to get him back on his feet. It would be professionally, never mind morally, wrong to think of him in any light other than as her patient.

A patient, she reminded herself.

Yet the butterflies in her stomach didn't go away.

With a quick, impatient flick of her wrist she dragged her brush through her hair. Kristian couldn't be an option even if he *was* single, and *not* her patient. It was ridiculous to romanticize or idealize him. She'd been married to a Greek and it ⸌ad been a disaster from the start. Their marriage had lasted ⸌o years but scarred her for nearly seven.

The memory swept her more than ten years back, to when, twenty-year-old New York socialite, she had been toasted ⸌e next great American beauty.

She'd been so young and inexperienced then, just a debutante entering the social scene, and she'd foolishly believed everything people told her. It would be three years before she fully understood that she was adored for her name and fortune, not for herself.

"No more Greek tycoons," she whispered to herself. "No more men who want you for the wrong reasons." Besides, marriage to a Greek had taught her that Mediterranean men preferred beautiful women with breasts and hips and hourglass figures—attributes slender, slim-hipped Elizabeth would never have.

With her hair a smooth pale gold curtain, she headed toward the library, since she didn't know where they were to eat tonight as the dining room had been converted into a fitness room.

Be kind, cordial, supportive, educational and useful, she told herself. But that is as far as your involvement goes.

Kristian entered the library shortly after she did. He was wearing dark slacks and a loose white linen shirt, and with his black hair combed back from his face his blue eyes seemed even more startling.

He wasn't happy, though, she thought, watching him push into the room, his wheelchair tires humming on the floor.

"Is something wrong?" she asked, still standing just inside the door, since she hadn't known where to go and didn't feel comfortable just sitting down. This was Kristian's refuge, after all, the place he spent the majority of his time.

He grimaced. "Now that I want to walk, I don't want to use the wheelchair."

"But you can't give up the chair yet. Though I bet yc tried," she guessed, her tone sympathetic.

"I suppose I thought that, having stood, I could probably walk."

"And you will. It'll take some time, but, considering your determination, it won't be as long as you think."

Pano appeared in the doorway to invite them to dinner. They followed him a short distance down the hall to a spacious room with a soaring ceiling hand-painted with scenes from the New Testament, in bold reds, blues, gray-greens and golds, although in places the paint was chipped and faded, revealing dark beams beneath.

A striking red wool carpet covered the floor, and in the middle of the carpet was a table set with two place-settings and two wood chairs. Fat round white candles glowed on the table and in sconces on the wall, and the dishes on the table were a glazed cobalt blue.

"It looks wonderful in here," she said, suddenly feeling foolish in her gray plaid skirt with its velvet trim. She should be wearing something loose and exotic—a flowing peasant skirt, a long jeweled top, even casual linen trousers came to mind. "The colors and artwork are stunning. This is the original ceiling, isn't it?"

"I had it saved."

"Is the building very old?"

"The tower dates to the 1700s while this part, the main monastery building, was put into service in 1802." Kristian drew a breath, held it, and just listened. After a moment he added more quietly. "Even though I can't see what's around me—the old stone walls, the beamed and arched ceilings. I feel it."

"That's good," she answered, feeling a tug on her heart. She could see why he loved the renovated monastery. It was atmospheric here, but it was so remote that she worried that Kristian wasn't getting enough contact with the outside world. He needed stimulation, interaction. He needed…a life.

But he's still healing, she reminded herself as they sat

down at the table, her place directly across from Kristian's. Just over a year ago he'd lost his brother, his cousin and numerous friends in the avalanche. He'd been almost fatally injured when his helicopter had crashed trying to look for survivors. Kristian had been badly hurt, and in the blunt trauma to his head he'd detached both retinas.

Sometimes, when she thought about it, it took her breath away just how much he'd lost in one day.

The housekeeper served the meal, and Pano appeared at Kristian's elbow, ready to assist him. Kristian sent him away. "We can manage," he said, reaching for the wine.

Kristian held the bottle toward Elizabeth, tilting it so she could read the label. "Will a glass hurt, Nurse Hatchet?"

His tone was teasing, but it was his expression which made her pulse quicken. He looked so boyish it disarmed her.

"A glass," she agreed cautiously.

He laughed and carefully reached out, found her glass, maneuvering the bottle so it was just over the rim. He poured slowly and listened carefully as he poured. "How is that?" he asked, indicating the glass. "Too much? Too little?"

"Just right."

He slowly poured a glass for himself, before finding an empty spot on the table for the bottle.

The next course was almost immediately served, and he was attentive during the meal, asking her questions about work, her travels, her knowledge of Greek. "At one point I spent a lot of time in Greece," she answered, sidestepping any mention of her marriage.

"The university student on holiday?" Kristian guessed.

She made a face. "Everyone loves Greece."

"What do you like most about it?" he persisted.

A half-dozen different thoughts came to mind. The v

The people. The climate. The food. The beaches. The warmth. But Greece had also created pain. So many people here had turned on her during her divorce. Friends—close friends—had dropped her overnight.

A lump filled her throat and she blinked to keep tears from forming. It was long ago, she told herself. Seven years. She couldn't let the divorce sour her on an entire country. Maybe her immediate social circle hadn't been kind when she and Nico separated, but not everyone was so judgmental or shallow.

"You've no answer?" he said.

"It's just that I like it all," she said, smiling to chase away any lingering sadness. "And you? What do you like best about your country?"

He thought about it for a moment, before lifting his wine glass. "The people. And their zest for life."

She clinked her glass against his, took another sip, and let the wine sit on her tongue a moment before swallowing. It was a red wine, and surprisingly good. She knew from the label it was Greek, but she wasn't as familiar with Greece's red wines as she was the white, as Nico preferred white. "Do you know anything about this wine?"

"I do. It's from one of my favorite wineries, a local winery, and the grape is *ayroyitiko,* which is indigenous to the Peloponnese."

"I didn't realize there were vineyards here."

"There are vineyards all over Greece—although the most famous Greek wines come from Samos and Crete."

"That's where you get the white wines, right?"

"Samian wine is, yes, and the most popular grape there is *moshato.* Lots of wine snobs love Samian wine."

was all she could do not to giggle. Nico, her former nd, was the ultimate wine snob. He'd go to a restaurant, order an outrageously priced bottle, and if he didn't think it up to snuff imperiously send it away. There had been times when Elizabeth had suspected there was absolutely nothing wrong with the wine. It was just Nico wanting to appear powerful.

"You're a white wine drinker?" Kristian asked.

"No, not really. I just had…friends…who preferred white Greek wine to red, so I'm rather ignorant when it comes to the different red grape varieties."

Kristian rested his forearms on the table. The corner of his mouth tugged. "A friend?" His expression shifted, suddenly perceptive. "A *male* friend?"

"He was male," she agreed carefully.

"And Greek?"

"And Greek."

He laughed softly, and yet there was tension in the sound, a hint that not all was well. "Greek men are sexual as well as possessive. I imagine your Greek friend wanted more from you than just friendship?"

Elizabeth blushed hotly. "It was a long time ago."

"It ended badly?"

Her head dipped. Her face burned. "I don't know." She swallowed, wondered why she was protecting Nico. "Yes," she corrected. "It did."

"Did this prejudice you against Greek men?"

"No." But she sounded uncertain.

"Against me?"

She blushed, and then laughed. "Maybe."

"So that is why I got the fleet of battleaxe nurses."

She laughed again. He amused her. And intrigued her. A if he wasn't her patient she'd even admit she found him v very attractive. "Are you telling me you didn't deserve the tleaxe nurses?"

"I'm telling you I'm not like other Greek men."

Her breath suddenly caught in her throat, and her eyes grew wide. Somehow, with those words, he'd changed everything—the mood, the night, the meal itself. He'd charged the room with an almost unbearable electricity, a hot tension that made her fiercely aware of him. And herself. And the fact that they were alone together.

"You can't judge all wine based on one vintner or one bottle. And you can't judge Greek men based on one unhappy memory."

She felt as though she could barely breathe, and she struggled to find safer topics, ones that would allow her more personal distance. "What kind of wine do *you* like?"

"It's all about personal preference." He paused, letting his words sink in. "I like many wines. I have bottles in my cellar that are under ten euros which I think are infinitely more drinkable than some eighty-euro bottles."

"So it's not about the money?"

"Too many people get hung up on labels and names, and hope to impress each other with their spending power or their knowledge."

"We are talking about wine?" she murmured.

"Do you doubt it?" he asked, his head lifting as though to see her, study her, drink her in.

She bit into her lower lip, her cheeks so warm she felt desperate for a frozen drink or a sweet icy treat. Something to cool her off. Something to take her mind off Kristian's formidable physical appeal.

And, sitting there, she could see how someone like 'ista, someone young and impressionable, might be at-
 ed to Kristian. But to threaten him? Attempt to black-
 him? Impossible. Even blinded, with shattered bones

and scarred features, he was too strong, too overpowering. Calista was a fool.

And, thinking of the girl's foolishness, Elizabeth began to giggle, and then her giggle turned into full blown laughter. "What was Calista thinking?" she wheezed, touching her hand to her mouth to try and stifle the sound. "How could someone like Calista think she could get away with blackmailing *you?*"

Kristian sat across the table from Elizabeth and listened to her laugh. It had been so long since he'd heard a laugh like that, so open and warm and real. Elizabeth in one day had made him realize how much he'd been missing in life. He hadn't even known he'd become so angry and shut down until she'd arrived and begun insisting on immediate changes.

He'd at first resented her bossy manner, but it had worked. He'd realized he didn't want or need someone else giving him orders, or attempting to dictate to him. There was absolutely no reason he couldn't motivate himself.

Although he was still incredibly suspicious of Cosima, and mistrusted her desire to have him walking and returning to Athens, he was also grateful for her interference. Cosima had brought Elizabeth here, and, as it turned out, Elizabeth was the right person at the right time.

He needed someone like her.

Maybe he even needed *her.*

Sitting across the table from her, he focused on where he pictured her to be sitting. He hoped she knew that even if he couldn't see, he was listening. Paying attention.

He'd never been known for his sensitivity. But it wasn't that he didn't have feelings. He just wasn't very good at expressing them.

He liked this room, and he was enjoying the meal. Even he couldn't see, he appreciated the small touches made

Pano and Atta, his housekeeper—like the low warm heat from the candles, which smelled faintly of vanilla.

He knew they were eating off his favorite plates. He could tell by the size and shape that they were the glazed ceramic dinnerware he'd bought several years ago at a shop on Santorini.

The weave and weight of the table linens made him suspect they were also artisan handicrafts—purchased impulsively on one of his trips somewhere.

Despite his tremendous wealth, Kristian preferred simplicity, and appreciated the talent of local artists, supporting them whenever he could.

"Now you've grown quiet," Elizabeth said, as Atta began clearing their dishes.

"I'm just relaxed," he said, and he was. It had been so long since he'd felt this way. Months and months since he'd experienced anything so peaceful or calm. He'd forgotten what it was like to share a meal with someone, had forgotten how food always tasted better with good conversation, good wine and some laughter.

"I'm glad."

The warm sincerity in her voice went all the way through him. He'd liked her voice even in the beginning, when she had insisted on calling him Mr. Koumantaros every other time she opened her mouth.

He also liked the scent she wore. He still didn't know what was, although he could name all the other battleaxes' rite fragrances: chlorine, antiseptic, spearmint, tobacco vhat was probably the worst of all, an annoyingly rose-scented hand lotion.

eth also walked differently than the battleaxes. Her m, precise, confident. He could almost imagine her sallying forth through a crowded store, decisive and determined as she marched through Fortnum and Mason's aisles.

He smiled a little, amused by this idea of her in London. That was where she lived. His smile faded as the silence stretched. He wished he could see her. He suddenly wondered if she was bored. Perhaps she wanted to escape, return to her room. She had passed on coffee.

As the seconds ticked by, Kristian's tension grew.

He heard Elizabeth's chair scrape back, heard her linen napkin being returned to the table. She was leaving.

Grinding his teeth, Kristian struggled to get to his feet. It was the second time in one day, and required a considerable effort, but Elizabeth was about to go and he wanted to say something—to ask her to stay and join him in the library. It was very possible she was tired, but for him the nights were long, sometimes endless. There was no difference between night and day anymore.

He was on his feet, gripping the table's edge with his fingers. "Are you tired?" he said, his voice suddenly too loud and hard. He hadn't meant to sound so brusque. It was uncertainty and the inability to read her mood that was making him harsh.

"A little," she confessed.

He inclined his head. "Goodnight, then."

She hesitated, and he wondered what she was thinking, wished he could see her face to know if there was pity or resentment or something else in her eyes. That was the thing about not being able to see. He couldn't read people the way he'd used to, and that had been his gift. He wasn't verbally expressive, but he'd always been intuitive. He didn't trust intuition anymore, nor his instinct. He didn't know how to go on either without his eyes.

"Goodnight," she said softly.

He dug his fingers into the linen-covered table. Nodded. Prayed she couldn't see his disappointment.

After another moment's hesitation he heard her footsteps go.

Slowly he sat back down in his wheelchair, and as he sat down something cracked in him. A second later he felt a lance of unbelievable pain.

How had he become so alone?

Gritting his teeth, he tried to bite back the loss and loneliness, but they played in his mind.

He missed Andreas. Andreas had been his brother, the last of his family. Their parents had died a number of years earlier—unrelated deaths, but they had come close together—and their deaths had brought he and Andreas, already close, even closer.

He should have saved Andreas first. He should have gone to his brother's aid first.

If only he could go back. If only he could undo that one decision.

In life there were so many decisions one took for granted—so many decisions one made under pressure—and nearly all were good decisions, nearly all were soon forgotten. It was the one bad decision that couldn't be erased. The one bad decision that stayed with you night and day.

Slowly he pushed away from the table, and even more slowly he rolled down the hall toward the library—the room he spent nearly all his waking hours in.

Maybe Pano could find something on the radio for him? perhaps there was an audio book he could listen to. tian just wanted something to occupy his mind.

t once in the library he stopped pushing and just sat near le, with his papers and books. He didn't want the radio, lidn't want to listen to a book on tape. He just wanted to be himself again. He missed who he was. He hated who he'd become.

"Kristian?" Elizabeth said timidly.

He straightened, sat taller. "Yes?"

"You're in here, then?"

"Yes. I'm right here."

"Oh." There was the faintest hitch in her voice. "It's dark. Do you mind if I turn the lights on?"

"No. Please. I'm sorry. I don't know—"

"Of course you don't know."

He heard her footsteps cross to the wall, heard her flip the switch and then approach. "I'm not really that sleepy, and I wondered if maybe you have something I could read to you. The newspaper, or mail? Maybe you even have a favorite book?"

Kristian felt some of the tension and darkness recede. "Yes," he said, exhaling gratefully. "I'm sure there is."

CHAPTER SEVEN

THAT night began a pattern they'd follow for the next two weeks. During the day Kristian would follow a prescribed workout regimen, and then in the evening he and Elizabeth would have a leisurely dinner, followed by an hour or two in the library, where she'd read to him from a book, newspaper or business periodical of his choice.

Kristian's progress astounded her. If she hadn't been there to witness the transformation, she wouldn't have believed it possible. But being here, observing the day-to-day change in Kristian, had proved once and for all that attitude was everything.

Every day, twice a day, for the past two weeks, Kristian had headed to the spacious dining room which had been converted into a rehabilitation room. Months ago the dining room's luxurious carpets had been rolled back, the furniture cleared out, and serious equipment had been hauled up the mountain face to dominate the space.

Bright blue mats covered the floor, and support bars had ⸺en built in a far corner to aid Kristian as he practiced ⸺king. The nine windows overlooking the garden and valley ⸺ were always open, and Kristian spent hours at a time ⸺ room.

⸺ sports trainer Kristian had hired arrived two days after

Elizabeth did. Kristian had found Pirro in Sparta, and he had agreed to come and work with Kristian for the next four weeks, as long as he could return to Sparta on the weekends to be with his wife and children.

During the week, when Pirro was in residence, Kristian drove himself relentlessly. A trainer for the last Greek Olympic team, Pirro had helped rehabilitate and train some of the world's most elite athletes, and he treated Kristian as if he were the same.

The first few days Kristian did lots of stretching and developing core strength, with rubber balls and colored bands. By end of the first week he was increasing his distance in the pool and adding free weights to his routine. At the end of the second week Kristian was on cardio machines, alternating walking with short runs.

From the very beginning Elizabeth had known Kristian would get on his feet again. She hadn't expected it would only take him fifteen days.

Elizabeth stopped by the training room on Friday, early in the afternoon, to see if Pirro had any instructions for her for the two days while he returned to Sparta for the weekend.

She was shocked to see Kristian running slowly on a steep incline on the treadmill.

Pirro saw her enter and stepped over to speak with her. *"Ti Kanis?"* he asked. "How are you?"

"Kalo." Good. She smiled briefly before pointing to Kristian on the treadmill. "Isn't that a bit extreme?" she asked worriedly. "He could hardly stand two weeks ago. Won't t running injure him?"

"He's barely running," Pirro answered, glancing ove shoulder to watch Kristian's progress. "Notice the ex incline? This is really a cross training exercise. Yes working on increasing his cardio, but it's really to strengthen and develop the leg muscles."

Elizabeth couldn't help but notice the incline. Nor Kristian's intense concentration. He was running slowly, but without support, with his shoulders squared, his head lifted, his gaze fixed straight ahead. And even though sweat poured off him, and his cheeks glowed ruddy red, she didn't think he'd ever looked better—or stronger. Yes, he was breathing hard, but it was deep, regular, steady.

She walked closer to the machine, glanced at the screen monitoring his heart-rate. His heart-rate was low. She returned to Pirro's side. "So it's really not too much?" she persisted, torn between pride and anxiety. She wanted him better, but couldn't help fearing he'd burn out before he got to where he wanted to be.

"Too much?" Pirro grinned. "You don't know Kirie Kristian, do you? He's not a man. He's a monster."

Monster.

Pirro's word lingered in her mind as she turned to leave Kristian to finish his training. It was the same word Kristian had used when she'd first met him—the day he'd torn the bandages from his head to expose his face. Monster. Frankenstein.

Yet in the past two weeks he'd demonstrated that he was so far from either…

And so much more heroic than he even knew.

Soon he'd be returning to Athens. To the woman and the fe that waited for him there. He'd eventually marry sima—apparently his family had known her forever—and h luck he'd have many children and a long, happy life.

ut thinking of him returning to Athens put a heaviness in eart. Thinking of him marrying Cosima made the heav- even worse.

But that was why she was here, she reminded herself, swallowing hard around the painful lump in her throat, that lump that never went away. She'd come to prepare Kristian for the life he'd left behind.

And he was ready to go back. She could see it even if he couldn't.

The lump grew, thickening, almost drawing tears to her eyes.

Kristian, the Greek tycoon, had done this to her, too. She hadn't expected to feel this way about him, but he'd amazed her, impressed her, touched her heart with his courage, his sensitivity, as well as those rare glimpses of uncertainty. He made her feel so many emotions. But most of all he made her feel tender, good, hopeful, new. *New*.

"Shall I give him a message for you?" Pirro asked, his attention returning to Kristian.

And Elizabeth looked over at Kristian, this giant of a man who had surprised her at every level, her heart doing another one of those stunning free falls. He was so handsome it always touched a nerve, and that violent scar of his just made him more real, more beautiful. "No," she murmured. "There's no message. I'll just see him at dinner."

But as Elizabeth turned away, heading outside to take a walk through the gardens, she wondered when she'd find the courage to leave.

She had to leave. She'd already become too attached on him.

Putting a hand to her chest, she tried to stop the surge of pain that came with thinking of leaving.

Don't think of yourself, she reminded herself. Think him. Think of his needs and how remarkable it is that he do so much again. Think about his drive, his assertiveness ability to someday soon live independently.

And, thinking this way, she felt some of her own s

lifted. He and his confidence were truly amazing. You wouldn't know he couldn't see from the way he entered a room, or the way he handled himself. In the past couple of weeks he'd become more relaxed and comfortable in his own skin, and the more comfortable he felt, the more powerful his physical presence became.

She'd always known he was tall—easily over six feet two—but she'd never felt the impact of his height until he'd begun walking with a cane. Instead of stumbling, or hesitating, he walked with the assurance of a man who knew his world and fully intended to dominate that world once more.

Her lips curved in a rueful smile as she walked through the garden, with its low, fragrant hedges and rows of magnificent trees. No wonder a monastery had been built here hundreds of years ago. The setting was so green, the views breathtaking, the air pure and clean.

Pausing at one of the stone walls that overlooked the valley below, Elizabeth breathed in the scent of pine and lemon blossoms and gazed off into the distance, where the Messenian plain stretched.

Kristian had told her that the Messenian plain was extraordinarily fertile and produced nearly every crop imaginable, including the delicious Kalamata olive. Beyond the agricultural plain was the sea, with what had to be more beautiful beaches and picturesque bays. Although Elizabeth had never planned on returning to Greece, now that she was here she was anxious to spend a day at the water. There was nothing like a day spent enjoying the beautiful Greek sun and sea.

"Elizabeth?"

Hearing her name called, she turned to discover Kristian ·ading toward her, walking through the gardens with his ·g narrow cane. He hadn't liked the cane initially, had said it emphasized his blindness, but once he'd realized the cane gave freedom as he learned to walk again, he had adapted to it with remarkable speed.

His pace was clipped, almost aggressive, bringing to mind a conversation she'd had with him a few days ago. She'd told him she was amazed by his progress and his confident stride. He'd shrugged the compliment off, answering, "Greeks like to do things well or not at all."

She couldn't help smiling as she remembered his careless confidence, bordering on Greek arrogance. But it had been a truthful answer and it suited him, especially now, as she watched him walk through the garden.

"Kristian, I'm here," she called to him, "I'm at the wall overlooking the valley."

It didn't take him long to reach her. He was still wearing the white short-sleeve T-shirt and gray baggy sweat pants he'd worked out in. His dark hair fell forward on his brow and his skin looked burnished with a healthy glow. Her gaze searched his face, looking for signs of exhaustion or strain. There were none. He just looked fit, relaxed, even happy. "You had a grueling workout," she said.

"It was hard, but it felt good."

"Pirro can be brutal."

Kristian shrugged. "He knows I like to be challenged."

"But you feel okay?"

White teeth flashed and creases fanned from his eyes. "I feel great."

And there went her heart again, with that painful little flutter of attraction, admiration and sorrow. He wasn't hers. He'd never be hers. All she had to do was watch one of hi exhausting physical therapy sessions to see that his desire heal was for his Cosima. And although that knowledge stu she knew before long she'd be back in her office and immersed in her administrative duties there.

The desk would be a good place for her. At her desk she'd be busy with the phone and computer and email. She wouldn't feel these disturbing emotions there.

"You were in the training room earlier," he said. "Everything all right?"

The soft breeze was sending tendrils of hair flying around her face, and she caught one and held it back by her ear. "I just wanted to check with Pirro—see if he had any instructions for me over the weekend."

"Did he?"

"No."

"I guess that means we've the weekend free."

"Are you making big plans, then?" she asked, teasing him, knowing perfectly well his routine didn't vary much. He was most confident doing things he knew, walking paths he'd become familiar with.

"I'm looking forward to dinner," he admitted.

"Wow. Sounds exciting."

The corner of his mouth lifted, his hard features softening at her gentle mockery. "Are you making fun of me?"

"Me? No. Never. You're Mr. Kristian Koumantaros—one of Greece's most powerful men—how could I even consider poking fun at you?"

"You would," he said, grooves paralleling his mouth. "You do."

"Mr. Koumantaros, you must be thinking of someone else."

"Mmm-hmm."

"I'm just a simple nurse, completely devoted to your lbeing."

"Are you?"

"Of course. Have I not convinced you of that yet?" She'd meant to continue in her playful vein, but this time the words came out differently, her voice betraying her by dropping, cracking, revealing a tremor of raw emotion she didn't ever want him to hear.

Instead of answering, he reached out and touched her face. The unexpected touch shocked her, and she reared back, but his fingers followed, and slowly he slid his palm across her cheek.

The warmth in his hand made her face burn. She shivered at the explosion of heat within her even as her skin felt alive with bites of fire and ice.

"Kristian," she protested huskily, more heat washing through her—heat and need and something else. Something dangerously like desire.

She'd tried so hard to suppress these feelings, knowing if she acknowledged the tremendous attraction her control would shatter.

Her control *couldn't* shatter.

"No," she whispered, trying to turn her cheek away even as she longed to press her face to his hand, to feel more of the comfort and bittersweet pleasure.

She liked him.

She liked him very much. Too much. And, staring up into his face, she felt her fingers curl into her palm, fighting the urge to reach up and touch that beautiful scarred face of his.

Kristian, with his black hair and noble but scarred face, and his eyes that didn't see.

She began talking, to try to cover the sudden awkwardnes between them. "These past two weeks you've made suc great strides—literally, figuratively. You've no idea how pro I am of you, how much I admire you."

"That sounds suspiciously like a goodbye speech."

"It's not, but I *will* have to be leaving soon. You're virtually independent, and you'll soon be ready to return to your life in Athens."

"I don't like Athens."

"But your work—"

"I can do it here."

"But your family—"

"Gone."

She felt the tension between them grow. "Your friends," she said quietly, firmly. "And you do have those, Kristian. You have many people who miss you and want you back where you belong." Chief among them Cosima.

Averting his head, he stood tall and silent. His brows tugged and his jaw firmed, and slowly he turned his face toward her again. "When?"

"When what?"

"When do you intend to leave?"

She shrugged uncomfortably. "Soon." She took a quick breath. "Sooner than I expected."

"And when is that? Next week? The week after that?"

She twisted her fingers together. "Let's talk about this later."

"It's that soon?"

She nodded.

"Why?" he asked.

"It's work. I've a problem in Paris, and my case manager is fed up, threatening to walk off the job. I can't afford to lose her. I need to go and try to sort things out."

"So when is this? When do you plan to go?"

Elizabeth hesitated. "I was thinking about Monday." The lump was back in her throat, making it almost impossible to breathe. "After Pirro returns."

Kristian just stood there—big, imposing, and strangely silent.

"I've already contacted Cosima," she continued. "I told her that I've done all I can do and that it'd be wrong to continue to take her money." Elizabeth didn't add that she'd actually authorized her London office to refund Cosima's money, because it was Kristian who'd done the work, not she. It was Kristian's own miracle.

"Monday is just days away," Kristian said, his voice hard, increasingly distant.

"I know. It is sudden." She took a quick breath, feeling a stab of intense regret. She wished she could reach out and touch him, reassure him, but it wasn't her place. There were lines that couldn't be crossed, professional boundaries that she had to respect, despite her growing feelings for him. "You know you don't need me, Kristian. I'm just in your way—"

"No."

"Yes. But you must know I'm in awe of you. You said you'd walk in two weeks, and I said you couldn't. I said you'd need a walker, and you said you wouldn't." She laughed, thinking back to those first two intense and overwhelming days. "You've made a believer out of me."

He said nothing for a long moment, and then shook his head. "I wish I *could* make a believer out of you," he said, speaking so quietly the words were nearly inaudible.

"Monday is still three days from now," she said, injecting a note of false cheer. "Do we have to think about Monday today? Can't we think of something else? A game of blind-man's bluff?"

Kristian's jaw drew tight, and then eased. He laughed most reluctantly. "You're a horrible woman."

"Yes, I know," she answered, grateful for humor.

"Most challenging, Cratchett."

"I'll take that as a compliment."

"Then you take it wrong."

Elizabeth smiled. When he teased her, when he played her game with her, it amused her to no end. Moments ago she'd felt so low, and yet she was comforted and encouraged now.

She loved his company. It was as simple as that. He was clever and sophisticated, handsome and entertaining. And once he'd determined to return to the land of the living, he had done so with a vengeance.

For the past week she'd tried to temper her happiness with reminders that soon he'd be returning to Athens, and marriage to Cosima, but it hadn't stopped her heart from doing a quick double-beat every time she heard his voice or saw him enter a room.

"I'm not sure of the exact time," Kristian said, "but I imagine it's probably close to five."

Elizabeth glanced at her silver watch. "It's ten past five now."

"I've made plans for dinner. It will mean dressing now. Can you be ready by six?"

"Is this for dinner here?"

"No."

"We're going *out?*" She gazed incredulously at the valley far below and the steep descent down. Sure, Pirro traveled up and down once a week to work with Kristian. But she couldn't imagine Kristian bumping around on the back of a mule or in a donkey's cart.

His expression didn't change. "Is that a problem?"

"No." But it kind of *was* a problem, she thought, glancing at the dwindling light. Where would they possibly go to eat? It would take them hours to get down the mountain, and it would be dark soon. But maybe Kristian hadn't thought of that, as his world was always dark.

Kristian heard the hesitation in Elizabeth's voice and he

tensed, his posture going rigid. He resented not being able to see her, particularly at times like this. It hadn't been until he couldn't see that he'd learned how much he'd depended on his eyes, on visual cues, to make decisions.

Why was she less than enthusiastic about dinner?

Did she not want to go with him? Or was she upset about something?

If only he could see her face, read her expression, he'd know what her hesitation meant. But, as it was, he felt as though he were stumbling blindly about. His jaw hardened. He hated this feeling of confusion and helplessness. He wasn't a helpless person, but everything was so different now, so much harder than before.

Like sleep.

And the nightmares that woke him up endlessly. Or, worse, the nightmares he couldn't wake from—the dreams that haunted him for hours when, even when he told himself to wake, even when he said in the dream, *This is just a dream,* he couldn't let go, couldn't open his eyes and see. Day or night, it was all the same. Black. Endless pitch-black.

"If you'd rather not go…" he said, his voice growing cooler, more distant. He couldn't exactly blame her if she didn't want another evening alone with him. She might say he didn't look like Frankenstein, but the scar on his face felt thick, and it ran at an angle, as though his face had been pieced together, stitched with rough thread.

"No, Kristian. No, that's not it at all," she protested, her hand briefly touching his arm before just as swiftly pulling away. And yet that light, faint touch was enough. It warmed him. Connected him. Made him feel real. And, God knew, between the darkness and the nightmares and the grief of losing Andreas, he didn't feel real, or good, very often anymore.

"I'd like to go," she continued. "I want to go. I just wasn't sure what to wear. Is there a dress code? Casual or elegant? How are you going to dress?"

He pressed the tip of his cane into the ground, wanting to touch her instead, wanting to feel the softness of her cheek, the silky texture that made him think of crushed rose petals and velvet and the softest lace edged satin. His body ached, his chest grew tight, pinched around his heart.

"I won't be casual." His voice came out rough, almost raw, and he winced. He'd developed edges and shadows that threatened to consume him. "But you should dress so that you're comfortable. It could be a late night."

In her bedroom, Elizabeth practically spun in circles.

They were going out, and it could be a late night. So where were they going and exactly how late was late?

Her stomach flipped over, and she felt downright giddy as she bathed and toweled off. It was ridiculous, preposterous to feel this way—and yet she couldn't help the flurry of excitement. It had been a little over two weeks since she'd arrived, and she was looking forward to dinner out.

Knowing that Kristian wouldn't be dressed casually, she flipped through her clothes in the wardrobe until she decided she'd wear the only dress she'd brought—a black cocktail-length dress with a pale lace inset.

Standing before the mirror, she blew her wet hair dry and battled to keep her chaotic emotions in check.

You're just his nurse, she reminded herself. Nothing more than that. But her bright eyes in the mirror and the quick beat of her pulse belied that statement.

Her hair shimmered. Elizabeth was going to leave it down, but worried she wouldn't appear professional. At the last minute she plaited her hair into two slender braids, then twisted the braids into an elegant figure-eight at the back of her head, before pulling some blonde wisps from her crown so they fell softly around her face.

Gathering a light black silk shawl and her small handbag, she headed for the monastery's library. As she walked through the long arched hallways she heard a distant thumping sound, a dull roar that steadily grew louder, until the sound was directly above and vibrating through the entire estate. Then abruptly the thumping stopped and everything was quiet again.

Elizabeth discovered Kristian already in the library, waiting for her.

He'd also showered and changed, was dressed now in elegant black pants and a crisp white dress shirt, with a fine leather black belt and black leather shoes. With his dark hair combed and his face cleanshaven, Elizabeth didn't think she'd ever met a man so fit, strong, or so darkly handsome.

"Am I underdressed?" he asked, lifting his hands as if to ask for her approval.

"No." Her heart turned over. God, he was beautiful. Did he have any idea how stunning he really was?

Kristian moved toward her, his cane folded, tucked under his arm. He looked so confident, so very sure of himself. "What are you wearing…besides high heels?"

"You could tell by the way I walked?" she guessed.

"Mmmm. Very sexy."

Blushing, she looked up into his face, glad he couldn't see the way she looked at him. She loved looking at him, and she didn't even know what she loved most about his face. It was just the way it came together—that proud brow, the jet-black eyebrows, the strong cheekbones above firm, mobile lips.

"I'm wearing a dress," she said, feeling suddenly shy. She'd

never been shy around men before—had never felt intimidated by any man, not even her Greek former husband. "It's
black velvet with some lace at the bodice. Reminds me of the
1920s flapper-style dress."

"You must look incredible."

The compliment, as well as the deep sincerity in Kristian's
voice, brought tears to her eyes.

Kristian was so much more than any man she'd ever met.
It wasn't his wealth or sophistication that impressed her,
either—although she did admit that he wore his clothes with
ease and elegance, and she'd heard his brilliant trading and
investments meant he'd tripled his family fortune—those
weren't qualities she respected, much less admired.

She liked different things—simple things. Like the way his
voice conveyed so much, and how closely he listened to her
when she talked to him. His precise word choice indicated he
paid attention to virtually everything.

"Not half as incredible as you do," she answered.

His mouth quirked. "Ready?"

"Yes."

He held out his arm and she took it. His body was so much
bigger than hers, and warm, the muscles in his arm dense and
hard. Together they headed through the hall to the front
entrance, where Pano stood, ready to open the front door.

At the door Kristian paused briefly, head tipped as he gazed
down at her. "Your chariot awaits," he said, and with another
step they crossed the monastery's threshold and went
outside—to a white and silver helicopter.

CHAPTER EIGHT

A HELICOPTER.

On the top of one of Taygetos's peaks.

She blinked, shook her head, and looked again, thinking that maybe she'd imagined it. But, no, the silver and white body glinted in the last rays of the setting sun.

"I wondered how you got up and down the mountain," she said. "You didn't seem the type to enjoy donkey rides."

Kristian's deep laugh hummed all the way through her. "I suppose I could have sent the helicopter for you."

"No, no. I would have hated to miss hours bumping and jolting around in a wood cart.

He laughed again, as though deeply amused. "Have you been in a helicopter before?"

"I have," she said. "Yes." Her parents had access to a helicopter in New York. But that was part of the affluent life she'd left behind. "It's been a while, though."

The pilot indicated they were safe to board, and Elizabeth walked Kristian to the door. Once on board, he easily found his seatbelt and fastened the clip. And it wasn't until they'd lifted off, heading straight up and then over, between the mountain peaks, that Elizabeth remembered that the worst of

Kristian's injuries had come from the helicopter crash instead of the actual avalanche.

Turning, she glanced into his face to see what he was feeling. He seemed perhaps a little paler than he had earlier, but other than that he gave no indication that anything was wrong.

"You were hurt in a helicopter accident," she said, wondering if he was really okay, or just putting up a brave front.

"I was."

She waited, wondering if he'd say more. He didn't, and she touched the tip of her tongue to her upper lip. "You're not worried about being in one now?"

His brows pulled. "No. I know Yanni the pilot well—very well—and, being a pilot myself…"

"You're a pilot?"

His dark head inclined and he said slowly, "I was flying at the time of the crash."

Ah. "And the others?" she whispered.

"They were all in different places and stages of recovery." His long black lashes lowered, hiding the brilliant blue of his eyes.

She waited, and eventually Kristian sighed, shifted, his broad shoulders squaring. "One had managed to ski down the mountain to a lower patrol. Cosima…" He paused, took a quick short breath. "Cosima and the guide had been rescued. Two were still buried in snow and the others…were located but already gone."

The details were still so vague, and his difficulty in recounting the events so obvious that she couldn't ask anything else. But there were things she still wanted to know. Like, had he been going back for his brother when he crashed? And how had he managed to locate Cosima so quickly but not Andreas?

Thinking of the accident, she stole a swift side-glance in Kristian's direction. Yes, he was walking, and, yes, he was physically stronger. But what if he never saw again?

What if he didn't get the surgery—or, worse, did have it and the treatment didn't work? What if his vision could never be improved? What then?

She actually thought Kristian would cope—it wouldn't be easy, but he was tough, far tougher than he'd ever let on—but she wasn't so sure about Cosima, because Cosima desperately wanted Kristian to be "normal" again. And those were Cosima's words: "He must be normal, the way he was, or no one will ever respect him."

How would Cosima feel if Kristian never did get his sight back?

Would she still love him? Stay with him? Honor him?

Troubled, Elizabeth drew her shawl closer to her shoulders and gazed out the helicopter window as they flew high over the Peloponnese peninsula. It was a stunning journey at sunset, the fading sun painting the ground below in warm strokes of reddish-gold light.

In her two years of living in Greece she'd never visited the Peloponnese. Although the Peloponnese was a favorite with tourists, for its diverse landscape and numerous significant archeological sites, she only knew what Kristian had been telling her these past couple weeks. But, remembering his tales, she was riveted by three "fingers" of land projecting into the sea, the land green and fertile against the brilliant blue Mediterranean.

"We're almost there," Kristian suddenly said, his hand briefly touching her knee.

She felt her stomach flip and, breath catching, she glanced down at her knee, which still felt the heat of his fingers even though his hand was no longer there.

She wanted him to touch her again. She wanted to feel his hand slide inside her knee, wanted to feel the heat of his hand, his palm on her knee, and then feel his touch slide up the inside of her thigh. And maybe it couldn't happen, but it didn't make the desire any less real.

Skin against skin, she thought. Touch that was warm and concrete instead of all these silent thoughts and intense emotions. And they were getting harder to handle, because she couldn't acknowledge them, couldn't act on them, could do nothing but keep it in, hold it in, pretend she wasn't falling head over heels in love. Because she was.

And it was torture. Madness.

Her heart felt like it was tumbling inside her chest—a small shell caught in the ocean tide. She couldn't stop it, couldn't control it, could only feel it.

With an equally heart-plunging drop, the helicopter descended straight down.

As the pilot opened the door and assisted her and then Kristian out, she saw the headlights of a car in front of them. The driver of the car stepped out, and as he approached she realized it was Kristian's driver.

Whisked from helicopter to car, Elizabeth slid through the passenger door and onto the leather seat, pulse racing. Her pulse quickened yet again as Kristian climbed in and sat close beside her.

"Where are we?" she asked, feeling the press of Kristian's thigh against hers as the driver set off.

"Kithira."

His leg was much longer than hers, his knee extending past hers, the muscle hard against hers.

"It's an island at the foot of the Peloponnese," he added. "Years ago, before the Corinth Canal was built in the late nineteenth century, the island was prosperous due to all the ships stopping. But after the canal's construction the island's population, along with its fortune, dwindled."

As the car traveled on quiet roads, beneath the odd passing yellow light, shadows flickered in and through the windows. Elizabeth couldn't tear her gaze from the sight of his black trouser-covered leg against hers.

"It's nice to be going out," he said, as the car began to wind up a relatively steep hill. "I love living in the Taygetos, but every now and then I just want to go somewhere for dinner, enjoy a good meal and not feel so isolated."

She turned swiftly to look at him. There were no streetlights on the mountain road and she couldn't see his face well. "So you *do* feel isolated living so far from everyone?"

He shrugged. "I'm Greek."

Those two words revealed far more than he knew. Greeks treasured family, had strong ties to family, even the extended family, and every generation was respected for what it contributed. In Greece the elderly rarely lived alone, and money was never hoarded, but shared with each other. A father would never let his daughter marry without giving her a house, or land, or whatever he could, and a Greek son would always contribute to his parents' care. It wasn't just an issue of respect, but love.

"That's why Cosima wants you back in Athens," Elizabeth said gently. "There you have your *parea*—your group of friends." And, for Greeks, the circle of friends was nearly as important as family. A good *parea* was as necessary as food and water.

But Kristian didn't speak. Elizabeth, not about to be put off, lightly touched his sleeve. "Your friends miss you."

"My *parea* is gone."

"No—"

"Elizabeth." He stopped her. "They're gone. They died with my brother in France. All those that perished, suffocating in the snow, were my friends. But they weren't just friends. They were also colleagues."

Pained, she closed her eyes. Why, oh why did she push? Why, oh, why did she think she knew everything? How could she be so conceited as to think she could counsel him? "I'm sorry."

"You didn't know."

"But I thought… Cosima said…"

"Cosima?" Kristian repeated bitterly. "Soon you will learn you can't believe everything she says."

"Even though she means well."

Silence filled the car, and once again Elizabeth sensed that she'd said the wrong thing. She pressed her fists to her knees, increasingly uncomfortable.

"Perhaps I should tell you about dinner," Kristian said finally, his deep chest lifting as he squared his shoulders. "We're heading to a tiny village that will seem virtually untouched by tourism or time. Just outside this village is one of my favorite restaurants—a place designed by a Greek architect and his artist wife. The food is simple, but fresh, and the view is even better."

"You could go anywhere to eat, but you choose a rustic and remote restaurant?"

"I like quiet places. I'm not interested in fanfare or fuss."

"Have you always been this way, or…?"

"It's not the result of the accident, no. Andreas was the extrovert—he loved parties and the social scene."

"You didn't go with him?"

"Of course I went with him. He was my brother and my best friend. But I was content to let him take center stage, entertain everyone. It was more fun to sit back, watch."

As Kristian talked, the moon appeared from behind a cloud. Elizabeth could suddenly see Kristian's features, and that rugged profile of his, softened only by the hint of fullness at his lower lip.

He had such a great mouth, too. Just wide enough, with perfect lips.

To kiss those lips…

Knots tightened inside her belly, knots that had less to do with fear and more to do with desire. She felt so attracted to him it was hard to contain her feelings, to keep the need from showing.

What she needed to do was scoot over on the seat, put some distance between them—because with him sitting so close, with their thighs touching and every now and then their elbows brushing, she felt so wound up, so keenly aware of him.

She looked now at his hand, where it rested on his thigh, and she remembered how electric it had felt when his hand had brushed her knee, how she'd wanted his hand to slide beneath the hem of her dress and touch her, tease her, set her on fire…

That hand. His body. Her skin.

She swallowed hard, her heart beating at a frantic tempo, and, crossing her legs, she fought the dizzying zing of adrenaline. This was ridiculous, she told herself, shifting again, crossing her legs the other way. She had to settle down. Had to find some calm.

"You seem restless," Kristian said, head cocking, listening attentively.

She pressed her knees together. "I guess I am. I probably just need to stretch my legs. Must be the sitting."

"We're almost there."

"I'm not complaining."

"I didn't think you were."

She forced a small tight smile even as her mind kept spinning, her imagination working overtime. She was far too aware of Kristian next to her, far too aware of his warmth, the faint spice of his cologne or aftershave, the formidable size of him…even the steady way he was breathing.

"You're not too tired, are you?" he asked as the car headlights illuminated the road and what seemed to be a nearly barren slope before them.

"No," she said, as the car suddenly turned, swinging onto a narrow road.

"Hungry?"

She made a soft sound and anxiously smoothed the velvet hem of her dress over her knees. "No. *Yes*. Could be." She laughed, yet the sound was apprehensive. "I honestly don't know what's wrong with me."

He reached out, his hand finding hers in the dark with surprising ease. She thought for a moment he meant to hold her hand but instead he turned it over and put his fingers on the inside of her wrist, checking her pulse. Several seconds passed before his mouth quirked. "Your heart's racing."

"I know," she whispered, staring at her wrist in his hand as the lights of a parking lot and restaurant illuminated the car. His hand was twice the size of her own, and his skin, so darkly tanned, made hers look like cream.

"You're not scared of me?"

"No."

"But maybe you're afraid to be alone with me?"

Her heart drummed even harder, faster. "And why would that be?"

His thumb caressed her sensitive wrist for a moment before releasing her. "Because tonight you're not my nurse, and I'm not your patient. We're just two people having dinner together."

"Just friends," she said breathlessly, tugging her hand free, suddenly terrified of everything she didn't know and didn't understand.

"Can a man and a woman be just friends?"

Elizabeth's throat seized, closed.

The driver put the car into "park" and came around to open their door. Elizabeth nearly jumped from the car, anxious to regain control.

At the restaurant entrance they were greeted as though they were family, the restaurant owner clasping Kristian by the arms and kissing him on each cheek. "Kyrios Kristian," he said, emotion thickening his Greek. "*Kyrie*. It is good to see you."

Kristian returned the embrace with equal warmth. "It is good to be back."

"*Parakalo*—come." And the older man, his dark hair only peppered with gray, led them to a table in a quiet alcove with windows all around. "The best seats for you. Only the best for you, my son. Anything for you."

After the owner left, Elizabeth turned to Kristian. "He called you *son?*"

"The island's small. Everyone here is like family."

"So you know him well?"

"I used to spend a lot of time here."

She glanced out the window and the view was astonishing. They were high on a hill, perched above a small village below. And farther down from the village was the ocean.

The lights of the village twinkled and the moon reflected off the white foam of the sea, where the waves broke on the rocks and shore.

The restaurant owner returned, presenting them with a gift—a bottle of his favorite wine—pouring both glasses before leaving the bottle behind.

"*Yiassis,*" she said, raising her glass and clinking it with his. *To your health.*

"*Yiassis,*" he answered.

And then silence fell, and the stillness felt wrong. Something was wrong. She just knew it.

Kristian shifted, and a small muscle suddenly pulled in his cheek. Elizabeth watched him, feeling a rise in tension.

The mood at the table was suddenly different.

Kristian suddenly seemed so alone, so cut off in his world. "What's wrong?" she asked nervously, fearing that she'd said something, done something to upset him.

He shook his head.

"Did I do something?" she persisted.

"No."

"Kristian." Her tone was pleading. "Tell me."

His jaw worked, the hard line of his cheekbone growing even more prominent, and he laughed, the sound rough and raw. "I wish to God I could see you."

For a moment she didn't know what to say or do, as heat rushed through her. And then the heat receded, leaving her chilled. "Why?" she whispered.

"I just want to see you."

Her face grew hot all over again, and this time the warmth stayed, flooding her limbs, making her feel far too sensitive. "Why? I'm just another battleaxe."

"Ohi." No. "Hardly."

Her hand shook as she adjusted her silverware. "You don't know that—"

"I know how you sound, and smell. I know you barely reach my shoulder—even in heels—and I know how your skin feels—impossibly smooth, and soft, like the most delicate satin or flower."

"I think you've found your old pain meds."

His dark head tipped. His blue eyes fixed on her. "And I think you're afraid of being with me."

"You're wrong."

"Am I?"

"Yes." She reached for her water glass and took a quick sip of the bubbly mineral water, but drank so much that the bubbles ended up stinging her nose. "I'm not afraid," she said, returning the glass to a table covered in white crisp linen and flickering with soft ivory candlelight and shadows. "How could I be afraid of you?"

His lips barely curved. "I'm not nice, like other men."

Her heart nearly fell. She looked up at him from beneath her lashes. "I'm not going to even dignify that with a response."

"Why?"

"Because you're baiting me," she said.

He surprised her by laughing. "My clever girl."

Her heart jumped again, and an icy hot shiver raced through her. Liquid fire in her veins. *His clever girl.* He was torturing her now. Making her want to be more than she was, making her want to have more than she did. Not more things, but more love.

His love.

But he was promised, practically engaged. And she'd been through hell and back with one man who hadn't been able to keep his word, or honor his commitments. Including his marriage vows.

"Kristian, I can't do this." She would have gotten up and run if there had been anywhere to go. "I can't play these games with you."

His forehead furrowed, emphasizing the scar running down his cheek. "What games?"

"These…this…whatever you call this. Us." She shook her head, unable to get the words out. "I know what you said earlier, that tonight we're not patient and nurse, we're just a man and…woman. But that's not right. You're wrong. I *am* your nurse. That's all I am, all I can be."

He leaned back and rested one arm on the table, his hand relaxed. His expression turned speculative. "And will you still be my nurse when you return to London in two days?"

"Three days."

"Two days."

She held her breath, her fingers balling into fists and then slowly exhaled.

His mouth tugged and lines deepened near his lips, emphasizing the beautiful planes of his face. "Elizabeth, *latrea mou,* let us not play games, as you say. Why do you have to go back?"

"I have a business to run—and, Kristian, so do you. Your officers and board of directors are desperate for you to return to Athens and take leadership again."

"I can do it from Taygetos."

She shook her head, impatient. "No, you can't. Not properly. There are appointments, conferences, press meetings—"

"Others can do it," he said dismissively.

Staring at him, she felt her frustration grow. He'd never sounded so arrogant as he did now. "But *you* are Koumantaros. You are the one investors believe in and the one your business partners want to meet with. *You* are essential to Koumantaros Incorporated's success."

He nearly snapped his fingers, rejecting her arguments. "Did Cosima put you up to this?"

"No. Of course not. And that's not the issue here anyway. The issue is you resuming your responsibilities."

"Elizabeth, I still head the corporation."

"But absent leadership?" She made a soft scoffing sound. "It's not effective, and, frankly, it's not you."

"How can one little Englishwoman have so many opinions about things she knows so little about?"

Elizabeth's cheeks flamed. "I know you better than you think," she flashed.

"I'm referring to the corporate world—"

"I am a business owner."

It was his turn to scoff. "Which we've already established isn't well managed at all."

Hurt, she abruptly drew back and stared at him. "That was unkind. And unnecessary."

He shrugged off her rebuke. "But true. Your agency provided me with exceptionally poor care. Propositioned and then blackmailed by one nurse, and demeaned by the others."

She threw her napkin down and pushed her chair back. "Maybe you were an exceptionally poor patient."

"Is that possible?"

"Possible?" she repeated, her voice quavering with anger and indignation. "My God, you're even more conceited than I dreamed. *Possible?*" She drew a swift breath. "Do you want the truth? No more sugar-coated words?"

"Don't start mincing words now," he drawled, sounding as bored as he looked.

Her fingers flexed, and blood pumped through her veins. She wanted to smack him, she really did. "Truth, Kristian— *you* were impossible. You were the worst patient in the history of my agency, and we take care of hundreds of patients every year. I've had my business for years, and never encountered anyone as self-absorbed and manipulative as you."

She took another quick breath. "And another thing—do you think I *wanted* to leave my office, put aside my obligations, to rush to your side? Do you think this was a holiday for me to come to Greece? No. And no again. But I did it because no one else would, and you had a girlfriend desperate to see you whole and well."

Legs shaking, Elizabeth staggered to her feet. "Speaking of your girlfriend, it's time you gave her a call. I'm done here. It's Cosima's turn to be with you now!"

CHAPTER NINE

ELIZABETH rushed out of the restaurant, past the three other tables of patrons. But no sooner had she stepped outside into the decidedly cooler night air than she felt assailed by shame. She'd just walked out on Kristian Koumantaros, one of Greece's most powerful and beloved tycoons.

As gusts of wind whistled past the building, perched on the mountain edge, she hugged her arms close, chilled, overwhelmed. She'd left a man who couldn't see alone, to find his own way out. And worst of all, she thought, tugging windblown tendrils behind her ears, she'd left in the middle of the meal. Meals were almost as sacred as family in Greece.

She was falling apart, she thought, putting a hand to her thigh to keep her skirt from billowing out. Her feelings were so intense she was finding it difficult to be around Kristian. She was overly emotional and too sensitive. And this was why she had to leave—not because she couldn't still do good here, but because she wondered if she couldn't manage her own emotions, how could she possibly help him manage his?

In London things would be different.

In London she wouldn't see Kristian.

In London she'd be in control.

A bitter taste filled her mouth and she immediately shook

her head, unable to bear the thought that just days from now she'd be gone and he'd be out of her life.

How could she leave him?

And yet how could she remain?

In the meantime she was standing outside Kristian's favorite restaurant while he sat alone inside. God, what a mess.

She had to go back in there. Had to apologize. Try to make amends before the evening was completely destroyed.

With a deep breath, she turned and walked through the front door, out of the night which was rapidly growing stormy. Chilly. She rubbed at her arms and returned to their table, where Kristian waited.

He was sitting still, head averted, and yet from his profile she could see his pallor and the strain at his jaw and mouth.

He was as upset as she was.

Heart sinking, Elizabeth sat down. "I'm sorry," she whispered, fighting the salty sting of tears. "I'm sorry. I don't know what else to say."

"It's not your fault. Don't apologize."

"Everything just feels wrong—"

"It's not you. It's me." His dense black lashes dropped. He hesitated, as though trying to find the right words. "I knew you'd need to go back, but I didn't expect you'd say it was so soon—didn't expect the announcement today."

She searched his face. It was a face she loved. *Loved.* And while the word initially took her by surprise, she also recognized it was true. "Kristian, I'm not leaving *you*. I'm just returning to my office and the work that awaits me there."

He hesitated a long time before picking up his wine glass, but setting it back down without taking a drink. "You couldn't move your office here?"

"Temporarily?"

"Permanently."

She didn't understand. "I didn't make this miracle, Kristian. It was you. It was your focus, your drive, your hours of work—"

"But I didn't care about getting better, didn't care about much of anything, until *you* arrived. And now I do."

"That's because you're healing."

"So don't leave while I'm still healing. Don't go when everything finally feels good again."

She closed her eyes, hope and pain streaking through her like twin forks of lightning. "But if I move my office here, if I remain here to help you..."

"Yes?"

She shook her head. "What about me? What happens to me when you're healed? When you're well?" She was grateful he couldn't see the tears in her eyes, or how she was forced to madly dash them away before anyone at the restaurant could see. "Once you've gotten whatever you need from me, do I just pack my things and go back to London again?"

He said nothing, his expression hard, grim.

"Kristian, forgive me, but sometimes being here in Greece is torture." She knotted her hands in her lap, thinking that the words were coming out all wrong but he had to realize that, while she didn't want to hurt him, she also had to protect herself. She was too attached to him already. Leaving him, losing him, would hurt so much. But remaining to watch him reunite with another woman would break her heart. "I like you, Kristian," she whispered. "Really like you—"

"And I like you. Very much."

"It's not the same."

"I don't understand. I don't understand any of this. I only know what I think. And I believe you belong here. With me."

He was saying words she'd wanted to hear, but not in the context she needed them. He wanted her because she was convenient and helpful, supportive while still challenging. Yet the relationship he was describing wasn't one of love, but usefulness. He wanted her company because it would benefit him. But how would *she* benefit by staying?

"Elizabeth, *latrea mou,*" he added, voice deepening. "I need you."

Latrea mou. Darling. Devoted one.

His voice and words were buried inside her heart. Again tears filled her eyes, and again she was forced to brush them swiftly away. "No wonder you had mistresses on every continent," she said huskily. "You know exactly what women want to hear."

"You're changing the subject."

She wiped away another tear. "I'm making an observation."

"It's not accurate."

"Cosima said—"

"This isn't working, is it? Let's just go." Kristian abruptly rose, and even before he'd straightened the restaurant owner had rushed over. "I'm sorry," Kristian apologized stiffly, his expression shuttered. "We're going to be leaving."

"*Kyrie,* everything is ready. We're just about to carry out the plates," the owner said, clasping his hands together and looking from one to the other. "You are sure?"

Kristian didn't hesitate. "I am sure." He reached into his pocket, retrieved his wallet and cash. "Will you let my driver know?"

"Yes, Kyrie Kristian." The other man nodded. "At least let me have your meal packed to go. Maybe later you will be hungry and want a little plate of something, yes?"

"Thank you."

Five minutes later they were in the car, sitting at opposite ends of the passenger seat as the wind gusted and howled outside. Fat raindrops fell heavily against the windshield. Kristian stonily faced forward while Elizabeth, hands balled against her stomach, stared out the car window at the passing scenery, although most of it was too dark to see.

She didn't understand what had happened in the restaurant tonight. Everything had been going so well until they'd sat down, and then...

And then...what? Was it Cosima? Her departure? What?

As the car wound its way back down the mountain, she squeezed her knuckled fists, her insides a knot of regret and disappointment. The evening was a disaster, and she'd been so excited earlier, too.

"What happened?" she finally asked, breaking the miserably tense silence. "Everything seemed fine in the helicopter."

He didn't answer and, turning, she looked at him, stared at him pointedly, waiting for him to speak. He had to talk. He had to communicate.

But he wouldn't say a word. He sat there, tall, dark, impossibly remote, as though he lived in a different world.

"Kristian," she whispered. "You're being horrible. Don't do this. Don't be like this—"

His jaw hardened and his lashes flickered, but that was his only response, and she thought she could hate him in that moment—hate him not just now, but forever.

To be shut out, to be ignored. It was the worst punishment she could think of. So unbelievably hard to bear.

"The weather is going to be a problem," he said at last. "We won't be able to fly. Unfortunately we are unable to return to Taygetos tonight. We'll be staying in the capital city, Chora."

The driver had long ago merged with traffic, driving into

and through a harbor town. If this was the capital city it wasn't very big. They were now paralleling the coast, passing houses, churches and shops, nearly all already closed for the night. And far off in the distance a vast hulking fortress dwarfed the whitewashed town.

As the windshield wipers rhythmically swished, Elizabeth gazed out the passenger window, trying to get a better look at the fortress. It sat high above the city, on a rock of its own. In daylight the fortress would have an amazing view of the coast, but like the rest of Chora it was dark now, and even more atmospheric, with the rain slashing down.

"You've booked us into a hotel?" she asked, glimpsing a church steeple inside the miniature walled town.

"We won't be at a hotel. We'll be staying in a private home."

She glanced at him, her feelings still hurt. "Friends?"

"No. It's mine." He shifted wearily. "My home. One of my homes."

They were so close to the fortress she could see the distinct stones that shaped the mammoth walls. "Are we far from your home?"

"I don't think so, no. But I confess I'm not entirely sure where we are at the moment."

Of course—he couldn't see. And he wouldn't automatically know which direction they were going, or the current road they were traveling on. "We're heading toward a castle."

"Then we're almost there."

"We're staying near the castle?"

"We're staying *at* the castle."

"Your home is a castle?"

"It's one of my properties."

Her brows pulled. "How many properties do you have?"

"A few."

"Like this?"

"They're all a bit different. The monastery in Taygetos, the castle here, and other estates in other places."

"Are they all so…grand?"

"They're all historic. Some are in ruins when I purchase them; some are already in operation. But that's what I do. It's one of the companies in the Koumantaros portfolio. I buy historic properties and find different ways to make them profitable."

Elizabeth turned her attention back to the fortress, with its thick walls and towers and turrets looming before them. "And this is a real castle?"

"Venetian," he agreed. "Begun in the thirteenth century and finished in the fifteenth century."

"So what do you do with it?"

He made a soft, mocking sound. "My accountants would tell you I don't do enough, that it's an enormous drain on my resources, but after purchasing it three years ago I couldn't bear to turn it into a five-star luxury resort as planned."

"So you stay here?"

"I've reserved a wing for my private use, but I haven't visited since before the accident."

"So it essentially sits empty?"

The wind suddenly howled, and rain buffeted the car. Elizabeth didn't know if it was the weather or her question, but Kristian smiled faintly. "You're sounding like my accountants now. But, no, to answer your question. It's not empty. I've been working with an Italian architect and designer to slowly—carefully—turn wings and suites into upscale apartments. Two suites are leased now. By next year I hope to lease two or three more, and then that's it."

The car slowed and then stopped, and an iron gate

opened. The driver got out and came round to open their door. "We're here."

A half-dozen uniformed employees appeared from no-where. Before Elizabeth quite understood what was happening, she was being whisked in one direction and Kristian in another.

Left alone in an exquisite suite of rooms, she felt a stab of confusion.

Where on earth was she now?

The feeling was strongly reminiscent of how she'd been as a child, the only daughter of Rupert Stile, the fourth richest man in America, as she and her parents had traveled from one sumptuous hotel to the next.

It wasn't that they hadn't had houses of their own—they'd had dozens—but her mother had loved accompanying her father on his trips, and so they had all traveled together, the young heiress and her nannies too.

Back then, though, she hadn't Elizabeth Hatchet but Grace Elizabeth Stiles, daughter of a billionaire a hundred times over. It had been a privileged childhood, made only more enviable when she had matured from pampered daughter status to being the next high-society beauty.

Comfortable in the spotlight, at ease with the media, she'd enjoyed her debutante year and the endless round of parties. Invitations had poured in from all over the world, as had exquisite designer clothes made for her specifically.

It had been so much power for a twenty-year-old. Too much. She'd had her own money, her own plane, and her own publicist. When men wined her and dined her—and they *had* wined and dined her—the dates had made tabloid news.

Enter handsome Greek tycoon Nico. Being young, she'd had no intention of settling down so soon, but he'd swept her off her feet. Dazzled her completely with attention, affection, tender gifts and more. Within six months they'd been engaged. At twenty-three she'd had the fairytale wedding of her dreams.

Seven and a half months after her wedding she had discovered him in bed with another woman.

She'd stayed with him because he'd begged for another chance, promised to get counseling, vowed he'd change. But by their first anniversary he'd cheated again. And again. And again.

The divorce had been excruciating. Nico had demanded half her wealth and launched a public campaign to vilify her. She was selfish, shallow, self-absorbed—a spoiled little rich girl intent on controlling him and embarrassing him. She'd emasculated him by trying to control the purse strings. She'd refused to have conjugal relations.

By the time the settlement had been reached, she hadn't been able to stand herself. She wasn't any of the things Nico said, and yet the public believed what they were told—or maybe she'd begun to believe the horribly negative press, too. Because by the end, Grace detested her name, her fortune, and the very public character assassination.

Moving to England, she'd changed her name, enrolled in nursing school and become someone else—someone stable and solid and practical.

But now that same someone was back in Greece, and the two lives felt very close to colliding.

She should have never returned to Greece—not even under the auspices of caring for a wounded tycoon. She definitely shouldn't have taken a helicopter ride to a small Greek island. And she definitely, *definitely* shouldn't have agreed to stay in a thirteenth-century castle in the middle of a thunderstorm.

Exhausted, Elizabeth pivoted slowly in her room like a

jewelry box ballerina. Where had Kristian gone? Would she see him again tonight? Or was she on her own until morning?

As if on cue, the bedroom lights flickered once, twice, and then went out completely, leaving her in darkness.

At first Elizabeth did nothing other than move toward the bed and sit there, certain at any moment the power would come back on or one of the castle staff would appear at her room, flashlight, lantern or candle in hand. Neither happened. No power and no light. Minutes dragged by. Minutes that became longer.

Unable even to read her own watch, Elizabeth didn't know how much time had gone by, but she thought it had to have been nearly an hour. She was beyond bored, too. She was hungry, and if no one was coming to her assistance, then she would go to them.

Stumbling her way toward the door, she bumped into a trunk at the foot of the bed, a chair, a table—ouch—the wall, tapestry on the wall, and finally a door.

The hall was even darker than her room. Not a flicker of light anywhere, nor a sound.

A rational woman would return to her room and call it a night, but Elizabeth was too hungry—and a little too panicked—to be rational, and, taking a left from her room, began a slow, fearful walk down the hall, knowing there were stairs somewhere up ahead but not certain how far away, nor how steep the staircase. She couldn't even remember if there was one landing or two.

Just when she thought she'd found the stairs she heard a noise. And it wasn't the creak of stairs or a door opening, but something live, something breathing. Whimpering.

She stopped dead in her tracks. Her heart raced and, reaching for the wall, her hand shook, her skin icy and clammy.

There was something—someone—in the stairwell, something—someone—waiting.

She heard a heavy thump, and then silence. Ears, senses straining, she listened. It was breathing harder, heavier, and there was another thump, a muffled cry, not quite human, followed by a scratch against the wall.

Elizabeth couldn't take anymore. With one hand out, fingertips trailing the wall, she ran back down the hall toward her room—and yet as she ran she couldn't remember exactly where her room was, or where the door was located. She couldn't remember if there were many doors between her room and the stairs, or even if she'd left her bedroom door open or not.

The terror of not knowing where she was, of whatever was in the stairwell and what might happen next, made her nearly frantic. Her heart was racing, pounding as if it would burst, and she turned in desperate circles. Where was her room? Why had she even left it? And was that thing in the stairs coming toward her?

There was a thump behind her, and then suddenly something brushed her arm. She screamed. She couldn't help it. She was absolutely petrified.

"Elizabeth."

"Kristian." Her voice broke with terror and relief. "Help me. Help me, please."

And he was there, hauling her against him, pulling her into the circle of his arms, his body protecting her. "What is it? What's wrong?"

"There's something out there. There's something…" She could hardly get the words out. Her teeth began chattering and she shivered against him, pressed her face against his cheek, which was hard and broad and smelled even better than it felt. "Scary."

"It's your imagination," he said, his arm firmly around her waist, holding her close.

But the terror still seemed so real, and it was the darkness and her inability to see, to know what it was in the stairwell. If it was human, monster or animal. "There was something. But it's so dark—"

"Is it dark?"

"Yes!" She grabbed at his shirt with both hands. "The lights have been out for ages, and no one came, and they haven't come back on."

"It's the storm. It'll pass."

Her teeth still chattered. "It's too dark. I don't like it."

"Your room is right here," he said, his voice close to her ear. "Come, let's get you bundled up. I'm sure there's a blanket on the foot of the bed."

He led her into her room and found the blanket, draping it around her shoulders. "Better?" he asked.

She nodded, no longer freezing quite as much. "Yes."

"I should go, then."

"No." She reached out, caught his sleeve, and then slid her fingers down to his forearm, which was bare. His skin was warm and taut, covering dense muscle.

For a long silent minute Kristian didn't move, and then he reached out, touched her shoulder, her neck, up to her chin. His fingers ran lightly across her face, tracing her eyebrow, then moving down her nose and across her lips.

"You better send me away," he said gruffly.

She closed her eyes at the slow exploration of his fingertips, her skin hot and growing hotter beneath his touch. "I'll be scared."

"In the morning you'll regret letting me stay."

"Not if I get a good night's sleep."

He rubbed his fingers lightly across her lips, as if learning the curve and shape of her mouth. "If I stay, you won't be sleeping."

She shivered even as nerves twitched to life in her lower back, making her ache and tingle all over. "You shouldn't be so confident."

"Is that a challenge, *latrea mou?*"

He strummed her lower lip, and her mouth quivered. The heat in his skin was making her insides melt and her body crave his. Instinctively her lips parted, to touch and taste his skin.

She heard his quick intake when her tongue brushed his knuckle, and another intake when she slowly drew that knuckle into her mouth. Having his finger in her mouth was doing maddening things to her body, waking a strong physical need that had been slumbering far too long.

She sucked harder on his finger. And the harder she sucked the tighter her nipples peaked and her womb ached. She wanted relief, wanted to be taken, seized, plundered, sated.

"Is this really what you want?" he gritted from between clenched teeth, his deep voice rough with passion.

She didn't speak. Instead she reached toward him, placed her hand on his belt and slowly slid it down to cover his hard shaft.

Kristian groaned deep in his throat and roughly pulled her against him, holding her hips tight against his own. She could feel the surge of heat through his trousers, feel the fabric strain.

Control snapped. He covered her mouth with his and kissed her hard, kissed her fiercely. His lips were firm, demanding, and the pressure of his mouth parted her lips.

She shuddered against him, belly knotting, breasts aching, so that she pressed against him for desperate relief, wanting closer contact with his body, from his thighs to his lean hips to his powerful chest and shoulders. Pressed so closely, she could feel his erection against the apex of her thighs, and as exciting as it felt, it wasn't enough.

She needed him—more of him—more of everything with him. Touch, taste, pressure, skin. "Please," she whispered, circling his waist and slowly running her hands up his back. "Please stay with me."

"For how long?" he murmured, his head dropping to sweep excruciatingly light kisses across the side of her neck and up to the hollow beneath her ear. "Till midnight? Morning? Noon?"

The kisses were making it impossible to think. She pressed her thighs tight, the core of her hot and aching. Years since she'd made love, and now she felt as though she were coming apart here and now.

His mouth found hers again, and the kiss was teasing, light, and yet it made her frantic. She reached up to clasp his head, burying her fingers in his thick glossy hair. "Until as long as you want," she whispered breathlessly.

She'd given him the right answer with her words, and the kiss immediately deepened, his mouth slanting across hers, parting her lips again and drawing her tongue into his mouth. As he sucked on the tip of her tongue she felt her legs nearly buckle. He was stripping her control, seizing her senses, and she was helpless to stop him.

She'd given him a verbal surrender, she thought dizzily, but it wasn't enough. Now he wanted her to surrender her body.

CHAPTER TEN

KRISTIAN felt Elizabeth shiver against him, felt the curve of her hips, the indentation of her waist, the full softness of her breasts.

He'd discovered earlier she was wearing her hair pulled back, with wisps of hair against her face. Kissing her, he now followed one of the wisps to her ear, and he traced that before his fingers slid down the length of her neck.

He could feel her collarbone, and the hollow at her throat, and the thudding of her heart. Her skin was even softer than he remembered, and he found himself fantasizing about taking her hair down, pulling apart the plaits and letting her hair tumble past her shoulders and into his hands.

He wanted her hair, her face, her body in his hands. Wanted her bare and against him.

"Kristian," she said breathlessly, clasping his face in her hands.

Instantly he hardened all over again, his trousers too constricting to accommodate his erection. He wanted out of his clothes. He wanted her out of hers. *Now.*

Elizabeth shuddered as Kristian's hand caressed her hip, down her thigh, to find the hem of her velvet dress. As he lifted the hem she felt air against her bare leg, followed immediately by the heat of his hand.

She let out a slow breath of air, her eyes closing at the path his hand took. His fingers trailed up the outside of her thigh, across her hipbone to the triangle of curls between her legs.

Tensing, shivering, she wanted his touch and yet feared it, too. It had been so long since she'd been held, so long since she'd felt anything as intensely pleasurable as this, that she leaned even closer to him, pressing her breasts to his chest, her tummy to his torso, even as his fingers parted her cleft, finding the most delicate skin between. She was hot, and wet, and she pressed her forehead to his jaw as his fingers explored her.

She couldn't help the moan that escaped her lips, nor the trembling of her legs. She wanted him, needed him, and the intensity of her desire stunned her.

Flushed, dazed, Elizabeth pulled back, swayed on her feet. "The bed," she whispered breathlessly, tugging on his shirt. They walked together, reaching the bed in several steps.

As they bumped into the mattress Kristian impatiently stripped her dress over her head. "I want your hair down, too."

Reaching up, she unpinned her hair and pulled the elastics off the plaits. It was hard to pull her hair apart when Kristian was using her own body against her. With her arms up, over her head, he'd taken her breasts in his hands, cupping their fullness and teasing the tightly ruched nipples.

Gasping at the pressure and pleasure, she very nearly couldn't undo her hair. She hadn't worn a bra tonight due to the sheer lace at her bodice, and the feel of his hands on her bare skin was almost too much.

Hair loose, she reached for Kristian's belt, and then the button and zipper of his trousers. Freeing his shaft, she stroked him, amazed by his size all over again.

But Kristian was impatient to have her on the bed beneath him, and, nudging her backward, he sent her toppling down, legs still dangling over the mattress edge. With her knees parted he kissed her inner thigh, and then higher up, against her warm, moist core. He had a deft touch and tongue, and his expertise was almost more than she could bear. Suddenly shy, she wanted him to stop, but he circled her thighs with his arms, held her open for him.

The tip of his tongue flicked across her heated flesh before playing lightly yet insistently against her core. Again and again he stroked her with his tongue and lips, driving her mad with the tension building inside her. She panted as the pressure built, reached for Kristian, but he dodged her hands, and then, arching, hips bucking, she climaxed.

The orgasm was intense, overwhelming. She felt absolutely leveled. And when Kristian finally moved up, over her, she couldn't even speak. Instead she reached for his chest, slid her fingers across the dense muscle protecting his heart, up over his shoulder to pull him down on top of her.

His body was heavy, hard and strong. She welcomed the weight of him, the delicious feel of his body covering hers. Her orgasm had been intense, but what she really wanted—needed— was something more satisfying than just physical satisfaction. She craved him. The feeling of being taken, loved, sated by him.

He entered her slowly, harnessing his strength to ensure he didn't hurt her. Elizabeth held him tightly, awed by the sensation of him filling her. He felt so good against her, felt so good *in* her. She kissed his chest, the base of his throat, before he dipped his head, covering her mouth with his.

As he kissed her, he slowly thrust into her, stretching his body out over hers to withdraw and then thrust again. His chest grazed her breasts, skin and hair rubbing across her sensitive nipples. She squirmed with pleasure and he buried himself deeper inside her.

Elizabeth wrapped her legs around his waist as his hips moved against her. She squeezed her muscles, holding him inside, and the tantalizing friction of their bodies, the warm heated skin coupled with the deep impenetrable darkness, made their lovemaking even more mysterious and erotic.

As Kristian's tempo increased, his thrusts becoming harder, faster, she met each one eagerly, wanting him, as much of him as he would give her.

No one had ever made her feel so physical, so sexual, or so good. It felt natural being with him, and she gave herself over to Kristian, to his skill and passion, as he drove them both to a point of no return where muscles and nerves tightened and the mind shut out everything but wave after wave of pleasure in the most powerful orgasm of her life.

For those seconds she was not herself, not Grace Elizabeth, but bits of sky and stars and the night. She felt thrown from her body into something so much larger, so much more hopeful than her life. It wasn't sex, she thought, her body still shuddering around him, with him. It was possibility.

Afterwards, feeling dazed and nearly boneless, she clung to Kristian and drew a great gulp of air.

Amazing. That had been so amazing. He made her feel beautiful in every way, too. "I love you," she whispered, against his chest. "I do."

Kristian's hand was buried in her hair, fingers twining through the silken strands. His grip tightened, and then eased, and, dropping his head, he kissed her nose, her brow, her eyelid. "My darling English nurse. Overcome by passion."

"I'm not English," she answered with a supremely satisfied yawn, her body relaxing. "I'm American."

He rolled them over so that he was on the mattress and her weight now rested on him. "What?"

"An American."

"You're *American?*" he repeated incredulously, holding her firmly by the hips.

"Yes."

"Well, that explains a lot of things," he said with mock seriousness. "Especially your sensitivity. Americans are so thin-skinned. They take everything personally."

Her hair spilled over both of them, and she made a face at him in the dark. "I think you were the one who was very sensitive in the beginning. And you were attached to your pain meds—"

"Enough about my pain meds. So, tell me, your eyes… blue? Green? Brown?"

She felt a pang, realizing he might never really know what she looked like. She'd accepted it before, but now it seemed worse somehow. "They're blue. And I'm not that tall—just five-four."

"That's it? When you first arrived a couple weeks ago I was certain you were six feet. That you made Nurse Burly—"

"Hurly," she corrected with a muffled laugh.

"Nurse Hurly-Burly seem dainty."

Elizabeth had to stifle another giggle. "You're terrible, Kristian. You know that, don't you?"

"So you and a half-dozen other nurses keep telling me."

Grinning, she snuggled closer. "So you really had no clue that I was raised in New York?"

"None at all." He kissed the base of her throat, and then up by her ear. "So is that where home is?"

"Was. I've lived in London for years now. I'm happy there."

"Are you?"

"Well, I don't actually live in London. I work in Richmond, and my home is in Windsor. It's under an hour's train ride each way, and I like it. I read, take care of paperwork, sort out my day."

He was stroking her hair very slowly, leisurely, just listening to her talk. As she fell silent, he kissed her again. "My eye specialists are in London."

She wished she could see his face. "Are you thinking of scheduling the eye surgery?"

"Toying with the idea."

"Seriously toying…?"

"Yes. Do you think I should try?"

She considered her words carefully before answering. "You're the one that has to live with the consequences," she said, remembering what Pano had said—that Kristian needed to have something to hope for, something to keep him going.

"But maybe it's better to just know." He exhaled heavily, sounding as if the weight of the world rested on his shoulders. "Maybe I should just do it and get it over with."

Elizabeth put her hand to his chest, felt his heart beating against her hand. "The odds…they're not very good, are they?"

"Less than five percent," he answered, his voice devoid of emotion.

Not good odds, she thought, swallowing hard. "You're doing so well right now. You're making such good progress. If the surgery doesn't turn out as you hoped, could you cope with the results?"

He didn't immediately answer. "I don't know," he said at last. "I don't know how I'd feel. But I know this. I miss seeing. I miss my sight."

"I'm sure you do."

"And I'd love to get rid of the cane. I don't like announcing to the world that I can't see. Besides, I'm sure I look foolish, tapping my way around—"

"That's a ridiculous thing to say!" She pulled away, sat up cross-legged. "First of all, the cane doesn't look foolish, and secondly, it's not about appearances, either. Life and love shouldn't be based on looks. It's about kindness, courage, humility, strength." She paused, drew an unsteady breath. "And you have all those qualities in abundance."

With that, power restored, the lights suddenly flickered and came on.

Elizabeth looked down at them, aware that Kristian couldn't see what she could see and that she should have been embarrassed. They were both naked, he stretched out on his back, she sitting cross-legged, with his hand resting on her bare thigh. But instead of being uncomfortable she felt a little thrill. She felt so right with him. She felt like his—body and soul.

"The power's back," she said, gazing at Kristian, soaking up his dark erotic beauty. His black hair, the strong classic features, impossibly long eyelashes and that sensual mouth of his. "We have lights again."

"Am I missing anything?" he drawled lazily, reaching for her and pulling her back on top of him.

As she straddled his hips he caressed the underside of her breast, so that her nipple hardened and peaked. The touch of his hand against her breast was sending sharp darts of feeling throughout her body, making her insides heat, and clench, and begin to crave relief from his body again.

"No," she murmured, eyes closing, lips helplessly parting as he tugged her lower, allowing him to take her nipple into his mouth. His mouth felt hot and wet against the nipple, and she gripped his shoulders as he sucked, unable to stifle her whimper.

Her whimper aroused him further. Elizabeth could feel him grow hard beneath her. And all she could think was that she wanted him—again. Wanted him to take her—hard, fast— take her until she screamed with pleasure.

He must have been thinking the same thing, too, because,

shifting, he lifted her up, positioned her over him and thrust in. She groaned and shivered as he used his hands to help her ride him. She'd tried this position years ago and hadn't liked it, as she hadn't felt anything much but foolish, and yet now the positions and their bodies clicked. Elizabeth's cheeks burned hot, and her skin glowed as they made love again.

She came faster than before, in a cry of fierce pleasure, before collapsing onto his chest, utterly spent.

Her heart hammering, her body damp, she could do nothing but rest and try to catch her breath. "It just keeps getting better," she whispered.

He stroked her hair, and then the length of her back, until his hand rested on her bottom. "I think I've met my match," he said.

She pushed up on her elbow to see his face. "What does that mean?"

He cupped her breast, stroked the puckered aureola with his thumb. "I think you enjoy sex as much as I do."

"With you. You're incredible."

"It takes two to make it incredible." Reaching up, he pulled her head down to his and kissed her deeply, his tongue teasing hers in another sensual seduction.

In the middle of the kiss, her stomach suddenly growled. Elizabeth giggled apologetically against his mouth. "Sorry. Hungry."

"Then let's find our dinner. I'm starving, too."

They dressed in what they'd left strewn about the floor earlier. Elizabeth bent to retrieve their clothes before handing Kristian first his pants and then his shirt. Slipping on her dress, she struggled to comb her hair smooth with her fingers.

"I feel like I'm in high school," she said with a laugh. And then, and only then, it hit her—Cosima.

"My God," she whispered under her breath, blood draining, her body going icy cold. What had she done? What had she just done?

"Elizabeth?"

She pressed her hand to her mouth, stared at him as he struggled to rebutton his shirt. He'd got it wrong.

"What's the matter?" he demanded.

She could only look at him aghast, shocked, sickened.

She'd behaved badly. *Badly.* He wasn't hers. He'd never been hers. All along he'd belonged to another woman….

"Elizabeth?" Kristian's voice crackled with anger. "Are you still here? Or have you left? Talk to me."

He was right. He couldn't see. Couldn't read her face to know what she was thinking or feeling. "What did we just do, Kristian?" *What did I do?*

His hands stilled, the final button forgotten. A look of confusion crossed his features. "You already have…regrets?"

Regrets? She nearly cried. Only because he wasn't hers.

"Do you have someone waiting for you in London?" he asked, his voice suddenly growing stern, his expression hardening, taking on the glacier stillness she realized he used to keep the world at bay.

"No."

"But there is a relationship?"

"No."

Even without sight he seemed to know exactly where he was, he crossed to her, swiftly closing the distance between them. He took her by the shoulders.

She stiffened, fearing his anger, but then he slid his arms around her, held her securely against him. He kissed her cheek, and then her ear, and then nipped playfully at a particularly sensitive nerve in her neck. "What's wrong, *latrea mou?* Why the second thoughts?"

She splayed her fingers against his chest. Her heart thudded ridiculously hard. "As much as I care about you, Kristian, I cannot do this. It was wrong. *Is* wrong. Just a terrible mistake."

His arms fell away. He stepped back. "Is it because of my eyes? Because I can't see and you pity me?"

"No."

"It's something, *latrea mou*. Because one moment you are in my arms and it feels good, it feels calm and real, like a taste of happiness, and now you say it was…terrible." He drew a breath. "A *mistake*." The bitterness in his voice carved her heart in two. "I think I don't know you at all."

Eyes filling with tears, she watched him take another step backward, and then another. "Kristian." She whispered his name. "No, it's not that. Not the way you make it sound. I loved being with you. I wanted to be near you—"

"Then *what?* Is this about Cosima again? Because, God forgive me, but I can't get away from her. Every time I turn around there she is…even in my goddamn bedroom!"

"Kristian."

"*No.* No. None of that *I'm so disappointed in you* garbage. I've had it. I'm sick of it. What is it with you and Cosima? Is it the contract? The fact that she paid you money? Because if it's money, tell me the amount and I'll cut her a check."

"It's not the money. It's…you. You and her."

He laughed, but the sound grated on her ears. "*Cosima?* Cosima—the Devil Incarnate?"

"You're not a couple?"

"A couple? You're out of your mind, *latrea mou*. She's the reason I couldn't get out of bed, couldn't make myself walk, couldn't face life. Why would I ever want to be with a woman who'd been with my brother?"

Her jaw dropped. Her mouth dried. "Your…*brother?*"

Kristian had gone ashen, and the scar on his cheek tightened. "She was Andreas's fiancée. He's dead because she's alive. He's dead because I went to her aid first. I rescued her for him."

Elizabeth shook her head. Her mouth opened, shut. Of course. *Of course.*

Still shaking her head, she replayed her conversations with Cosima over again. Cosima had never said directly that she was in love with Kristian. She said she'd cared deeply for him, and wanted to see him back in Athens, but she never had said that there was more than that. Just that she hoped…

Hoped.

That was all. That was it.

"So, do you still have to go to Paris on Monday? Or was that just an excuse?" Kristian asked tersely, his features so hard they looked chiseled from granite.

"I still have to go," she answered in a low voice.

"And you still have regrets?"

"Kristian—"

"You do, don't you?"

"Kristian, it's not that simple. Not black and white like that."

"So what *is* it like?" Each word sounded like sharp steel coming from his mouth.

"I…" She closed her eyes, tried to imagine how to tell him who she'd been married to, how she'd been vilified, how she'd transformed herself to escape. But no explanation came. The old pain went too deep. The identities were too confusing. Grace Elizabeth Stiles had been beautiful and wealthy, glamorous and privileged, but she'd also been naïve and dependent, too trusting and too easily hurt.

"You *what?*" he demanded, not about to let her off the hook so easily.

"I can't stay in Greece," she whispered. "I can't."

"Is this all because of that Greek *ornio* you met on your holiday?"

"It was more serious than that."

He stilled. "How serious?"

"I married him."

For a long moment he said nothing, and then his lips pulled and his teeth flashed savagely. "So this is how it is."

She took a step toward him. "What does that mean?"

"It means I'm not a man to you. Not one you can trust or respect—"

"That's not true."

"It *is* true." His shoulders tensed. "We spent two weeks together—morning, noon and night. Why didn't you tell me you were married before? Why did you let me believe it was a simple holiday romance, a little Greek fling gone bad?"

"Because I...I...just don't talk about it."

"Why?"

"Because it hurt me. Badly." Her voice raised, tears started to her eyes. "It made me afraid."

"Just like swimming in the deep end of the pool?"

She bit her bottom lip. He sounded so disgusted, she thought. So irritated and impatient.

"You don't trust me," he added, his tone increasingly cold. "And you don't know me if you think I'd make love to one woman while involved with another."

Her heart sank. He was angry—blisteringly angry.

"What kind of man do you think I am?" he thundered. "How immoral and despicable am I?"

"You're not—"

"You thought I was engaged to Cosima."

"I didn't want to think so."

"But you did," he shot back.

"Kristian, please don't. Please don't judge me—"

"Why not? You judged me."

Tears tumbled. "I love you," she whispered.

He shrugged brusquely. "You don't know the meaning of love if you'd go to bed with a man supposedly engaged to another woman."

Elizabeth felt her heart seize up. This couldn't be happening like this, could it? They couldn't be making such a wretched mess of things, could they? "Kristian, I can't explain it, can't find the words right now, but you must know how I feel—how I really feel. You must know why I'm here, and why I even stayed this long."

"The money, maybe?" he mocked savagely, opening the door wider.

"*No.* And there is no money, I'm not taking her money—"

"Conveniently said."

He didn't know. He didn't see. And maybe that was it. He couldn't see how much she loved him, and how much she believed in him, and how she would have done anything, just about anything, to help him. Love him. Make him happy. "Please," she begged, reaching for him.

But there was no reaching him. Not when he put up that wall of his, that huge, thick, impenetrable ice wall of his, that shut him off from everyone else. Instead he shrugged her off and walked down the hall toward the distant stairwell.

His rejection cut deeply. For a moment she could do nothing but watch him walk away, and then she couldn't just let him go—not like that, not over something that was so small.

A misunderstanding.

Pride.

Ego.

None of it was important enough to keep them apart. None

of it mattered if they truly cared for each other. She loved him, and from the way he'd held her, made love to her, she knew he had to have feelings for her—knew there was more to this than just hormones. For Pete's sake, neither of them were teenagers, and both of them had been through enough to know what mattered.

What mattered was loving, and being loved.

What mattered was having someone on your side. Someone who'd stick with you no matter what.

And so she left the safety of her door, the safety of pride and ego, and followed him to the stairs. She was still wiping away tears, but she knew this—she wasn't going to be dismissed, wasn't going to let him get rid of her like that.

She chased after him, trailing down the staircase. Turning the corner of one landing, she started down the next flight of stairs even as a door opened and footsteps crossed the hall below.

"Kristian!" A man said, his voice disturbingly familiar. "We were just told you'd arrived. What a surprise. Welcome home!"

Nico?

Elizabeth froze. Even her heart seemed to still.

"What are *you* doing here?" Kristian asked, his voice taut, low.

"We—my girlfriend and I—live here part-time," Nico answered. "Didn't you know we'd taken a suite? I was sure you'd been told. At least, I know Pano was aware of it. I talked to him on the phone the other day."

"I've been busy," Kristian murmured distractedly.

Legs shaking, Elizabeth shifted her weight and the floorboard squeaked. All heads down below turned to look up at her.

Elizabeth grabbed the banister. This couldn't be happening. Couldn't be.

Nico, catching sight of her, was equally shocked. Staring up at Elizabeth, he laughed incredulously. "Grace?"

Elizabeth could only stare back.

Nico glanced at Kristian, and then back to his ex-wife. "What's going on?" he asked.

"I don't know," Kristian answered tightly. "You tell me."

"I don't know either," Nico said, frowning at Elizabeth. "But for a moment I thought you and Grace were…together."

"Grace who?" Kristian demanded tersely.

"Stile. My American wife."

Kristian went rigid. "There's no Grace here."

"Yes, there she is," Nico answered. "She's standing on the landing. Blonde hair. Black lace dress."

Elizabeth felt Kristian's confusion as he swung around, staring blindly up at the stairwell. Her heart contracted. "Kristian," she said softly, hating his confusion, hating that she was the source of it, too.

"That's not Grace," Kristian retorted grimly. "That's Elizabeth. Elizabeth Hatchet. My nurse."

"Nurse?" Nico laughed. "Oh, dear, Koumantaros, it looks like she's duped you. Because your Elizabeth is my ex-wife, Grace Stile. And a nasty gold-digger, too."

CHAPTER ELEVEN

KRISTIAN felt as though he'd been punched hard in the gut. He couldn't breathe, couldn't move, could only stand there, struggling to take in air.

Elizabeth wasn't Elizabeth? Elizabeth was really Grace Stile?

He tried to shake his head, tried to clear the fuzz and storm clouding his mind.

The woman he'd fallen in love with wasn't even who he thought she was. Her name wasn't even Elizabeth. Maybe she wasn't even a nurse.

Maybe she was a gold-digger, just like Nico said.

Gold-digger. The word rang in Elizabeth's head.

Shocked, she went hot, and then cold, and hot again. "I'm no gold-digger," she choked, finally finding her voice. Legs wobbling, she took one step and then another until she'd reached the hall. "*You* are," she choked. "You, you... you're..." But she couldn't get the words out, couldn't defend herself, could scarcely breathe, much less think.

Nico had betrayed *her.*

Nico had married *her* for her money.

Nico had poisoned the Greek media and public against her.

Stomach roiling, she was swept back into that short brutal marriage and the months following their divorce.

He'd made her life a living hell and she'd been the one to pay—and pay, and pay. Not just for the divorce, and not just his settlement, but emotionally, physically, mentally. It had taken years to heal, years to stop being so hurt and so insecure and so angry. *Angry.*

And she had been angry because she'd felt cheated of love, cheated of the home and the family and the dreams she'd cherished. They were supposed to have been husband and wife. A couple, partners.

But she'd only been money, cash, the fortune to supplement Nico's dwindling inheritance.

Nico, though, wasn't paying her the least bit of attention. He was still talking to Kristian, a smirk on his face—a face she'd once thought so handsome. She didn't find him attractive anymore, not even if she was being objective, because, next to Kristian, Nico's good-looks faded to merely boyish, almost pretty, whereas Kristian was fiercely rugged, all man.

"She'll seduce you," Nico continued, rolling back on his heels, his arms crossed over his chest. "And make you think it was your idea. And when she has you in bed she'll tell you she loves you. She'll make you think it's love, but it's greed. She'll take you for everything you're worth—"

"That's enough. I've heard enough," Kristian ground out, silencing Nico's ruthless character assassination. He'd paled, so that the scar seemed to jump from his cheekbone, a livid reminder of the tragedy that had taken so much from him over a year ago.

"None of it is true," Elizabeth choked, her body shaking, legs like jelly. "Nothing he says—"

"I said, *enough.*" Kristian turned away and walked down the hall.

Elizabeth felt the air leave her, her chest so empty her heart seized.

Somehow she found her way back to her room and stumbled into bed, where she lay stiff as a board, unable to sleep or cry.

Everything seemed just so unbelievably bad—so awful that it couldn't even be assimilated.

Lying there, teeth chattering with shock and cold, Elizabeth prayed that when the sun finally rose in the morning all of this would be just a bad, bad dream.

It wasn't.

The next morning a maid knocked on Elizabeth's door, giving her the message that a car was ready to drive her to meet the helicopter.

Washing her face, Elizabeth avoided looking at herself in the mirror before smoothing the wrinkles in her velvet dress and heading downstairs, where the butler ushered her to the waiting car.

Elizabeth had been under the impression that she'd be traveling back alone, but Kristian was already in the car when she climbed in.

"Good morning," she whispered, sliding onto the seat but being careful to keep as much distance between them as she could.

His head barely inclined.

She ducked her head, stared at her fingers, which were laced and locked in her lap. Sick, she thought, so sick. She felt as though everything good and warm and hopeful inside her had vanished, left, gone. Died.

Eyes closing, she held her breath, her teeth sinking into her lower lip.

She only let her breath out once the car started moving, leaving the castle for the helicopter pad on the other side of town.

"You were Nico's wife," Kristian said shortly, his deep rough voice splitting the car's silence in two. There was a brutality in his voice she'd never heard before. A violence that spoke of revenge and embittered passion.

Opening her eyes, she looked at Kristian, but she couldn't read anything in his face—not when his fiercely handsome features were so frozen, fixed in hard, remote, unforgiving lines. It was as if his face wasn't a face but a mask.

The car seemed to spin.

She didn't answer, didn't want to answer, didn't know *how* to answer—because in his present frame of mind nothing she said would help, nothing she said would matter. After all, Kristian Koumantaros was a Greek man. It wouldn't matter to him that she was divorced—had been divorced for years. In his mind she'd always be Nico's wife.

Elizabeth glanced down at her hands again, the knuckles white. She was so dizzy she didn't think she could sit straight, but finally she forced her head up, forced the world's wild revolutions to slow until she could see Kristian on the seat next to her, his blue eyes brilliant, piercing, despite the fact that she knew he couldn't see.

"I'm waiting," he said flatly, finality and closure in his rough voice.

Tears filling her eyes, she drew another deep breath. "Yes," she said, her voice so faint it sounded like nothing.

"So your name isn't really Elizabeth, is it?"

Again she couldn't speak. The pain inside her chest was excruciating. She could only stare at Kristian, wishing everything had somehow turned out differently. If Nico hadn't been one of the castle's tenants. If Cosima hadn't stood between them. If Elizabeth had understood just who and what Cosima really was...

"I'm still waiting," Kristian said.

Hurt and pain flared, lighting bits of fire inside her. "Waiting for what?" she demanded, shoulders twisted so she could better see him. "For some big confession? Well, I'm not going to confess. I've done nothing wrong—"

"You've done *everything* wrong," he interrupted through gritted teeth. "Everything. If your name isn't really Elizabeth Hatchet."

Colder and colder, she swallowed, her eyes growing wide, her stomach plummeting.

"If Nico was your husband, that makes you someone I do not know."

Elizabeth exhaled so hard it hurt, her chest spasming, her throat squeezing closed.

When she didn't answer, he leaned toward her, touched the side of her head, then her ear and finally her cheekbones, her eyes, her nose, her mouth. "You are Grace Stile, aren't you?"

"Was," she barely whispered. "I was Grace Stile. But Grace Stile doesn't exist anymore."

"Grace Stile was a beautiful woman," he said mockingly, his fingertips lingering on the fullness of her soft mouth.

She trembled inwardly at the touch. "I am not her," she said against his fingers. Last night he'd made her feel so good, so warm, so safe. *Happy.* But today...today it was something altogether different.

He ground out a mocking laugh. "Grace Stile, daughter of an American icon—"

"No."

"New York's most beautiful and accomplished debutante."

"Not me."

"Even more wealthy than the Greek tycoon she married."

Elizabeth stopped talking.

"Your father, Rupert Stile—"

She pulled her head away, leaned back in her seat to remove herself from his touch. "Grace Stile is gone," she said crisply. "I am Elizabeth Hatchet, a nursing administrator, and that is all that is important, all that needs to be known."

He barked a laugh, far from amused. "But your legal name isn't even Elizabeth Hatchet."

She hesitated, bit savagely into her lower lip, knowing she'd never given anyone this information—not since that fateful day when everything had changed. "Hatchet was my mother's maiden name. Legally I'm Grace Elizabeth."

He laughed again, the sound even more strained and incredulous. "Are you even a registered nurse?"

"Of course!"

"Of course," he repeated, shaking his head and running a hand across his jaw, which was dark with a day's growth of beard.

For a moment neither spoke, and the only sound was Kristian's palm, rubbing the rough bristles on his chin and jaw.

"You think you know someone," he said, after a tense minute. "You think you know what's true, what's real, and then you find out you know nothing at all."

"But you do know I am a nurse," she said steadfastly. "And I hold a Masters Degree in Business Administration."

"But I don't know that. I can't see. You could be just anybody...and it turns out you are!"

"Kristian—"

"Because if I weren't blind you couldn't have pulled this off, could you? If I could see I would have recognized you. I would have known you weren't some dreary, dumpy little nursing administrator, but the famously beautiful heiress Grace Stile."

"That never crossed my mind—"

"No? Are you sure?"

"Yes."

He made a rough, derogatory sound. His mouth slanted, cheekbones pronounced. The car had stopped. They were at the small airport, and not far from their car waited the helicopter and pilot. As the driver of the car turned off the ignition, Kristian laid a hand on Elizabeth's thigh.

"Your degrees," he said. "Those are in which name?"

She felt the heat of his hand sear her skin even as it melted her on the inside. She cared for him, loved him, but couldn't seem to connect anything that was happening today with what had taken place in her bed last night.

"My degrees," she said softly, referring to her nursing degree and then the degree in Business Administration, "were both earned in England, as Elizabeth Hatchet."

"Very clever of you," he taunted, as the passenger door opened and the driver stood there, ready to provide assistance.

Elizabeth suppressed a wave of panic. It was all coming to an end, so quickly and so badly, and she couldn't figure out how to turn the tide now that it was rushing at her, fierce and relentless.

"Kristian," she said urgently, touching his hand, her fingers attempting to slide around his. But he held his fingers stiff, and aloof, as though they'd never been close. "There was nothing clever about it. I moved to England and changed my name, out of desperation. I didn't want to be Grace Stile anymore. I wanted to start over. I *needed* to start over. And so I did."

He didn't speak again. Not even after they were in the helicopter heading for Athens, where he'd told her a plane awaited. He was sending her home immediately. Her bags were already at Athens airport. She'd be back in London by mid-afternoon.

It was a strangely silent flight, and it wasn't until they were on the ground in Athens, exiting the helicopter, that he broke the painful stillness.

"Why medicine?" he demanded.

Kristian's question stopped her just as she was about to climb the private jet's stairs.

Slowly she turned to face him, tucking a strand of hair behind her ear even as she marveled all over again at the changes two weeks had made. Kristian Koumantaros was every inch the formidable tycoon he'd been before he was injured. He wasn't just walking, he stood tall, legs spread, powerful shoulders braced.

"You didn't study medicine at Smith or Brown or wherever you went in the States," he continued, naming universities on the East Coast. "You were interested in antiquities then."

Antiquities, she thought, her teeth pressed to the inside of her lower lip. She and her love of ancient cultures. Wasn't that how she'd met Nico in the first place? Attending a party at a prestigious New York museum to celebrate the opening of a new, priceless Greek exhibit?

"Medicine's more practical," she answered, eyes gritty, stinging with tears she wouldn't let herself cry.

And, thinking back to her move across the Atlantic, to her new identity and her new choices, she knew she'd been compelled to become someone different, someone better...more altruistic.

"Medicine is also about helping others—doing something good."

"Versus exploiting their weaknesses?"

"I've never done that!" she protested hotly.

"No?"

"No." But she could see from his expression that he didn't

believe her. She opened her mouth to defend herself yet again, before stopping. It didn't matter, she thought wearily, pushing another strand of hair back from her face. He would think what he wanted to think.

And, fine, let him.

She cared about him—hugely, tremendously—but she was tired of being the bad person, was unwilling to be vilified any longer. She'd never been a bad woman, a bad person. Maybe at twenty-three, or twenty-four she hadn't known better than to accept the blame, but she did now. She was a woman, not a punching bag.

"Goodbye," she said *"Kali tihi."* Good luck.

"Good luck?" he repeated. "With what?" he snapped, taking a threatening step toward her.

His reaction puzzled her. But he'd always puzzled her. "With everything," she answered, just wanting to go now, needing to make the break. She knew this could go nowhere. Last night she should have realized that nothing good would come out of an inappropriate liaison, but last night she hadn't been thinking. Last night she'd been frightened and uncertain, and she'd turned to him for comfort, turned to him for reassurance. It was the worst thing she could have done.

And yet Kristian still marched toward her, his expression black. "And just what is *everything?*"

She thought of all he had still waiting for him. He could have such a good life, such a rich, interesting life—sight or no sight—if he wanted.

Her lips curved in a faint, bittersweet smile. "Your life," she said simply. "It's all still before you."

And quickly, before he could detain her, she climbed the stairs, disappearing into the jet's cool, elegant interior where she settled into one of the leather chairs in the main cabin.

Except for the flight crew, the plane was empty.

Elizabeth fastened her seatbelt and settled back in the club chair. She knew it would be a very quiet trip home.

Back in London, Elizabeth rather rejoiced in the staggering number of cases piled high on her desk. She welcomed the billing issues, the cranky patients, the nurses needing vacations and personal days off, as every extra hour of work meant another hour she couldn't think about Kristian, or Greece, or the chaotic two weeks spent there.

Because now that she was back in England, taking the train to work at her office in Richmond every day, she couldn't fathom what had happened.

Couldn't fathom how it had happened.

Couldn't fathom why.

She wasn't interested in men, or dating, or having another lover. She wasn't interested in having a family, either. All she wanted was to work, to pay her bills, to keep her company running as smoothly as possible. Her business was her professional life, social life and personal life all rolled into one, and it suited her just fine.

Far better to be Plain Jane than Glamorous Grace Stile, with the world at her feet, because the whole world-at-your-feet thing was just an illusion anyway. As she'd learned the hard way, the more people thought you had, the more they envied you, and then resented you, and eventually they lobbied to see you fall.

Far better to live simply and quietly and mind your own business, she thought, shuffling papers into her briefcase.

She was leaving work early again today, tormented by a stomach bug that wouldn't go away. She'd been back home in England just over two months now, but she hadn't felt like herself for ages. Since Greece, as a matter of fact.

Her secretary glanced up as Elizabeth opened the office door.

"Still under the weather, Ms. Hatchet?" Mrs. Shipley asked sympathetically, pushing her reading glasses up on her head.

Mrs. Shipley had practically run the office single-handedly while Elizabeth was gone, and she couldn't imagine a better administrative assistant.

"I am," Elizabeth answered with a grimace, as her insides did another sickly, queasy rise and fall that made her want to throw up into the nearest rubbish bin. But of course she never had the pleasure of actually throwing up. She wasn't lucky enough to get the thing—whatever it was—out of her system.

"If you picked up a parasite in Greece, you'll need a good antibiotic, my dear. I know I'm sounding like a broken record, but you really should see a doctor. Get something for that. The right antibiotic will nip it in the bud. And you need it nipped in the bud, as you look downright peaky."

Mrs. Shipley was right. Elizabeth felt absolutely wretched. She ached. Her head throbbed. Her stomach alternated between nausea and cramps. Even her sleep was disturbed, colored with weird, wild dreams of doom and gloom.

But what she feared most, and refused to confront, was the very real possibility that it wasn't a parasite she'd picked up but something more permanent. Something more changing.

Something far more serious.

Like Kristian Koumantaros's baby.

She'd been home just over two months now and she hadn't had her period—which wasn't altogether unusual, since she was the least regular woman she knew—but she couldn't bring herself to actually take a pregnancy test.

If she wasn't pregnant—fantastic.

If she was...

If she was?

The next morning her nausea was so severe she huddled next to the toilet, managing nothing more than wrenching dry heaves.

Her head was spinning and she was gagging, and all she could think was, What if I really am pregnant with Kristian Koumantaros's baby?

Kristian Koumantaros was one of the most wealthy, powerful, successful men in Europe. He lived in ancient monasteries and castles and villas all over the world. He traveled by helicopter, private jet, luxury yacht. He negotiated with no one.

And she knew he wouldn't negotiate with her. If he knew she was pregnant he'd step in, take over, take action.

And, yes, Kristian *ought* to know. But how would he benefit from knowing? Would the baby—if there really was a baby—benefit?

Would *she?*

No. Not when Kristian viewed her as a heartless mercenary, a gold-digger, someone who preyed upon other's weaknesses.

Elizabeth somehow managed to drag herself into work, drag listlessly through the day, and then caught the train home to Windsor.

Sitting on the train seat, thirty minutes away from her stop, it hit her for the first time. She was pregnant. She knew deep down she was going to have a baby.

But Kristian. What about Kristian?

A wave of ice flooded her. What would he say, much less do, if he knew about the baby? He didn't even like her. He despised her. How would he react if he knew she carried his child?

Panic flooded her—panic that made her feel even colder and more afraid.

She couldn't let him find out. She wouldn't let him find out.

Stop it, she silently chastised herself as her panic grew. It's not as though you'll bump into him.

You live on opposite ends of the continent. You're both on islands separated by seas. No way to accidentally meet.

As heartless as it sounded, she'd make sure they wouldn't meet, either.

He'd take the baby. She knew he'd take the baby from her. Just the way Nico had taken everything from her.

Greek men were proud, and fierce. Greek men, particularly Greek tycoons, thought they were above rules and laws. And Kristian Koumantaros, now that he was nearly recovered, would be no different.

Elizabeth's nausea increased, and she stirred restlessly in her seat, anxious to be home, where she could take a long bath, climb into bed and just relax.

She needed to relax. Her heart was pounding far too hard.

Trying to distract herself, she glanced around the train cabin, studying the different commuters, before glancing at the man next to her reading a newspaper. His face was hidden by the back of the paper and her gaze fell on the headlines. Nothing looked particularly interesting until she read, *Koumantaros in London for Treatment*.

Koumantaros.

Kristian Koumantaros?

Breath catching, she leaned forward to better see the article. She only got the first line or two before the man rudely shuffled the pages and turned his back to her preventing her from reading more.

But Elizabeth didn't need to read much more than those first two lines to get the gist of the article.

Kristian had undergone the risky eye surgery at Moorfield's Hospital in London today.

CHAPTER TWELVE

WALKING from the train station to her little house, Elizabeth felt her nerves started getting the best of her. For the past three years she'd made historic Windsor her home, having found it the perfect antidote to the stresses of her career, but today the walk filled her with apprehension.

Something felt wrong. And it wasn't just thinking about the baby. It was an uneasy sixth sense that things around her weren't right.

Picking up her pace, she tried to silence her fears, telling herself she was tired and overly imaginative.

No one was watching her.

No one was following her.

And nothing bad was going to happen.

But tugging the collar of her coat up, and crossing her arms over her chest to keep warm, she couldn't help thinking that something felt bad. And the bad feeling was growing stronger as she left the road and hurried up the crushed gravel path toward her house.

Windsor provided plenty of diversion on weekends, with brilliant shopping as well as the gorgeous castle and the riverside walks, but as she entered her house and closed the door behind her, her quiet little house on its quiet little lane seemed very isolated.

If someone had followed her home, no one would see.

If someone broke into her house, no one would hear her cries for help.

Elizabeth locked the front door, then went through the kitchen to the back door, checking the lock on that before finally taking her coat off and turning the heat up.

In the kitchen she put on the kettle for tea, and was just about to make some toast when a knock sounded on her door.

She froze, the loaf of bread still in her hands, and stood still so long that the knock sounded again.

Putting the bread on the counter, and the knife down, she headed for the door, checking through a window first before she actually opened it.

A new model Jaguar was parked out front, and a man stood on her doorstep, his back to her as he faced the car. But she knew the man—knew his height, the breadth of his shoulders, the length of his legs, the shape of his head.

Kristian.

Kristian here.

But today was his surgery…he was supposed to have had surgery…the paper had said…

Unless he'd backed out.

But he wouldn't back out, would he?

Heart hammering, she undid the lock and opened the door, and the sound of the lock turning caught his attention. Kristian shifted, turning toward her. But as he faced her his eyes never blinked, and his expression remained impassive.

"Kristian," she whispered, cold all over again.

"Cratchett," he answered soberly.

And looking up into his face, a face so sculpturally perfect, the striking features contrasted by black hair and blue eyes, she thought him a beautiful but fearsome angel. One sent to judge her, punish her.

Glancing past him to the car, the sleek black Jaguar with tinted windows, she wondered how many cars he had scattered all over the world.

"You're…here," she said foolishly, her mind so strangely blank that nothing came to her—nothing but shock and fear. He couldn't know. He didn't know. She'd only found out today herself.

"Yes, I am." His head tipped and he looked at her directly, but still without recognition. She felt her heart turn over with sympathy for him. He hadn't gone through with the surgery. He must have had second thoughts. And while she didn't blame him—it was a very new, very dangerous procedure— it just reaffirmed all over again her determination to keep the pregnancy a secret…at least for now.

"How did you know I lived here?"

"I had your address," he said blandly.

"Oh. I see." But she didn't see. Her home address was on nothing—although she supposed if a man like Kristian Koumantaros wanted to know where she lived it wouldn't take much effort on his part to find out. He had money, and connections. People would tell him things, particularly private detectives—not that he'd do that…

Or would he?

Frowning, bewildered, she stared up at him, still trying to figure out what he was doing here in Windsor—on her doorstep, no less.

From the kitchen, her kettle began to whistle.

His head lifted, his black brows pulling.

"The kettle," she said, by way of explanation. "I was just

making tea. I should turn it off." And without waiting for him to answer she went to the kitchen and unplugged the kettle, only to turn around and discover Kristian right there behind her, making her small, old-fashioned kitchen, with its porcelain farm sink and simple farmhouse table, look tired and primitive.

"Oh," she said, taking a nervous step back. "You're here."

The corner of his mouth twisted. "I appear to be everywhere today."

"Yes." She pressed her skirt smooth, her hands uncomfortably damp. How had he made his way into the kitchen so quickly? It was almost as if he knew his way already—or as if he could actually see...

Could he?

Her pulse quickened, her nerves strung so tight she felt disturbingly close to falling apart. It had been such an overwhelming day as it was. First her certainty about the baby, and now Kristian in her house.

"Have you been in England long?" she asked softly, trying to figure out just what was going on.

"I've spent part of the last month here."

A month in England. Her heart jumped a little, and she had to exhale slowly to try to calm herself. "I didn't know."

One of his black eyebrows lifted, but he said nothing else. At least some things hadn't changed, she thought. He was still as uncommunicative as ever. But that didn't mean she had to play his game.

"The surgery—it was scheduled for today, wasn't it?" she asked awkwardly.

"Why?"

"I read it in the paper...actually, it was on the train home. You were supposed to have the treatment done today in London."

"Really?"

She felt increasingly puzzled. "It's what the paper said," she repeated defensively."

"I see." He smiled benignly. And the conversation staggered to a stop there.

Uncertainly, she turned to pour her tea.

Good manners required her to ask if he'd like a cup, but the last thing she wanted to do was prolong this miserable visit.

She wrestled with her conscience. Good manners won. "Would you like some tea?" she asked, voice stilted.

White teeth flashed in a mocking smile. "I thought you'd never ask."

Hands shaking, she retrieved another cup and saucer from the cupboard before filling his cup.

He couldn't see…could he?

He couldn't possibly see…

But something inside her, that same peculiar sixth sense from earlier, made her suspicious.

"Toast?" Her voice quavered. She hated that. She hated that suddenly everything felt so wildly out of control.

"No, thank you."

Glancing at him, she put the bread away, too nervous now to eat.

"You're not going to eat?" he asked mildly.

"No."

"You're not hungry?"

Her stomach did another uncomfortable freefall. How did he know she wasn't going to eat?

"The surgery," she said. "You didn't have it today."

"No." He paused for the briefest moment. "I had it a month ago."

Her legs nearly went from beneath her. Elizabeth put a

hand out to the kitchen table to support herself. "A month ago?" she whispered, her gaze riveted to his face.

"Mmmm."

He wasn't helping at all, was he? She swallowed around the huge lump filling her throat. "Can you, can you…see?"

"Imperfectly."

Imperfectly, she repeated silently, growing increasingly light-headed. "Tell me…tell me…how much do you see?"

"It's not all dark anymore. One eye is more or less just shadows and dark shapes, but with the other eye I get a bit more. While I'll probably never be able to drive or pilot my own plane again, I can see you."

"And what do you see…now?" Her voice was faint to her own ears.

"You."

Her heart was beating so hard she was afraid she'd faint.

"The colors aren't what they were," he added. "Everything's faded, so the world's rather gray and white, but I know you're standing near a table. You're touching the table with one hand. Your other hand is on your stomach."

He was right. He was exactly right. And her hand was on her stomach because she felt like throwing up. "Kristian."

He just looked at her, really looked at her, and she didn't know whether to smile for him or burst into tears. He could see. Imperfectly, as he'd said, but something was better than nothing. Something meant he'd live independently more easily. He'd also have more power in his life again, as well as control.

Control.

And suddenly she realized that if he could see her, he'd eventually see the changes in her body. He'd know she was pregnant…

Her insides churned.

"Is that why you're here tonight?" she asked. "To tell me your good news?"

"And to celebrate your good news."

She swayed on her feet. "My good news?"

"You do have good news, don't you?" he persisted.

Elizabeth stared at Kristian where he stood, just inside the kitchen doorway. Protectively she rubbed her stomach, over her not yet existent bump, trying to stay calm. "I...I don't think so."

"I suppose it depends on how you look at it," he answered. His mouth slanted, black lashes lowering to conceal the startling blue of his eyes. "We knew each other only two weeks and two days, and that was two months and two weeks ago. Those two weeks were mostly good. But there was a disappointment or two, wasn't there?"

She couldn't tear her eyes off him. He looked strong and dynamic, and his tone was commanding. "A couple," she echoed nervously.

"One of the greatest offenses is that we flew to Kithira for dinner and we never ate. We were in my favorite restaurant and we never enjoyed an actual meal."

Elizabeth crossed her arms over her chest. "That's your *greatest* disappointment?"

"If you'd ever eaten there, you'd understand. It's truly great food. Greek food as it's meant to be."

She blinked, her fingers balling into knuckled fists. "You're here to tell me I missed out on a great meal?"

"It was supposed to be a special evening."

He infuriated her. Absolutely infuriated her. Pressing her fists to her ribs, she shook inwardly with rage. Here she was, exhausted from work, stressed and sick from her pregnancy, worried about his sight, deeply concerned about the future, and all he could think of was a missed meal?

"Why don't you have your pilot take you back to Kithira and you can *have* your delicious dinner?" she snapped.

"But that wouldn't help you. You still wouldn't know what a delicious meal you'd missed." He gestured behind him, to the compact living room. "So I've brought that meal to you."

"What?"

"I won't have you flying in your state, and I'm worrying about the baby."

"What baby?" she choked, her veins filling with a flood of ice water.

"Our baby," he answered simply, turning away and heading for the living room, which had been transformed while they were in the kitchen.

The owner of the Kithirian restaurant, along with the waiter who had served them that night, had set up a table, chairs, covering the table in a crisp white cloth and table settings for two. The lights had been turned down and candles flickered on the table, and on the side table next to her small antique sofa, and somewhere, she didn't know where, music played.

They'd turned her living room into a Greek taverna and Elizabeth stood rooted to the spot, unable to take it all in. "What's going on?"

Kristian shrugged. "We're going to have that dinner tonight. Now." He moved to take one of the chairs, and pulled it out for her. "A Greek baby needs Greek food."

"Kristian—"

"It's true." His voice dropped, and his expression hardened. "You're having our baby."

"My baby."

"Our baby," he corrected firmly. "And it is *our* baby." His blue gaze held hers. "Isn't it?"

With candles flickering on the crisp white cloth, soft Greek music in the background, and darkly handsome Kristian here before her, Elizabeth felt tears start to her eyes. Two months without a word from him. Two months without apology, remorse, forgiveness. Two months of painful silence and now this—this power-play in her living room.

"I know you haven't been feeling well," he continued quietly. "I know because I've been in London, watching over you."

Weakly she sat down—not at the table, but on one of her living room chairs. "You think I'm a gold-digger."

"A gold-digger? Grace Stile? A woman as wealthy as Athina Onassis Roussel?"

Elizabeth clasped her hands in her lap. "I don't want to talk about Grace Stile."

"I do." He dropped into a chair opposite her. "And I want to talk about Nico and Cosima and all these other sordid characters appearing in our own little Greek play."

The waiter and the restaurant owner had disappeared into the kitchen. They must have begun warming or preparing food, as the smell coming from the back of the house made her stomach growl.

"I know Nico put you through hell in your marriage," Kristian continued. "I know the divorce was even worse. He drove you out of Greece and the media hounded you for years after. I don't blame you for changing your name, for moving to England and trying to become someone else."

She held her breath, knowing there was a *but* coming. She could hear it in his voice, see it in the set of his shoulders.

"But," he added, "I minded very much not being able to see you. Much more not being able to see—and assess—the situation that night at the Kithira castle for myself."

She linked her fingers to hide the fact they were trembling.

"That evening was a nightmare. I just want to forget it. Forget them. Forget Grace, too."

"I can't forget Grace." His head lifted and his gaze searched her face. "Because she's beautiful. And she's you."

The lump in her throat burned, swelled, making everything inside her hurt worse. "I'm not beautiful."

"You were beautiful as a New York debutante, and you're even more beautiful now. And it has nothing to do with your name, or the Stile fortune. Nothing to do with your marriage or your divorce or the work you do as an administrator. It's you. Grace Elizabeth."

"You don't know me," she whispered, trying to silence him.

"But I do. Because for two weeks I lived with you and worked with you and dined with you, and you changed me. You saved me—"

"No."

"Elizabeth, I didn't want to live after the accident. I didn't want to feel so much loss and pain. But you somehow gave me a window of light, and hope. You made me believe that things could be different. Better."

"I wasn't that good, or nice."

"No, you weren't nice. But you were strong. Tough. And you wouldn't baby me. You wouldn't allow me to give up. And I needed that. I needed you." He paused. "I still do."

Her eyes closed. Hot tears stung her eyelids.

He reached over, skimmed her cheeks with his fingers. "Don't cry," he murmured. "Please don't cry."

She shook her head, then turned her cheek into his palm, biting her lip to keep the tears from falling. "If you needed me, why did you let me go?"

"Because I didn't feel worthy of you. Didn't feel like a man who deserved you."

"Kristian—"

"I realized that night that if I'd been able to see, I would have been in control at the castle in Kithira. I could have read the situation, understood what was happening. Instead I stood there in the dark—literally, figuratively—and it enraged me. I felt trapped. Helpless. My blindness was creating ignorance. Fear."

"You've never been scared of anything," she protested softly.

"Since the accident I've been afraid of everything. I've been haunted by nightmares, my sleep disturbed until I thought I was going mad, but after meeting you that began to change. I began to change. I began to find my way home—my way back to me."

She simply stared at him, her heart tender, her eyes stinging from unshed tears.

"I am a man who takes care of his woman," he continued quietly. "I hated not being able to take care of you. And you are my woman. You've been mine from the moment you arrived in the Taygetos on that ridiculous donkey cart."

Her lips quivered in a tremulous smile. "That was the longest, most uncomfortable ride of my life."

"Elizabeth, *latrea mou,* I have loved you from the very first day I met you. You were horrible and wonderful and your courage won me over. Your courage and your compassion. Your kindness and your strength. All those virtues you talked about in Kithira. You told me appearances didn't matter. You said there were virtues far more important and I agree. Yes, you're beautiful, but I couldn't see your beauty until today. I didn't need your beauty, or the Stile name, or your inheritance to win me. I just needed you. With me."

"Kristian—"

"I still do."

Eyes filmed by tears, she looked up, around her small living room. Normally it was a rather austere room. She lived off her salary, having donated nearly all of her inheritance to charity, and it never crossed her mind to spoil herself with pretty things. But tonight the living room glowed, cozy and intimate with candlelight, the beautifully set table and strains of Greek music, even as the most delectable smells wafted from the kitchen.

The restaurant owner appeared in the doorway. "Dinner is ready," he said sternly. "And tonight you both must eat."

Elizabeth joined Kristian at the table, and for the first time in weeks she enjoyed food. How could she not enjoy the meal tonight? Everything was wonderful. The courses and flavors were beyond brilliant. They shared marinated lamb, fish with tomatoes and currants, grilled octopus—which Elizabeth did pass on—and as she ate she couldn't look away from Kristian.

She'd missed him more than she knew.

Just having him here, with her, made everything feel right. Made everything feel good. Intellectually she knew there were problems, issues, and yet emotionally she felt calm and happy and peaceful again.

It had always been like this with him. It wasn't what he said, or did. It was just him. He made her feel good. He made her feel wonderful.

Looking across the table at him, she felt a thought pop into her head. "You know, Cosima said—" she started to say, before breaking off. She'd done it again. Cosima. Always Cosima. "Why do I keep talking about her?"

"I don't know. But you might as well tell me what she said. I might as well hear all of it."

"It's nothing—not important. Let's forget it."

"No. You brought it up, so it's obviously on your mind. What did Cosima say?"

Elizabeth silently kicked herself. The dinner had been

going so well. And now she'd done the same thing as at the castle in Kithira. Her nose wrinkled. "I'm sorry, Kristian."

"So tell me. What does she say?"

"That before you were injured you were an outrageous playboy." She looked up at him from beneath her eyelashes. "That you could get any woman to eat out of your hand. I was just thinking that I can see what she meant."

Kristian coughed, a hint of color darkening his cheekbones. "I've never been a playboy."

"Apparently women can't resist you…ever."

He gave her a pointed look. "That's not true."

"So you didn't have two dates, on two different continents, in the same day?"

"Geographically as well as physically impossible."

"Unless you were flying from Sydney to Los Angeles."

Kristian grimaced. "That was a one-time situation. If it hadn't been for crossing the time zones it wouldn't have been the same day."

Elizabeth smiled faintly, rather liking Kristian in the hot seat. "Do you miss the lifestyle?"

"No—God, no." Now it was his turn to smile, his white teeth flashing against the bronze of his skin. Sun and exercise had given him the most extraordinary golden glow. "Being a playboy isn't a picnic," he intoned mockingly. "Some men envied the number of relationships I had, but it was really quite demanding, trying to keep all the women happy."

She was amused despite herself. "You're shameless."

"Not as shameless as you were last August, checking me out by the pool…*despite* us having a deal."

"I *wasn't* looking."

"You were. Admit it."

She blushed. "You couldn't even see."

"I could tell. Some things one doesn't need to see to know. Just as I didn't need to see you to know I love you. That I will always love you. And I want nothing more than to spend the rest of my life with you."

Elizabeth's breath caught in her throat. She couldn't speak. She couldn't even breathe.

Kristian stood up from the table and crossed around to kneel before her. He had a ring box in his hand. "Marry me, *latrea mou*," he said. "Marry me. Come live with me. I don't want to live without you."

His proposal shocked her, and frightened her. It wasn't that she didn't care for him—she did, oh, she did—but *marriage*. Marriage to another Greek tycoon.

She drew back in her chair. "Kristian, I can't... I'm sorry, I can't."

"You don't want to be with me?"

All she wanted was to be with him, but marriage terrified her. To her it represented an abuse of power and control, and she never wanted to feel trapped like that again.

"I do want to be with you—but marriage..." Her voice cracked. She felt the old pressure return, the sense of dread and futility. "Kristian, I just had such a terrible time of it. And it shattered me when it ended. I can't go that route again."

"You can," he said, rising.

"No, I can't. I really can't." She slid off her chair and left the table. She felt cornered now, and she didn't know where to go. He was in her house. The restaurant owner and the waiter were in her house. And it was a little two-bedroom house.

Elizabeth retreated to the only other room—her bedroom—but Kristian followed. He put his hand out to keep her from closing the door on him.

"You accused *me* of being a coward by refusing to recover," he said, holding the door ajar. "You said I needed to get on my feet and back to the land of living. Maybe it's time you took your own advice. Maybe it's time you stopped hiding from life and starting living again, too."

Firmly, insistently, he pushed the door the rest of the way open and entered her room. Elizabeth scrambled back, but Kristian marched toward her, fierce and determined. "Being with you is good. It feels right and whole and healthy. Being with you makes me happy, and I know—even if I couldn't see before—it made you happy, too. I will not let happiness go. I will not let you run away, either. We belong together."

She'd backed up until there was nowhere else to go. She was against her nightstand, cornered near her bed, her heart thundering like mad in her chest.

"You," he added, catching her hands in his and lifting them to his mouth, kissing each balled fist, "belong with me."

And as he kissed each of her fists she felt some of the terrible tension around her heart ease. Just his skin on hers calmed her, soothed her. Just his warmth made her feel safe. Protected. "I'm afraid," she whispered.

"I know you are. You've been afraid since you lost your parents, the year before your coming-out party. That's why you married Nico. You thought he'd protect you, take care of you. You thought you'd be safe with him."

Tears filmed her eyes. "But I wasn't."

He held her fists to his chest. "I'm not Nico, and I could never hurt you. Not when I want to love you and have a family with you. Not when I want to spend every day of the rest of my life with you."

She could feel his heart pounding against her hands. His body was so warm, and yet hard, and even with that dramatic scar across his cheek he was beautiful.

"Everything I've done," he added, tipping his head to brush his lips across her forehead, "from learning to walk again to risking the eye surgery, was to help me be a man again—a man who was worthy of you."

"But I'm not the right woman—"

"Not the right woman? *Latrea mou*, look at you! You might be terrified of marriage, but you're not terrified of me." His voice dropped, low and harsh, almost mocking. "I know I'm something of a monster, I've heard people say as much, but you've never minded my face—"

"I *love* your face."

His hands tightened around hers. "You don't bow and scrape before me. You talk to me, laugh with me, make love with me. And you make me feel whole." His voice deepened yet again. "With you I'm complete."

It was exactly how he made her feel. Whole. Complete. Her heart quickened and her chest felt hot with emotion.

"You make sense to me in a way no one has ever made sense," he added, even more huskily. "And if you love me, but really can't face marriage, then let's not get married. Let's not do anything that will make you worry or feel trapped. I don't need to have a ceremony or put an expensive ring on your finger to feel like you're mine, because you already are mine. You belong with me. I know it, I feel it, I believe it—it's as simple and yet as complicated as that."

Elizabeth stared up at him, unable to believe the transformation in him. He was like a different man—in every way—from the man she'd met nearly three months ago.

"What's wrong?" he asked, seeing her expression. "Have I got it wrong? Maybe you don't feel the same way."

The sudden agony in his extraordinary face nearly broke

her heart. Elizabeth's chest filled with emotion so sharp and painful that she pressed herself closer. "Kiss me," she begged.

He did. He lowered his head to cover her mouth with his. The kiss immediately deepened, his touch and taste familiar and yet impossibly new. This was her man. And he loved her. And she loved him more than she'd thought she could ever love anyone.

Kissing him, she moved even closer to him, his arms wrapping around her back to hold her firmly against him. His warmth gave her comfort and courage.

"I love you," she whispered against his mouth. "I love you and love you and love you."

She felt the corner of his mouth lift in a smile.

"And I don't care if we get married," she added, "or if we just live together, as long as we're together. I just want to be with you, near you, every day for the rest of my life."

He drew his head back and smiled down into her eyes. "They say be careful what you wish for."

"Every day, forever."

"Grace Elizabeth…"

"Every day, each day, until the end of time."

"Done." He dropped his head and kissed her again. "There's no escaping now."

She wrapped her arms around him, reassured by the wave of perfect peace. "I suppose if you're not going to let me escape, we might as well make it legal."

Kristian drew his head back a little to get a good look at her face. "You've changed your mind?"

A huge knot filled her throat and she nodded, tears shimmering in her eyes. "Ask me again. Please."

"Will you marry me, *latrea mou?*" he murmured, his voice husky with emotion.

"Yes."

He kissed her temple, and then her cheek, and finally her mouth. "Why did you change your mind?"

"Because love," she whispered, holding him tightly, "is stronger than fear. And, Kristian Koumantaros, I love you with all my heart. I don't want to be with anyone but you."

The Antonides
Marriage Deal

ANNE MCALLISTER

Award-winning author **Anne McAllister** was once given a blueprint for happiness that included a nice, literate husband, a ramshackle Victorian house, a horde of mischievous children, a bunch of big friendly dogs and a life spent writing stories about tall, dark, handsome heroes. "Where do I sign up?" she asked, and promptly did. Lots of years later, she's happy to report the blueprint was a success. She's always happy to share the latest news with readers at her website – www.annemcallister.com – and welcomes their letters there or at PO Box 3904, Bozeman, Montana 59772, USA (SAE with return postage appreciated).

Don't miss Anne McAllister's exciting new novel,
***The Virgin's Proposition*, out in June 2010**
from Mills & Boon® Modern™.

For Aunt Billie
With love forever

CHAPTER ONE

"YOUR father is on line six."

Elias Antonides stared at the row of red lights blinking on his desk phone and thanked God he'd declined the ten-line option he'd been offered when he'd begun renovating and converting the riverside warehouse into the new Brooklyn-based home of Antonides Marine International nine months ago.

"Right," he said. "Thanks, Rosie. Put him on hold."

"He says it's important," his assistant informed him.

"If it's important, he'll wait," Elias said, reasonably confident that he wouldn't do anything of the sort.

Aeolus Antonides had the staying power of a fruit fly. Named for the god of the wind, according to him, and "the god of hot air," in Elias's view, Aeolus was as charming and feckless a man as had ever lived. As president of Antonides Marine, he enjoyed three-hour lunches and three olive martinis, playing golf with his cronies and taking them out in his sailboat, but he had no patience for day-to-day routine, for turning red ink into black, for anything that resembled a daily grind. He didn't want to know that they would benefit from some ready cash or that Elias was contemplating the purchase of a small marine outfitter that would expand their holdings. Business bored him. Talking to his son bored him.

And chances were excellent today that, by the time Elias had dealt with the other five blinking lights, his father would have hung up and gone off to play another round of golf or out for a sail from his Hamptons home.

In fact, Elias was counting on it. He loved his father dearly, but he didn't need the old man meddling in business matters. Whatever his father wanted, it would invariably complicate his life.

And he had enough complications already today—though it wasn't much different from any other.

His sister Cristina, on line two, wanted him to help her set up the financing for a bead store.

"A *bead* store?" Elias thought he'd heard everything. Cristina had variously wanted to raise rabbits, tie-dye T-shirts and go to disk-jockey school. But the beads were new.

"So I can stay in New York," she explained perfectly reasonably. "Mark's in New York."

Mark was her latest boyfriend. Elias didn't think he'd be her last. Famous for racing speedboats and chasing women, Mark Batakis was as likely to be here today and gone tomorrow as Cristina's bead-store aspirations.

"No, Cristina," he said firmly.

"But—"

"No. You come up with a good business plan for something and we'll talk. Until then, no." And he hung up before she could reply.

His mother, on line three, was arranging a dinner party on the weekend. "Are you bringing a girlfriend?" she asked hopefully. "Or shall I arrange one."

Elias gritted his teeth. "I don't need you arranging dates for me, Mother," he said evenly, knowing full well as he did so that his words fell on deaf ears.

Helena Antonides's goal in life was to see him married and providing her with grandchildren. Inasmuch as he'd been married once disastrously and had no intention of ever being married again, Elias could have told her she was doomed to fail. She had other children, let them have the grandchildren she was so desperate for.

Besides, wasn't it enough that he was providing the financial support for the entire Antonides clan to live in the manner to which three generations of them had become accustomed? Apparently not.

"Well—" she sniffed, annoyed at him as usual "—you don't seem to be doing a very good job yourself."

"Thank you for sharing your opinion," Elias said politely.

He never bluntly told his mother that he was not ever getting married again, because she would have argued with him, and as far as Elias was concerned, the matter wasn't up for debate. He had been divorced for seven years, had purposely made no effort at all to find anyone to replace the duplicitous, avaricious Millicent, and had no intention of doing so.

Surely after seven years his mother should have noticed that.

"Don't go all stuffy on me, Elias Antonides. I've got your best interests at heart. You should be grateful."

As that didn't call for an answer, Elias didn't supply one. "I have to go, Mom, I have work to do."

"You always have work to do."

"Someone has to."

There was a dead silence on the other end of the line. She couldn't deny it, but she wouldn't agree, either. At last Helena said firmly, "Just be here Sunday. I'll provide the girl." She was the one who hung up on him.

His sister, Martha, on line four, was brimming with ideas for her painting. Martha always had ideas—and rarely had the means to see them through.

"If you want me to do a good job on those murals," she told him, "I really should go back to Greece."

"What for?"

"Inspiration," she said cheerfully.

"A vacation, you mean." Elias knew his sister. Martha was a good artist. He wouldn't have asked her to cover the wall of the foyer of his building, not to mention one in his office and the other in his bedroom if she were a hack. But he didn't feel like subsidizing her summer holidays, either. "Forget it. I'll send you some photos. You can work from them."

Martha sighed. "You're such a killjoy, Elias."

"Everyone knows that," he agreed. "Deal with it."

On line five Martha's twin, Lukas, didn't want to deal with it. "What's wrong with going to New Zealand?" Lukas wanted to know.

"Nothing's wrong with it," Elias said with more patience than he felt. "But I thought you were going to Greece?"

"I did. I'm in Greece," Lukas informed him. "But it's boring here. There's nothing to do. I met some guys at the taverna last night. They're heading to New Zealand. I thought I'd go, too. So do you know someone there—in Auckland, say—who might want to hire me for a while?"

"To do what?" It was a fair question. Lukas had graduated from college with a major in ancient languages. None of them was Maori.

"Doesn't matter. Whatever," Lukas said vaguely. "Or I could go to Australia. Maybe go walkabout?"

Which seemed to be pretty much what he was already doing, Elias thought, save for the fact that he wasn't confining his wandering to Australia as their brother Peter had.

"You could come home and go to work for me," Elias suggested not for the first time.

"No way," Lukas said not for the first time, either. "I'll give you a call when I get to Auckland to see if you have any ideas."

Ted Corbett—on line one—the only legitimate caller as far as Elias was concerned, was fortunately still there.

"So, what do you think? Ready to take us over?" That was why he was still there. Corbett was eager to sell his marine outfitters business and just as eager for Elias to be the one to buy it.

"We're thinking about it," Elias said. "No decision yet. Paul has been doing some research, running the numbers."

His projects manager loved ferreting out all the details that went into these decisions. Elias, who didn't, left Paul to it. But ultimately Elias was going to have to make the final decision. All the decisions, in the end, were his.

"I want to come out and see the operation in person," he said.

"Of course," Corbett agreed. "Whenever you want." He chattered on about the selling points, and Elias listened.

He deliberately took his time with Corbett, eyeing the red light on line six all the while. It stayed bright red. When he finally finished with Corbett it was still blinking. Probably the old man just walked off and left his phone on. That would be just like him. But Elias punched the button anyway.

"My, you're a busy fellow," Aeolus boomed in his ear.

Elias shut his eyes and mustered his patience. His father must have been doing the crossword to wait so long. "Actually, yes. I've been on the phone way too long, and now I'm late for a meeting. What's up?"

"Me, actually. Came into the city to see a friend. Thought I'd stop by. Got something to discuss with you."

The last thing Elias needed today was his father making a personal appearance. "I'm coming out on the weekend," Elias said, hoping to forestall the visit. "We can talk then."

But Aeolus was otherwise inclined. "This won't take long. See you in a bit." And the phone clicked in Elias's ear.

Damn it! How typical of his father. It didn't matter how busy you were, if he wanted your attention, Aeolus found a way to get it. Elias banged the phone down and pinched the bridge of his nose, feeling a headache gathering force back behind his eyes.

By the time his beaming father breezed straight past Rosie and into Elias's office an hour later, Elias's headache was raging full-bore.

"Guess what I did!" Aeolus kicked the door shut and did one of the little soft-shuffle steps that invariably followed his sinking a particularly tricky putt.

"Hit a hole in one?" Elias guessed. He stood up so he could meet his father head-on.

At the golf reference, Aeolus's smile grew almost wistful. "I wish," he murmured. He sighed, then brightened. "But, metaphorically speaking, I guess you could say that."

Metaphorically speaking? Since when did Aeolus Antonides speak in metaphors? Elias raised his eyebrows and waited politely for his father's news.

Aeolus rubbed his hands together and beamed. "I found us a business partner!"

"What!" Elias stared at his father, appalled. "What the hell do you mean, business partner? We don't need a business partner!"

"You said we needed ready cash."

Oh, hell. He *had* been listening. "I never said anything about a business partner! The business is doing fine!"

"Of course it is," Aeolus nodded. "Couldn't get a partner if it weren't. No rats want to board sinking ships."

Rats? Elias felt the hair on the back of his neck stand up. "What rats?"

"Nothing. No rats," Aeolus said quickly. "Just a figure of speech."

"Well, forget it."

"No. You work too hard, Elias. I know I haven't done my part. It's just…it's not in me. I—" Aeolus looked bleak.

"I know that, Dad." Elias gave his father a sincere, sympathetic smile. "I understand." Which was the truth. "Don't worry about it. It's not a problem."

Not now at least. Eight years ago it had cost him his marriage.

No, that wasn't fair. His father's lack of business acumen had been only one factor in the breakup with Millicent. It had begun when he'd toyed with quitting business school to start his own boat-building company, to do what his grandfather had done. Millicent had been appalled. She'd been passionate about him finishing school and stepping in at Antonides. But that was when she'd thought it was worth something. When she found out its books were redder than a sunset, she'd been appalled, and livid when Elias had insisted on staying and trying to salvage the firm.

No, his father's business incompetence had only highlighted the problems between himself and Millicent. The truth was that he should have realized what Millicent's priorities were and never married her in the first place. It was a case of extraordinary bad judgement and one Elias was not going to repeat.

"But I do worry," his father went on. "We both do, your mother and I. You work so hard. Too hard."

Elias had never spoken of the reasons for the divorce, but his parents weren't fools. They knew Elias had worked almost 24/7 to salvage the business from the state it had slid to due to his father's not-so-benign neglect. They knew that the financial reality of Antonides Marine did not meet the expectations of their son's social-ladder climbing wife. They knew she had vanished not long after Elias dropped out of business school to work in the family firm. And within weeks of the divorce being final, Millicent had married the heir to a Napa Valley winery.

Of course no one mentioned any of this. For years no one had spoken her name, least of all Elias.

But shortly after Millicent's marriage, the fretting began—and so had the parade of eligible women, as if getting Elias a new wife would make things better, make his father feel less guilty.

As far as Elias was concerned, his father had no need to feel guilty. Aeolus was who he was. Millicent was who she was. And Elias was who he was—a man who didn't want a wife.

Or a business partner.

"No, Dad," he said firmly now.

Aeolus shrugged. "Sorry. Too late. It's done. I sold forty percent of Antonides Marine."

Elias felt as if he'd been punched. "*Sold it?* You can't do that!"

Aeolus's whole demeanor changed in an instant. He was no longer the amiable, charming father Elias knew and loved. Drawing himself up sharply with almost military rigidity, he looked down his not inconsiderable nose at his furious son.

"Of course I can sell it," Aeolus said stiffly, his tone infused with generations of Greek arrogance that even his customary amiable temperament couldn't erase. "I own it."

"Yes, I know that. But—" But it was true. Aeolus did own Antonides Marine. Or fifty percent of it anyway. Elias owned ten percent. Forty percent was in trust for his four siblings. It was a family company. Always had been. No one whose name was not Antonides had ever owned any of it.

Elias stared at his father, feeling poleaxed. Gutted. Betrayed. He swallowed. "Sold it?" he echoed hollowly. Which meant what? That his work of the past eight years was, like his marriage, gone in the stroke of a pen?

"Not all of it," Aeolus assured him. "Just enough to give you a little capital. You said you needed money. All last Sunday at your mother's dinner party you were on the phone talking to someone about raising capital to buy some outfitter."

"And I was doing it." Elias ground out.

"Well, now I've done it instead." His father rubbed his hands together briskly. "So you don't have to work so hard. You have breathing room."

"Breathing room?" Elias would have laughed if he hadn't already been gasping. His knees felt weak. He wanted to sit down. He wanted to put his head between his knees and take deep desperate breaths. But instead he stood rigid, his fingers balled into fists, and stared at his father in impotent fury, none of which he allowed to show on his face.

"You didn't need to sell," he said at last in measured tones that he congratulated himself did not betray the rage he felt. "It would have been all right."

"Oh, yes? Then why did we move here?" Aeolus wrinkled his nose as he looked around the newly renovated offices in the riverside warehouse Elias had bought and which until today his father had never seen.

"To get back to our roots," Elias said through his teeth. There was no reason at all to pay midtown Manhattan prices when his business could be better conducted from Brooklyn. "This is where *Papu* had his first offices." His grandfather had never wanted to be far from water.

Aeolus didn't seem convinced. "Well, it's obvious that things aren't what they used to be," he said with a look around. "I wanted to help."

Help? Dear God! Elias took a wild, shuddering breath, raked

a hand through his hair. With help like this he might as well throw in the towel.

Of course, he wouldn't.

Antonides Marine was his life. Since he'd shelved his dream of building his own boats, since Millicent had walked out, it was the only thing he'd focused on. She would have said, of course, that it was the only thing he'd focused on *before* she'd left him. But that wasn't true. And he'd done it in the first place for her, to try to give her the life she'd wanted. How was he to know she'd just been looking for an excuse to walk out?

Now it was all he had. All he lived for. He was determined to restore it to the glory his great-grandfather and his grandfather had achieved. And he was almost there.

But it hadn't been an easy road so far, and he shouldn't expect it would start now. Deliberately he straightened his tie and pasted a smile on his face and told himself it would be all right.

This was just one more bump in the road. There had been plenty of bumps—and potholes—and potential disasters in the road since he'd taken over running Antonides Marine.

With luck he could even work out a deal to buy the shares Aeolus had sold away. Yes. That was a good idea. Then there would be no more opportunity for his father to do something foolish behind his back.

Elias flexed his shoulders, worked to ease the tension in them, took another, calmer breath and then turned to his father, prepared to make the best of it.

"Sold it to whom?" he asked politely.

"Socrates Savas."

"The hell you say!"

So much for calm. So much for polite. So much for making the best of it!

"Socrates Savas is a pirate. A scavenger! He buys up failing companies, guts them, then sells off what's left for scrap!" Elias was yelling. He knew he was yelling. He couldn't help it.

"He does have a certain reputation," Aeolus admitted, the characteristic smile not in evidence now.

"An entirely deserved reputation," Elias snarled. He stalked around the room. He wanted to punch the walls. Wanted to punch his father. "Damn it to hell! Antonides Marine is *not* failing!"

"So I hear. Socrates said it was doing very well indeed. He had to give me a pile for it," Aeolus reflected with considerable satisfaction. "So much that he complained about it. Said he should have bought it five years ago. Said it was too bad he hadn't known about it then."

Which had been the whole point. One look at the Antonides Marine's books eight years ago, and Elias had known their days as a company were numbered unless he could drag them back into the black.

He'd done it. But it had meant long long hours and cost-cutting and streamlining and reorganization and doing all of it without allowing the company to look as if it were in any trouble at all. He'd spent years trying to stay under Socrates Savas's radar. For all the good it had done him.

"Good thing for us Socrates didn't notice it then," Aeolus reflected, as if it had just occurred to him.

"Good thing," Elias agreed sarcastically, for once taking no pains to spare his father's feelings.

Aeolus looked momentarily chagrined, but then brightened again and looked at his son approvingly. "You should be proud. You pulled us out of the abyss, Socrates says. Though I don't know as I'd have called it an abyss," he reflected.

"I would've," Elias muttered.

Obviously Savas had had his eye on the business for a while whether Elias had known it or not. Circling like a vulture, no doubt. Not that he'd ever given any indication. But he was a past master at spotting prey, waiting for the right moment, then snapping up a floundering company.

For the past year Elias had dared to breathe easier knowing that Antonides Marine wasn't floundering anymore. And now his father had *sold* the blackguard forty percent of it anyway?

Damnation!

So what did Savas intend to do with it? The possibilities sent chills down Elias's spine. He wouldn't let himself imagine. And he certainly wouldn't hang around to watch. Knowing he couldn't bear it gave him the resolve to say words he never ever thought he'd say.

"Fine," he said, looking his father in the eye. "He can have it. I quit."

His father gaped at him, his normally rosy countenance going suddenly, starkly white. "Quit? *Quit?* But…but, Elias…you *can't* quit!"

"Of course I can." Elias had been blessed with his own share of the Antonides arrogance and hauteur, and if Aeolus could sell the business that his son had rescued from the scrap pile without so much as a nod in his direction, then by God, Elias could certainly quit without looking back!

"But…" Aeolus shook his head helplessly, his hands waving in futility. "You can't." His words were almost a whisper, his face still ashen. There was a pleading note in his voice.

Elias frowned. He had expected *sturm und drang,* not a death mask.

"Why can't I?" he asked with studied politeness, a hint of a not very pleasant smile on his lips.

"Because—" Aeolus's hands fluttered "—because it's…it's written in the contract that you'll stay on."

"You can't sell me with the company, Dad. That's slavery. There're laws against it. So, I guess the contract is null and void?" Elias smiled a real smile now. "All's well that ends well," he added, managing—barely—to restrain himself from rubbing his hands together.

But Aeolus didn't look pleased and his color hadn't returned. His fingers knotted and twisted. His gaze dropped. He didn't look at his son. He looked at the floor without a word.

"What is it?" Elias said warily in the silence.

Still nothing. Not for a long, long time. Then, at last, his father lifted his head. "We'll lose the house."

Elias scowled. "What do you mean, you'll lose the house? What house? The house on Long Island?"

His father gave an almost imperceptible negative shake of his head.

No? *Not* the Long Island house?

Then that meant...

"*Our* house?"

The family home on Santorini? The one his great-grand-father, also called Elias, had built with his bare hands? The one each succeeding generation of Antonides men and women had added to, so that it was home to not only their bodies but their history, their memories, their accomplishments?

Of course, they'd had the house on Long Island for years. They'd had flats in London, in Sydney and in Hong Kong.

But they only had one home.

But his father couldn't mean that. The house on Santorini had nothing to do with the business! Never had. It belonged to his father now as it had belonged to his father and his father's father before him. For four generations the house had gone from eldest son to eldest son.

It would be Elias's someday. And, though he'd saved the company and all its holdings, none of them mattered to him as much as that single house. It held memories of his childhood, of summer days spent working building boats with his grandfather, of the dreams of youth that were pure and untarnished, though life was anything but. The house on Santorini was their strength, their refuge—the physical heart of the Antonides family.

It was the only *thing* Elias loved.

His fingers curled into fists. It was the only way he could keep from grabbing his father by the front of his emerald-green polo shirt and shaking him. *"What have you done to our house?"*

"Nothing," Aeolus said quickly. "Well, nothing if you stay on at Antonides." He shot Elias a quick, hopeful glance that skittered away at once in the face of his son's burning black fury. He wrung his hands. "It was just a small bet. A sailboat race. A bet I made with Socrates. Which boat—his or mine—could sail to Montauk and back faster. I'm a better sailor than Socrates Savas!"

Which Elias had no doubt was true. "So what happened?"

"The bet was about the boats," his father said heavily.

"I know. You raced the boats. So?"

Aeolus shot him an exasperated look. "I'm a better sailor than *Socrates* Savas. I don't hold a candle to his son Theo!"

Elias whistled. "Theo Savas is Socrates's son?"

Even Elias had heard of Theo Savas. Anyone who knew anything about sailing knew Theo Savas. He had sailed for Greece in the Olympics. He had crewed in several America's Cup races. He had done windsurfing and solo sailing voyages that caught the hearts and minds of armchair adventurers everywhere. He was also lean, muscular and handsome, a playboy without equal and, naturally—according to Elias's sisters—the ideal of Greek manhood.

No matter that he had been raised in Queens.

"Theo won," Aeolus said, filling his cheeks with air, then exhaling sharply and shaking his head. "And he gets clear title to the house—unless you agree to stay on as managing director of Antonides Marine for two years."

"Two years!"

"It's not much!" Aeolus protested. "Hardly a life sentence."

It might as well be. Elias couldn't believe it. His father was asking him to simply sit here and watch as Socrates Savas gutted the company he had worked so hard to save!

"What the hell did I ever do to him?" Elias demanded.

"Do to him? Why, nothing at all. What do you mean?"

"Nothing. Never mind." There was no reason to take it personally. Socrates Savas did this sort of thing all the time. Still Elias ground his teeth. He felt the pulse pound in his temple and deliberately unclenched his jaw and took a deep, calculated breath.

Two years. It was a price he could pay. He'd paid far bigger ones. And this wasn't just about his life, it was the life of his whole family.

He'd done everything else. How could he not do this?

"All right," he said at last. "I'll stay."

His father beamed, breathed again, pounded him on the back. "I knew you would!"

"But I'm not answering to Socrates Savas. He's *not* running things!"

"Of course not!" His father said, relieved beyond belief. "His daughter is!"

The new president of Antonides Marine International hadn't slept a wink all night.

Tallie had lain awake, grinning ear to ear, her mind whirling with glorious possibilities and the satisfaction of knowing that her father was finally acknowledging she was good at what she did.

She knew it wasn't easy for him. Socrates Savas was as traditional as a stubborn, opinionated Greek father could be—even though he was two generations removed from the old country.

In her father's mind, his four sons were the ones who were supposed to follow his footsteps into the family business. His only daughter, Thalia, ought to stay at home, mend clothes and cook meals and eventually marry a nice, hardworking Greek man and have lots of lovely little dark-haired, dark-eyed Greek grandchildren for Socrates to dandle on his knee.

It wasn't going to happen.

Oh, she would have married. If Lieutenant Brian O'Malley's plane had not crashed seven years ago, she certainly would have married him. Life would have been a lot different.

But since Brian's death she'd never met anyone who'd even tempted her. And not for her father's lack of trying. Sometimes she thought he'd introduced her to every eligible Greek on the East Coast.

"Go pester the boys," she told him. "Go find them wives."

But Socrates just muttered and grumbled about his four sons. They were even more of a mystery to him than Tallie was. If she desperately wanted to follow him into business, Theo, George, Demetrios and Yiannis, had absolutely no interest in their father's footsteps—or his business—at all.

Theo, the eldest, was a world-class open-ocean sailor. Tie him to an office or even stick him in a city and he would die. Socrates wasn't sympathetic. He considered that his oldest son just "mucked about in boats."

George was a brilliant physicist. He was unraveling the universe, one strand at a time. Socrates couldn't believe people actually had theories about strings.

Demetrios was a well-known television actor with an action-adventure series of his own. His face—and a whole lot of his bare, sculpted torso—had recently been on a billboard in Times Square. Socrates had averted his eyes and muttered, "What next?"

But he wouldn't have believed it if anyone had told him.

Yiannis, the youngest of Tallie's four older brothers, who was as city-born and -bred as the rest of them, had, five years ago, finished a master's degree in forestry and was living and working at the top of a Montana mountain!

It was Tallie who had always been determined to follow in her father's footsteps. She was the one with the head for business. She was the one who had worked in stockrooms and storerooms, in warehouses and shipping offices, doing everything she could to learn how things worked from the ground up.

And she was the one her father had fired more than once when he'd found her working in one of his companies.

"No daughter of mine is going to work here," he'd blustered and fumed.

So she'd gone to work for someone else.

He hadn't liked that any better. But Tallie was as stubborn as her old man. She'd gone to university and done a degree in accounting. She'd taken a job in California, crunching numbers for a mom-and-pop tortilla factory. And while she was there, she'd learned everything from how to make tortillas to a thousand ways to cook with them to the cleverest way to market them. Then she'd gone back and got her MBA, working on the side for a Viennese baker who taught her everything he knew. If she were ever going into business for herself, Tallie decided, it would be in baking. She loved making cakes and tortes and pastries. But she preferred that as her relaxation.

Eighteen months ago, MBA in hand, she'd applied for another job with one of her father's companies—and had been turned down.

So she'd gone to work for Easley Manufacturing, one of his biggest competitors. She'd been doing well there and had recently been promoted. She was on the fast track, the boss had told her. She'd hoped word would get back to Socrates.

Obviously it had.

Two weeks ago he'd rung and invited her to dinner after she got off work.

"Dinner?" she'd echoed. "With whom?"

Had he dredged up another eligible Greek, in other words?

"Just me," Socrates said, offended. "I'm in the city. Your mother is in Rome with her art group. I'm lonely. I thought I'd call my daughter and invite her to a meal."

It sounded perfectly innocent, but Tallie had known her father for twenty-nine years. She knew suppressed excitement when she heard it in his voice. She accepted, but not without reservations.

And when she'd met him at Lazlo's, a Hungarian restaurant on the Upper East Side he'd suggested, she had looked around warily for stray males before she went to sit at the table with him.

But Socrates hadn't come bearing Greeks for a change. Instead he'd offered her a job.

"A job?" Tallie had done her best to hide her incredulity while she found herself glancing outside to see if the late-May sun was still shining. The words h*ell froze over* were flitting around in her brain. "What sort of job?"

Her father waited until the server had brought their dinners. Then he said in his characteristic blunt fashion. "I've just acquired forty percent of Antonides Marine International. They build boats. As major stockholder, I get to name the president." He paused, smiling. "You."

"Me?" Tallie's voice squeaked. She blinked rapidly. Now she was sure that hell had frozen over. Or that she'd lost her mind.

But Socrates picked up his knife and fork and cut into his

chicken paprika and said with a shrug, "You've always said you wanted to come into the business."

"Yes, but—"

"So now you're in."

Tallie shook her head, mind still whirling. "I meant…I *didn't* mean I expected you to buy me a company, Dad!"

"I didn't buy you a company," he said, enunciating every word. "I acquired *part* of a company. And so, I have a say in how it's run. I want you to run it."

Tallie wet her lips. Her brain spun with possibilities, with potential—with panic. She tried to get a toehold on her thoughts. "I don't— It's so…sudden."

"The best opportunities often are."

"I know." But still…she needed to think. To consider. To—

"So, what do you say?"

"I—" Her tongue seemed welded to the roof of her mouth.

Socrates smiled gently and regarded her over a forkful of chicken. "Or maybe you were just talking. Maybe you don't think you can do it."

By God, yes, she could do it!

And she'd said so.

Socrates had beamed, the way a shark must beam when an unsuspecting little fish swims straight into his mouth. Tallie knew it. She could almost hear his jaws snap shut. But she didn't care.

Whatever agenda her father had in offering her this job, she had her own agenda—to do the best damned job she could do and prove to him that she was worthy of his trust.

The two weeks she had to spend working out her notice at Easley's had given her time to break in a replacement and do a crash course of reading everything she could get her hands on about Antonides Marine International.

What she'd learned about its history had made her even more eager to get to work. It was an old and respected boat-building company that had fallen on hard times and over the past eight years had been in the process of righting itself and moving ahead. While there was no change in leadership—Aeolus Antonides was still president (until today!)—his son had been running things. And apparently the son had done rather well. He'd economized and streamlined things, getting back to basics, redefining and refocusing the company's mission. Recently she'd read that AMI appeared poised to branch out, to test the waters in areas other than strictly marine construction. It was on the brink of expansion.

Tallie could hardly wait to be part of the process.

And now, she thought as she stood on the pavement and stared up at the old Brooklyn warehouse that was the home of the offices of Antonides Marine International, she was.

Amazingly the address was only nine blocks from her flat. She had expected some mid-Manhattan office building. Six months ago, she knew, she would have been right. But then AMI had moved across the East River to Brooklyn.

Tallie understood it was a cost-cutting move. But there was a certain rightness to it being here in DUMBO, the neighborhood acronym for its location "down under the Manhattan Bridge."

DUMBO was a vital, happening place—lots of urban renewal going on, considerable gentrification of the old brownstones and even older warehouses that sat on or near the edge of the East River. It was that energy, as well as the more reasonable rents, that had drawn her to DUMBO. She imagined it had drawn the management of AMI as well.

But looking around in the crisp early morning light, Tallie could see that it belonged here anyway, in the old five-story brick warehouse in the process of being restored. Within sight of the old Navy Shipyards, it was where a shipbuilding company—even the corporate offices thereof—ought to be.

Feng shui, her friend Katy who knew these things, would have said. Or maybe that was just inside buildings and where you put your bed. But it felt right. And that made Tallie smile and feel even better.

She was early—way early—but she couldn't wait any longer. She pushed open the door and went in.

It was like stepping across the ocean. Expecting the traditional neutral business environment, she was startled to find herself in a foyer painted blue—and not the soft pale blue one usually found on walls—but the deep vibrant blue of the Mediterranean. From floor to ceiling there was blue sea and blue sky—and dotted here and there were brown islands out of which seemed to grow impossibly white buildings and blue-domed churches. All very simple and spare, and almost breathtaking in its unexpectedness. And in it appropriateness.

Tallie had never been to the Greek homeland of her forebears. She'd never had time. But she knew it at once and found it drawing her in. Instinctively she reached out a finger and traced the line of rooftops, then a bare hillside, then one lone white building at the far end of one island. As if it were a sentry. A lookout.

She'd never particularly wanted to go to Greece. It had seemed the source of all the tradition she'd spent her life battling. But now she could see there was more to it than that. And suddenly the notion tempted her.

But not as much as punching the elevator button and hitting 3.

The elevator was apparently part of the refurbishment, all polished wood and carpet that still smelled new. When the door slid open three floors later she saw that the renovation was still a work in progress. The floor was bare, unfinished wood. The walls were plastered but unpainted. She could hear hammering coming from behind a closed door down the hall.

She thought briefly that whoever was doing it, she'd have to get his name and pass it on to her landlord. Arnie was trying to get some renovations done on one of the apartments and couldn't find a workman who would show up before noon.

She passed several offices—an accountant, a magazine publisher, a dentist—before she found the new heavy glass door of Antonides Marine International. The door was locked. At six-forty in the morning she could hardly expect otherwise.

No matter. She had a key. A key to her company. Well, a key to the company she was president of.

Now all she had to do was prove herself worthy of it.

Taking a deep breath and feeling the rightness of the moment, Tallie set her briefcase down and shifted the bag in her arm to get out the key. Then she turned it in the lock, pushed open the door and went in.

She was late.

First day on the job and the new hotshot president of Antonides Marine couldn't even be bothered to show up!

Elias prowled his office, coffee mug in hand, grinding the teeth with which he'd intended to take a bite out of her. So much for the "eager beaver" his father had assured him Socrates insisted she was.

He supposed he ought to be pleased. If she wasn't there, she couldn't screw things up. He'd spent the past two weeks trying to make sure she had as little opportunity to interfere as possible.

Once it had been clear that there was no way out of the mess his father had created, Elias had done his best to limit the damage. That meant defining the limits of the problem and making sure it didn't get bigger. So he'd readied the big office overlooking the river—the one he'd hoped to move into someday but which was too far from the hub of the office to be practical now. That was for when things were running themselves.

Or for when he was running them and needed to stick a figurehead president as far from the action as possible, he thought grimly. With her conveniently out of the way, he could get on with running the company. Which he ought to be doing right now, damn it! But he wanted her settled and disposed of first.

He had expected she'd at least be there by nine, but it was already half past. He'd been at his desk since eight, ready to deal with the interloper. Rosie, his assistant, had been there when he came in and had coffee brewing—obviously trying to impress the new "boss."

She told him to make his own damn coffee on a daily basis. She'd even put a plate of fancy cookies by the coffeemaker.

Elias had considered giving her grief over them, but they

were damn good. Some buttery chocolate kind with a hint of cinnamon, and some with almonds, and the traditional American favorite, peanut butter criss-cross.

His stomach growled now just thinking about them, and he went out to snatch another one only to find everyone else already there.

His normally spit-and-polished researcher, Paul Johanssen, was talking with his mouth full. Lucy, who oversaw the contracts and accounting, was deciding to go on her diet tomorrow. Dyson, who did blueprints and development for AMI projects, had crumbs in his mustache, and even the temp steno girls, Trina and Cara and the very-pregnant-and-about-to-deliver-any-moment Giulia were sneaking into reception to steal a cookie or two.

Elias thought it was no wonder Rosie had always refused to even make coffee in the office. If they'd known the extent of her talents, they wouldn't have let her do anything else.

Well, Ms Thalia Savas was sure to be impressed—provided she managed to show up before the coffee and cookies were gone.

But he was done waiting. It was time she realized this wasn't business school. Real work got done in the real world.

"We'll go into the boardroom," he said to Paul and Dyson. They jumped guiltily at the sound of his voice, and Paul surreptitiously wiped his mouth.

Elias grinned, taking a bit of perverse satisfaction in the tardy Ms Savas missing out on the cookies made especially for her. Not to mention that Rosie had gone to all that trouble only to have her efforts gobbled up by the rest of the staff.

"Very impressive," he said as he passed her on his way to the boardroom. "I can see why you don't do it all the time."

Rosie looked up. "I didn't do it at all."

Elias gave her a sceptical look, but she stared him down so sternly that he turned to Paul. "Don't tell me you baked them?"

Paul laughed. "I can't boil water."

"Don't look at me," Dyson backed away, shaking his dreadlocks and grinning.

"Maybe the new girl made them," Trina suggested as she headed back to her office with her arms full of files.

"What new girl?" Elias knew they were going to send one to fill Giulia's spot, but he didn't know she'd arrived.

"I guess that would be me." A cheerful, unfamiliar voice from the hallway made them all turn around. She was not the usual temp agency girl. She was older for one thing. Late twenties probably. She didn't resemble a stick insect, either. She was slender but definitely curvy. She also wasn't wearing a nose ring or sporting a hank of blue hair. Her hair, in fact, though pulled back and tied down and even anchored, had a will of its own. And even the army of barrettes she'd enlisted to tame it wasn't up to the job. Her hair was thick and wild and decidedly sexy.

She looked as if she'd just got out of bed.

Elias found himself imagining what she would be like *in* bed. The thought brought him up short. He was as appreciative of a beautiful woman as the next man, but he didn't usually fantasize about taking them to bed within moments of meeting them.

Then Ms Temp smiled brightly at him, at the same time giving her head a little shake so that her hair actually danced. And the urge to pull out those pins and tangle his fingers in that glorious hair hit him harder.

He shoved his hands in his pockets. He knew better than to mix business and pleasure.

"*You* made the cookies?" he demanded.

She nodded, still smiling. "Did you like them?"

"They're good," he acknowledged gruffly. But he didn't want her getting the idea she could use them as a ticket to something more. "But they aren't necessary. You only have to do your job."

"My job?" She looked blank.

So she had a temp brain apparently. "Filing," he said patiently. "Typing. Doing what you're told."

"I don't type. I hate to file. And I rarely do what I'm told," she said cheerfully.

Elias frowned. "Then what the hell are you doing here?"

She stuck out her hand to shake his. "I'm Tallie Savas. The new president. It's nice to meet you."

CHAPTER TWO

DAMN Socrates, anyway.

One look at Elias Antonides and Tallie knew she'd been had. So much for her father finally taking her seriously.

Now she knew what he was really up to. The presidency of Antonides Marine was nothing more than a means to throw her into the path of a Greek god in khakis and a blue oxford cloth shirt.

Elias Antonides was definitely that—an astonishingly handsome Greek god with thick, wavy, tousled black hair, a wide mobile mouth, strong cheekbones and an aquiline nose that was no less attractive for having been rearranged at some earlier date. Its slight crook only made him look tough and capable—like the sort of god who could quell sea monsters on the one hand while sacking Troy on the other.

And naturally he wasn't wearing a wedding ring, which just confirmed her suspicions. Well, she certainly couldn't say her father didn't have high aspirations.

But he must have lost his mind to imagine that a hunk like Elias Antonides would be interested in *her!*

In the looks department, Tallie knew she was decidedly average. Passable, but certainly not head-turning. Some men liked her hair, but they rarely liked the high-energy, high-powered brain beneath it. More men liked her father's money, but they seldom wanted to put up with a woman who had a mind of her own.

Only Brian had loved her for herself. And until she found another man who did, she wasn't interested.

When the right man came along, he wouldn't be intimidated by her brain or attracted only by her hair or her father's millions. He would love her.

He certainly wouldn't be looking at her, appalled, as Elias Antonides was, like she was something nasty he'd found on the bottom of his shoe. At least she didn't have to worry that Elias was in on her father's little game.

But if he found her presence so distasteful, why hadn't he just told her father—and his—no? As managing director—not to mention the man who had pulled Antonides Marine back from the edge of the financial abyss over the past eight years—surely he had some say in the matter.

Maybe he was just always surly.

Well, Tallie wasn't surly, and she was determined to make the best of this as a business opportunity, regardless of what her father's hidden agenda was.

So she grabbed Elias's hand and shook it firmly. "You must be Elias. I'm glad to meet you at last. And I'm glad you liked the cookies. I thought I should begin as I mean to go on."

"Making cookies?" He stared at her as if she'd lost her mind, then scowled, his brow furrowing, which would have made the average man look baffled and confused. It made Elias Antonides look brooding and dangerous and entirely too tempting. Silently Tallie cursed her father.

"Yes," she said firmly. "I've always found that people like them—and so they enjoy coming to work."

Elias's brows lifted, and he looked down his patrician nose at her. "Enjoyment is highly overrated, Ms Savas," he said haughtily.

Tallie let out a sigh of relief. Oh, good, if he was going to be all stiff and pompous, he would be much easier to resist.

"Oh, I don't agree at all," she said frankly. "I think it's enormously important. If employee morale is low," she informed him, "the business suffers."

His teeth came together with a snap. "Morale at Antonides Marine is not low."

"Of course it isn't," Tallie agreed. "And I want to keep it that way."

"Cookies do not make morale."

"Well, they don't hurt," she said. "And they certainly improve the quality of life, don't you think?" She glanced around at the group who had been scarfing down her best offering and was gratified to see several heads nod vigorously.

A glare from Elias brought them to an abrupt halt. "Don't you have work to do?" he asked them.

The heads bobbed again, and the group started to scatter.

"Before you go, though," Tallie said. "I'd like to meet you."

Elias didn't look pleased, but he stuffed his hands in his pockets and stood silently while she introduced herself to each one, shook hands and tried to commit all their names to memory.

Paul was blond and bespectacled and crew-cut and personified efficiency. "I hope you'll be very happy here," he told her politely.

Dyson was black with flying dreadlocks and a gold hoop earring. "You're good for my morale," he told her with a grin, and snagged another cookie.

Rosie was short and curvy with flame-coloured hair. It was her job, she said, to keep everyone in line. "Even him." She jerked her head at Elias. "I never make coffee," she told Tallie. "Or cookies." Then she confided that she might—if she could have these recipes.

"Sure, no problem," Tallie said.

Lucy wore her silver hair in a bun and had a charm bracelet with a charm for every grandchild. Trina had long black hair with one blue streak, while Cara's was short and spiky and decidedly pink. Giulia looked as if she were going to deliver triplets any minute.

"Boy or girl?" Tallie asked her.

"Boy," Giulia said. "And soon, I hope," she added wearily. "I want to see my feet."

Tallie laughed. "My friend Katy said the same thing."

They were a nice group, she decided after she'd chatted with them all. Friendly, welcoming. Everyone said they were happy to have her. Well, everyone except Elias Antonides.

He never said a word.

Finally, when the group began to head back to their various jobs, she looked at him. He was studying her as if she were a bomb he had to defuse.

"Perhaps we should talk?" she suggested. "Get acquainted?"

"Perhaps we should," he said, his voice flat. He raked a hand through his hair, then sighed and called after Paul and Dyson, "Just keep going on the Corbett project. We'll meet later."

"If you need to meet with them, don't let me interrupt," Tallie said.

"I won't."

No, not really very welcoming at all.

But Tallie persisted, determined to get a spark of interest out of him. "I apologize for not letting you know I was already here," she said. "I came in about seven. I could hardly wait," she confided. "I was always getting to school on the first day hours early, too. Do you do that?"

"No."

Right. Okay, let's take a different tack.

"I found my office. Thank you for the name plaque, by the way. I don't think I've ever had a plaque before. And thank you for all the fiscal reports. I got them from my father, so I'd already read them and I have a few questions. For example, have you considered that Corbett's, while a viable possible acquisition, might not be the best one to start with? I thought—"

"Look, Ms Savas," he said abruptly, "this isn't going to work."

"What isn't going to work?"

"This! This question-and-answer business! You baking cookies, for God's sake, then coming in with questions concerning things you know nothing about! I don't have time for it. I have a business to run."

"A business I am president of," she reminded him archly.

"On account of a bet."

Tallie stopped dead. "Bet? What bet?"

Hard dark eyes met hers accusingly. "You don't know?"

But before she could do more than begin to shake her head, his jaw tightened and he sighed. "No, probably you don't." He opened his mouth, then shut it again. "Not here," he muttered, glancing around the open break room. "Come on."

And he grabbed her arm, steered her out the door and down the hallway, past the chattering temps and his flame-haired, goggle-eyed secretary and straight into his office. He shut the door with a definite click.

Elias Antonides's office was far smaller than the one he'd given her. It didn't even have a window. It had a desk overflowing with papers and files, two filing cabinets, a blueprint cabinet, three bookcases and one glorious wall painted by the same artist who had done the murals in the entry downstairs.

"Wow," Tallie said involuntarily.

Elias looked startled. "Wow?"

She nodded at the mural. "It's unexpected. Breathtaking. You don't need a window."

"No." He stared at the mural a long moment, his jaw tight. Then abruptly he turned his gaze back to her and gestured toward a chair. "Sit down."

It was more a command than an invitation. But it didn't seem worth fighting about, so Tallie sat, then waited for him to do likewise. But he didn't. He cracked his knuckles and paced behind his desk. A muscle worked in his jaw. He opened his mouth to speak, then stopped, paced some more and finally came to a stop directly behind the desk where at last he turned to face her. But he still didn't speak.

"The bet?" Tallie prompted, not sure she wanted to know this, but reasonably certain it would shed light on why Elias was so upset.

"My father fancies himself a racing sailor," he said at last. "And after he sold forty percent of Antonides Marine without telling anyone of his intentions—"

Uh-oh.

"—he hadn't screwed things up badly enough yet. So he and

your father made a little bet." Elias cracked his knuckles again. She got the feeling he wished he was cracking his father's head.

"What sort of bet?" Tallie asked warily. Dear God, her father hadn't bet her hand in marriage, had he? He hadn't done anything quite that outrageous yet in his attempt to marry her off, but she wouldn't put it past him.

"The winner got the other's island house and the presidency of Antonides Marine."

"But that's ridiculous!" Tallie protested. "What on earth would my father want with another house?" He had five now—if you counted what the family called "the hermitage" on a little island off the coast of Maine.

"I have no idea," Elias said grimly. "I don't think the houses had anything to do with it…even though," he added bitterly, "in our case it was our family's home for generations."

"So why did they do it? Because of the presidency?"

Elias shrugged. "Not my father."

But hers would have cared a great deal, she thought. She didn't say so, however. "Then why would your father bet?"

"Because he thought he'd win!" Elias's dark eyes flashed in anger. He shoved his hands through his hair. "He likes a good challenge. Especially when he's got what he considers a sure thing. He didn't count on your brother, the Olympic sailor," Elias added heavily. He flung himself down in his chair and glared at her as if it were her fault.

Tallie knew whose fault it was. "Oh, dear. Daddy got Theo to race."

It wasn't a question. Of course he had got Theo to race—because just like Aeolus Antonides, Socrates Savas *always* played to win. And in this case, Aeolus had something that Socrates wanted far more than any house—the presidency for his daughter—and the consequent proximity to Aeolus's Greek godson.

At least he hadn't offered her hand in marriage.

But what he had done was almost worse.

"Then we'll just call it off," Tallie said firmly. As much as she wanted the chance to prove herself, she was damned if she wanted the opportunity this way. "I'll quit and you can have your house back."

Elias looked surprised at her suggestion. Then he surprised *her* by shaking his head. "Won't work."

"Why not?"

"Because it's your father's. He won it, fair and square." Elias's mouth twisted as he said that. "Or as fair as Socrates Savas is likely to be."

"My father doesn't cheat!" Tallie defended her father fiercely on that count. He manipulated with the best of them. He played all the angles, pushed the edges of the envelope. But he didn't cheat.

Elias shrugged. "Whatever. He's got the house. And he's going to keep the house."

"I'll tell him not to. If I can't hand it back to you, I'll quit. I won't take the job."

"You have to take the job."

"Why?"

"Because that's the deal. That's the only way he'll deed it back."

Deals? Bets? She wanted to strangle her father.

"Tell me," she said grimly.

"He told my father he'd deed it back in two years…" Elias stopped and shook his head.

"If…?" Tallie prompted. She knew there was an *if*. There was always an *if*.

Elias ground his teeth. "If I stay on as managing director of Antonides," Elias said at last. "And you stay on as president."

"For *two* years?"

Obviously her father didn't have much confidence in her if he figured she would need two years to get Elias to the altar, Tallie thought wryly. Or maybe he thought it would take him two years to convince her that it was a good idea.

It *wasn't* a good idea. And she had no intention of doing any such thing!

"That's absurd," she said at last. "We don't have to play their games."

"The house—"

"It can't be that great a house!" she objected.

"There are a thousand others like it," he agreed readily.

"Well then—"

Elias steepled his hands. "My father was born there. His father was born there. His grandfather was born there. The only reason I wasn't born there was because my folks came to New York the year before I was born. But generations of Antonides have lived and loved and died in that house. We go back all the time. I built boats with my grandfather there when I was a boy." There was no tonelessness in his voice now. All the emotion he had so carefully reined in earlier was ragged in his voice now. "My parents were married there, for God's sake! It's our history, our heart."

"Then your father had no business *betting* it." Tallie was almost as mad at his father as he was.

"Of course he didn't! And your father had no business taking advantage of a man who shouldn't be let out alone."

They glared at each other.

It was true, Tallie reflected, what Elias just said. Her father had always had an eye for the main chance. His own dirt-poor immigrant parents had taught him that. If the Antonides family had an ancestral home to lose, it was more than Socrates's family had ever had. Tallie had been brought up on stories of how hard they'd worked for little pay. So when opportunities came along, you took them, Socrates said. And luck—well, that you made yourself.

Tallie didn't doubt for a minute that her father thought taking advantage of Aeolus Antonides was a prime bit of luck.

"So what do you propose we do?" she asked politely, since she had no doubt he'd tell her anyway.

"I don't propose *we* do anything," Elias said sharply. "I've been doing just fine for the past eight years on my own. I've pulled Antonides Marine out of the red, I've made it profitable, and I'll continue to do so. And since you have to be here, Ms

President, you can sit in your office or you can bake cookies—or file your fingernails."

"I'm *not* going to be filing my fingernails!"

"Whatever. Just stay out of my way."

She gaped at him. "I'm the president!"

"You're an interloper," Elias said flatly. " Why'd your old man stick you in here anyway?"

Tallie coloured, certain she knew the real reason. But it wasn't the one she gave him. "Because I can do the job!"

That was the truth, just not all of it.

Elias snorted. "You don't know a damned thing about the marine business."

"I'm learning. I read every report my father sent. I researched AMI in journals and business weeklies. I spent the morning reading the financial statements you put in my office. And I told you I have some concerns—"

"Which are not necessary."

"On the contrary, they are. If Antonides Marine is going to move out of strictly boat building, I think we should be considering a variety of options—"

"Which I have done."

"—and we need to examine the whole marketing strategy—"

"Which I have done."

"—before we make a decision."

"And I will make a decision."

Once more they glared at each other.

"Look," Tallie said finally, mustering every bit of patience she could manage. "We both agree that I can't leave—for our own reasons," she added quickly, before he could speak. "So I'm staying. And since I am, I'm getting involved. I'm president of Antonides Marine, whether you like it or not. And I won't be shunted aside. I won't let you do it."

Elias's jaw worked. He glowered at her. Tallie glowered right back. And they might have gone right on glowering if the phone hadn't rung.

Elias snatched it up. "What?" he barked.

Whatever the answer was, it didn't please him. He listened, drummed his fingers on the desktop, then ground his teeth. "Yeah, okay. Put her through." He punched the hold button and looked at Tallie. "It's my sister. I have to talk to her."

From the look on his face, Tallie didn't think she'd want to be Elias Antonides's sister right now. Or any other time for that matter.

"Fine," she said. "Go right ahead."

She needed time to come to terms with the things she'd learned this morning, anyway. It was far worse than she'd thought—the bet, the house, the deal, the arrogant unsuspecting Greek god her father had his eye on as a prospective son-in-law, not to mention said Greek god's "file your fingernails" attitude about what her role should be at Antonides Marine. Oh, yes, she had her work cut out for her.

She stood up. "I'll be in my office if you need me."

"Yeah, that'll happen," Elias muttered.

She shot him a hard look, but he was already back on the telephone with his sister.

"No," Elias said.

It was what he always said to Cristina. It wasn't the bead shop this time. As he'd suspected, that had been a momentary whim. But this conversation wasn't going any better. Whenever he talked to his sister Cristina, they ended up at loggerheads. Usually it happened sooner. Like within a minute.

This time it had taken ten, but mostly because he was distracted, his mind still playing over the frustrating encounter with Ms President while Cristina rabbited on about how she'd been out sailing off Montauk last week, and wasn't it beautiful at Montauk this time of year, and on and on.

Waiting for her to get to the point, Elias had tried to think how he could have handled the irritatingly sanguine Ms Savas differently. Surely there had to be some way to convince her to leave well enough alone and not meddle in Antonides Marine affairs. But he couldn't think of one.

She'd flat-out said, "I don't follow directions well," and then she'd pretty much proved it. Annoying woman!

"It was a beaut," Cristina enthused. "You'd love it. You should come with us next time."

Elias dragged his brain back from Tallie Savas long enough to say, "No time."

"Oh, for heaven's sake, Elias. Get a life."

"I have a life," Elias said stiffly, even though he was sure Cristina wouldn't consider working seventy hours a week on Antonides Marine and another thirty or forty renovating the building much of a life at all.

"Sure you do." Cristina sniffed. "Come on, Elias. Mark would love to take you."

So she was still with Mark? After what—two months now? Elias supposed it was some sort of record.

"You could bring Gretl," she suggested enthusiastically. "We saw her this weekend, Mark and I. I don't know why you dumped her."

And he wasn't going to tell her, either.

When he'd met Gretl Gustavsson at a South Street Seaport bar one night, she'd just broken up with her boyfriend and had no interest in getting serious again anytime soon. As Elias had no interest in getting serious at all, they'd enjoyed each other's company.

Their relationship, which Elias didn't even want to describe with that word, had gone on for the past two years—until Gretl started acting as if there was more to it than there was.

"I've wasted two years on you, Elias," she'd told him a couple of months ago.

Elias hadn't considered them a waste, but if that was the way she wanted to look at it, so be it. He'd said goodbye, and that was that. He hadn't seen her since.

"She's so sweet. She asked about you." Cristina waited hopefully and got no response. She sighed. "Well, if you don't want Gretl, fine. We'll find you someone else."

"No, you won't," Elias said sharply. "I don't need you setting me up with a woman. Besides, I'm busy. I've got work up to my eyebrows. And it just got harder. In case you haven't heard, we have a new president of Antonides Marine."

"Daddy told me. And it's a woman!" Amazement didn't even begin to cover Cristina's feelings about that. She giggled. "Do you think *he's* setting you up?"

"No, I damned well don't!" Though the thought had certainly occurred to him. Still, his father was rarely that subtle. Aeolus took a more shove-the-woman-in-his-face approach.

And the truth was, Tallie Savas would never be his father's choice in a woman.

Aeolus loved his wife, but he had never stopped ogling tall, big-busted Nordic beauties. He'd thought Gretl was stunning, which she had been. But Elias had never fantasized going to bed with her. Because he'd *gone* to bed with her, he told himself. There had never been any speculation. Never any mystery with Gretl.

Whereas with Tallie Savas and her miles of wild curly hair—

"Maybe I'll come and check her out. What's she like?" Cristina said eagerly.

"Nothing special." Elias made sure his tone was dampening. Then he cleared his throat. "She's an MBA. A CEO. All business."

"Battle-ax, hmm?"

"Pretty much."

"Oh." Cristina's disappointment was obvious. "I wonder what Daddy was thinking then."

"I doubt he *was* thinking."

Cristina laughed. "He's not that bad, Elias. He likes Mark."

"Which proves my case."

"It does not," Cristina said, but she didn't sound as defensive as she usually did about her boyfriends. "You don't know him. He knows a lot about boats. If the lady prez is a hard worker, you'll have some time off now. You can come out with Mark and me."

"No." Which brought them back to where they'd started. Elias pinched the bridge of his nose. "Look, Cristina, I've got work to do—"

"You won't even meet him," she accused.

"I've met him," Elias said wearily. "I went to Yale with him."

"So I heard. He said he's changed since Yale."

Elias hoped so. At Yale Mark had been a drunken reveler who'd only got in because his father knew someone who knew someone. What was it with Greek fathers?

"If you want me to meet him again, bring him out to the folks' on Sunday." He'd managed to avoid his mother's last Sunday dinner by pleading a work overload. He wasn't going to get out of this one and he knew it.

"I'm not sure that's a good idea," Cristina mumbled.

"I thought you said the old man liked him."

"Yes, but only because he can beat Mark at golf."

Elias laughed. "Well, there you go. Something to build on. You'll work it out, Crissie. I have to go. I'll see you Sunday."

"I'll bring Mark if you bring Ms President."

"Goodbye, Crissie." Elias hung up before his sister got any more bright ideas.

He had other far more important things to deal with—like convincing Thalia Savas, aka Ms President, that despite what she thought, it was a better idea to spend the next two years filing her fingernails than trying to meddle in the business of Antonides Marine.

If she thought she'd done her homework, Elias thought, rubbing his hands together in anticipation, she had another think coming.

He'd show her homework. And he knew exactly where to start.

"For me?" Tallie looked up and smiled brightly when Elias appeared in her office late that afternoon with a three-foot-high-stack of reports and folders.

"For you," Elias agreed cheerfully, thumping them on her desk. "Since you want to be involved in the decisions, you'll want to get up to speed.

"Of course I will," she agreed promptly. "Thank you very much."

He gave her a hard-eyed gaze, but she smiled in the face of it and finally he just shrugged. "My pleasure." He turned toward the door, then paused and glanced back. "I'll have more for you tomorrow."

Tallie's determined smile didn't waver. "I can hardly wait."

In fact, she was having a very good time. After he'd finished his phone call with his sister, he'd gone into the boardroom to meet with Paul and Dyson. He hadn't invited her, but she had gone in anyway. He'd looked startled when she'd opened the door and very much like he'd like to throw her out. But finally he'd shrugged and said, "Pull up a chair."

Tallie had pulled up a chair and taken out a notepad and pen. She'd listened intently, making notes but not saying a word, though from the way Elias angled a glance at her periodically, she knew he was expecting her to stick her oar in.

She never did.

The first order of business she'd learned from her father was to look and listen before saying anything at all. It had stood her in good stead before. She intended to do the same thing here.

Listening today was quite enough. She was impressed with how thorough Elias was and how he was able to take the information Paul provided and examine it from different angles. He had, as he'd told her, done a thorough job of considering many of the ramifications of the purchase of Corbett's.

She still wasn't convinced that it was a good move. It seemed a little too far afield, but she would listen and consider and do more work on her own, and then she'd comment.

In the meantime, she'd read the stack of material he left her.

She wouldn't have been surprised if he'd given her three feet of invoices and grocery lists to read. But she wouldn't know unless she skimmed every single piece. So she spent the rest of the afternoon in her office doing just that.

Some of the reports seemed little more than she'd expected. But some were significant. They outlined in far greater detail than the material her father had given her what the financial status of Antonides Marine had been when Elias had come in eight years ago—and what it was now.

She got a far clearer understanding of just how dire the straits had been when Elias had taken over, and an even greater appreciation for how astute his business handling was. He'd seen what needed to be done, and he'd done it—even when it had meant cutting out some very appealing but not terribly lucrative lines.

The venture into luxury yacht construction that his father had spent vast amounts on was obviously one of Aeolus's pet projects. It had drained the company's assets, though, and had brought in very little.

When Elias took over, it had been the first thing to go.

There was nothing in the papers he gave her that spelled out in words his father's opposition. But in the "who was in favor of what" pieces, it was clear that Elias's decision had met with considerable parental opposition.

She wondered if she dared point it out to him as something the two of them had in common. Somehow she doubted it. But the more she read, the less she blamed him for his attitude. And when at last she leaned back in her chair and contemplated the skyline of Manhattan against the setting sun, she had to admit that if she were Elias Antonides, she'd resent an interloper coming in, too.

At eight o'clock when she gathered up the stack of papers she intended to take home for further study. It was a foot and a half high, but every bit could be all important. When she finally opened her mouth, she wanted to have her facts straight. Giving the stack a little pat, she went in search of a box to put it in.

The office was deserted. Rosie had left ages ago, but not without poking her head in to remind Tallie to bring the recipes tomorrow.

She'd promised them to Paul, too, who thought his fiancée would like them, and to Dyson who'd said he didn't have a fiancée, but who needed one? If you wanted cookies badly enough—and they were good enough—you just baked them yourself.

"I'm liberated," he'd told Tallie.

She smiled now at the memory, glad she'd brought them, determined to bring others tomorrow. They were good for morale.

And they were an excellent way to connect with the staff, even if some people, she thought as she opened the supply closet, looked down their once-broken noses at them.

"Ah, excellent," she muttered, discovering a box behind the paper supplies. She fished it out, then stood up and turned, slamming into a hard male chest.

"Can I help you find something?" Elias's tone was polite, his meaning was anything but. Loosely translated, Tallie knew, he wanted to know what the hell she was doing.

She smiled brightly at him. "You're still here, too? I was just getting a box to take some work home." She tried to step around him.

He blocked her way. "What work?"

"Some of that reading material you provided. Excuse me." Her tone was polite, too, but when he didn't move, she sidestepped him and—accidentally, of course—knocked the box into his solar plexis. "Oh! Sorry."

Not exactly the truth, but if he was going to stand in her way... She heard him mutter under his breath as she hurried back down the hall with the box in her arms.

Footsteps came after her. "You don't need to take things home." He stopped in the door of her office, scowling as she piled the papers into the box.

"Well, I don't plan to stay here all night."

"You're taking way too much trouble."

"It's not trouble. It's my job."

His jaw bunched, and she knew he was itching to say, "No, it's mine."

But he didn't say anything, just exhaled sharply and rocked back on his heels before muttering something under his breath, then turning and stalking off down the hall.

"Welcome to your first wonderful day at Antonides Marine," Tallie murmured to herself as she watched him stalk away.

No question about it—Tallie Savas was going to be a pain.

Who the hell needed a president who baked cookies? Who came to meetings and sat there, scribbling furiously on a notepad and never said a word? Who buried herself in her office with the piles and piles of reports he'd given her and actually read them? *And* took them home with her?

Elias stood glaring after her from his office as she tottered toward the door, the box full of files balanced on top of her briefcase, and three empty cookie tins teetering precariously on top of that.

A gentleman would help her with it.

Elias didn't feel much like a gentleman. He would have liked to have seen her collapse in a heap.

But the way his life was going at the moment, his father would probably want to pay all her medical bills with money Elias hadn't made yet!

Grimly he strode after her. "Allow me," he said with frigid politeness and opened the door for her.

"Thanks." She gave him a sweet smile that was completely at odds with her stubborn refusal to go home and let him get on with the job. "Have a good evening."

"Oh, yeah," he said drily.

She turned her head to grin at him. The top cookie tin teetered, and she nearly dropped them all, rescuing it.

Against his better judgment, Elias said grudgingly, "Do you want some help?"

Tallie shook her head—and the cookie tins and the briefcase and the box. "No, thanks." And she wobbled off down the hall.

Oddly annoyed at having his offer refused, Elias shut the door behind her. But he didn't move away. He continued to watch her through the glass. If she dropped the damn things, she'd have to let him help her.

But at that moment one of the doors down the hall opened and a man came out. Elias recognized Martin de Boer instantly from his tweedy elbow-patched jacket and his floppy earnest-and-intense-journalist-too-busy-to-get-a-haircut hair.

Martin wrote for the snooty monthly opinion mag, *Issues and Answers,* that rented a group of offices down the hall. When Elias had leased to them, he'd figured they'd be congenial tenants, and the people who worked on the physical magazine were. He even played recreational league basketball with the layout director.

But the journalists who wrote for *Issues and Answers* were a different story. They thought everyone else had issues but only they had answers. And from the few conversations Elias had had with him, Martin de Boer had more answers than most. As far as Elias could see, de Boer was a pompous, arrogant know-it-all who stuck his oar in where it wasn't needed.

And his opinion didn't improve as he watched Martin smile and speak to Tallie, obviously offering to help carry her box. In this case he got a brilliant smile in return and a reply that permitted him to whisk the box out of her arms gallantly and cradle it in his own.

Hell! Elias glared. She'd practically kicked his shins when he'd offered! He was half tempted to stalk down the hall and jerk the damn box out of de Boer's skinny arms.

Good thing his cell phone rang.

Bad thing to hear his father's voice, jovial and upbeat, booming down the line. "Well how'd it go today with our new president?"

Elias, watching Tallie disappear into the elevator with Martin the Bore, bit out two words: "Don't ask."

CHAPTER THREE

THE PHONE began ringing right after she came in the door.

"Just wanted to see how things went," Socrates said. Her father's tone was deliberately casual and offhand but at the same time simply simmering with curiosity.

Tallie, who was feeding a very hungry and indignant cat who thought he should have eaten two hours before, scooped some fishy-smelling glop onto a plate and set it on the floor. Harvey fell on it ravenously. She straightened and took a deep breath. "Just fine."

She would have left it at that, but she knew from experience that that wasn't the way to handle Socrates. Less was never more with her father. And letting him ask questions was worse than telling him more than enough to lead him astray.

So she launched into a full-scale report on almost everything—about the office, the murals, the furniture, the history of Antonides Marine—in short, more about the history of Antonides Marine than she was sure he ever wanted to know.

And about everything, in other words, except what she knew he wanted to hear.

To give him credit, he waited patiently through the whole recitation. It was his gift, she thought, knowing when to pounce. She made sure she gave him nothing to pounce on.

"Well, well. You certainly seem to have had a good day," he said heartily when she finally wound down. Harvey had long

since finished his dinner and was eyeing the bacon and eggs she
was making for herself.

Tallie shook her head and gave him a stern look. He gave her
a gimlet-eyed glare that reminded her uncannily of Elias's hard-
eyed stare, the one that said Antonides Marine was *his,* not hers.

My eggs. My bacon, she mouthed at him silently.

"So you like them?" Socrates pressed on in her ear. "The
people? Companies are made of people, Thalia. What about the
people?"

A small nudge to get her closer to what he wanted to know.

So Tallie obediently rattled on about the people. She started
with Dyson: "an absolutely charming naval architect," and went
on to Paul: "obviously has a strong work ethic. Solid midwest-
ern values," and then to Rosie, Lucy, the accountant and even the
temp girls. She talked and talked about everyone but—

"And Aeolus's son?" he finally had to ask. "Elias was there,
wasn't he?"

"Elias? Oh, yes," Tallie agreed, as determinedly offhand as her
father, damn it. "Elias was there."

Foaming at the mouth. Furious that you bet his daft father our
piddly island getaway against their ancestral home, and then got
Theo to make sure you won it—and the presidency to boot.

"Ah, good. And he was…helpful?" There was a certain guard-
edness in Socrates's tone now.

"He gave me a lot to read." Which was nothing but the truth.

"To read?"

"Reports. On the business."

"Oh. Oh, good. So he, ah, seemed to accept you, then?"

"As president, you mean?" Tallie said guilelessly. Then, "Apparently you didn't give him any choice, Dad."

Her tone told him she was onto him.

"Oh, now, that's not true!" Socrates blustered.

"Yeah, right. You didn't use Theo to get what you wanted?
And tack on the presidency, as well, and then tell Aeolus
Antonides that you'd deed his ancestral home back to him if—
and only if—Elias remained on as managing director for two
years?"

There was a minute's silence while her father apparently tried to figure out how to handle the damage control that was clearly necessary.

"I did it for you, Thalia. It is an opportunity for you. You've always wanted to go into business!" he said at last.

"As if that was the real reason you did it."

Socrates sputtered and muttered, but no words came out.

"Stop trying to manipulate my life, Dad," Tallie said evenly. "Stop trying to shove men down my throat."

"I never! I merely provided an—"

"Eligible man," Tallie filled in for him.

"So he is eligible? So what? I cannot make you marry him, can I? Or vice versa."

"But you would if you could."

There was another pause. Then, "Marriage is a wonderful thing," Socrates said. "Your mother and I—"

"Are meant for each other." And a good thing, too. Tallie couldn't imagine her parents with anyone else. " No one else would put up with you," she told him. "And I'm very happy you and Mom have each other. And if Brian had lived, I would have married him, but—"

"He would not want you to stay single forever, Thalia."

"I know that! But he wouldn't want me to marry just anyone, either!"

"Of course not. But—"

"Stop it, Dad. Just stop."

There was a long pause, then: "I am stopped."

Yeah, right.

"We'll see," she murmured. Then she said briskly, "I have to go now, Dad. I have a lot of work to do. All that reading Elias gave me to do."

"Oh, yes?" Socrates shifted gears right along with her. "Yes. Good. I've been concerned about Antonides' intention to diversify."

So he hadn't bought the company only to shove her down Elias's throat and vice versa? He was actually interested in the business. Tallie shouldn't have been surprised. Her father never ignored the bottom line.

"I hear he is considering a buy-out of another company," Socrates said. "Tell me about it. I might know the men in this other company. What did you say it was?"

"I didn't."

There was a brief silence which Tallie didn't fill. "And what is it?" her father finally asked.

"I can't say."

"Can't say? What do you mean, you can't say?" Socrates was clearly surprised by that.

"Business is business. What goes on in the office is confidential. You know that, Dad. You taught me it yourself."

"Yes, yes. Confidential. Business is confidential. But, Thalia, not when I *own* forty percent of it!"

"Even then," Tallie said firmly. "You're on the board. You're not involved in the day-to-day running of the company."

"But—"

"No one wants to have the board second-guessing their every move. You would hate it."

"Yes, but—"

"Come to the next shareholders' meeting, Dad," she said sweetly. "We'll tell you everything you need to know there."

It was no big deal, Elias told himself every morning. So Tallie Savas's name was now on the letterhead as president of Antonides Marine.

So what? It didn't make any difference to the way he ran things.

But the truth of the matter was, it did.

It wasn't that Dyson and Paul were "yes" men. It was that they didn't see things the same way Tallie did. Dyson was theoretical and Paul was nuts and bolts. And Tallie was…well, Tallie.

She saw things from a different perspective.

"A woman's perspective," she said with a shrug, as if it, too, was no big deal.

But irritatingly, it was. She brought up things he didn't pay as much attention to—people things, like how to balance job and family issues.

Balance was not something Elias was familiar with. When he was at work, he thought about work. When he wasn't at work, he thought about work.

"Work matters. Pure and simple," he told her.

"Get a life," she told him.

They glared at each other.

But the truth was, for the first time in years, Elias found that he was having to cope with a distraction. Of course, he could claim that the distraction was work by another name—but work had never had a woman attached to it before.

And this one was definitely distracting.

Elias was ordinarily happy to appreciate a beautiful woman. But he had always—until now—been able to choose the time and place. He had never mixed business with pleasure. He was still trying not to.

It wasn't easy.

Now, at the damnedest, most inconvenient times, he'd be sitting there in a meeting, trying to focus on what Paul or Dyson was saying and he'd glance across the room at Tallie. And his attention would take a sharp turn away from the work at hand.

He would find himself transfixed by those wayward strands of hair that had a habit of escaping from the confines of whatever she was trying to tame them with that day. And the next thing he knew, he would be imagining what it would be like to see her hair untamed, wild and glorious. And it was a quick jump to imagining what it would be like to unpin it and run his fingers through it.

And then, inevitably, Dyson would say, "So what do you think, Elias?"

And he'd be caught flat-footed, dazed and confused, without a clue about what Dyson had just said. It had happened more than once.

Last Tuesday he had been watching Paul make one of his intricate charts on the whiteboard, which was not exactly fascinating. And his gaze had drifted over to Tallie and locked on the sight of her crossing her legs. The glimpse of smooth tanned thighs as she shifted was enough to make him lose track of all of Paul's lines and curves and squiggles.

"With me so far?" Paul asked, turning to face them.

Tallie had nodded, tapping the end of her pen against her front teeth, and Elias closed his eyes and squashed his errant thoughts and did his best to bully his brain cells into paying attention.

It was almost like being in high school again!

It made him furious. Though whether he was more furious with Tallie for being there or himself for being unable to ignore her was a question he didn't ever ask. So he challenged her, asked her tough, demanding questions.

And she gave him thoughtful, considered answers that showed she was paying attention, even if he wasn't. Further irritation.

"That Tallie's one sharp cookie," Dyson said to him one afternoon after a meeting in which she had once more pointed out things the rest of them hadn't seen.

Elias grunted. That was another thing. Cookies!

They were another part of the problem. She hadn't just brought them the first day. She brought them *every* day. Or if she didn't bring cookies, she brought strudels or cakes or tortes.

"Other offices have a candy dish," Elias grumbled. "We have a damned Viennese bakery."

"No one's complaining but you," Tallie pointed out unrepentantly.

Which was true, of course. But that didn't make it right. Or healthy! "They will when they get their cholesterol checked."

But instead of quitting, she offered to bring in fresh vegetables, too. And after that, she showed up every day with some baked delicacy and a tray of carrot and celery sticks, broccoli and cauliflower pieces and green and red pepper strips.

Elias didn't like it. "We don't have the budget for this sort of thing."

"The office isn't paying. It's my treat."

He muttered things about precedents, but she just smiled and kept on hauling the stuff in. And how was he supposed to forbid her to bring it in? She was the bloody president!

Of course, once the largesse began arriving regularly, everyone in the office seemed to materialize and stuff their faces.

And talk.

He'd never heard so much talking going on. He thought he'd always run a pretty easygoing office where people could speak their minds. But he'd never achieved the level of communication Tallie did with her damn cookies!

Ideas were exchanged. Thoughts were expressed. The staff didn't just talk about last night's Yankees game or how the Mets were doing or how Paul's wedding plans were going or what Lucy's grandchildren were doing. They talked about business, too. Sometimes reasonably good ideas actually emerged because of Tallie's cookies.

"Your old man is smarter than we thought." Dyson didn't know the whole story of how Tallie got to be president of Antonides Marine, but he did know that it was Aeolus's doing. He probably thought Aeolus picked her because she could bake. Little did he know.

Elias grunted. "Dumb luck."

"Could be," Dyson allowed with a grin. "But I'm not complaining." He leaned one hip on the edge of Elias's desk as he watched Tallie across the hall talking to Rosie. "She's good for this place. And she's one fine-looking woman."

Elias scowled. "You can't say that in the office."

"Tallie wouldn't care. She'd just tell me I was a fine-lookin' man." Dyson laughed in smug self-satisfaction.

Elias banged a drawer shut. "Which just shows how bad her taste is."

Dyson's grin broadened. He cocked his head. "You been a little grumpy ever since she got here. You jealous?"

Elias would have liked to have banged another drawer. "Not a chance. And we don't pay you to stand around spouting nonsense. Get to work."

"Just saying." Still chuckling, Dyson saluted and left.

"Shut the door," Elias called after him, and was glad when it banged shut, though he'd have preferred to do the slamming himself.

It was true what Dyson said. Tallie would probably say he was a fine-looking man. She joked with Dyson all the time. He even let her call him by his first name, Rufus, which absolutely no one else got away with. She laughed at his silly puns and corny jokes.

She spent hours with everyone on the staff discussing not just business matters, but their lives.

Elias would be sitting at his desk, trying to concentrate on work, and he'd hear Rosie nattering on about her boyfriend problems, and Tallie would be right there listening and clucking sympathetically. He'd be getting a cup of coffee so he could focus on the quarterly reports, and he'd overhear Dyson talking to her about old Jimmy Cliff movies and some girl named Sybella who was giving him a hard time. Or he'd go looking for Paul to discuss the information he was gathering about going back to using teak in their boats, and Paul would be in Tallie's office discussing wedding plans.

Hell, he hadn't even known Paul was getting married!

Tallie knew. She knew Paul's fiancée's name. She knew Lucy's grandchildren's names. She knew what Giulia had named the baby she'd finally had last Saturday.

"Giacomo," Tallie had told him, "after Vincent's father."

Elias didn't even know who Vincent was.

Tallie even knew the name of Cara's hair colourist.

"Why? Planning to color your hair pink?" Elias had asked her sarcastically when Cara had gone back to work.

Tallie had grinned. "Actually, I was making sure it wasn't anyone I let anywhere near my hair."

But that was the only time she'd grinned at him. Every other time she'd been business—all business.

And he had to admit that when she worked, she worked hard.

She came to work early and she left late. Because she spent damn near the whole workday listening to peoples' problems, Elias thought irritably.

But if he couldn't fault her diligence, he certainly didn't think much of her taste in men.

She was hanging around with Martin the Bore.

After pompous, irritating Martin had been the macho hotshot who'd carried her box of papers downstairs, he'd stopped by the office later that week to see if she was free for lunch.

"No, she's not," Elias said flatly before she could answer.

Tallie had looked at him, surprised.

"We have a lunch meeting."

"Really? I didn't know that." She looked at Martin and shrugged, smiling ruefully. "Sorry. I guess I can't."

"Dinner then?" Martin had lifted shaggy eyebrows hopefully.

Elias's jaw clenched. It was still clenched when Tallie turned to him, her look questioning.

"What?" he demanded.

She smiled guilelessly. "I just wondered if we might have a dinner meeting I don't know about, too?"

"No," he said curtly. "We don't."

"Fine." She turned away. "Then I'd love to go out with you," she said to Martin.

Elias, grinding his teeth, had turned and stalked away. But he knew she'd gone out with the Bore that night. He learned later she'd gone with him to the opera on the weekend.

"Opera?" Elias had choked on the word when she'd mentioned it on the following Monday morning

"Well, I prefer jazz," Tallie had said with a shrug. "But it was an educational experience. Martin knows a lot about opera."

"I'll bet," Elias had muttered, shaking his head. She really did have lousy taste in men.

Not that it mattered to him.

He was not—repeat, *not!*—interested in Tallie Savas. She was trouble, with a capital *T*. He was working with her because he had to. Just *working!* Nothing else.

But she was getting under his skin. He thought about her all the time. He hadn't thought about a woman this much since he'd been crazy in love with Millicent. And look what a disaster that had been, he reminded himself.

He put Tallie Savas firmly off-limits.

All the same, it was good he had the building renovations to work on. Tearing out walls became an excellent way to spend his evenings. It used up a lot of excess energy that his hormones would have preferred to spend another way. He hadn't ripped Martin the Bore's head off yet, either. And every night that Elias worked like a maniac, banging and slamming and ripping and hammering with Elvis Costello at full volume, he didn't hear the phone and didn't have to talk to his sisters or his father or his mother, either.

Hell, life was just about perfect.

Knowledge was power, wasn't it?

So if Tallie knew her father was setting her up and if she knew he hoped she would fall for Elias Antonides, all she had to do was resist.

Right?

Piece of cake.

In fact, that turned out to be the operative word. Or one of them, at least.

Cake. Cookies. Bread. Muffins. Scones. *Linzertorte. Gugelhupf. Striezel. Buchtel. Powidlkolatschen. Semmel. Vanillekipferln,* courtesy of her Viennese baker friend, Klaus. And *baklava, ravani, koulourakia and megthalpeta,* courtesy of her mother.

You name it, Tallie baked it.

Every night when she got home from the office, she fed Harvey, fixed her own dinner, did her Pilates to relieve stress. And then she went into the kitchen and got out the flour and sugar and butter and spices and undid all the work Pilates had done—because baking was how she really relieved stress.

And Tallie was stressed.

Or maybe, she thought grimly, she was frustrated.

Who wouldn't be if they had to spend days looking at—and not touching—as fine a specimen of the male of the species as Elias Antonides?

Well, she supposed Dyson and Paul weren't.

And Rosie had a boyfriend, and Lucy had a husband, and Trina and Cara drooled over boy bands and one of the new young Latin ballplayers on the New York Mets. None of them even seemed to notice that Elias Antonides simply oozed sex appeal.

Lucky them.

Unfortunately Tallie noticed. She noticed the way Elias had of furrowing his brow when he was deep in thought. She noticed the dimple in his cheek that flashed when he grinned. She sat in the meetings, and while she was supposed to be listening, she was noticing what large capable hands Elias had and that he had calluses on his fingers which no man who pushed a pen all day should have.

More than she wanted to, Tallie noticed muscles flexing beneath his shirt that he hadn't got from pushing any pen, either. There was not much about Elias Antonides that she didn't notice, more's the pity.

Worse, he challenged her. He was constantly staring at her as if he wished she would just disappear. And then he'd ask some pointed question or wait until Paul had outlined some particularly boring facts, and then Elias would look at her and say, "And what do you think, Ms Savas?"

After being caught out the first time and blushing bright red, then having to make up something on the spot that, fortunately, wasn't too far off base because she'd done a lot of reading the night before, she had vowed never to be caught again.

It was almost a game to her now—watching him surreptitiously, waiting for him to pounce with his question, then answering him with all the wisdom and forethought she could muster.

She began to look forward to it, determined to pick up on things he might not have noticed, to show him she was good at what she did, too.

Some days after a meeting she felt like she'd been in a sparring match with the two of them, challenging and feeding off each other. Elias Antonides got her adrenaline flowing.

And that was even scarier.

Brian used to get her adrenaline flowing. Lieutenant Brian O'Malley had been the last man Tallie would have imagined she'd fall for. But he'd always had a way of challenging her, of making her think about things differently, of making her mad and then of making her laugh.

He had loved her for herself, not the companies her father owned. He had helped her find the best part of herself. When his plane had crashed on a training exercise seven months before their wedding, a part of Tallie had died with him. No one had ever made her feel as alive as Brian had.

Until now.

Not that Elias was anything like Brian!

He wasn't. Was...not. Period.

He was handsome—far handsomer than her tough, redheaded, freckle-faced Brian. He was smooth and arrogant, which Brian had never been. Besides, Elias was her father's choice, not hers. And if he sparred with her, it was because he was stuck with her for the next two years.

It was not an ideal situation.

She came home tired but edgy, running whatever Elias had said that day over in her mind, thinking about how she might have answered him better, sharper, quicker. Almost always she could think of something.

At the time, though, she was often distracted by the physical Elias Antonides as much as the sharp-as-a-whip managing director. Hormones that had been dormant since Brian's death.

It was disconcerting, to say the least.

It was particularly disconcerting to have it happen at work. Nothing—not even Brian—had distracted her from her work before. Of course Brian had never been where she'd worked. But Elias was. And Elias did.

She'd even found herself fantasizing about what he looked

like without his oxford cloth shirts and his well-pressed khakis. She wondered what he looked like *naked!*

So she baked. Furiously. And she went out with Martin.

She never fantasized about Martin.

He wasn't bad looking. He was actually reasonably nice looking in a pigeon-chested, pinch-lipped sort of way. He had an engaging grin when it could be teased out of him. And he had very nice hazel eyes. She liked his eyes. But had she thought about him naked?

No. Never.

He looked as if he could use a square meal, but he never ate one. He ate a lot of macrobiotic things like brown rice and bulgar with bean sprouts. It was healthy, he told her. He didn't think her baking was healthy at all, but he went out with her anyway.

"To convince me of the error of my ways," she told Harvey.

Martin, she discovered early on, could pontificate on any topic—and did. At length. He was interesting in a long-winded sort of way. His favorite topic was his view of the world and how it was failing to live up to his standards.

Tallie herself was in danger of not living up to them, too, because the night he took her to the opera she very nearly fell asleep.

She should have stayed home and gone over the material Elias had given her—her "homework" for the weekend. But she'd spent most of the day on Saturday doing just that—and found herself distracted with thoughts of the way Elias had looked holding Giulia's baby when she'd brought him into the office to show him off the day before.

It hadn't been Elias's idea. The women had been passing Giacomo around, cooing and gooing over him. Trina had been holding him when Elias stuck his head out of his office and wondered sarcastically when they had started providing child care and when Trina was going to finish typing up the material he'd given her that morning.

Tallie would have said something pithy and sarcastic right back. But Trina, in her haste to do the right thing, actually did something better.

"Oh, gosh, right now," she'd said—and thrust the baby into Elias's arms as she'd darted back to the steno office to get to work.

Tallie didn't know who looked more shocked, Elias or the baby. She'd thought he would hand Giacomo straight back to his mother.

But he didn't. After a moment's stunned silence, he'd shifted the baby awkwardly until he had it settled more comfortably in his arms, and then they regarded each other solemnly.

And then he'd smiled.

Elias had smiled—not the baby!

It was the most amazing thing. She could close her eyes and still see the tender look on his face. There was no impatience, no irritation. None of the things he most commonly aimed at her.

And that was when she'd realized it hadn't been a good thing Trina had done at all, because it had the unfortunate effect of making him even more appealing than he usually was—and in a different way.

It had been reasonably easy to resist a man who was simply physically attractive. It was a lot harder to ignore her attraction when she saw him with a baby.

He also listened patiently to phone calls from his sisters or requests from his mother. For all of Elias's hard-nosed attitude in business, he was, Tallie had realized after being there just a few days, a soft touch when it came to his family.

Of course, he had to be, or he'd never have stayed on as managing director of Antonides Marine. But it wasn't just his faimly. That same afternoon, after Giulia left, Tallie caught him on the phone agreeing to buy cookie dough from some school fundraiser for one of his mother's friends' granddaughters.

Then he'd noticed her listening and had scowled fiercely at her.

Tallie had grinned. It was like verifying the Big Bad Wolf liked sentimental old movies.

But it was also worrisome. And it had made her say yes when Martin wanted her to go with him to some totally boring lecture at Cooper Union on global warming.

* * *

His mother had stopped trying to set him up with women.

Used to her perennial efforts to get herself a new daughter-in-law, Elias was at first relieved by the sudden lack of women being shoved down his throat.

And then he realized why.

His mother didn't have to find him a suitable wife because she thought his father already had. And Elias couldn't keep saying, as he'd said to all her earlier efforts, "No, Mom. No, I'm not interested. No. No. No."

Because if he did, they'd know she was getting to him.

He knew what he needed to do. He needed to find his own woman.

Not to marry, God forbid. He was adamant about that. But to go out with, to flirt with, to charm and tease and have sex with.

Man did not live by work alone, as his father was often inclined to tell him.

Elias knew that. He'd had Gretl, hadn't he?

But it had been months since he'd had Gretl or any other woman. Obviously he needed to find one—a recreational partner—not a life mate.

And definitely not the president of Antonides Marine!

So on Monday he went out after work instead of heading down to the second floor where he was knocking out the walls of one of the offices . There was a bar called Casey's down the block, and he dropped in and had a beer and studied the unattached women at the bar.

The noise was appalling. The women, when he talked to them, were brainless. And none of them had hair that made him want to run his fingers through it. So he finished his beer and went back and knocked down another wall.

Tuesday he tried a different place—a club that had a jazz quartet. He liked jazz and he thought he might meet a more kindred spirit. He did not think about the woman in his office who liked jazz but went to see an opera with Martin the Bore.

There was a girl called Abigail at the jazz place. She hit on him and he didn't resist. He spent the evening listening to her talk about her crazy roommates and her annoying mother and he wondered if Tallie played jazz CDs while she was baking. Abigail gave him her phone number. He discovered later he'd left it on the bar and he didn't even care.

Wednesday evening he went to the local health club. Ordinarily he played basketball when he went. But there were no women on his basketball team. So instead he played racquetball with a French teacher called Clarice from Bordeaux.

They played hard, and she looked pretty enticing sweaty, and he thought that was promising, so he invited her out for a meal after.

She shook her head, batted her lashes, held out her hand and purred, "Let's go to my place instead."

God knew what would have happened at Clarice's place—and Elias did, too—if he had got there.

But as they left the health club and were walking toward Clarice's flat, his mother rang him on his cell phone. "I should take it," he told Clarice. She could think it was business. And the truth was, if he didn't take it, his mother would just call back at an even less opportune time.

"Have you heard from Martha?" Helena demanded.

"Nope. Not a word." Which wasn't exactly a disappointment. Elias heard from all his family far too often, as far as he was concerned.

"She just broke up with Julian," his mother went on, her voice rising. "She's very upset."

"She'll get over it," Elias said wearily. He shot Clarice an apologetic glance. "She's a big girl." Besides, his own disastrous marriage didn't qualify him to solve anybody's relationship problems. "I've got to go."

But Helena wasn't going to be easily dismissed. "You've got to talk to her, Elias. Calm her down. She listens to you."

Then she was the only one, Elias thought. "She'll work it out, Ma. She'll be fine."

"I don't think so. You know Martha."

Yes, he did. He knew all the hysterical members of his family who thought the world revolved around them. "Ma, I have to go."

But it was too late. He could already see Clarice withdrawing. Whether it was the "Ma" that did it (what woman wanted to take a man home who spent the walk there listening to his mother?) or something else, Elias didn't know. But by the time he managed to shut his mother up, Clarice was remembering she'd promised to play canasta with her elderly neighbor tonight.

"She's a real card shark. And lonely. I shouldn't disappoint her," Clarice was smiling and backing away.

Elias could take a hint. "Some other time, then."

"Of course," Clarice agreed.

But not Thursday. Because all day Thursday Elias was at Tom Corbett's factory with Paul and Tallie, making notes, talking to Corbett and his production manager, getting a hands-on feel for the place.

While he asked question after question and Paul went over the books and charts, Tallie just wandered around, chatted with the employees, poked her nose in this and that and smiled.

She'd brought along some sort of star-shaped cookies that smelled of cinnamon for Corbett and his minions, and the next thing Elias knew she was trading recipes with one of the shipping clerks.

"She's the president?" Corbett said doubtfully. He also seemed to be appreciating Tallie's figure a little more than Elias thought was entirely necessary.

"She is," he said sharply.

"Don't know how you keep your mind on business," Corbett said frankly. "Or your hands off her."

It was one of those totally politically incorrect things that no one these days was supposed to say. It was also unfortunately and annoyingly true.

Tallie Savas was tempting the hell out of him.

And every day it was getting worse.

CHAPTER FOUR

SHE WASN'T there.

Here it was, ten past ten Friday morning—ten past the time he and Paul and Dyson and Ms President of Antonides Marine were supposed to be having their meeting about the Corbett's acquisition—and she hadn't stuck her nose in the door!

Hadn't bothered to call, either.

How responsible was that?

Of course, Elias reminded himself, he shouldn't be surprised. When his father had first sprung Tallie-Savas-is-our-new-president on him, he had been sure it wouldn't last. He'd thought she'd treat it as a lark, a game rich girls played.

The way she'd acted for the past three weeks, though, had made Elias wonder if he'd been wrong. During that time Tallie had given every indication of taking the job seriously.

Still, she hadn't asked Corbett any questions yesterday. She'd wandered off, poked around, hadn't focused on any of the really important issues he and Corbett and Paul had discussed.

She hadn't said anything much on the way back in the car, either. And every time he'd slanted her a glance, she'd turned her gaze out the window. Bored, he supposed now.

And this morning she simply hadn't bothered to show up!

As he had come in prepared to steel himself against whatever enticing baked delicacy she would bring, not to mention what skirt she would be wearing that would show off her lovely long legs, he felt unaccountably annoyed. The least she could have done was call.

But she'd done nothing. There had been no whiff of cinnamon, no hint of cardamom or apple when he pushed open the door. There had been no cheery good-morning to Rosie, no request for a play-by-play on the latest of Paul's wedding plans. Nothing.

Because she didn't appear.

Everyone else did. Dyson, Paul, Rosie, Lucy and all the temp girls all stuck their heads into his office to ask where she was.

"How would I know?" Elias replied irritably.

"Haven't you heard from her?"

"Not a word."

He didn't know where she was. He didn't *care* where she was, he told himself firmly. He set down his pen, leaned back in his chair and took a deep breath, the first he'd taken since his father had sprung the awful news on him, and felt lighter.

Emptier.

Emptier?

Nonsense. He had just grown used to the continual buzz Tallie created in the office. It was a relief not to have her stirring things up. It would just take a little readjustment. That was all.

The phone rang, and for once he hoped it was his father so he could tell the old man that the president of Antonides Marine hadn't bothered to show up.

But the gruff male voice that boomed in his ear said, "Savas here."

Elias straightened in his chair. "Yes, Mr. Savas," he said crisply to Tallie's father. "What can I do for you?"

"Put my daughter on the phone."

Elias frowned. "I beg your pardon."

"I want to talk to Thalia." Pause. "She's not answering her cell phone because she knows it's me."

Elias's brows lifted. "Why?" he couldn't help asking.

"Because you've told her to, I would guess," Socrates retorted.

Because *he* had told he to? Elias's mind boggled.

"Blasted girl," Socrates went on. "Won't say a word."

A word about what? Elias wondered.

Socrates told him. "Goes on and on about what doesn't matter. This architect with dreadlocks and some girl with blue hair. But about the business—nothing! And you—" There was another abrupt pause. Then "What do you think of my daughter?"

Um. Er. "She's...very sharp."

"Of course she is sharp. She's a Savas! Beautiful, too, don't you think?"

"She's a beautiful woman," Elias agreed with as much dispassionate indifference as he could manage. She was drop-dead gorgeous, but he wasn't going to say that to her old man.

"That's what I tell her. So why does she want only to be a businessman? She is a *woman!* One hundred percent woman! A woman like my Thalia should be married, should have children. She will make a good wife and mother someday, yes?"

Visions of Tallie Savas with little weedy, floppy-haired Martins flickered across Elias's brain. He took a death grip on the receiver. "If she wants. Who knows?" he said casually.

"I know!" Clearly Socrates had his mind made up.

Elias felt a momentary pang of sympathy for Tallie Savas. Her father was as bad as his mother.

"And when she is married I will not be worrying about her, wondering where she is," Socrates went on. "That will be her husband's job. You tell her to call me." It was an order, not a suggestion.

"I'll give her the message."

Elias could just imagine what Tallie would say to him delivering a message from her old man. In fact the thought made him smile and shove back his chair. He went out into the reception area, glad he had an excuse to find out where the hell she was.

"Call Ms Savas," he instructed Rosie. "Tell her she's late."

While he stood there tapping his foot, Rosie rang Tallie's home phone and her cell phone. Apparently she wasn't answering his calls, either.

"Do you suppose she's sick?" Paul asked.

"She'd be home in bed if she were sick, wouldn't she?" Elias snapped. "I'm sure she's just got better things to do."

"Like what?" Paul looked bewildered.

"How the hell should I know? We're not waiting." Elias turned and stalked into the boardroom. "We had a meeting scheduled. She knew it. If she can't be bothered, that's her problem. Come on."

Obediently, but worriedly, Dyson and Paul followed.

The meeting went as all pre-Tallie meetings had gone. One of them, in this case Dyson, acted as the disinterested bystander. He had done no research on Corbett's. He had nothing to gain, nothing to lose. He was there to observe, to ask questions, to pull things together. Paul was there to discuss the financial issues, the market, the reasons for buying Corbett's from his standpoint, and the reasons against. And Elias was there to run through what he had discovered from talking to Corbett, to lay out all the pros and cons from the broader scope of the company.

They'd done it before—lots of times.

It should have been second nature. It was, really, Elias assured himself. It was just that they'd got used to Tallie saying, "Yes, but what about kids?" Or, "Have you considered that women don't always want to go out and sail around in boats in the freezing cold and get wet?"

Stuff that, frankly, they hadn't considered.

There were odd, awkward pauses, now and then, that made it feel to Elias as if they were actually waiting for her input.

And then the door cracked open.

All three of them looked up.

Something silver poked its way through the door. There was a thump and a bonk and a female mutter of annoyance. Suddenly Rosie was pushing the door wide-open and saying, "Here. For heaven's sake, let me get that! What happened? What are you doing here?"

"I work here!" It was Tallie's voice, defiant and determined and—

What the hell?

They all stared, astonished, as Tallie, leaning heavily on a pair of crutches, thumped her way into the room. There was an instant's total shock. Then all three men leaped to their feet.

Dyson pulled out a chair for her. "Here. Sit."

Paul said, "Let me," and eased her into it.

Elias contented himself with looming over her, demanding, "What the hell happened to you?"

She was a mess. She was tattered and disheveled, her face was flushed and there was a scrape on her cheek, her normally ruthlessly tamed hair was poking out from its pins, her legs were bare of pantyhose, both had skinned knees, and her lower left leg was in a bright-purple cast the ended just below the knee.

Tallie smiled ruefully. "I got run over by a truck."

Elias gaped at her. *"You what?"*

She laughed a little painfully and shifted carefully into the chair that Paul had helped her to. "Well, not really run over. Just knocked down, really. I was crossing the street and some guy was turning and—" she shrugged "—he didn't seem to notice I was in the crosswalk."

"Good God!" Elias wasn't sure if it was a prayer or a cry of exasperation. "Didn't you notice *him,* for Christ's sake? You could have been killed!"

"Well, I wasn't." She gave him a bright smile that was way too ragged around the edges for Elias's satisfaction. "Fortunately," she added reflectively after a moment, "or not. I suppose it depends on your point of view. You probably wish he'd done a better job of it."

"Don't be an ass," Elias snapped. He was furious now, though he wasn't sure at whom. He snapped his pencil in half and stalked up and down the length of the room. "What the hell are you doing here? Why aren't you in the hospital?"

"Don't yell." Tallie winced. "And stop pacing. It gives me a headache."

He stopped and spun around. "Are you concussed? Did you hit your head? Your cheek is cut," he noticed. Quickly he crouched down beside her to get a better look and discovered her big brown eyes just inches from his own. Abruptly he stood up. "Why aren't you in the hospital?"

It was all he could do to moderate his tone. He wanted to strangle someone. Preferably the guy with the truck.

"Because," Tallie said levelly, "they don't keep people in hospitals these days. They patch them up and send them home.

And—" she held up a hand and forestalled his next question before he could even get it out of his mouth "—there was no point in sitting home when I can sit here just as well. It's only a broken ankle. And a few bumps and bruises." She shifted in her chair and winced, then managed another smile. "No big deal."

Elias stared. So did Paul and Dyson.

"You could have been killed, you idiot woman!" he yelled.

"I realize that," Tallie said quietly, and there was the slightest quaver in her voice. "But I wasn't. So obviously I've been spared for a purpose—" she offered Elias a faint grin "—like making your life hell?"

Elias snorted and raked a hand through his hair. He cracked his knuckles and picked up another pencil and began pacing again. How could she expect he'd just stand still? "I can deal with you," he muttered. Or he would be able to if she'd stop doing such stupid things and go home and rest or file her nails or bake her damn cookies or—

He snapped the pencil in half.

"It'll be okay. Really." Now she sounded as if she was soothing him! "I'm all right. I've broken my ankle before. I'm an old hand at it actually. Done it three times now. The bad thing in this instance," she said sadly, "is that my cinnamon rolls and bear claws all landed in the gutter."

"That's the bad thing, is it?" Elias still wanted to throttle her. "No one needs your damned cinnamon rolls!"

"I'll bet they were good," Dyson said with a grin.

Tallie ignored Elias and smiled back at Dyson. "I'll make some more," she promised.

"Excellent!"

"That'll be great!" Paul was beaming now, all eagerness, too.

Didn't the idiot notice the cuts on her hands? The cast on her leg? Elias ground his teeth. "She's hurt. She isn't going to be making cinnamon rolls!"

"Well, I didn't mean right away," Paul said hastily. "I just meant, when she's feeling better—"

"When I'm feeling better, I'll make more," Tallie reiterated. Then she turned to Elias. "Don't make faces."

He barred his teeth at her. "Why? Does that give you a headache, too?"

"Actually, it does. Look, could we just go on with the meeting? I'm sorry I'm late. I was—"

"Hit by a truck," Elias snarled before she could say it again. "Have you called your father?"

"Of course not!" Tallie looked as if the idea had never occurred to her.

"He doesn't know?"

"No one knows. Well, except the staff at the emergency room, the EMTs and you guys. I didn't take out an ad in the *Times!* Or call my folks. Frankly, my father is the last person I'd tell. He'd fuss."

"He already has. He rang this morning."

The little colour in her cheeks seemed to fade completely. Elias thought she might faint. "He called here?"

"Looking for you. Worrying about you. Said you were avoiding him." It had been more satisfying when he'd thought she had been avoiding Socrates. But maybe she had, even before the truck incident. "Don't call if you don't want to," Elias said. "I've dealt with him."

"You have?" She looked stricken.

"Yes, so don't worry about him. Come on," he said. "You need to go home."

"I'm *not* going home. I came to work to attend this damn meeting, and I'm going to do it."

"Afraid I'll do something you wouldn't approve of?" he challenged her.

She met his gaze. "Afraid you won't think I'm holding up my end of the deal," Tallie replied.

Which was exactly what he had thought. Elias ground his teeth, then shrugged. "Fine. Be stupid." He turned his gaze to Paul. "Keep going. If Ms Savas wants to be a pigheaded, obstinate idiot, that's entirely her affair."

Paul didn't seem to remember where he was. "Um, let's see—" He fumbled with his notes, punched a couple of keys on his computer to see where he was in the presentation. "I'm not sure— I don't—" He looked around helplessly.

"The waterproof-clothing line," Elias prompted.

"Oh, er, right." Paul found the spot in his notes and the right material on the screen. Squaring his shoulders and sparing one more worried glance at Tallie, he launched into his report once more.

Elias didn't listen.

Stupid, stupid woman. What the hell did she think she was doing coming to work after she'd nearly been killed? He couldn't take his eyes off her as Paul droned on. He knew he should be paying attention. It was important.

But he couldn't. He sat watching Tallie while Paul's words flowed over him like water over a rock, but with less effect.

Tallie, of course, sat straight in her chair, pen in hand, notebook on her lap, purple-casted leg and foot stuck out in front of her. Her gaze was fixed on Paul and she was listening intently. Probably hanging on his every word, Elias thought irritably. She even made notes.

But now and then he saw her wince or grimace, then shift in her chair as if trying to find a comfortable spot. The only spot she was likely to be comfortable in was her bed. She had to be in pain. A sane woman would have left the hospital and gone straight home.

He waited for her to smile gamely and call it quits. She never did. She sat still and breathed carefully, shallowly and every now and then ran her tongue along her upper lip.

What the hell was she trying to prove?

Well, actually he knew what she was trying to prove. She was trying to prove herself to her father, who didn't think she ought to be in the business world at all.

And—Elias flexed his shoulders guiltily here—he knew she was also trying to prove herself to him. He'd made things hard on her over the past few weeks. He'd challenged her, doubted her, pushed her.

And she had responded with determination. She had done the job.

She didn't need to sit here turning white around the mouth, a sheen of perspiration on her forehead.

Abruptly Elias stood up. "Okay, that's it. I need a little more time to digest this. Thanks, Paul. We'll finish up on Monday," he said to his shocked assistant. Then he turned to Tallie, "Come on, Prez, we're going home."

It took a second for Tallie to even react, which, as far as Elias was concerned, just proved his point.

Then her brow furrowed and, naturally, she objected. "What? What are you talking about?"

"Time to close the shop." He was flicking down the blinds in the windows and opening the door to the reception area as he spoke. "We're ending the meeting. Heading out. It's Friday. We close early on Fridays in the summer."

"Since when?"

"Since now," Elias said in a tone that brooked no argument. He fixed a glare on Dyson and Paul that dared them to dispute it.

Dyson grinned broadly and rubbed his hands. "That's right! I nearly forgot. I'm outa here!"

Paul, still looking a little dazed, was fumbling with his notes. "Uh, yeah, but—"

"But *I'm* the president," Tallie protested.

"And you can be president from your house just as well." Elias stood by her chair and held out a hand. "Let's go."

She looked at it but didn't put hers in it. Figured. Stubborn woman.

"Tallie." Elias tapped his foot impatiently.

Sighing, she finally took his hand and he helped her to her feet. But when she tugged her hand to get free, he didn't go away. He fitted her crutches under her arms and held the door for her.

"But I'm not leaving," Tallie said "I'm having lunch with Martin."

"Like hell!"

"I am," Tallie insisted, trying to maneuver the corner on her crutches. But the effects of the accident finally seemed to be taking their toll. She was wobblier now than when she'd come in. She teetered and would have fallen if Elias hadn't caught her.

Whoa.

Tallie Tough-As-Nails Savas was incredibly soft. Round. Delectable. Her father's words echoed in Elias's head: *One hundred percent woman.*

Oh, yes.

"Steady now," he said gruffly, shifting her away from him, turning his head so he would stop breathing in the soft citrus scent of her shampoo.

"I am steady," she muttered, her knuckles white as she gripped the hand bars on the crutches.

"Sure you are." He steered her carefully out the meeting room door and into the main office. Rosie and Dyson and Paul and the temp girls all looked on nervously.

"What are you looking at? Don't you have work to do?" Elias demanded.

They all shook their heads.

"They were just leaving," Tallie said impishly. "Weren't you?"

"On our way," Dyson agreed. But not one moved, watching rapt as Tallie and Elias lurched through the office, like a stumbling man in a three-legged race. This was never going to work.

"Here," Elias said to Dyson. And in one swift movement he slipped Tallie's crutches out from under her arms, thrust them at Dyson, then scooped the president of Antonides Marine into his arms and headed for the door.

"What do you think you're doing?" she demanded furiously.

Elias kicked the door open. "Taking you home."

"Martin—"

"Can bore somebody else," he said as Paul held the door for him to go out and down the hall.

"Elias, stop!" Tallie wriggled in his arms, giving him some very interesting tactile sensations that did nothing to make him want to let her go. Then suddenly she sucked in a sharp breath and stopped.

"What's wrong? Does it hurt?" he demanded, staring down into the dark-brown eyes only inches from his.

She swallowed. Their gazes were still locked. "If I say yes will you put me down?"

"Not a chance."

She made a face. "I feel like an idiot," she muttered as he carried her toward the elevator.

"Because you are," Elias said flatly. "You broke your leg, you stupid woman. You should never have come in at all. You should have gone home!" The elevator door opened and he stepped inside. Paul followed with the crutches.

"I broke my *ankle,*" Tallie corrected. "It's not a big deal. It hurts, yes. It's swollen, yes. But I'm not going to die from it. Besides, if I'd gone home you'd have thought I was shirking my duty."

He glared at her.

She gave him a saccharine smiled in return. Then she resolutely turned her head away from him again, as if not looking at him would allow her to believe she wasn't being cradled in his arms.

Well, she might be able to deny it, but Elias couldn't. She was too solid, too soft, too *real* to deny. And when she turned her head he got another noseful of soft curly hair. He held his breath.

The elevator bumped and the door opened. Paul sprinted ahead. "I'll flag down a taxi." He shot out the door just as Martin de Boer was coming in.

"Tallie!" De Boer, looking windblown and very journalist-about-town with his leather briefcase and his bomber jacket, stared, horrified.

"Oh, Martin! Hi. I broke my ankle. About lunch today—"

"She won't be able to make it," Elias said, shouldering past Martin and out onto the sidewalk.

"Wait!" Tallie elbowed him sharply in the ribs and craned her neck to look back. "I need to talk to Martin."

"Phone him."

But there was no need because de Boer had come after them. "My God, Tallie. What happened?"

"I had a small accident." She was wriggling around, trying to see de Boer over his shoulder.

"She got hit by a truck," Elias said flatly. "Hold still, damn it," he snapped at her, for which he got another elbow.

"Dear God." De Boer looked appalled.

"I'm fine," Tallie said.

"She could have been killed, of course," Elias added conversationally.

"But I wasn't!"

De Boer, whose eyes went from one to the other as if he were watching a tennis match, didn't seem capable of saying anything at all.

"I was going to call you, Martin," Tallie said earnestly. "To let you know that I probably shouldn't go out—"

"Sanity rears its head at last," Elias muttered.

"But," Tallie went on forcefully, ignoring his comment, "if you want, we could eat at my place."

Sanity obviously didn't last.

Elias didn't even give de Boer a chance to respond to that idiotic suggestion. He headed for the curb where Paul had flagged down a taxi.

De Boer tagged along like a junkyard dog, patting Tallie's arm awkwardly. "Well, thank you, but, er, I don't think so." He gave her his hopeless grin. "All things considered, I think we should reschedule. Is she really all right?" he asked Elias doubtfully. "Did she fall on her head?"

"I'm fine!" Tallie insisted as Elias lowered her into the back seat.

"She's fine," Elias echoed, deadpan, "as you can see."

De Boer looked from Tallie in the cab to Elias, taking the crutches from Paul and climbing in beside her, and backed away. "Well, it, um, looks as if things are under control," he said to Tallie. "I'll give you a call."

"They're not—"

But Elias slammed the door shut.

"Where to?" the driver asked.

Elias looked at Tallie to give her address. She glared mutinously back at him. He looked at the driver and shrugged.

The driver rolled his eyes. "Ain't got all day, folks."

Tallie's jaw tightened, but finally she muttered her address and the taxi shot away.

Tallie's apartment was only about half a dozen blocks away. Elias was surprised at that. He'd pegged her as a hotshot, fast-track Upper-West-Sider. So she was walking to work and got hit? Where? he wondered, studying the street corners as they passed.

Tallie was looking out the window, determinedly ignoring

him. Probably wishing he'd let bloody de Boer bring her home, he thought irritably.

She didn't say a word until they were on her block. Then she leaned forward and said to the driver, "This one," and gestured to a four-story brick building right on the East River's edge. Like many of the buildings in the neighborhood—including the one that housed Antonides Marine International—this one was a converted warehouse, home to a funky used-clothing store, a kitchenwares shop, a music store and a pizza place on the ground floor with three stories of loft apartments and businesses above. Elias paid the taxi and climbed out, then reached back to get the crutches, but Tallie already had them.

"I can manage," she said, a mulish look on her face.

"You'll fall on your face." She was as pale as a ghost. "Don't be ridiculous. Just give me the crutches and—"

She gave him the crutches—one of them—right where he least expected it. Or wanted it!

"God almighty!"

Elias jumped back and nearly doubled over. Good thing she hadn't put any force behind it. If she had, she'd have settled his mother's "isn't it about time you got me some grandchildren" issue once and for all. And not in the way his mother would have preferred.

Not the way *he* would prefer, either. "Bloody hell!" He gritted his teeth and waited for the pain to subside.

"Sorry." Tallie's cheeks flushed. "Are you…all right?"

"No, damn it. I'm not all right," Elias said through his teeth. "You fight dirty, Prez."

She had the grace to look ashamed, but then she lifted her chin and said haughtily, "Well, if you'd get out of my way—"

When Elias could move again, he did just that. "Fine. Do it yourself. Be my guest." He stood back watching as she wriggled and squirmed and eventually made her way out of the back seat of the taxi one slow, painful inch at a time.

The taxi driver, waiting, shot Elias despairing looks and tapped his fingers impatiently on the steering wheel.

Elias just shrugged.

"You ain't no gentleman," the driver told him.

"And she's no lady."

The cab driver who had seen her jab with the crutch barked a laugh. "Ain't that the truth!"

Tallie glowered at them both. Then she concentrated on extricating herself from the taxi and negotiating the curb. Elias let her do it. Then he slammed the door shut and the cab sped away.

"Now you'll just have to flag down another one," Tallie pointed out.

Elias ignored her. He crossed the sidewalk to the door of her building, then turned and wordlessly held out his hand for her key.

The look she gave him promised a fight. But apparently the logistics of dealing with the door and the key and the crutches were—for the moment—more than she wanted to deal with.

With a long-suffering sigh, Tallie handed over the key.

Elias opened the door, held it for her, got a muttered ungracious "Thank you" for his trouble. Then he followed her into the building.

The foyer was utilitarian. Brick and steel, clean and spare, with a door to the stairs and an elevator at the far end. Tallie turned and gave him a level but annoyed look.

"Okay. I'm here. You've seen me to the door. Mission accomplished. Thank you again. I'll see you on Monday."

"Not a chance." Elias stepped around her and headed for the elevator, leaving her behind. He pushed the button and waited while it whirred to life overhead and begin its descent.

Tallie glared at him. "You're a pain in the ass, Antonides."

"So I've been told."

She looked longingly toward the door that said Stairs on it.

Go for it, sweetheart, Elias thought irritably. *See how far you get.* He turned back to the elevator.

A full thirty seconds passed before her crutches thumped his way across the tile. She reached him just as the door of the elevator opened. He held it open silently. Tallie hobbled past him and gave him a fulminating glare on her way in.

Elias stepped in after her. "Would've been a hike," he said conversationally.

She pressed the button marked three. "I would have loved to do it just to spite you," she admitted, surprising him. Then she shrugged. "But when I thought about what would happen if I fainted halfway up…" She gave him a wry, weary grin. A ghost of a smile, really.

"You wouldn't faint," he said, and somehow believed it was true. She was tough, was Tallie Savas. He might fight her, but he respected her. Looking at her now, he saw that she was white around the mouth again and there was really very little colour left in her cheeks at all.

"Are you okay?" he asked warily, discovering that he much preferred the spitfire Ms Savas to the one who looked as if she were in danger of keeling over.

"Yes, of course," she said with some asperity. "I didn't take the stairs because I know my limits."

He grinned his relief. "That's my girl."

"I am *not* your girl!"

Which was exactly what he knew she'd say, which was exactly why he'd said it. His grin broadened.

The elevator shuddered to a halt and the door slid open. They stepped out into a small vestibule painted a bright poppy red. There were three doors besides the elevator. Tallie nodded at the purple door opposite it.

"That's mine," she said and, bowing to the inevitable, waited while he unlocked it and pushed it open. She went in, then turned back to offer him a real, if wan, smile this time. "Now I really am home, and I didn't faint, and while it wasn't necessary for you to accompany me, I suppose I should appreciate it."

"I suppose you should," he said. "And I'm sure you *won't* appreciate this, Prez, but I'm not leaving."

CHAPTER FIVE

WHAT was she supposed to do? Throw herself in front of him and stop him?

Tallie had done enough throwing of herself for one day, thank you very much, even if the throwing hadn't been her idea.

She *hurt*, damn it.

Her ankle was throbbing, her head ached, the scrapes on her hands and arm were stiff and smarting. It felt like rigor mortis setting in.

But she had sucked it up and gone to the office—had never considered *not* going in to work today. As long as she was alive and breathing—and unhospitalized—she had been determined to go to work, to prove to Mr. All-Work-and-No-Play Antonides that her level of commitment to the job equaled his.

But a woman's strength and stamina and grit only went so far. And then she was done. Shot. Kaput.

Tallie was kaput. It was true what she'd said in the elevator. She might have fainted had she tried the stairs—and God knew she'd *wanted* to take the stairs and prove herself independent and whole!

But she was feeling less independent and whole by the minute. And right now if she didn't sit down soon she was going to fall down and she knew it.

After having been carried—*carried!*—through the streets of New York (well, thank God, actually only Brooklyn) and in front of Martin (who had been shot at by terrorists and made it sound like a walk in the park) Tallie didn't think she could stand further humiliation today. Not and survive.

So she just looked at Elias's straight back as he walked past her into her living room and did the only thing she could—she stuck out her tongue.

Then she turned ever so carefully on her crutches because, even though she'd used crutches plenty of times before and knew it was a skill that would come back quickly, she wasn't swift on them at the moment. She was decidedly shaky. Her arms, unaccustomed to bearing her weight, were fatigued. The scrapes she'd sustained were stinging. And her ankle, which the doc had said to rest, elevate and use ice on, was now throbbing beyond belief.

He had given her painkillers. But she had adamantly refused any at the hospital. She'd been determined to have all her wits about her in the meeting. Now her wits seemed expendable. Where was that bottle of pills?

"Where's my briefcase?" She looked around, but didn't see it.

Elias was looking around her apartment, probably making more judgments about her competence based on the fact that she furnished from thrift shops and the Goodwill. At least he didn't seem offended that Harvey was walking around him, sniffing, checking him out.

"Where is it?" she demanded again, feeling a little panicky now. "Elias?"

"Oh, give it a rest. You're not going to work now." He had stopped staring around the apartment and was looking straight at her. His hands were jammed into the pockets of his khakis, which had the effect of making him look very masculine and gunfighterish.

The last thing Tallie needed was a gunfighter. Unless he could shoot her and put her out of her misery.

She took a breath. "I know I'm not going to work," she said with all the patience she could muster. "I just need my briefcase. My pain pills are in it."

"Then why the hell didn't you say so? It's at the office. I'll call Rosie. She can bring it over." Elias dug his mobile phone out of his pocket and punched in a number, then waited, tapping his foot, looking at Tallie for signs that she might explode before his eyes.

She tried to look more patient than she felt.

There was apparently no answer because Elias continued to wait. He tapped. Waited some more. Muttered to himself about bloody answering machines, then punched in the number again and waited some more, until finally in disgust he flicked the phone off and stuffed it back in his pocket.

"Where the hell is she?" he demanded furiously.

"I believe," Tallie said with a faint smile, "that on Fridays in the summer everyone has the afternoon off."

"Damn it!" Elias raked a hand through his hair, then stalked across the room to loom above her.

He wasn't actually *that* much taller than she was—four inches, maybe five—but he could loom with the best of them. She wondered if he'd taken looming lessons. Did they give looming lessons? Where?

Oh, God, she was losing her mind. She needed to get off her feet and get some drugs!

"I'll go get your pills. You sit down," Elias commanded.

"I'd love to," Tallie looked longingly at the armchair and sofa across the room.

Her apartment was bright and airy—and not a lot bigger than a postage stamp. Ordinarily. Now the sofa looked as far away as the moon. The armchair was in another galaxy. Harvey, after one curious glance in their direction, was in it, fast asleep.

Elias's gaze followed hers, then came back to zero in on her. "Give me the crutches."

"Why? So I can fall over?"

"No. I'll carry you. Give me the crutches."

"Don't be so bossy."

"Then fall over, damn it." He looked as if he'd rather strangle her than carry her. "I'll help you to the sofa, Prez, but not if you've got weapons."

"Oh." The penny dropped. And Tallie noticed suddenly that, even though he seemed to be looming, Elias was keeping out of her crutches' reach. "Once bitten, twice shy?" she ventured with a faint grin.

"Let's just say you're not getting another chance." There was a flicker of remembered pain in his eyes that made her momentarily remorseful. And she really did need to sit down.

"Here." She thrust them at him. He caught them and tossed them aside, then scooped her into his arms.

And for the second time she was in Elias Antonides's arms. Worse, she was glad to be there, grateful for the muscular hard strength of them cradling her, for the solid expanse of chest against which she leaned, for the strong firm jaw that—

Whoa! Hold on a minute, girl! The strong, firm jaw had nothing to do with him getting her to the sofa.

Of course, she knew that. She was just delirious with pain. Or…or something.

Still she was aware of feeling his heart beating as he carried her to the sofa. She watched his Adam's apple move when he swallowed as he lowered her onto the cushions. And she noticed that he had cut himself shaving. There was a tiny nick on the edge of his jaw. There was also a longer older scar on the underside of his chin.

Instinctively she touched it.

Elias jerked. His brows drew down.

"Sorry," Tallie said quickly. "I saw the scar. I just wondered… what happened?"

"When I was ten I stopped a hockey puck with my face."

"Ouch." The very thought made her wince.

"Yeah, that about covered it. No big deal," he said, echoing her earlier words.

He lowered her carefully to the sofa. His face was less than a foot from her own. And, scar and all, he was, without a doubt, the most handsome man she'd ever seen. Even her pain-fogged brain could register that. So did her body. All unbidden, it seemed to lean toward him.

Their eyes met. And something arced between them. Oh, help!

But before she could bend her mind around it, Elias straightened quickly and stepped back. If she'd been a hot potato, he couldn't have backed off faster.

"I'll get you some pillows." He made a production of gathering up her assortment of gaily covered throw pillows from around the room and piled them at the foot of the sofa. When he had built a small mountain, he stepped back and waited for her to lift her ankle up onto it. It might as well have been Everest.

And Elias seemed to realize that at the same moment she did. Gently he grasped her ankle and carefully—hot potato carefully—lifted her casted ankle to rest on them.

"Thank you." Tallie breathed a sigh of relief.

"Okay. I'll go back to the office and get your pills. Don't go anywhere."

Tallie just looked at him. "As if."

He should send them back via messenger. Call a car and have the driver take them over and bring them up. It was smarter than going back himself.

It was bad enough to lust after Tallie Savas when she was across the room from him at a meeting—even though it was wholly inappropriate. But it was something else entirely, now that he knew just how soft and warm she really was.

The feel of her body against his chest as he had carried her to the taxi was imprinted on his memory. And the short journey from the door of the apartment to the sofa—which he'd been determined to do to prove to himself how unaffected by her charms he actually was—proved the complete opposite instead.

When he'd lowered her to the sofa, it was all he could do not to kiss her and lie right down beside her. Muscle memory, he assured himself. In the past whenever he'd lowered a woman to a sofa or bed, it had always been a prelude to joining her, to making love with her.

And there was a direction his thoughts definitely needed to stay away from. Make love with Tallie Savas? Ye gods.

Talk about complicating his life!

He'd get her pain pills—and her damned briefcase—and wish

her the joy of them. Then he'd go home and ring up what was her name—Denise? Patrice?

Oh, yeah. Clarice. The woman he'd met at the gym.

Right. He'd take Clarice out. And then go back to her place. And he wouldn't answer his phone this time! They would have an uninterrupted evening, and he would forget all about Tallie Savas's soft curves. It seemed like such a good idea he rang her from the office while he was picking up Tallie's pills.

"It's Elias," he said. "How about meeting me at Casey's? We could have a drink or two. Go out for dinner?"

"Sounds lovely," Clarice purred. "I will look forward to it."

So would he. And it didn't matter where it went after dinner, he told himself as he walked the six blocks back to Tallie's flat, as long as it blotted Tallie Savas's big brown eyes and kissable lips and soft breasts right out of his brain.

Tallie was still lying on the sofa with the cat—Harvey, she had called him—sprawled next to her. She had her ankle up on the pillow, but she was barefoot now—and she'd unpinned her hair. It cascaded in all its luxuriant tangled glory against the buttery tan leather as she held the phone to her ear.

All thoughts of Clarice went right out of Elias's head. Hell.

Tallie waggled her fingers at him, applauded the sight of the briefcase, then motioned frantically for the pill bottle and a glass of water. At the same time she continued talking on the phone.

"Yes, Mom," she was saying. "No, Mom."

Three bags full, Mom, her expression seemed to say.

Elias understood. Was it just Greek parents, he wondered, who were ready to step in at a moment's notice to run your life for you? He gave her a wry, knowing smile.

Tallie sighed and winced as she moved her leg. "I'm fine, Mom. Really. It's not a bad break. Of course I can manage. No, I don't need to come home. I *am* home!"

Elias went to the kitchen to get the glass of water. There was some baklava on a cake plate under glass. He remembered the baklava all too well. It was the one thing she'd brought in this week he'd been powerless to resist. Even now his stomach growled. Determinedly he ignored it and fetched the water, then opened Tallie's briefcase, took out the bottle of pills, shook one into his palm and carried them back to the living room.

Tallie was still on the phone. "No, Mom. You do not need to come and take care of me. I have help. Don't worry. There will be someone here."

She took the glass when Elias held it out, popped the pill and mouthed her thanks. "Look, Mom. I really have to go. I'll talk to you tomorrow. I love you, too, and Daddy. Be sure to tell Daddy everything is fine, too. Tell him *I'm* fine, and I'm taking care of business. Tell him he is *not* to meddle!" She hung up as if the receiver was on fire. "They think I'm seven," she grumbled.

"Parents do."

"I guess. It just gets old. Thank you for bringing my brief-case and my pills."

"Not a problem." Elias carried the glass back to the kitchen and put the bottle of pain medication on the counter. "You should do what she said, though," he counseled when he returned. "Rest. Take it easy. Don't overdo. It's a good thing you've got some help coming in. You'll need it."

"Yes, Daddy."

"Don't push your luck," Elias warned her. He didn't feel in the least fatherly, and he wished she'd stop stretching her arms over her head that way. It lifted her breasts, made them all too notice-able, made him remember their softness. "It's true," he insisted.

Tallie shifted on the sofa, tipped her head back against the cushions giving him a view of a long, elegant neck. She shut her eyes. "Mmm. Yeah."

What? No argument?

Then she opened them again and smiled at him. The painkill-ers must have kicked in. She sure hadn't smiled at him like that earlier. Earlier she'd tried to kill him. Or maim him at least. He winced now, remembering.

That had been bad. This—this staring at her, having her smile at him—was worse. This was temptation. God, her hair was gorgeous.

Elias wiped his palms down the sides of his khakis. "So," he said briskly, "is there anything I can get you before I take off."

"A pizza."

He stared. "A what?"

"A pizza." Tallie looked hopefully at him, then smiled. "I'm starving. I ate half a grapefruit for breakfast. I thought I'd eat one of the cinnamon rolls at the office. But, well, we all know how that turned out." She grimaced. "And then you wouldn't let me have lunch with Martin."

Yeah, but still… "A pizza?"

"There's a pizza place right downstairs. If you don't mind?" she added hesitantly. It was the most hesitancy he'd heard from her since he'd met her. That little hint of vulnerability. Was she doing it on purpose?

Whatever she was doing, it was working.

Elias rubbed a hand against the back of his neck. "Oh, hell. All right."

He could bring her up a pizza and still get over to Casey's to meet Clarice when she got off work.

"Great! What do you like on your pizza?"

"What would *I*—?"

"You haven't had lunch, either," she reminded him, then squinted at him assessingly. "Are you the goat cheese and pineapple type?"

"I am the pepperoni type. With double cheese," he said flatly. "None of that sissy stuff."

Tallie laughed. "Whatever you want, then. Tell them to put it on my account."

The last thing he was going to do was let Tallie Savas pay for the pizza. He supposed he could eat a piece or two while he waited until whoever was coming to stay with her turned up.

"The number is on the refrigerator magnet." She waved a hand toward the kitchen. "Sal's All You Ever Wanted In A Pizza. You can call it in."

"I'll go down." If he was going to stay here, he needed a little space, a little breathing room. A little less Tallie. "Stay put."

She smiled and gave him a lady-of-the-manor wave of her hand. "I believe I will."

When he got back with the pizza half an hour later she was asleep. She looked younger and surprisingly defenseless but just as mindblowingly beautiful. He kept his distance. It was better that way. But then she opened her eyes and smiled vaguely at him. Her face was flushed. Her hair was everywhere.

"You," she told him, smiling muzzily when she saw the pizza box, "are a regular prince."

"And you're drunk on painkillers," Elias said. He could see it in her eyes, in the loopy smile she was giving him. He got plates from the kitchen and carried them and the pizza box over to the coffee table in front of the sofa and set them down. Then he opened the box.

Tallie leaned forward, sniffing appreciatively. "I looooove pepperoni. Martin thinks it's plebeian."

"Martin would. So… you and the Bore had pizza at the opera?"

"*De* Boer," Tallie corrected primly. Then after a moment, "Duh Bore." She giggled. It was a very girlish infectious giggle. Elias wasn't used to thinking of Tallie Savas as girlish any more than he was used to thinking of her as defenseless. He watched her warily.

"We had pizza for lunch one day. Martin likes Gorgon-Gorgonzola," Tallie stumbled over the word. Her eyes looked glassy. "And smoked oysters. He says they're an aphro—" she looked around the room for inspiration, found none and shrugged vaguely "—whatever."

"Aphrodisiac?" Elias didn't like the sound of that.

Tallie giggled again. "Silly, isn't it? Do you s'pose he needs aphro-whatevers?" Her voice was getting a little slurred.

If she didn't know, that was good.

"I wouldn't be surprised," Elias said.

Tallie nodded sagely. Big exaggerated nods, her chin bumping her chest. "Me, neither." She reflected on that while she chewed her pizza. "Do you need 'em?"

"*What?*" Elias dropped the pizza in his lap. "Damn it." He

jumped up, swiping ineffectually at the grease and tomato sauce with a paper towel.

Tallie watched his every move. Then she said, as if she'd been considering it, "No, you prob'ly don't." She looked straight at him. "You're pretty sexy as is."

Of course it was the painkiller talking, and she was going to regret like hell having said that in the morning—if she even remembered in the morning.

Elias rubbed a hand against the back of his neck. "Um, thanks. I think."

The loopy smile returned. "You're welcome." She looked at him expectantly.

He wished he knew what she was expecting. Then immediately he thought it was probably better that he didn't.

"Eat your pizza," he ordered gruffly.

Tallie smiled at him—one of those smiles that made all his hormones go on alert.

Deliberately he focused on his pizza. He finished it quickly, then wiped his hands on the paper towel and glanced at his watch. It was close to four and he had to go back to his place, grab a shower and change his clothes for something without tomato sauce before meeting Clarice.

Getting to his feet he said, "Look, I really should be heading out. When's your help coming?"

Tallie who had been dozing, opened her eyes and frowned. "My help?"

"You told your mother you were having help."

"I did. You. You brought pizza."

"Me? I'm not— Listen, Prez, you need someone with you."

"You're with me."

"I'm not staying."

"Oh." The light went out of her eyes.

Elias felt as if he'd taken candy from a child. He raked a hand through his hair. "I can't!"

"Of course." She waved a vague hand toward the door. "Well,

goodbye, then," And she dismissed him as if he didn't matter and went back to eating her pizza.

If anything proved that she shouldn't be left on her own, it was that. She didn't even know she needed to have someone there.

"Oh, hell." Elias stalked into the kitchen, grabbed his phone and punched in Clarice's number. When she answered, he said, "I can't make it. Something's come up. Business." This *was* business, damn it. Tallie was president of the company.

Clarice made a tsking sound. "Ah, *mon cher,* you work too hard. But," she reminded him, "at least this time it is not your mother."

No, God help him, it wasn't.

But this might well be worse.

CHAPTER SIX

TALLIE was having the oddest dream.

She was dreaming she was swimming. But not swimming easily the way she always had. No, this time she was dragging an anchor, barely able to move. And though there was water, she was thirsty, parched, desperate for a drink.

She thrashed, trying to reach land, to reach the oasis, the cool shade of the beach and rest. And water. Dear God, she wanted water.

And then Elias Antonides, of all people, handed her a glass.

She took it, drank it quickly, took pills he offered her, let him wipe her forehead, let him straighten her pillows, let him shift the purple anchor and make the ache go away.

It was amazing how quickly it vanished.

Because Elias was there.

"Do you do magic?" she asked him.

"What?" He looked rumpled and worried. His shirt was hanging loose, and his tie was gone. There was a shadow of stubble on his jaw. He was even handsomer in her dreams than he was in real life. Figured.

He was nicer than he was in real life, too. She smiled muzzily at him. "You must do magic," she said. "You make the pain go away."

A corner of his mouth quirked. "Me and the little white pills."

She tried to focus on the pills. But she didn't see them clearly. It was because she was dreaming.

It was the first time she'd dreamed of Elias in her bedroom. Usually she had dreams about the two of them at work. Sometimes they were, um, interesting dreams. But they'd never gone as far as she'd have been interested in taking them. In her dreams, of course!

"Nice pills," she murmured.

"Apparently," Elias's tone was dry. But he was smiling at her. He almost never smiled at her. He had a lovely smile. "You might want to eat something with them," he suggested. "Are you hungry?"

"Don't want," she said, then frowned. What was it she remembered about pizza? Had she and Elias had pizza? No. She and Martin had had pizza. But she remembered something about Elias bringing her pizza.

Or maybe that was another dream. She tried to remember, but she was too tired. She shut her eyes. But she was hungry. His having mentioned food made her think about it.

"Baklava," she said woosily. She wondered if she had the strength to get up and get some. Maybe she could just dream she was eating it. That would be wonderful. But she didn't much feel like moving.

"Here." A gruff voice penetrated the fog that was her mind.

She opened her eyes. No, she didn't. She must be still dreaming because Elias was still here. In fact he was standing besides the bed with a plate of something in his hand.

She blinked at him. "Whazzat?"

"Baklava. You said you wanted some."

What a dream! What a spectacular dream. Not only was Elias Antonides starring in it, all rumpled and gorgeous looking, he was bringing her baklava in bed!

Tallie accepted the plate, but it wobbled precariously in her grasp.

"Here," he said. "Give it back." And the next thing she knew, he was holding the plate again and sitting beside her on the bed.

Bemused at how real it all seemed, albeit slightly fuzzy around the edges, Tallie took a piece of the baklava and bit into it. Ambrosial…if she did say so herself.

"Mmm." She shut her eyes, savoring the sweetness, and licked the honey off her lips. A slightly strangled sound made her open her eyes again. Elias was looking at her, a rather odd, definitely desperate look on his face.

"Oh," she said. "Sorry. I should have offered you some."

"No, it's okay. I'm—"

"You must be hungry. Eat." She held out what was left of her piece of baklava, waving it under his nose, brushing it against his lips.

"Tal—" But that was as far as he got, because she poked the baklava in his mouth. His lips touched her fingers. His mouth shut in surprise and he half coughed before he managed to swallow and then chew the unexpected treat. "Thank you," he said when he'd swallowed again. He sounded very polite and rather strained.

"Stop that," she told him.

His brow furrowed. "Stop what?"

"Acting all stiff and proper. This is my dream and you aren't supposed to behave that way."

He looked almost startled. But then he shrugged slightly and his lips quirked. "I'm not? How am I supposed to behave?"

"You're supposed to be nice," she told him firmly. "Well, you have been, I guess. Bringing me the baklava. But sometimes at work you're cranky."

"I apologize."

"See? There. You're doing it again. Smile," she commanded. He barred his teeth.

"Not like that. Are you ticklish?"

"What?" His eyes went wide.

"I asked if you were ticklish. If I tickled you and you laughed, that would be as good as a smile."

"I'm not ticklish," he said dampeningly.

"Pity." She picked up the last piece of baklava and broke it in two and held a piece of it out level with his mouth, inviting him to take another bite.

He hesitated a moment, then leaned forward and did just that.

Only this time he wasn't surprised. She was. Because this time he didn't just nibble at the baklava—he nibbled her fingers!

The feeling was so unexpected and so surprisingly intimate that she jerked back, shocked. "Elias!"

He grinned.

Oh my, yes. It was even better than a smile. Elias Antonides's grin was glorious. It was memorable. She hoped to goodness this was one of those dreams she could recall after she woke up!

"Here," he said, and began to brush the crumbs off the bed-clothes and into his hand. It necessitated him touching the light-weight duvet that was covering her. It necessitated him brushing his hands over her breasts, over her belly and her thighs. It seemed almost as intimate as his nibbling her fingers had.

And then, somehow he was leaning right over her, his face very close, nearly in her own, and his deep, dark eyes met hers, locked with hers. His lips were just inches from her own—right where they had been before he'd kissed her.

Kissed her?

What?

Good Lord, another dream? A dream within a dream? She blinked rapidly. Gave her head a little shake.

Elias straightened up. "What's wrong? Got something in your eye?"

Tallie shook her head again, dazed, trying to think. To remember. But it was gone. Whatever she'd thought she was remembering she couldn't.

It was just the feeling, she thought. It was how she used to feel when Brian had kissed her. There had been that moment of connection, of anticipation, of need. That was what she was remembering!

She was missing Brian. Her gaze sought the picture on her dresser. It was too dark in the room, though, with only the small reading lamp illuminated. She couldn't see her 5-by-7 inch Brian in the shadows. She could only see Elias, tall and strong and devastatingly sexy, looking down at her worriedly.

He was too vivid, too present to allow her to focus on anything—or anyone—else. Memories of Brian slid away as memories of Brian had been doing lately. And this was only a dream, anyway.

She might as well enjoy her dream.

She reached out and took hold of his shirtfront and pulled him down toward her again.

"Tallie?"

"Shh. Just testing," she murmured, and then she pressed her lips to his.

It was indeed the dream to end all dreams, she thought dizzily as the kiss went on and on and became better and better.

Even dreaming she remembered thinking he was the last man in the world she ought to have anything to do with. But Elias Antonides kissed as good as he looked. Better, in fact. The best since Brian.

Possibly, her traitorous thoughts proclaimed, even better than Brian—though she *loved* Brian.

Still, she had to admit, for a dream kiss, it was the best she'd ever had. She didn't know why she didn't dream about kissing more often if she was so good at conjuring up kisses like this!

The last man she'd kissed for real had been Martin—if you could call the dry press of his mouth against hers a kiss. What she remembered most about that was the aftertaste of goat cheese.

Elias's kiss, on the other hand, was the sort she could take out and replay to keep her warm on subzero nights in Antarctica. Con Ed could use it to light up all of Manhattan and have enough wattage left over for Brooklyn and the Bronx besides.

It threatened to burn them both right down to the ground. And Tallie knew she would go willingly and die with a smile on her face.

Her hands slid underneath his shirt. She ran her fingers through the soft, springy hair on his chest, savored the heat of his body, the ripple of his muscles as he caught his breath. His fingers came up to tangle in her hair, to weave and thread and curl the strands, to tug lightly on them, to bring her closer, to bring the two of them together.

She wanted more. She wanted it all. And so, it seemed, did

he. But as she began to fumble with his buttons, there was a thump, and Harvey—her subscious in feline form, no doubt—landed on the bed. A shred of sanity reminding her that even in her dreams there were some things she shouldn't do.

Apparently, the dream Elias thought the same thing because he pulled back abruptly, then stared at her looking as dazed as she was. She was aware—and pleased—that he looked as shattered as she felt. At least in her dreams she could disconcert him.

"Bad idea, Prez. Really, really bad," he said raggedly. And then he'd straightened up and walked out of the room.

Watching him go, Tallie found herself wishing that her subconscious cat hadn't disturbed them. It would have been more than interesting to make love with Elias Antonides. She touched her tingling lips, thinking how real they felt, how well kissed.

"Killjoy," she muttered to Harvey.

Then she closed her eyes and willed herself back into the dream, curious now. If she could get back to the level where she and Elias were kissing, well, she thought with a smile, she might never want to wake up.

Unfortunately she did.

Her ankle was throbbing. It took her a moment to figure out why. To remember the accident. The ambulance. The hospital. The purple Barney of a cast that felt like a lead weight on her leg. The meeting at the office. That mortifying journey out of the building and the trip home in the taxi with Elias and then him having to go back and get her pain pills for her.

Thank God today was Saturday. She wouldn't have to face him again until Monday.

Wincing, Tallie carefully rolled her aching bruised body over in her bed and stared in horror at the rumpled, stubble-jawed man sound asleep in *Yiayia* Savas's old rocking chair next to her bed.

Oh, dear God.

Tallie squeezed her eyes shut, disbelieving the sight before her eyes, trying desperately to subdue the pounding behind her eye-

lids that seemed to make her hallucinate. But when she opened
them again, he was still there—Elias Antonides!—in her bedroom!

But…that was a dream!

Please, God, it had been a dream!

But even as she thought it, Tallie had a gut-twisting feeling
that it hadn't been a dream at all. Her heart hammered. That was
anxiety. Her head pounded. She felt as if she had the mother of
all hangovers. And that was, she knew, the aftereffects of the pain
medication.

She never should have taken any. The pills worked—good
heavens, yes, she knew they worked. Give her one and she was
blessedly pain free—but they also did a number on her head.

She knew from past experience that they made her hazy,
blurry, loopy, crazy and absolutely irresponsible for anything that
she said or did.

Which was exactly why she'd refused to take any until she
got home. She had known she would need all her wits about her
at the office. She would never have been able to pay attention or
make sense if her brain was buzzing. That was why she'd rung
her parents, too, before Elias had returned with them. She wanted
to sound with it and sensible so they wouldn't come and hover
over her.

So she'd got, what? Elias instead?

Dear God.

A kaleidoscope of more dizzy impressions crowded into her
still-pounding head. She tried to think, to sort, to remember.
He'd brought her the pills she'd left in her briefcase at the office.
He'd brought her pizza. A good satisfying pepperoni pizza with
lots of gooey cheese, not one of those designer pizzas like she
and Martin the Bore—de Boer—had shared, and she'd told him
about Martin and the aphrodisiacs and—

Her face burned as she remembered that conversation.

And then, blessedly, Elias had said he had to leave. But he'd
been determined to wait for the person coming to take care of her.
And she'd had to admit she'd made it up to reassure her mother.

"You mean no one will be here?" he'd demanded.

And when she'd shaken her head, assuring him she'd be fine, he'd snorted and stalked off to the kitchen. She vaguely remembered him cleaning up the pizza and talking on the phone. And then he'd come back and sat down in the chair opposite the sofa.

"Go away," she'd said.

But of course he hadn't listened. He'd picked up a magazine and had started to read. She didn't remember anything more because the bloody little pill had done its trick and she'd fallen asleep on the sofa.

But she wasn't on the sofa now. She was in her bed—in a nightgown she couldn't remember putting on—and a man she remembered dreaming about kissing was no dream at all. He was sound asleep barely a foot away.

Tallie moaned.

Elias jerked. His eyes flicked open. For just an instant he looked as confused as she'd been feeling, but then clarity unclouded his gaze and he pushed himself upright. "You're awake. You need another pill?" He was already heading on autopilot for wherever he'd put them.

"No!" Good God, no! She'd made a big enough idiot of herself already.

At her desperate shout he turned back. "You sure?" He sounded doubtful.

His dark hair was sticking up in spikes. His shirttails hung out. Only three buttons were done up on his shirt and his tie was gone. The stubble on his jaw was even darker than it had been when she'd kissed him—

Remembering that it wasn't a dream, Tallie moaned again.

"I'm getting you a pill," Elias said.

"No! Really. I don't need any pills. I'm…fine." She struggled to push herself up against the headboard of her bed.

Elias moved to help her, then stopped abruptly, jammed his hands in the pockets of his khakis and remained where he was.

Probably afraid he was going to get attacked again. Should she acknowledge what she'd done? Pass it off with a laugh? Or was it better to pretend it had never happened?

Because one look at him told her that, no matter how gorgeous he was and how tempting it would be to kiss him again, Elias had no desire for a repeat performance.

Nor did she! He was the man her father had set his sights on for her. She didn't love him. She was attracted to him—on a purely physical level. And that was all. She loved Brian.

Who was dead, a tiny voice inside her head reminded her.

True. But even so…she did *not* love Elias Antonides! Getting involved with him would be disastrous. It would complicate everything.

And it would make her father even more power-mad than he already was.

So, what was she going to do about the kiss?

Nothing. Elias had to know she hadn't meant it, that if she'd been in her right mind, she'd never have done it. So if she acted as if she didn't remember, they would both be spared some needless embarrassment. And if he should happen to bring it up, she could laugh it off, say she'd been "under the influence."

It was nothing but the truth.

"So," Elias said, "fine. No pills. Can I get you some water?"

"That would be nice." She gave him a polite determinedly distant smile. "Thank you."

He nodded wordlessly and left the room. When he came back with a glass of water, he had his shirt buttoned and neatly tucked in. He'd run his fingers through his hair, and while he hadn't necessarily tamed it, he looked proper and quite as determined to get things back on a businesslike footing as she was.

As it should be, Tallie reminded herself.

She drank the whole glass of water, handed it back, then looked up at him with what she hoped was the proper degree of businesslike equanimity. "It was very kind of you to stay last night."

"Not a problem."

"Still," she insisted, "you didn't have to."

Elias shrugged. "Somebody did."

Tallie was tempted to dispute that. But Elias didn't look as though he was going to give in on that argument. And if she tried, things might be brought up she had no desire to discuss. So she merely inclined her head. "Yes, well, it was above and beyond the call of duty. Thank you."

His mouth twisted briefly and she wondered which "beyond the call of duty" moments he was remembering. But he simply nodded. "You're welcome."

Their gazes met, locked. And the notion that painkillers had been solely responsible was hard to accept.

Abruptly Elias looked away. "So, you're okay today?" he asked briskly, all business. "How's your ankle?"

"It hurts, but I can live with it. No problem." Every muscle in her body ached, in truth. "I'll be fine."

"Right. Well then, I guess I'll take off. He sat down in the rocking chair and yanked on his socks and shoes, then stood up again. "If you decide you need them, your pills are by the sink in the bathroom. Your crutches are here by the bed." He poked them with his toe. "And your cell phone is on the nightstand. Do you want me to get you something to eat before I leave?"

"No, I can get something later."

"Sure?"

"Absolutely. Again, thank you very much."

It was all very polite now. Very businesslike and distant. And awkward as hell because she could remember the sandpapery feel of his jaw against her cheek, could remember the hungry press of his lips. And wanted, heaven help her, to feel them again.

She cleared her throat. "I'll see you Monday."

Elias opened his mouth, started to speak, then closed it again and nodded. "Right. See you Monday. Take care."

The woman was going to be the death of him—or at least of his better intentions!

Elias needed the whole weekend to recover his equilibrium, to stop remembering the taste of Tallie Savas's lips, the softness of her body, the smoothness of her skin.

Well, he did remember. But for odd isolated moments now and then he managed to focus on something else.

It took some effort.

Saturday, as soon as he left Tallie's apartment, he started working on the offices he was renovating. But that gave him far too much time on his own. Way too much opportunity to remember the way he'd spent the night—and how much more he'd wanted to do with Tallie that night.

And even reminding himself that he hadn't wanted to do it because it was *Tallie* and it would have been a huge mistake didn't give him reason enough to forget how much he'd enjoyed her touch, her kiss—*her!*

So he rang Dyson and woke him up. "You still want to show me that boat you're having built?"

A trip out to Long Island to see Dyson's pride and joy had been on the back burner too long. Dyson had invited him to come along to see it half a dozen times. But every time Elias had been too busy.

Now he heard Dyson yawn so loudly his jaw cracked. Then Dyson said, "Yeah. Pick you up in an hour."

They spent the day at the boatyard, which made Elias remember how much he had loved building boats with his grandfather and how sidetracked his life had become. Thinking about the past gave him some respite from memories of Tallie in his arms.

But it also reminded him of other dreams he'd had—of a life split between Santorini and New York, of building boats for a living, of marrying a woman who would love the same things he did and the family they would have together.

It hadn't happened the way he'd imagined. Not any of it.

And the memories of what he'd hoped for and what had actually happened made him surly.

"Not gonna bring you again," Dyson said on the way home. "You been scowling all day long. You look like hell, too. What'd you do last night?"

"Nothing," Elias said, staring out the window at the traffic heading into the city. It was the truth. He hadn't done what he'd wanted to do for a long, long time.

It was his own fault, of course. No one had forced him to do any of it. No one had held a gun to his head and made him marry Millicent. No one had demanded he take over Antonides Marine and abandon his dreams of his own boat-building business.

And no one would have stopped him if he'd made love with Tallie Savas last night—least of all Tallie.

It was his own bloody misguided sense of doing what was right. He needed to get over it, get past it, get a life. If he had a woman, he wouldn't be tempted by the likes of Tallie Savas.

So as soon as Dyson dropped him off, he rang Clarice.

"How about tonight?" he asked her. "I'll leave my phone at home. No mothers. No sisters. No business."

And definitely no Tallie!

"Mais, oui," Clarice said in her honeyed voice. "I would like that."

So would he, Elias promised himself. So would he.

He picked her up just before eight. They had a good meal. Very elegant. Very French. They had some interesting conversation. At least he thought they did. The trouble was, he kept losing his train of thought. His brain kept flashing back to the night before—to the pizza he'd shared with Tallie, to the totally nonsensical conversation they'd had when she hadn't been falling asleep—

"But you see, it is still a problem," Clarice said sadly.

Elias's mind jerked back to the present. "Problem?" What had he missed? "What problem?"

"The business," Clarice explained. "You said there would be no business. And yes, there is no business here. But you think about it—" she tapped the side of her head "—here, anyway."

He could hardly say it wasn't *business* he was thinking about!

His mouth twisted wryly. "I'm sorry. I'm just…distracted. We could go somewhere," he suggested, reaching for her hand across the table. "Do something that would blot business right out of my mind."

He was sure she knew what he meant. But she smiled ruefully and shook her head. "I would invite you back to my place," Clarice said, "but my sister is visiting from Paris."

"So you can come to mine."

Another shake of her head. "Not when my sister is visiting," Clarice said. "I cannot be gone all night."

Elias squeezed her hand. "Another time?"

She gave him a brilliant smile. "But of course."

He took her home and did manage at least to get a kiss before he left her on her doorstep. He told himself it was a start. But it might have been one more mistake, because it made him think about Tallie's kiss. This one was nowhere near as memorable.

No matter, he told himself resolutely as he walked home. He had a woman in his life again—a woman who promised a casual, easy relationship with no demands, no strings, no expectations.

Exactly what he wanted.

Monday brought Tallie in bright and early, as usual. With a Viennese delicacy, as usual. With carrot and celery sticks for him—as usual. She was bouncy and perky and, other than the silly purple cast on her ankle, she looked cheerful and well rested—as if Friday night had never happened at all.

Good. Because he wasn't going to think about it. Or her. He'd had two days to put the matter in perspective. And he had decided on the best course—he would forget it. And other than professionally, where he had no choice, he would ignore her.

Which was easier said than done when she was sitting right across from him at a two-hour meeting and his mind kept flashing back to memories of what it had felt like to tangle his fingers in her wild, untamable hair.

It was pinned and anchored today, of course. Only a few tendrils were escaping, but Elias's fingers clenched into fists as he remembered the silken softness of those tendrils, the vibrant springiness of them, the total temptation of them—

He jerked his thoughts back to the subject at hand. He didn't look at Tallie again. He was tempted. He resisted.

He was almost grateful when Rosie appeared halfway through the meeting to get him to take an urgent call. He was less grateful when it turned out to be Cristina.

"I need to talk to you!"

"Now?"

"You haven't been answering your phone. I've been calling you for days."

"I'm busy." And he'd had no desire to spend his weekend mopping up a series of family disasters. Besides the flood of messages from Cristina, there had been several from Lukas about problems in New Zealand, a half a dozen from Martha demanding that he call her, a surprising message from his brother Peter suggesting that they talk, and, of course, the requisite dinner invitation from his mother who wanted him to meet someone called Augusta, whom she described as his "soul mate." Elias seriously doubted that. Why would he want to answer any of them?

"Too busy for your family?" Cristina demanded.

Yes, damn it. "I'm in a meeting. What do you want?"

There was an infinitesimal pause. Then, "I want you to hire Mark."

"And I want a roast duck to fly over and fall into my mouth. Come on, Cristina. Get real. Not going to happen."

"See," she wailed. "I knew you'd do that. You won't even consider it!"

"No."

"But—"

"No, Cristina. I have to go. People are waiting." He drummed his fingers on Rosie's desk and glared at her for calling him out of the meeting.

"She said it was urgent," Rosie mouthed at him.

"You don't know him!" Cristina waited.

"I do know him," Elias reminded her. "That's the problem."

"But I love him!"

She *loved* Mark Batakis? Ye gods. Elias grimaced, then pinched the bridge of his nose and drew a deep breath. "And your undying love gives him what sort of job qualifications?" he asked politely.

"I don't know!" Cristina's voice wobbled. "But you don't have to be a smart-ass. Mark is no dummy. He can learn anything. He went to Yale after all. And...and he knows a lot about boats."

"He *races* boats, Cristina. Not the same thing."

"But boats are—"

"Cristina," Elias said with all the patience he could muster, "we *don't* race boats. We have nothing to do with racing boats."

"We could," she insisted.

"We could build a rocket ship and fly to the moon, too. But we're not going to."

"Even so. All I'm asking is for you to talk to him," Cristina said tightly.

"And give him a job."

"Well, yes, but—"

"No. Besides," he said with considerable relish, "even if I wanted to, I can't."

"You mean you won't!"

"No, I mean I can't." For the first time Elias felt kindly toward his father's idiotic bet with Socrates Savas. "I'm not the boss anymore."

"What do you mean you're not the boss?" Cristina demanded.

"Didn't you hear? Dad sold forty percent of the business."

"What? Dad *sold*—" His sister sputtered her disbelief.

"Sold," Elias reiterated. "Which makes him no longer president."

"Then you're—"

"No, I'm not," he said with considerable satisfaction. "You want to get your boyfriend a job at Antonides Marine, Cristina, you'll have to talk to the new CEO."

There was a pause, then Cristina said stoutly, "All right. I will. What's his name?"

"*Her* name is Tallie Savas."

It was going to be all right.

Tallie kept telling herself that as she kept trying to convince herself—and Elias—that she had no memory of what had happened that night in her apartment. She had come in today determined to act as if nothing at all had occurred.

And she thought Elias believed it.

He looked at her oddly once or twice, but when she gave no sign, he focused on business.

She wished she could.

She wished she could stop remembering how he had kissed her, how firm and warm his lips had been, how springy his hair was, how rough his stubbled jaw had been, how hot his skin had felt beneath her fingers.

She wished—

She wished a lot of things—mostly that she'd never heard of Antonides Marine, that she had never taken this job, that she had never met Elias Antonides. He made her want the things she had wanted with Brian, things she'd put aside after Brian's death, things she had promised herself she would only want again if another man worthy to step into Brian's shoes came into her life— a man who loved her for herself, who wanted her and not her father's money or his empire.

A man, in short, who was nothing like Elias Antonides!

She knew he didn't want her father's money or his empire. He simply wanted his own empire back! But he didn't want her—not in the way Brian had. He didn't care about her. Only about sex.

She wondered why he'd stopped.

God knew she wouldn't have been able to. She'd been daft enough to think Harvey was her subconscious alter ego, her common sense. Under the influence of painkillers she didn't have the common sense of a cat!

A thought that didn't make her feel any better.

At least spending time watching how her father handled himself in business had taught her that it was wise to give nothing away, to maintain her cool, to appear indifferent and unconcerned at all costs.

So she'd done that. She'd come bearing *apfelstrudel,* had chatted easily with Rosie and Lucy, had endured Dyson's teasing about losing a battle with a truck and had deflected Paul's sympathy for her pain by joking about her "Barney cast."

And she'd smiled politely at Elias. He had smiled politely at her. Sanity prevailed.

All the same she was glad when he had to go out of their meeting briefly to take a phone call. It was easier to concentrate when he wasn't in the room. When he came back, she felt immediately edgy and aware again. She forced herself to concentrate on Paul's charts and diagrams and endless monotonous commentary. She even managed to make a couple of points herself about her concern that Corbett's, while a good business in itself, was perhaps not the direction Antonides wanted to go in.

"Why not?" Elias demanded.

And so she explained her feeling of enervation. "And it's not just me," she said. "No one here is particularly excited about this. No one is champing at the bit to buy in."

"We're taking our time," Elias said, "working out the ramifications. Crunching the numbers."

"Fine," Tallie said. "But you've got to have more than numbers, even if they add up. You've got to want to do this, you've got to want to make seaworthy apparel."

Elias just stared at her as if she was crazy.

"You do," Tallie insisted. "You need passion." And then she remembered another kind of passion they had shared the other night and her face flamed. She could actually *feel* the heat of the blood that rushed to her face. She pressed her lips together and focused on Paul, on Dyson, on anyone or anything but Elias. "I think Corbett's is fine as a business, but maybe not *our* business," she added quickly. "I just don't think any of us wants to commit."

When she finally dared venture a glance in Elias's direction, he was staring at the whiteboard behind Paul, as if he were deliberately not remembering Friday night, too. Thank God.

Finally he looked around the room. No one else said anything either. "Yes? No?" They all looked at each other.

Dyson cleared his throat. "She might be right," he said slowly. "I mean, we've gone back to the drawing board on it how many times?"

"Lots," Paul muttered.

Elias didn't look totally convinced, but he didn't disagree, either. "Okay. I told Corbett we'd let him know," he said, finally allowing his gaze to meet Tallie's. "We can talk about it in the morning." He shoved back his chair and stood up. "Right now Dyson and I are heading out to Long Island."

Tallie felt an enormous sense of relief. So he wasn't going to be in the office all afternoon? Yippee. "What's there?"

"Nikos Costanides's boatyard."

"*The* Nikos Costanides?"

Elias raised his brows. "You know him?"

"Of him." Right around the time she had met Brian, Nikos had been on her father's short list of eligible Greeks. Because of Brian she'd never met him. Just as well because she had never been in Nikos Costanides's league. While she had been dating her Navy pilot, Nikos had been squiring around some of the world's most gorgeous women and being written up in scandal sheets on both sides of the Atlantic.

After Brian's death, when her father was again compiling his list, she learned that Nikos, the wild playboy, had in the meantime married, settled down, had kids and, thus, permanently removed himself from her father's eligible list.

"We went out and looked at the boat he's building for Dyson on the weekend." There was a light in his eyes that Tallie hadn't seen before. "You might be right about the enthusiasm bit," he told her.

"Oh?"

"We'll see. I'll leave my notes for you and we can go over them tomorrow morning, then call Corbett."

Tallie nodded. "That will be fine." Very proper. Very cool. Very businesslike. Whew.

Elias opened the door and she preceded him into the main reception area. A young woman was sitting there, idly flipping through a magazine.

"Nine o'clock? I'll just—" Elias broke off as the woman stood up. He scowled furiously at her. "What the hell are you doing here?"

"Nice to see you again, too, Elias, dear." She gave him a brilliant smile, sashayed toward him and kissed him on the cheek.

She was one of the most gorgeous women Tallie had ever seen. Tall and striking, with short spiky dark hair that had the casual ruffled elegance that only came with a high price tag, and cheekbones you only saw in magazine ads. Everything about her, from her trendy clothes to her perfectly applied makeup added up to make her one stunning young woman—exactly the sort who would attract a man like Elias. Even though he didn't seem especially delighted to see her, there was no denying they made a spectacular couple.

Was she the woman he'd stood up on Friday night?

Tallie vaguely remembered him making a phone call, telling someone he couldn't make something, apologizing. Maybe she'd told him off and they'd had a fight and that was why he was glowering at her now.

"Go home," he said brusquely.

"No. I won't. You said talk to the president!"

Elias's expression darkened. "For God's sake—"

"President?" Tallie frowned.

The young woman's gaze fixed on her, brown eyes alight with curiosity. "Is this—"

"Yes," Elias said through his teeth. "It is. And you can't talk to her now. She's busy."

"She doesn't look busy," the young woman said matter-of-factly. "Are you?" she asked Tallie.

"It's lunchtime," Elias said.

"Then we'll have lunch." She held out her hand to Tallie. Her nails were well shaped and beautifully manicured. Tallie's were short and utilitarian, good for kneading pastry dough. "I'm Cristina."

"Cristina?" Tallie looked to Elias for an explanation.

She got one—short and furious. "My sister!"

CHAPTER SEVEN

TALLIE Savas was having lunch with his sister.

The very thought made the hair on the back of Elias's neck stand straight up. What Cristina, with her big mouth and her ungovernable brain, might do or say to Tallie was horrifying to contemplate. There were plenty of loose-cannon genes in the Antonides family, but Cristina's were the loosest.

He had half a mind not to go to Long Island with Dyson at all. But he could hardly change his mind when Tallie was smiling delightedly and saying she'd *love* to have lunch with Cristina, and his sister was grinning like the Cheshire Cat and waggling her fingers at him and saying not to worry at all, that she knew just the place to take the new president of Antonides Marine.

He shuddered to think. In fact, he expected to spend the entire day distracted by what was happening back in Brooklyn.

But Nikos Costanides was a compelling man.

Elias had never met him before Saturday when Nikos had dropped by the boatyard to pick something up and had found Dyson there showing Elias his new, nearly finished boat. A twenty-two-foot gaff-rigged sailboat, it was every bit as fantastic as Dyson had claimed it would be. And when Nikos, who had only come to pick up some files he'd left at the office, discovered that Elias had a serious boat-building background, he'd invited them back this afternoon. And he was waiting for them when they arrived, eager to show them around.

Costanides Custom Boats was the stuff of Elias's childhood dreams. That it should have apparently been Nikos's dream, too, surprised him. While he hadn't known Nikos, he was acquainted with Stavros Costanides, Nikos's father. The elder Costanides was a friend of his own father. They played golf together now and then. It was always interesting to watch them because Aeolus always tried hard and enjoyed the exercise, and Stavros Costanides was there to win. No more, no less. He was everything Elias's father was not—tough, astute, hard as nails.

Nikos, from everything Elias had been, was a far different story. He was the star of every cautionary tale Elias had ever been told. Stories of Nikos the wild care-for-nothing playboy, bane of his father's existence, were legion and oft repeated.

"You don't be like that Nikos Costanides," his mother had said, shaking her finger at him. "You settle down with a nice girl. You work hard. You take care of business."

God knew he'd tried. He'd done everything the family had ever expected him to—and more. He'd had no choice, of course. Not if Antonides Marine were going to survive. For all the good it had done him.

Nikos, he decided, had got the better deal.

All those years he'd spent avoiding working for his old man— "the only work that matters" according to Stavros Costanides— Nikos had not simply spent squiring beautiful women around. He had been working as hard as his old man, just not for Costanides International. Virtually tossed out on his ear because he wouldn't toe the familial line, Nikos had gone to university in Glasgow to train as a naval architect, then set up a custom boat-building business with a friend in Cornwall.

He'd made a success of his business and of his life—on his own terms.

Elias wished he could have done the same. He'd longed to make his mark the way Nikos had—to build boats the way Nikos had—and then come into the family business when he was ready.

If he were given to envy, Elias could have envied Nikos

Costanides. For his fiscally healthy, financially sound Costanides empire. For his thriving custom-boat business. For his whole life.

Because Nikos had one.

His smiling dark-haired wife, Mari, and his three little stair-step sons came by the boatyard that afternoon on their way home from the dentist.

"I promised them if they were brave we'd come see Daddy," Mari told Elias and Dyson, watching with undisguised adoration as the three little boys clambered all over Nikos who clearly doted on them.

It was the life Elias had once envisioned he would have with Millicent. But when he'd had to drop out of school to take over at Antonides Marine, things had changed. Even then, he'd have been happy to have a child.

"Why not?" he'd said to Millicent. "It will give me someone to work for. It won't be just for the past. It will be for the future."

But Millicent had been horrified. "Bring a child into this chaos? Absolutely not!"

"Chaos?" Elias hadn't seen it that way. He'd seen it as a challenge, a whole hell of a lot of work, to be sure, but also as an opportunity, a way to do something important for his family.

"Everything's about your family," Millicent had complained.

Yes, it was. But she was a part of his family. It wasn't just about his parents and siblings. It was about making a future for her and their children, as well.

But Millicent didn't want anything to do with that. She hadn't, in very short order, wanted anything to do with him.

Antonides Marine, in its faltering state, wasn't the shining company she'd thought it was. So Elias wasn't the man she'd hoped he would be. No matter that he was doing his damnedest to bring it back, to make it work.

She didn't want it. She didn't want him.

She wanted a divorce.

He hadn't believed it when she'd told him. He'd argued passionately that it wasn't too late to work things out. "We can get counseling. We can make it work," he'd told her.

But she'd said no. Just no. She'd left him. Gone to California where her parents lived. And when he'd finally found her again, she'd still refused to come back to him.

"It's too late," she said. She didn't love him anymore. There was someone else.

And she was going to have his child.

His child. She'd been willing to bring a child into that, but not into her marriage to Elias!

The memory still had the power to cut him to the core.

So he didn't think about it. He'd moved on. And for the most part he forgot about it. But sometimes it came back to haunt him—like today when he'd seen Nikos and Mari and their boys.

And last Friday night in Tallie Savas's bedroom.

He shoved the thought away.

They got back into the city shortly before eight. Dyson dropped him off and went to pick up a date and tell her all about his beautiful boat.

Elias went back to the office and did what he did every night. He went to work.

The place was totally quiet. Everyone else had long since gone home. There were half a dozen messages on his desk and another dozen on his answering machine. He ran through them quickly, relieved that none was from Tallie complaining about his idiot sister.

None was from Cristina, either, also a good thing. It meant that Tallie had taken her duties as president seriously and had sent Cristina and her boat-racing, job-seeking boyfriend packing with enough firmness that Cristina now knew that calling him wasn't going to get her anywhere.

Hallelujah.

Instinctively he reached for the phone to call Tallie and thank her, then changed his mind. He wasn't contacting Tallie outside of business hours. But since he had the phone in his hand, he rang one of the sail suppliers in San Diego instead.

All the workaholics on the West Coast were still in their offices. He spent two hours on the phone with one after another. He got a lot of work done.

What else did he have to do with his life?

It was almost ten when he finally quit. The muscles in his neck were knotted. His back ached. He flicked off the light in his office and headed for the door. On his way out, he spied a single piece of Tallie's apple strudel sitting on the plate by the break room.

He hadn't eaten any this morning. It had been a matter of self-control. He wasn't going to be seduced by Tallie Savas in any way, shape or form.

Tonight he was hungry. He hadn't had any dinner. Mari Costanides had invited them to the house for a meal, but they'd declined.

Now he stared at the pastry and his stomach growled, tempted. He glared at it. It wasn't the apple in the Garden of Eden, for heaven's sake! Just a simple piece of pastry. He was making way too much of it.

Screw it, he thought, grabbed the strudel and took a savage bite, then stomped up the stairs.

When he'd bought the old warehouse, it had seemed like a terrific idea—renovate it, use part of it for the Antonides Marine offices, rent out enough of the rest to other businesses to pay the mortgage, and keep a loft apartment for himself upstairs. Very neat, very efficient.

He couldn't get away from work even if he tried.

He unlocked the door to his apartment and pushed it open.

When Elias had started renovations, he'd had great plans for his own space. Working with wood had always reminded him of boyhood days spent working with his grandfather on Santorini. It was as close to doing what he'd always wanted to do as he was ever going to get. So the first thing he'd done, once the walls were up, plastered and painted, was to order the wood and build a bar of quarter-sawn oak between the living room and kitchen. Then he'd built matching oak cabinets and installed them, as well.

The rest of the furnishings—the sofa, armchair, two bar stools and a bed—were utilitarian. But he'd begun to put up a wall of bookshelves when business had demanded more attention again a few months ago.

Five months later a lot of his belongings were still in boxes stacked in the shadows against the walls. Other than the mural of Santorini and the sea that he'd hired his sister Martha to paint on one wall, nothing else had been done.

It wasn't a home. It was a camping spot.

And he wasn't in it alone.

Someone was sitting in the shadows on the sofa. It was a woman—slowly starting to get up.

"Martha?"

"No, it's Tallie." She settled her crutches under her arms and crossed the room into the light.

Elias stared in disbelief. *"Tallie?"*

She put a finger to her lips and almost lost a crutch. "Shh. Not so loud. You'll wake her."

"What?" He stared. "Wake who?"

"Cristina." She tipped her head in the direction of his bedroom. "Your sister."

As if there were another one.

"What the hell is Cristina doing here? Why's she in my bedroom?"

"Shh!" Tallie hissed. "I told you—" she grabbed his arm hard enough to make him wince "—you have to be quiet. You'll wake her up."

"You're damned right I'll wake her up! What's she doing in my apartment? In my bed?"

Tallie didn't answer. She began pulling him into the kitchen— or trying to. She wasn't having much luck with doing anything but banging his shins with her crutches as she made the attempt.

"For God's sake, stop that! All right." He turned her and got her balanced on her crutches again, standing right in front of him. "I'm not shouting. What's going on? Is she sick?"

"No, she's not sick."

"Then what—?"

Tallie looked at him nervously. "It's…complicated. Well—" she balanced on one crutch and shoved a hand through her cloud of dark hair "—maybe it's not that complicated, but…would you like a cup of tea or something?"

"Tea?" He gaped. "What you talking about?"

"Tea is good in crises."

That this was a crisis seemed to go without saying. "I don't have tea."

"You do now," Tallie informed him, nodding at the box on the counter. She turned her back to hobble to the stove and put on a kettle he'd never seen before, either. There were two mugs there, as well. Those he recognized. Obviously already used. As he watched, she opened the door to one of his cupboards and got out another mug.

"Made yourself at home, did you?"

"I didn't think you'd mind," she said, then turned and gave him an arch look, "since you did the same at my place."

Elias scowled, then stuffed his hands in his pockets and rocked back on his heels. "Okay, fine. We'll have a cup of tea. And then you can tell me what the hell is going on and what my bloody sister is doing here."

"Well, that part's easy. She's waiting for Mark."

"Mark?" Elias practically shouted. "What's he coming for?"

Tallie made shushing gestures again. "He's coming to get her. But he's out in Greenport. Or he was. I didn't reach him until seven."

Why she'd bothered to reach him at all was a mystery to Elias. One of many, apparently. He waited until the water boiled and then he picked up the kettle before she could, so she didn't scald herself by trying to stand up on crutches and pour boiling water at the same time.

"Thank you," she said. "It's a little awkward."

"As I'm sure you know. You poured for Cristina, didn't you?"

Tallie looked away. "She was upset. She wasn't feeling well—"

"I thought you said she wasn't sick?"

"Upset and sick are not the same thing. Don't worry. She's going to be fine."

"Terrific," he said sarcastically. Elias picked up the two mugs and jerked his head toward the sofa in the living room. "Come on."

He set the steaming mugs on the packing box he was currently using for a coffee table, then waited until Tallie sat down clumsily on the sofa. For a brief moment he debated picking up his own mug again and going to sit far away from her in the chair. It would be the sane, sensible thing to do.

But sane and sensible had pretty much gone out the door when he'd come in and found Tallie in his apartment. So he deliberately sat down on the sofa and turned toward her. "All right. Let's hear it."

Tallie took a deep breath. "Well, as you know, we went out for lunch. To this place in the East Village Cristina knew. Very funky. New. Trendy. Like her."

"Uh-huh."

"And we got to know each other a bit. I like Cristina. She's very funny, your sister."

"A laugh a minute," Elias said drily.

Tallie shot him a disapproving look. "She thinks you don't like her."

"I love her. She just drives me crazy. She doesn't have a practical bone in her body. She flits from one thing to the next. And she always expects me to fund whatever stupid scheme she's got lined up next."

"Yes, that's what she said." Tallie leaned back against the sofa and wrapped her hands around the mug of tea.

Elias raised his brows. "She did?"

"Yes. But now she has to stop. She's determined to be staid and responsible."

"Cristina? What about Mark?"

"What about him?"

"I thought she was supposed to be telling you how wonderful *he* was."

"Oh, yes. She did. They're both going to be staid and responsible."

"Yeah, right."

"Don't be so cynical. You're not giving her much of a chance!"

"It's not my fault she's an impractical airhead."

"No, of course it's not. It's hers. I mean, she's not really an airhead. She's—" Tallie seemed to grope for the suitable word.

Elias waited, wondering what it would be.

Finally Tallie shrugged helplessly. "An airhead," she admitted, stifling a laugh.

And suddenly Elias felt the tension between his shoulders ease. He smiled wryly but felt an odd sort of relief that someone—even Tallie Savas—actually understood.

"But a sweet airhead," Tallie added quickly.

"A sweet airhead who is in my bed. Why? For that matter how?" He certainly hadn't given Cristina a key.

"She got…upset at lunch. We were talking…she *was* talking," Tallie corrected herself, "and she got a little, um…hysterical."

"Hysterical?" The tension came back with a vengeance.

"Pretty much. So I didn't think I ought to leave her there or send her home by herself. So I brought her with me. But having her in the office didn't seem like a very good idea either—"

Elias could believe that. Cristina's behavior had been every bit as bad as he'd feared.

"I considered taking her to my place. But Rosie said I should just bring her up here. To your place. I didn't even know you lived here," she added. "Rosie said she had a key and she got it for me. So I did. It wasn't Cristina's idea," she added firmly. "She said you'd be furious. But, well—" Tallie shrugged "—I didn't give her any choice."

Elias accepted that. He didn't like it—the Cristina part anyway—but he could deal with it. Once he had the whole story, at least. Which he knew he didn't have yet.

"Go on," he said.

Tallie twisted a lock of her hair around her finger. "I was afraid you'd say that." She smiled wryly. "This is the tricky bit."

Elias felt the tension in his neck tighten further.

"I'm not the one who should be telling you this. I shouldn't be involved at all." She stopped and stared at him, as if she could will him to tell her not to go on.

"But you are. So go on," he said implacably.

"Fine. All right." She took a deep breath. "Cristina's pregnant."

"What!" So, all right, it was a bellow. He couldn't help it.

Tallie strangled her mug. "Please! Hush. You'll wake her up."

"Damn right I will. *Pregnant?* That idiot! What the hell did she do that for?"

"I gather it wasn't, um, planned."

Elias's jaw clenched. "She can't be that stupid." But evidently she could be. He raked a hand through his hair. "I suppose it's Mark's?" He didn't want to think she might not know.

"It's Mark's. No question."

Apparently Cristina had been at pains to make sure Tallie understood that. But knowing it didn't make Elias much happier. He leaped up and paced around the room, raking his fingers through his hair. "The last thing Cristina needs is a boy toy for the father of her child."

"It would probably be better if you didn't mention that to her," Tallie said mildly.

Elias snorted. "It would be better if the child had any other parents on earth!"

"You don't know that," Tallie argued. "Sometimes parenthood is the making of people."

"Didn't do much for my old man," Elias muttered.

He had never in his life commented on the mathematical impossibility of his own conception having occurred after his parents' wedding day. Still, he shouldn't have mentioned it. "Forget I said that," he muttered, feeling disloyal.

"Of course." Tallie nodded and, thank God, didn't pursue it. "They're getting married."

Elias rolled his eyes. "And that's supposed to make me feel better?"

"I don't think it has much to do with your feelings at all," Tallie said frankly. "You're her brother, not her father or the father of her child."

"I'm the bank," Elias said grimly.

"No, you just run the bank. Or you did," she said reflectively.

Elias's brows snapped down. His gaze met hers. "You think you have more to say about this than I do?"

"No." Tallie shook her head. "I don't think either one of us has anything to say about it ultimately. We can be a stumbling block. Or not."

There was a quiet—but distinct—challenge in her words.

Elias mulled them over. He chewed on the inside of his cheek, trying to come to terms with what she had just told him. It rankled a bit that his sister had confided in Tallie when she hadn't been willing to talk to him.

Of course, Cristina might be an airhead, but she did have some instincts of self-preservation, and there was no doubt she knew what he'd say.

But Tallie was right. The child wasn't his. The decisions weren't his. He rubbed the back of his neck. "So when are they getting married?"

Tallie beamed. "I knew you'd be sensible."

Yeah, well, everyone knew that. When in his life hadn't Elias been sensible? It was what he was, while all the rest of his family went crazy around him. He just stared at her in stony silence.

"They're getting married tomorrow."

"Tomorrow?"

"Well, what point is there in waiting?" Tallie asked. She didn't expect him to answer, though. She went right on. "I told Cristina you'd stand up for them."

"You did *what?*" Elias was appalled.

But Tallie flabbergasted him further by continuing, "I knew you'd want to. It's what you do. You love her. And you take care of your family."

The words were simple, but she made them sound like a truth carved in stone. And then, just when he was about to protest, damned if she didn't reach out and take hold of his hand, squeezing it gently, then hanging on.

Elias stared at her, at her dark eyes so wide and intense, pleading with him. Then he dropped his gaze to her hand wrapped around his, her warm soft fingers curving around his hard cold ones.

He couldn't remember the last time anyone had touched him like that—intensely, personally, honestly. It touched not just his hand, but something deep inside him, stirred it, like a stick stirring the ashes of a nearly dead fire, sparking it, creating embers, heat.

He steeled himself against it.

"I know it's not what you want for her," Tallie went on earnestly, still clutching his hand. "She knows that. She said you have 'high expectations.'"

"I don't ask anyone for anything I wouldn't do myself."

"Of course not." Tallie smiled almost gently. "But Cristina doesn't have the same resiliency you do. Most people don't. Most people wouldn't take on saving a family business when they were, what? Twenty-five years old?"

"Twenty-four. But that's not the point."

"It's part of the point. It speaks to your strength, your determination, your love of your family. What you did by staying on at Antonides when my father foisted me off on you speaks of the same thing," she added with a wry little smile.

Elias scowled. "I love that house," he said, then shrugged. "Besides, it's not a big deal. As a president, you're doing all right." However annoying, it was the truth.

Tallie smiled faintly. "Thanks for the vote of confidence. But this isn't about me. Or about you, really. It's about Cristina and Mark and their child. She wants this child. And she wants to marry Mark. She would have liked for it to have happened differently. But sometimes life just…happens."

"Especially to Cristina," Elias said drily.

Tallie's fingers squeezed his lightly. "Especially to Cristina," she echoed with a smile. "But she's determined to make this work. And from what she told me, that's new to her. Isn't it?"

Slowly, reluctantly, Elias nodded. "But who says she will?"

He had wanted his marriage to work, too, but it hadn't. What he'd wanted hadn't mattered at all.

"Who says she won't?" Tallie countered quietly. "Especially if Mark wants it, too. From everything she said, I gather she has always happily, or not so happily, jumped from one thing to another—"

"And one guy to another," Elias added.

"—her whole life. She never felt any commitment to any of them." Tallie's fingers were massaging his gently, warming them. "She feels commitment to Mark. She loves Mark. And their child."

Elias raised his eyes and looked at her wordlessly. What was there to say? That he didn't believe it? He didn't. But what did he know?

He certainly hadn't known Millicent. If you didn't even know about your own wife or your own marriage—

It was true, what Tallie said about Cristina's lack of previous commitment. She had always had the staying power of a fruit fly. But who knew what anyone else felt, what anyone else was capable of?

"What the hell are my folks going to say?"

"Very little if you support her decision," Tallie predicted. "They'll be upset that she got married so quickly and without them there."

"What do you mean, without them there?"

"Cristina says she doesn't want them there under the circumstances. She says that she and your mother would just battle their way through all the preparations and drive each other crazy and it would be awful. But if it is a done deal—and you support them—then your mother will be fine. Cristina wants it to be fine."

Odd as it seemed, when he thought about it, Elias knew his sister was right. She had their parents pegged. Maybe she did know what she was doing.

"Well, they can't get married tomorrow," he said. "It takes longer than that to get a license, arrange a wedding."

"Mark has already done it."

"How?"

"No idea. When they talked on the phone, Mark said he'd arrange it, and he has. He called a couple of hours ago to say it was all set up for two o'clock tomorrow afternoon in some judge's chambers in Manhattan."

"We have a meeting with Corbett tomorrow at two."

Tallie just looked at him. "Elias." There was gentle reproach tone in her voice.

His mouth twisted, but before he could say anything else, the door buzzer sounded.

"Mark," Tallie predicted.

Elias's hand turned into a fist. "I'd like to punch his lights out."

Tallie curved her fingers around his fist. "I know." She gave it a gentle, knowing squeeze, then she let go of his hand and struggled to get to her feet. "But you won't," she concluded with more confidence in him than he had himself.

"I—"

"You answer the door. I'll wake Cristina."

The buzzer sounded again, short, sharp, impatient.

Elias gritted his teeth and stalked toward the door.

Mark Batakis looked very much as if he expected the punch Elias so desperately wanted to throw. An inch or so shorter than Elias, he was stockier, with dark hair and a nose that had obviously been punched in the past—though not, Elias hoped, for the same reason he wanted to.

"Go ahead," Mark said, reading his body language if not his mind. He thrust out his chin. "Hit me. Do whatever you want, but it isn't going to change anything. I'm still marrying your sister."

"So I hear." Elias stood aside and let the other man enter, then shut the door with a decided click. "So I'll save it—and give it to you later if you ever dare to hurt her."

Mark looked surprised at the reprieve, but no less determined. "I won't hurt her. I love her. Where is she?" He was looking around the dimly lit room with increasing apprehension. "Tina! Tina! What have you done to her?"

"*I*—" Elias's voice was icy "—haven't done anything to her."

The door to the bedroom flew open. "Here I am!" And Cristina ran tearfully into Mark's arms, which folded protectively around her. High drama all around. Elias winced, remembering how Millicent had hated the emotional intensity of Antonides family life.

She'd always found Cristina's outbursts annoying, his father's jovial backslapping irritating, his mother's hugs stifling.

"I'm just not like that, Elias," she'd said more than once. "It's uncomfortable."

But Tallie didn't seem uncomfortable. She went right up to the tearful couple and held out her hand to Mark. "I'm Tallie Savas. I spoke with you earlier. I'm glad to meet you."

And Tallie's matter-of-factness seemed to spark an answering chord in his loony sister. As Elias watched, dumbfounded, Cristina dried her tears and mustered the social skills that their mother had despaired of ever teaching her, introducing Tallie to Mark and vice versa.

She even told Mark how wonderful Tallie had been to her— to them, she corrected herself, giving Tallie a watery smile. Mark heartily agreed, shaking Tallie's hand, thanking her profusely.

"Don't thank me," Tallie said. "I was just doing what Elias would have done if he'd been here."

While none of them believed this for a minute, they were all apparently—even Cristina—on their best behavior and too polite to say so. In the awkward silence that followed Tallie's announcement, however, Cristina took Mark's hand and drew him over to where they could stand facing Elias together.

"I know you knew each other at Yale," she said. "And I know you might not have been friends. But this is different. This is family. This is my brother," she said to Mark, her voice a little wavery but determined. She swallowed, then turned an equally determined look on Elias. "Elias, I want you to meet—and welcome—Mark. My fiancé." There was more than a little defiance in her tone.

Before Elias could do more than grit his teeth, he felt something brush against his shirtsleeve and realized that Tallie had come to stand next to him. For moral support or to step on his foot if he misspoke? Probably the latter.

No matter. No one had ever done it before. He let out a deep breath and stuck out his hand to shake Mark's.

"Congratulations," he said, his voice a little rough.

Mark blinked his surprise, then a grin spread across his face and he gave Elias's hand a strong firm shake. "Thanks. You don't have to worry. I'll take care of your sister," he vowed. "And our child. All our children," he added. "I mean that."

All? Good God. There were going to be more? Elias suppressed a shudder at the thought of a horde of little Cristinas. But she was looking at him with such teary-eyed happiness that he managed an answering smile.

"See that you do," he said evenly to Mark, "and there will never be any problem."

"I'm sure he will." Tallie's voice was firm and cheerful, defusing the gunfighters-at-noon feel to the moment. "Why don't you tell Elias what the plans are so he can arrange to meet you tomorrow?" she suggested to Mark.

Briefly Mark did. What it amounted to was that Elias was expected to wear a dark suit, show up at the judge's chambers, witness the deed and sign the paper afterward. In other words, not a lot.

"And this is all right with you?" Elias asked his sister doubtfully. As weddings went, this was so spare it bore no resemblance to those she'd prattled on about in her girlish dreams.

But Cristina just nodded her head. "It's fine."

"And the parents?"

She bit her lip. "If they would come and not try to argue or run things or make me cry, I would ask them to be there," she said, meeting his gaze. "You know they won't."

Elias nodded. "All right," he said. "I'll be there tomorrow a little before two."

Cristina threw her arms around him and pressed a kiss to his cheek. "Oh, I love you, Elias. You're the best brother in the whole world."

"I'm glad you finally realize that," he said drily. Then because, damn it, he did care, he gave her a hard squeeze in return, then let her loose and said gruffly, "Go home, Cristina."

Giggling she gave his cheek another kiss. "I will. Don't be a grouch, Eli. Someday I hope you're as happy as I am."

"God forbid."

"You will be," she prophesied. "Just because that witch—"

"Cristina," he said sharply, "go home."

"I'm going," she said. Then, smiling, she hooked her arm in Mark's. "Let's go, darling." Then she turned back to Tallie. "Thank you, Tallie, for everything. You are the best."

"I'm glad you think so."

Mark looped an arm protectively around Cristina, opened the door, then stopped and looked back at Tallie. "Can we give you a lift home?"

"I—"

"I'll see that she gets home," Elias cut in.

Cristina's eyes got wide and round as dinner plates as she looked from him to Tallie and back again, then opened her mouth to stick her foot in it.

"Good night, Cristina," Elias said firmly before she could. "I'll see you tomorrow for your wedding." There was a finality to his tone that even his clueless sister seemed to recognize.

She nodded and blinked rapidly, her mascara sliding further down her cheeks as she smiled tremulously. "Good night. Thank you. Thank you both."

Then at last the door shut behind them.

And there was suddenly such complete silence that Elias thought he could hear his heart beat. Or maybe that was Tallie's.

She was still standing right next to him, close enough that their arms brushed. Close enough for him to make just a half turn to his left to come nearly mouth to nose with her. Close enough to remember all too vividly what it had felt like to be this close…to be even closer. To touch her lips with his.

And all thoughts he'd been trying not to think since Friday night came back with a vengeance as Tallie seemed almost to sway toward him.

It was the crutches, of course. She had no balance. But God, she had beautiful lips. Kissable lips.

Desperately he cleared his throat, tried to find his voice—and his equilibrium. "Thank you… for…for taking care of Cristina." He tried to sound calm and collected. He sounded rusty and out of breath.

"I was glad to do it." There was a huskiness in her voice, as well. Their gazes locked.

It was just like last Friday—only worse. Because this time there were no pain killers involved. There was no baklava.

There was only desire.

It was insane. A mistake. A very bad idea. All of the above.

He should put her in a taxi and see her home, because Tallie Savas was a complication he didn't need in his life. He knew that. If it wasn't smart, it wasn't sensible, it wasn't in the best interests of Antonides Marine or the Antonides family, Elias didn't do it.

For the first time in his adult life Elias didn't give a damn about Antonides Marine or the rest of the Antonides family. He didn't give a damn about being sane and sensible.

Just once…just one damn time, he was going to live for the moment, in the moment.

"To hell with it," he muttered.

He took Tallie's crutches and tossed them aside.

"Elias!"

He shook his head and wrapped his arms around her, drew her close, reveling in the slender curves and softness that seemed to fit so well against him. And then he bent his head and kissed Tallie Savas for all he was worth. His lips found hers and they melted together.

CHAPTER EIGHT

IT DIDN'T stop at kissing.

Tallie was glad about that.

She told herself she would regret it someday. But even as she tried to form those negative words in her head, she was on her way to the bedroom in Elias's arms, and what her mind was really saying was, "Yes, yes, yes."

Or were those her lips?

No, they were busy nuzzling his neck, kissing his jawline, learning the feel of the rough stubble one way and the silky softness the other. And then he was bending to lay her on his bed. She settled in, snuggled down, raised her hands toward him.

But he didn't drop down beside her. Instead Elias braced himself, hands on the duvet on either side of her arms, and looked down at her, his eyes hooded, his handsome face taut.

"This isn't sensible," he muttered.

Tallie shook her head. "No."

It was possibly the most senseless thing she'd done in her life. He was not Brian. He didn't love her the way Brian had. But this wasn't about love.

It was about coming back to life—feeling something again, wanting something...*someone*—again.

Just that.

She knew he felt the same way. She knew more about his demons now. This afternoon at lunch Cristina had explained why Elias was going to be so upset with her marrying Mark.

"He thinks marriages don't work. He was married," she'd gone on to explain, "to the world's biggest bitch. We called her 'the ice maiden.' She was grasping and demanding and she hated all of us. She wanted Elias—and Antonides Marine. And when it turned out the company had problems and Elias had to spend most of his life fixing them, she walked out!"

Cristina's eyes had flashed with anger. "He doesn't trust anyone now. He doesn't believe in happy endings. He doesn't believe in love."

Tallie believed in love. She'd had it with Brian. She didn't expect to ever have it like that again. She'd been in her own "ice chest" since his death.

But just recently the ice had begun to thaw. Not the emotional ice that held her heart. But the physical ice. At least her hormones were alive and well—and attracted to Elias. His looks, of course, were memorable. His body was hard and muscular. He was one gorgeous specimen of manhood.

But it was more than his looks or his physical attributes that attracted her. It was his energy, his determination, his dynamism. And his kindness to his family. How often had she seen him stop his work to deal with a family problem. He'd done it again today with Cristina.

And on Friday, taking her home, staying all night, nobly refusing what she had so eagerly offered, he had been kind to her.

Elias Antonides was a good man. And he came in a package that was, on every level, too tempting to resist.

She'd tried. God knew she'd done everything she could. She'd turned her back. She'd walked away. She'd dated Martin.

Suddenly she laughed. Her father had always told her never to turn her back on her problems. "It doesn't work," he said. "They always come back and bite you on the ass."

Elias had been nibbling her jaw, her neck her shoulders. Was he working his way south?

"Something funny?" he growled, lifting his head and noting her smile. His face was taut, his body was hard. She could feel tremors running through him where her hands pressed against his back.

"A little. I was thinking of something my father always said."

"Your father?" Elias pulled back abruptly. His eyes were glazed and he looked somewhere between pleasure and pain. But he was clearly aghast at the direction of her thoughts. A muscle jumped in his jaw. "You're thinking about *your father?*"

Tallie kissed the spot where the muscle was twitching. "Just for a moment." And while she often told her father when his advice was particularly apropos, she didn't think she'd mention this instance.

"Forget him," she muttered. And before Elias could pull back completely, she pulled Elias's head down and began kissing him again.

He resisted for only a moment, and then he came down beside her, as hungry and desperate and eager as she was. And Tallie welcomed him with open arms. She fumbled with the buttons of his shirt, wanting desperately to get her hands inside it, to run her fingers over his hot skin.

He didn't bother with her buttons, just tugged her top out of her trousers and slid his hands up under it. His fingers were calused, slightly rough. Working-man's hands. She'd noticed it before and had wondered how a man who ran a business got work-roughened hands.

Cristina had explained that he'd done most of the renovations on the building and all of them in his apartment. He had made those beautiful cabinets in the kitchen, that stunning bar between it and the living room.

He had talented hands. Good with wood—and good with her. They felt wonderful, made her skin tingle wherever they touched. Made her shiver with longing to have them touch her more.

She got his shirt undone, and he levered himself up enough to strip it off, then reached down and peeled hers off as well. Then he bent his head and began kissing her bare shoulders, her breasts, and Tallie shivered.

"Are you cold?" Elias's voice was muffled against her.

She shook her head. "Burning." She threaded her hands through his thick hair, then slid them down across his shoulders and traced the line of his spine. His back was smooth and hard with muscles. She spread her palms against them, kissed his shoulders, his jaw, his chin.

And then once more he captured her mouth with his and rolled her over so she lay on top of him. Deftly he reached behind her and unhooked her bra. And as it fell away, he cupped her breasts in his hands, lifted his head and kissed each one in turn, laved it softly with his tongue, made her shiver and grip his shoulders, tense with longing for him.

"Elias!" His name hissed between her teeth.

He lay back against the pillow and smiled up at her, watching her beneath hooded lids all the while that his fingers tracing patterns lightly on her sensitive skin, swirling over her breasts and down across her abdomen.

Mesmerized, Tallie held perfectly still, savoring the feel of them, their soft rough touch gliding over her skin, leaving fiery trails of longing in their wake. The fire built, grew hotter and more intense. And then he flicked open the button to her slacks and drew her zip down.

As his hands parted the fabric, instinctively Tallie rose up on her knees. He pushed the trousers down on her hips, then slid his fingers inside to delve beneath her silky panties and found her hot and wet and wanting. He touched her there.

A breath hissed through Tallie's teeth. She bit her lip and pressed against his questing fingers, whimpering as he stroked and rubbed and lifted his head to kiss her breasts, to take first one nipple and then the other in his mouth until she couldn't resist. Her body tensed and trembled, desperate, needy, aching.

It had been so long.

And yet she wasn't ready, resisted taking the release he offered. No! Not now. Not yet.

Deliberately she rolled to his side, but not away, wanting more—wanting him—and determined that, hungry as they were they were nowhere close to finished yet. He had made her burn for him. Now it was her turn.

She pressed kisses to his arm, to his shoulder, then raised up on one elbow to lean over and kiss his chest. He watched her, his dark eyes hooded, skin taut across his cheekbones. She smiled and drew squiggles over his chest with her fingers and lazy circles with her tongue. The breath hissed out between his teeth, and he tensed beneath her touch as she had under his.

"Tallie," he muttered, his fingers knotting in the duvet.

"Mmm? Want something?"

"You."

"You've got me." Lifting her head, she looked into his eyes and smiled. His own smile was strained, his breathing shallow. She stopped tracing with her fingers and walked them slowly down his chest and his hard belly to his belt. She undid it, then eased down the zip and bent her head to kiss the line of dark hair that disappeared beneath his boxers.

Elias jerked at the touch of her mouth. "Tallie!"

She didn't answer, just moved her head back and forth, brushing her hair against his belly. Then she slipped her hand beneath the elastic and felt hot, hard, straining flesh meet her fingers there. She curved her fingers around him, weighed and stroked his length. His hips arched. A sharp breath hissed between his lips. "Stop! Just…wait."

Tallie waited. She bent her head and kissed him lightly on the chest, then smoothed her hand up his body to feel his heart hammering beneath her fingers. Hammering for her. Wanting her.

Wordlessly Elias reached up and grasped her fingers and drew them to his lips, kissed them one after another, nibbled them, tasted them, heated her blood all over again.

And then he pulled her down against him and rolled them over. And somehow they managed to shed the rest of their clothes, no mean trick as it entailed getting her slacks down over her cast. But Elias did it. He was gentle but efficient as he worked her trouser leg down over the cast.

"Amazing. You're good at everything," Tallie murmured.

He grinned crookedly. "Glad you think so," he said, his voice ragged. And then he pressed a kiss to her knee above the cast and then to her toes as he slid the trouser leg over them. It nearly undid her.

And then he was sheathing himself to protect her, and she smiled again because it was so like Elias to, without a word, take the responsibility.

He caught her gaze. "What?"

She shook her head and held out her arms to him. And he came to her, settling between her thighs, eager now, pressing against her.

And Tallie reached for him, drew him down and in. It was as close as two people could be. And when he began to move, instinctively she moved with him, dug her fingers into his back, urged him closer, deeper, harder. Until he shattered and she shattered with him. And they were no longer separate.

They were one.

She hadn't expected that. That was how she had felt with Brian—as if their bodies, their hearts, their souls had merged.

She had been so lonely, so empty without him. And yet she'd grown accustomed to it, had—over the years—even taken refuge in her loneliness. It was safer than loving. Safer than caring.

She was very much afraid she was beginning to care about Elias Antonides.

And that wasn't safe—or sensible—at all.

It hadn't done the trick.

He'd made love with Tallie Savas to get her out of his system. To stop thinking about her. To stop closing his eyes and seeing her even then. To stop *wanting* her every minute of the day....

And within moments of having had her—of having been *inside* her—he had wanted to be there again.

They'd rested, they'd murmured, they'd touched, they'd stroked. And then he'd had her again. And she'd had him.

And still it hadn't been enough.

Making love with Tallie hadn't assuaged his desire. It had heightened it. Sharing intimacies with her had only whetted his appetite for more. He wanted to make her crazy. He wanted to feel her body respond to his. He wanted to feel her nails digging into his flesh as her body climaxed and shuddered beneath him. He wanted her over him, riding him. He wanted to wrap his fingers in her hair and bury his face against her neck and slide right back into the closest he'd ever felt to being whole.

And at the same time he wanted to run a million miles!

Tallie Savas was not for him.

He told himself that over and over all night long. Beyond their reluctant temporary partnership in Antonides Marine—a partnership of necessity—she didn't want a relationship. She was all about business. And so was he.

What the hell was the matter with him?

He'd gone to bed with a fair number of women since Millicent had left, and he'd *never* thought in terms of the future with any of them. The word *relationship* had never entered his mind. While he had always enjoyed the experience, he'd never lain beside a woman and wondered where things were going from here.

Not the way he lay next to Tallie now, wide-awake and staring at the ceiling while she slept soundly and, he hoped, satisfied, in his arms.

That should be enough. They had been attracted, yes. They'd felt an itch and they'd scratched it—very successfully, he reflected. Making love with Tallie Savas had been an exciting mix of give and take, of gentleness and passion. It had been beautiful and mind-blowing all at once.

He'd never experienced anything like it.

Which was probably why he wanted more. More lovemaking; that went without saying. The itch was very definitely still there. But so was this irritating niggling demand for something else. He wanted more…*more*…even as he knew it was a mistake.

It was all Nikos Costanides's fault, he decided.

Seeing Nikos and Mari together, happy, fulfilled, loving had reawakened all those long-buried memories. They had made him want the things he used to want—the things he thought he'd have by now with Millicent.

And because he was physically attracted to Tallie, those longings had simply attached themselves to her.

It was all very logical when he thought about it.

No matter that she was exactly the wrong woman. No matter that he didn't want any woman for more than a night. No matter, no matter, no matter.

Damn it to hell.

It was Cristina's fault, too. While he was passing around blame, she deserved her share. He was going to have to stand there and watch her get married in scant hours. To Mark Batakis, of all people, who raced fast boats, fought at the drop of a hat, could drink his entire college under the table, and had, conservatively, fifty girlfriends during their college years.

But Cristina loved him. And he said he loved her. So that made it all right. Elias snorted derisively.

What the hell did either one of them know about love? If you loved, you left yourself open for being gutted the way he'd been gutted by Millicent. You had hopes and dreams that depended on another person. And they let you down.

There were no numbers to crunch, no balance sheets to check, no projections to consider. There was nothing sensible to base it on. Nothing logical. It was all emotion and desire and *love*. They were idiots!

Tallie must have sensed his unrest, for she turned toward him in her sleep and nestled closer, her lips brushing his bare chest, the fresh scent of her shampoo teasing his nose. It drove him insane with wanting.

But it wasn't love, he assured himself. It was attraction. Lust. Animal passion. A release they had both needed because they had worked so hard, been so consumed with work, with sorting out what to do about Corbett's, with Cristina's little bombshell.

He was sure that was the way Tallie saw it. She certainly wasn't lying awake anguishing over what they'd done, was she?

Of course not.

But he was. And if he didn't get up and get out he was very much afraid he might wake her and do it all over again.

Carefully Elias eased himself out of bed. It was nearly seven. He could shave and shower and be dressed by the time she woke up. It would be easier to be distant and properly businesslike that way.

It was harder, though, than he imagined. *He* was harder. As he stood beneath the shower, he kept remembering his hands on her and hers on him, and he was tempted to go out and wake her, to bring her with him into the shower where he could touch her all over again and—

Damn, didn't this water get any colder?

His teeth were chattering by the time he had shaved and dressed and combed his hair. But at least he had his self-control firmly in place again.

Then he opened the door and confronted the sight of a rumpled and completely bare—except for her purple cast—Tallie easing herself into one of his shirts.

So much for self-control.

So much for cold showers. He'd need a glacier to get over this!

"Oh, good morning." Tallie flashed him a quick smile and continued to do up the buttons. The eager lover she'd been in bed was the breezy CEO now, even wearing his shirt.

"Morning." He hoped his voice wasn't as ragged as it sounded to his own ears.

"Hope you don't mind about the shirt. I just need something to wear until I've washed. I don't suppose you have a hair dryer?" She was talking quickly, papering over the awkwardness, apparently not about to do a postmortem—or postcoital—of the night before.

Not that he wanted to, but—one of the reasons for keeping business and pleasure separate, obviously.

He shook his head. "No hair dryer."

"Can't shower unless I can dry the cast with one," Tallie said ruefully. "How about a washer and dryer?"

"I've got a laundry room off the kitchen."

"Great. Could I throw my stuff in?"

"I'll do it." Much better than standing there looking at her wearing his shirt, wanting to rip it off her and take her back to bed. Swiftly Elias gathered up her clothes—and his—and bolted for the door. He had the laundry going and had just finished making coffee when she came into the kitchen. The shirt hit her above midthigh. He knew what was beneath it.

He cleared his throat. "Cup of coffee?"

"Please."

He poured two. "Bacon? Eggs? Toast? Oatmeal?" He didn't look at her again. A man could only stand so much temptation.

But Tallie was completely blasé. "Toast," she decided. He heard the clatter as she leaned her crutches against the bar, then one of the stools moved as she sat up on it. "Thanks," she said when he set a mug in front of her. "You have a great place here."

He put the bread in the toaster. "I'm working on it."

"Cristina told me. I had no idea you were doing all the work not just here, but in the whole building. I didn't even know you owned it."

He shrugged. "It was a good investment. And I haven't done all of it. I've hired out the wiring and stuff. I do the dirty work—and the wood."

"So you did all this?" She was looking at the kitchen cabinets and running her fingers appreciatively over the bar.

Elias tried not to remember what else her fingers had rubbed over. "I did all the woodwork."

"Then why are you wasting your time at Antonides Marine?"

He frowned and looked at her for the first time since she'd come into the room. "What?"

"I'm sorry. It's not a waste, I guess. It's just…this is beautiful. Way more beautiful than mergers and acquisitions." She stroked the gleaming wood again. "And you obviously love doing it." She smiled, understanding him.

He didn't want her understanding him. It undermined his resolve to keep this casual. He shrugged dismissively. "No time." Besides, he enjoyed the business, too, though admittedly—to himself at least—not as much as he'd enjoyed building boats. Not as much as he still enjoyed working with wood. The toast popped up. He put it on plates and got out butter and jam. "Besides, you can't make a living at it. Here. Help yourself."

Tallie buttered her toast, but she pressed on. "I'll bet you could," she argued. "Lots of people would kill to have something this beautiful in their home."

"Kill, maybe. Pay for? Not likely." Elias shook his head. But they paid Nikos—and paid him well, a little voice inside his head piped up. He shut it down. "It's just a hobby. I have more important things to do."

"Antonides Marine." Tallie said.

"That's right. And don't suggest I leave it all to you," he said sharply, unsure why the conversation made him feel edgier and more exposed than he'd felt naked in bed with her. It was easier to pick a fight with her.

But Tallie didn't oblige him. "You can't, can you?" she pointed out mildly. "Not if you want your house back."

Exactly. It all came back to the house. Last night's intimacy was simply a byproduct of a bloody business deal.

"That's right," he said gruffly. "And I ought to get to it right now." He shot back the cuff of his shirt to glance at his watch. "It's nearly eight. The wash is in there." He jerked his head toward the door to a small utility room off the kitchen. "It should be done in a few minutes. You can put it in the dryer."

He took one last swallow of coffee and felt it churn in his stomach as he set the mug on the counter and then brushed past Tallie to head for the door.

"I didn't intend to be rude, Elias," she said to his back.

He stopped at the door and turned, meeting her gaze, trying to focus on her eyes and not on her delectable body clad only in his shirt. He tried, too, to forget last night and remember that today was all about business. *They* were all about business. "I know that."

"Good." She paused. "And…about last night—" She stopped. He waited. Didn't breathe.

The colour rose in her cheeks. "It was…um…nice."

"Nice?" He stared at her. *Nice?*

"More than nice," she amended, deeply flushed now, agitated, too. She was strangling her toast. "Thank you."

Christ! What was he supposed to say to that? *Thank you, too?*

"Yeah." He gave a jerky nod. His teeth clenched. He had to consciously relax his jaw, then take a breath and let it out. "Take your time," he said at last. "We can have our meeting about Corbett's whenever you get there."

She flashed him a quick smile. "Thanks. Could you tell Mark I'll be a little late."

"Mark?"

Tallie rolled her eyes. "Your soon-to-be-brother-in-law, Mark."

"I thought the wedding wasn't until two."

"It isn't. So there's no reason he can't work until noon."

"What?" Elias gaped at her, disbelieving his own ears. "You didn't."

Tallie just shrugged happily. "Yes, I did. I hired him."

When she finally got her clothes clean and dried and made it into the office it was half past nine. She could have been a few minutes earlier, but she'd taken a side trip to buy bagels from the shop down the street.

"I was a little busy last night," she apologized to Rosie and Dyson, and hoped her blushes wouldn't betray her and that no one would remember she was wearing the same silk shirt and black trousers she'd had on yesterday—except for the bright pink scarf knotted at her neck. She'd just bought it from the street vendor in front to the bagel shop.

"You don't have to bring something every day," Rosie said even as she peered in the bag. "It's not like we expect it."

"Of course not," Dyson assured her, helping himself to a bagel, slicing it in half and slathering it with cream cheese. "However—" he took an enormous bite, chewed and swallowed, then grinned at her "—it's fine with me if you do."

Tallie grinned, too, then looked around. "Where's Paul?" which wasn't what she wanted to ask, but asking, "Where's Elias? Has he killed Mark yet?" didn't seem like the best question.

In fact, the door was closed to Elias's office and she didn't hear any shouting, which she hoped was a good thing.

Rosie said, "They went to meet a publicist."

Tallie's brows went up. "Publicist?"

Rosie nodded. "Someone Mark knew from his races. Said he thought the guy could do an ad campaign for the pleasure-craft line."

"Really?" It was better than she'd dared hope. After she'd told Elias she'd hired Mark, she'd tried to explain her reasoning.

"Having him work for the company, as long as he's willing, will give Cristina the sense that you accept him, that you have faith in him."

"I'm letting her marry him, damn it!" Elias had snarled.

Not that he could have stopped her, Tallie thought. But she forwent to pointing this out. She'd just nodded. "But this way you show you have confidence in him."

"And not that I just want to keep an eye on him?" Elias raised a brow.

Tallie had smiled. "Well, that, too," she agreed. "But he has things to offer. He's a racer. A proven winner."

"A playboy."

"A man who's attractive to women," she'd corrected.

"Who's marrying my sister," Elias retorted through his teeth.

"Who is in love and wants to spend the rest of his life with one woman. It's very romantic," Tallie revised.

Elias had given her a hard look.

"Look, we have a speedboat division in the pleasure-craft side. It's basic, not the luxury stuff your dad was doing. But it's there. And it's pretty stagnant from what I can see. It can be developed. It *should* be developed. Mark's handsome. Charming—"

Elias had contributed a couple more unprintable adjectives or two which Tallie determinedly ignored.

"—and he could be an excellent spokesman. It's worth considering."

He had grunted and left, unconvinced.

But apparently, against all odds, Mark had convinced him. It was cause for hope. And Elias not being there made it easier to get through the morning.

She wasn't used to waking up in mens' apartments. For that

matter, she wasn't used to going to bed with them. She hadn't made love with anyone but Brian. She'd almost resigned herself to never sleeping with anyone again.

And now she had.

With Elias Antonides of all people.

Undoubtedly a colossal mistake. She'd mixed business and pleasure. She'd slept with a man who clearly didn't want a relationship. And even knowing that, she knew she would do it again.

Was this how affairs started?

Tallie had never seen herself as the sort who had affairs. But probably, she thought honestly, most women didn't. They found themselves in situations and they *responded*. The way she had responded to Elias last night. The way she would probably respond if he walked into her office right now.

So it was a shock when there was a brisk rap on the door and before she could do more than look up a black-haired pirate strode in.

"Theo?" She stared, astonished and then delighted at the sight of her oldest brother. "Theo!" She leapt out of her chair, forgetting her cast, and nearly fell over the desk. Righting herself she waited for him to come to her. "What are you doing here?"

It had been months since she'd seen him. Theo Savas was as footloose as their father was tied down.

He kicked the door shut and crossed the room to haul her into his arms and give her a hug. "On my way to Newport. Testing a new boat there. Sailing her to Spain if I decide she's good. I called the old man from the airport but he was out wheeling and dealing, so I asked for you. Figured you might have finally wormed your way into the company."

"Not quite." Tallie smiled ruefully and shook her head.

"His secretary told me you were here." Theo frowned. "What the hell are you doing here of all places?" Then he glanced down, spotted her cast and demanded, "And what have you done to yourself now?"

"Lost a crosswalk to a truck?"

Theo looked at her, appalled. "You could have been killed!" It jolted how much he sounded like Elias.

"Well, I wasn't. Come sit down. I'll get some coffee. Tell me what you're doing here. You hate the city."

She would have gone down the hall, but Theo picked up her phone and asked Rosie to please bring some in. Then he hung up and caught the surprise on Tallie's face, and shrugged. "It's her job. She works for you," he said.

"I know that, but—when did you get so corporate?"

Theo grinned. "I can delegate when I have to. I don't haul all those sails myself." He waited for her to sit down, then dropped into one of the chairs and regarded the skyscrapers of Manhattan across the river. "Hell of a view, Tal."

"I owe it all to you."

"Me?" He raised a quizzical brow.

"My job. You won a boat race," she reminded him, "against Aeolus Antonides. For which you won a house…for the moment, anyway, and I got to be president of Antonides Marine."

"The son of a gun got you a presidency?" Theo shook his head, amazed. Then his mouth twisted. "Well, something good came out of it, anyway."

"You won the race," Tallie reminded him.

"Yeah."

She expected him to grin, relishing his triumph. But he just looked grim.

"Something wrong with that?" she asked. She was used to Theo looking a bit ragged and tired. The sea and the sun did that to a man. But she could see now that he looked agitated, too.

"Should've thrown it," he said unexpectedly. "Wish I'd never seen the damn thing."

"What thing?"

"The house on Santorini."

Tallie's eyes widened. "You've been there?"

Theo raked a hand through unruly black hair. "Yeah."

"I, um, thought it was supposed to be beautiful. Elias, the managing director, Elias Antonides," she clarified, doing her best to sound professional, "says his family is very fond of it."

"They are." Theo's voice was grim. He stood abruptly and began pacing the confines of her office like a panther trapped in a suitcase.

Tallie watched, fascinated. Theo was, except when it came to sailing, the most easygoing of men. She'd never seen anything ruffle Theo—not even her overbearing father—but something was definitely ruffling Theo now.

There was a tap on the door and Rosie appeared with coffee and bagels. She set the tray on the desk. And while she was doing it, she took a long and appreciative look at Theo. All women did.

And ordinarily Theo returned the compliment. Today, though, Theo just scowled out the window, not paying the least bit of attention. Rosie sighed and left, shutting the door behind her.

Tallie went back to the subject at hand. "What's wrong with the house?"

"Not what," Theo snapped. "Who!"

"Like there's a ghost in it?"

"Don't be an idiot!" Theo cracked his knuckles. "There's no ghost. There's a girl."

"You mean, like, a little girl?"

Maybe the housekeeper had a pesky daughter. Tallie could envision—remotely—a five-year-old would be impervious to Theo's charms. But it wouldn't last. And she didn't imagine a five-year-old would be living there alone.

Theo glared. "No, I don't mean a little girl."

"Well then," Tallie grinned, "you certainly ought to be able to handle her. Use the legendary Savas charm."

Theo snorted. He cracked his knuckles again. He paced.

Tallie was curious beyond belief. "Don't tell me she's impervious." She giggled at her brother's discomfiture. "Come on, Theo. Tell all!"

"No. It doesn't matter. Besides, when I get back she'll be gone." He turned to stare out across the river, shoulders hunched. "She damned well better be," he muttered more to himself than to her.

Tallie had often studied Theo's back as he'd stood onboard a sailboat staring out at the horizon. She'd always thought how strong and determined he looked, the captain of his ship, master of his destiny.

Today she thought he looked as if he were about to walk the plank.

It was not easy to contemplate. Theo, as the oldest of her brothers, had always been her protector, not teasers and tormenters, like Yiannis, Demetrios and George. She had hero worshiped Theo since she'd been old enough to trail around after him. He had always had the answer to all the world's problems—or he had been able to assure her that the problem she was obsessing about didn't really matter.

And now?

"Are you okay, Theo?" she asked him, concerned now.

"Swell." He flung himself back down in the chair and stared morosely at his hands.

"No," Tallie decided. "You're not. You need to do something fun."

Theo dragged his palms down his face. "What I need is to sleep. I've had a hell of a week. I just got off a plane from Athens. I've got to pick up a car to drive to Newport tonight so I can meet a crew there and test a new boat."

"Okay. You can take a nap at my place," Tallie decided, "and then we'll figure things out from there."

It was the distraction she needed. Elias was going to Cristina and Mark's wedding this afternoon. She was not. She had declined when Cristina had invited her, saying that she didn't think it was a good idea. And that was *before* she'd slept with Elias.

Thank God, she'd had a little bit of sense.

"Come on," she said to her brother and led the way down the hall. "We're going out for a while," she told Rosie.

Rosie nodded and eyed Theo again, then grinned broadly and said, "Have fun," in a knowing way.

This time Theo flashed his dimples and his grin and winked. "We will."

While Theo slept—or tried to—she baked a poppy seed cake and *kolaches* to take into work tomorrow. And while she baked, she made every effort to think about something other than Elias, which was well-nigh impossible.

It was a relief when Theo finally got up. He still looked tired and distracted. But any questions from her just made him scowl and tell her to mind her own business.

After being told that, she didn't much feel like asking his advice about hers. Besides, if Theo couldn't handle his relationships, which were far less complicated than hers, she could hardly expect him to help her figure things out.

She did ask him what he did to clear his head, though.

"Go sailing," he said promptly.

"No boat," she said just as promptly.

"Or sometimes, when I can't sail, I run."

Tallie looked at the cast on her ankle and sighed. "Well, that's out, too."

"What's the problem?" Theo was perched on a bar stool in her kitchen, eating a *kolache,* but studying her intently at the same time.

Aware of his scrutiny, Tallie turned away and concentrated on drying the dishes. "Nothing much. I'm all right." She shrugged lightly. "Just trying to figure things out. You know, new job and all."

Theo grinned. "You're the president now. You can do what you want."

"If only it were that simple."

"Old Man Antonides giving you problems?"

"Not really. He was a figurehead. His son runs—ran—" She shut her mouth.

"*He's* giving you trouble?" Theo looked as if he might punch Elias out.

"No, not really," Tallie said quickly. "We get along pretty, um, well now. It's just…complicated." And it was making her cheeks burn.

Theo looked at her narrowly. "Complicated how?"

"Never mind." She finished drying the dishes and hung the towel neatly on the rack with far more attention to getting its corners square than was entirely necessary.

When she turned back, Theo was still staring at her. Tallie met his gaze defiantly.

He looked away first. But his mouth twisted and he shook his head.

"We need a boat," he decided. "Let's go get some fresh air. But, kid, I'll tell you one thing—the old man has a lot to answer for."

Theo, being Theo, found a boat—not a sailboat, of course. But he took her rowing in Central Park.

It was the best he could do, he said ruefully, on short notice.

Tallie had never been rowing in Central Park. She nearly fell into the water trying to negotiate the dock and the tipping boat with the cast on her leg. But once she got in and settled, sitting there in the boat while Theo rowed them over the water was surprisingly soothing. With the late afternoon sun on her face, the blue sky overhead and the traffic and noise of the city at a distance, she felt calmer, more in control.

The emotion generated by her night with Elias seemed less acute. The problem, she could see now, was coming to terms with her expectations.

She had no right to expectations. They were two consenting adults who had shared a night of intimacy. And yes, she liked him. She wouldn't have gone to bed with him if she hadn't.

But she could deal with it. She wasn't going to throw herself at him—or off a bridge—no matter what. She was simply grateful to him for waking her up again, for making her feel alive again.

He had proved to her that there was life after Brian. She would find it. She was determined now to find it.

It just wouldn't be with him.

The realization settled her down. She caught Theo's eye and smiled across at him. "You're right. It helps."

"Does it?" he said wryly.

And then each of them went back to their own thoughts without a word being spoken.

They spent an hour on the small lake, then they had dinner at a little German place in Yorkville, and finally she accompanied him to pick up the hired car he'd arranged to drive out to Newport.

"I'll take you home on my way," he told her.

"No. You go on. It's a long drive. You don't need to mess with Brooklyn traffic, too." He looked as though he would have argued, but Tallie insisted. "I'll get a cab. Don't worry. And thank you. It was fun." She gave him a kiss and got a bone-crushing hug in return.

"Take care of yourself. Don't do anything I wouldn't do." Theo winked at her.

Tallie laughed. "License for everything, in other words." But she was all right now. Steady, balanced, sensible.

She had her equilibrium back—until the elevator door opened in front of her apartment and she saw Elias standing there.

CHAPTER NINE

"WHERE the hell have you been?"

It wasn't the way to start the conversation. Elias knew that. But it was nearly ten o'clock, for God's sake. She'd been gone for hours.

According to Dyson and the temp—Laura or Cora or something—who were still in the office when Elias came in from putting Cristina and bloody Mark on a plane to Bermuda, Tallie had left with a man in the middle of the afternoon.

"What man?" he'd demanded. "You mean Martin?"

The temp had giggled. "Oh, no. A real man."

"Not Martin," Dyson had concurred. "Some dark-haired stud. I didn't talk to him."

What stud?

Dyson hadn't known. "Never seen him before."

And there was no one else around to ask.

Not that it was any of his business, of course. Tallie had every right to go out with any stud she wanted.

But not in the middle of the day. Not when she was supposed to be working, being the bloody president of Antonides Marine! If she wasn't going to do her job, she ought to be fired.

When he'd stomped up to his apartment, he'd called her to find out, in an offhand way, what exactly was going on. But all he'd got was her answering machine.

Five times!

He had gone back down to the office to get her cell phone number from Rosie's phone book. But her cell phone was switched off.

Where the hell was the consummate businesswoman now?

Was she all right? he worried, concerned for her welfare. That was what sent him round to her apartment. He'd just wanted to make sure she was all right, that she hadn't been attacked by any dark-haired studly stranger.

But she wasn't there.

So he waited. And waited. For two damn hours—all the while imagining the worst!

And now here she was, looking wild and windblown, sun-burned and gorgeous. Not to mention astonished to see him.

"Elias?"

"No, the big bad wolf," he snarled. "Where have you been? Dyson said you left the office in the middle of the afternoon!"

"I told Rosie. Was there a problem?" She looked genuinely concerned as she fumbled to get her key out of her purse.

Elias's jaw bunched. "There damned well could have been."

She stopped and looked at him. "But there wasn't?"

"No." He clipped off the word. He knew he was making way too much out of this. "So, who was the stud?"

Tallie goggled. "Stud?"

Elias's teeth ground together. "The dark-haired stud—to quote Laura the temp—that you ran off with."

Tallie laughed. "Maura," she corrected him. "Her name is Maura."

He didn't care if her name was Rumplestiltskin, damn it! *"Who was he?"*

Tallie turned the key in the lock and pushed open the door. "Theo," she said. "My brother."

"Theo?" He didn't understand why his knees suddenly wob-bled. *"Your brother?"*

"Yes He was on his way to Newport. From Athens. Appar-ently he was at your house in Santorini." Tallie said this last as if she were reluctant to admit it, but Elias didn't give a damn about that. He didn't give a damn about anything other than that the dark-haired stud was her *brother*.

"Some girl there was giving him fits."

"Girl?" Elias echoed vaguely.

Tallie shrugged. "I don't know anything more than that. He muttered a bunch of stuff about a girl, but he wouldn't say any more. Maybe she lives in the village?"

"Maybe." Who cared? Not him. He followed her into her apartment. She looked a little surprised, a little curious, a little wary. She kicked off her shoes and tossed her bag on the little table next to the door. "Do you know her?" she asked.

"No."

She didn't matter. The only woman that mattered right now was standing across the room from him. Elias shut the door and leaned against it, just watching her, wanting her.

"Well, I don't know anything else," Tallie went on, talking rapidly. "Theo's my best brother, but he can be disgustingly closemouthed about things. I was just glad to see him. It's been ages. He was exhausted. So we came back here so he could grab a nap. I wasn't getting anything d—" She stopped abruptly and began again. "I came, too, because my ankle was aching. And…why are you leaning against the door?"

Because it seemed like a better idea than walking across the room, ripping her clothes off and having his way with her. But the minute he thought it, he knew he was wrong. There was no better idea than making love to Tallie.

"I'm not," he said, and pushed away from the door, strode across the room and swept her into his arms.

It was the first thing that had felt right all day.

"Elias!" She stiffened for just a moment, then melted into his embrace. She wrapped her arms around, hanging on to him, holding him close as her lips met his.

Kissing Tallie, touching Tallie, burying his face in her hair, breathing in the scent of her—it was heady and exhilarating and, oddly, like coming home, the more so because he'd spent the whole day dealing with things he'd rather not have dealt with—

like Mark and Cristina—and the last two hours imagining the worst about Tallie and her dark-haired stud.

And now she was here. In his arms. He was kissing her.

And she was kissing him in return.

She seemed just as eager, just as desperate as he was, pulling his shirttails out, sliding her hands up beneath it, stroking his hot skin, even as he was doing the same to her. Buttons popped; zippers slid.

"Tallie!"

"Mmm?"

"We're not going to make it to the bed if you— Tal!" His voice strangled as he sought to keep control.

She stopped. Took her hands off him, holding them up in the air like some bank robber under the sheriff's gun. Oh, God. He couldn't think and make love to Tallie Savas at the same time!

So who needed to think?

He scooped her up into his arms and staggered into her bedroom where he lowered her to the bed.

"Now, where were we?" she mused, smiling up at him. "Ah, yes, I remember." And then her hands began their feverish work again.

"Jeez, Tallie!" But it was exquisite what she was doing to him. Desperate for more, he slid between her thighs and into the warmth of her. And that place was the most right of all.

And then it was his turn to stop, to shake his head no when she urged him on. "I want," he said through his teeth, "to make...it last."

"Why?"

"Why?" Her question confounded him.

A smile touched her lips and she gave a little wriggle against the sheets. "The sooner you get started, the sooner we can do it all again!" She shrugged and looked at him hopefully. "Just trying to be logical."

Far be it from him to defy logic.

And when she kissed him again and urged him to respond, he knew he didn't need any urging at all.

"Whatever you say," he muttered. Then he bent his head and

kissed her again, long and deep and hard, as if he could imprint himself on her memory, as if he could brand her and make her his alone. And then he began to move.

He didn't make it last. He shattered in moments. So did Tallie, whispering his name as she arched into his final thrust. And then they lay, spent, still wrapped in each other's arms.

And still it wasn't enough.

He'd just had her—and he wanted her all over again.

"They're married! My baby is married! Cristina is married, Elias!" His mother's voice bleated in his ear, increasingly more shrill with every sentence.

And good morning to you, too, he thought wearily. She was not the first person he wanted to hear from today.

He wanted Tallie to breeze into his office and tempt him with some bakery confection—or something else. But that wasn't going to happen. She'd breezed in to the office, all right. She'd even brought some *kolaches* she'd made yesterday. But she had on her President Tallie hat. She was charming and friendly—and totally professional.

Which meant, he supposed, that they were having an affair: passionate, torrid sex at night, business as usual during the day.

He wouldn't have wanted it any other way, of course.

But still…

"Elias! Did you hear me?" His mother demanded.

"Yes, Ma. I know," he said now, regretting that he had allowed Rosie to put the call through in the first place. But it had seemed smarter to get it over with before his mother had a chance to work up to full-blown hysteria.

He had insisted yesterday, before he'd put them on the plane, that Cristina call their parents at once and tell them about the wedding.

"When we're in Bermuda," she'd promised. "I'll call them tomorrow. I want my wedding night without angst, Elias," she said firmly.

And he hadn't been able to argue with that.

She had obviously called bright and early this morning and given their parents the news. And just as obviously, whatever she'd said, it hadn't been enough, and he was going to have to do mop-up work. As usual.

"You were there," Helena accused. "She said you were invited!"

"They needed a witness."

"I would have witnessed!" Helena wailed. "Why didn't you tell me?" Elias had to hold the phone away from his ear.

"Because it wasn't my wedding, Ma," he said. "It wasn't my decision."

"Since when do you let your sister make foolish decisions."

"It's her life."

"You should have told me anyway. What sort of mother doesn't go to her own daughter's wedding?"

"One who doesn't know her daughter is getting married," Elias said logically.

"She didn't even have a dress. I suppose she got married in some tacky spandex and combat boots." Helena's complaint was somewhere between a question and an accusation.

"She looked fine," Elias said. "She had a dress."

"What sort of dress?"

He tried to remember. But he hadn't been thinking about his sister. He'd been thinking about Tallie, who should damned well have been there witnessing the wedding with him. After all, it was her fault Mark now had a job in the firm and was part of his family.

And Cristina's dress? He couldn't remember much.

"I think it was purple," he ventured.

"Purple?" Helena invariably lapsed into Greek when the stakes were high. She lapsed now, rattling on furiously, making it sound as if the fashion police would arrest Cristina the moment she set foot again on New York soil.

"She looked great," Elias cut in. "And it was her wedding, so it was her choice. Mark liked it."

God knew why he was going out of his way to defend his sister. He had no great hopes that the marriage would last. But the deed was done. And he had to admit that Cristina looked more determined than he had ever seen her. And Mark had said his vows with a firmness that had surprised Elias.

Of course, a ceremony did not a marriage make, as he well knew.

"I should have been there," his mother muttered.

"You can be there for the baby."

"*Baby?* What baby?"

Oh, hell. He'd forgotten she didn't know about that.

"Well, of course there will be a baby eventually," he said hastily. "They're bound to have one. Cristina loves kids. So does Mark," he improvised. "And you'll know all about it. It isn't as if they can sneak off and do it. You'll see it coming."

"A baby." Helena's voice had lost its shrillness and took on a gentle, musing quality. "Yes, I suppose they might."

"Of course they will." And Elias devoutly hoped she continued to sound that delighted whenever Cristina got around to telling her about the impending arrival. "Look, Mom, I've got a lot of work waiting for me…"

"Yes, of course," Helena said. "Not so much work these days, though? Now that Dad has hired that nice president girl to help you."

Nice president girl? Tallie? Whom his father had "hired" to *help* him?

Elias wondered, not for the first time, just exactly what his father told his mother about the business. He also wondered what Tallie would think of her job description. He grinned, looking forward to telling her.

"She works hard," he told his mother, because that was very very true.

"Good. So you will have time now. Yes?" Helena sounded as if she were rubbing her hands together in anticipation.

"Mom, I—"

"Yes," Helena answered her own question. "Now you will have time to find yourself a wife."

"I had a wife," Elias reminded her.

"Bah. She was never the wife for you, Elias," Helena said. She didn't say *I told you so* because she hadn't. But she'd always been concerned about his decision to marry Millicent, though all she had said was, "Are you sure she will make you happy, my son?"

What she should have asked, Elias thought, was, can you make *her* happy? Because obviously he had not.

Now he shut his eyes. "Don't start, Ma—"

"She hurt you, Elias. But you cannot hide away forever."

"I'm *not* hiding!"

"No, you are working. You are working every single hour of the day! And maybe that is not hiding precisely, but it does the trick."

He couldn't argue. She wouldn't listen. "I have to go."

But Helena, thwarted by her daughter, was not about to let Elias's disastrous first marriage destroy the possibility of a second one.

"I know the perfect woman. I was having my hair done last week. You know Sylvia Vrotsos who cuts my hair? She has a cousin who has a daughter—"

"Mom! Stop!"

"Beautiful girl. Sylvia had her picture there. You will love her. She's smart. Beautiful and smart. Sylvia says she is getting an MBA!"

Elias already knew a beautiful smart woman who had an MBA. He was sleeping with her.

"I will invite her to dinner on Sunday," Helena rattled on. "You can meet her then."

"I don't—"

"And if you don't like her, Sophia Yiannopolis has a daughter who is a stockbroker who just broke off her engagement to a lawyer from New Haven."

"Mom!"

But she was too caught up in her own ideas to even hear him. Thank God Rosie tapped on the door, then opened it and poked her head in.

"Someone to see you. Says it's important. How long?" she mouthed silently.

"Now," Elias mouthed back. "Mom, I have to go. I have a business to run."

"But the president girl—"

"Goodbye, Mom." He banged down the phone and glared at it. Then he looked up at Rosie. "Send him in."

She turned to the man in reception. "Mr. Antonides will see you now." Then she stepped aside and a lankier, scruffier Antonides strolled in.

"Hey, bro! How's it goin'?"

"Peter?"

His brother was wearing faded blue jeans with holes in the knees and a bright-red Hawaiian shirt with palm trees on it. His jaw was unshaven, his black hair windblown and in need of cutting.

"Don't look so surprised. I told you I wanted to talk to you. You never called me back." The voice was mildly accusing.

"I'm busy."

Peter looked around. "So I see." He held out his hand, and Elias shook it, still feeling a bit numb because "surprised" didn't quite cover it.

He hadn't seen his brother in, what, three years? Peter had gone to Hawaii for college ten years ago—as far away from home as he could get and still be in America, he'd told Elias. He'd been back perhaps half a dozen times since. On the rare occasions he had been home, stopping by to see Elias at work had never been high on his list of priorities.

He'd visited the Manhattan office once, about six years ago, and had hightailed it back to Hawaii the next day, confessing to Elias in a phone call weeks later that the mere sight of his brother neck deep in red ink and business ledgers while trying to sustain the family business had totally spooked him.

"I don't know how you do it," he'd said.

"Someone has to," Elias had replied sharply.

"Well, better you than me," Peter's tone had been fervent.

Elias had only seen him once since. A few Christmases ago on his way out of the city, Peter had stopped by his old flat on the Upper West Side to see if Elias could lend him some money—money that, so far, he hadn't paid back.

And he didn't need to think he was going to get more this

time! Elias had had it up to here with irresponsible relatives. He sat down again and gestured toward the chair on the other side of the desk. But Peter didn't sit down. He stared at the mural Martha had painted.

"Nice. She does good work." He didn't have to ask who had done it.

"Yes, she does." Elias straightened the papers on his desk, then picked up his pen and rolled it between his fingers, waiting for the other shoe to drop.

But Peter wasn't ready to drop it yet, apparently. He prowled around the office, juggled Elias's sea-glass paperweight, tapped his fingers on the doorjamb, then shoved his hands in his pockets. Elias watched him warily.

"Smart move coming over to Brooklyn," his brother said finally. "Hell of a good view of Manhattan."

"Yes," Elias agreed. "But I didn't come for the view."

"Obviously," Peter said, taking in Elias's windowless room. "It's all about finances, isn't it?"

"They are a consideration," Elias kept his voice even.

Peter nodded. "So how'd you like to be on the next big boom? Make a bundle. Sound good?"

Peter? Talking money? Talking about *making* money? Elias tried to bend his mind around that.

"Spell it out," he said at last.

"I've been working on a windsurfer."

Working on a windsurfer seemed, to Elias, an oxymoron. Windsurfers were play, no matter how much time you spent on them and how much money you went through while you were doing it instead of getting a real job.

But he held his tongue as Peter rambled on, talking about how he'd come up with this new idea while he was repairing an old one. His brother, in the throes of enthusiasm, had always been hard to follow. He waited, strangling his pen.

"Look," Peter said. "I'll show you what I mean." He went back out into the reception office and returned carrying a two-foot-square portfolio, which he proceeded to open on Elias's desk.

There were drawings, lots of them, surprisingly detailed and with lots of numbers and arrows and references to velocity and wind power, and Peter seemed intent on explaining it all to him— how it was a departure from current windsurfers, how it was faster and more maneuverable, and how it would be easy to manufacture and very appealing to the market. Peter covered all the bases, rambled on for half an hour at least. Then he stood back and looked down at Elias.

"So," he asked, "what do you think?"

Elias, who had actually been thinking about how he could get Tallie to come to his place tonight—maybe work late and offer to make her supper blinked. "Think? About what?"

"About the windsurfer," Peter said with barely controlled impatience. "Didn't you hear anything I said?"

"Yes, of course." Well, sort of. Elias shrugged. "It's...interesting."

"So, do you want to do it?"

"Do what?" Surely Peter wasn't asking him to go windsurfing.

"Oh, for God's sake, Elias! I came all the way from Honolulu to show you the plans, to give you first shot—"

"First shot? At what? At building windsurfers?" Elias stared at him.

"Yes, damn it!" Peter snapped at him.

"Then, no, damn it, I don't."

It was Peter's bad luck to be the last straw. Elias was fed up with the lot of them—with his father, who only wanted to play golf, do lunch and sail; with his mother, who only wanted grandchildren and expected him to provide them; with Cristina, who was already irresponsibly providing a grandchild no one was supposed to know about yet; and now Peter, Mr. Surfer Dude, who only put in an appearance when he wanted something and now had some lame-brained idea for a windsurfer that would undoubtedly support his beach-bum lifestyle while draining money away from Antonides Marine!

Peter's jaw clenched, his eyes flashed. Then with barely controlled violence, he shuffled the papers back into a stack, slammed the portfolio shut and gripped it under his arm. "Thank you for your serious consideration," he said, sarcasm dripping.

"It's been so good to see you, so heartening to know you're as supportive as ever. Don't bother to see me out."

Everything in the room rattled when the door slammed behind him.

For a long moment Elias didn't move. He just sat there in the silence and wondered what the hell else could happen.

Would Martha show up to announce that she was running away with the gypsies? Would Lukas send a telegram from the back of the beyond saying that he was going to live out his life on a Himalayan mountainside and eat nothing but betel nuts.

There probably weren't betel nuts in the Himalayas, but when had logic ever governed anything the rest of the Antonides family wanted to do?

Elias stared at the door, waiting for disaster and wishing for Tallie to push it open and smile at him and make him whole again.

She didn't.

Because, he reminded himself, life wasn't like that. So he opened the folder on his desk and tried to concentrate.

He couldn't.

CHAPTER TEN

"TALLIE? You're not listening!"

"Of course I'm listening, Dad." Well, sort of. Trying to at any rate. In fact, her brain was wrestling with a far more important issue—what had happened during last night's lovemaking with Elias.

"Then answer me, damn it. I got the report Elias sent. I'm concerned about the profits."

"Um…" Tallie fumbled with the papers on her desk.

Report? Elias had sent a report? Yes, she guessed he had. She had mentioned her father wanting one and obviously he'd sent one. Responsible Elias.

Irresponsible Tallie. Foolish Tallie. Blind, idiotic Tallie.

And none of those Tallies was in the least interested in talking business with her father this morning. She couldn't even think about it.

All she could think about was Elias—and that somehow she had fallen in love with him.

"The overall profits of Antonides Marine were flat last quarter, you know," Socrates went on.

It hadn't happened in a blinding flash the way it had with Brian. They had seen each other across the proverbial crowded room. They had walked toward each other as if destiny was pulling them together. They had smiled. They had spoken. They had felt an instant connection that had endured for the rest of Brian's life.

She had known she loved him from the moment she saw him.

Elias had sneaked up on her. Of course, he was handsome. Certainly he had a body to die for. He was smart, intense, dynamic, hardworking, determined. He cared about his family, his staff, even the interloper president who had come in and taken over what should have been his job.

The wonder wasn't that she loved him. The wonder was that it had taken her so long to realize it.

But knowing, she had no idea what to do.

Elias wasn't like Brian. He didn't wear his heart on his sleeve. On the contrary, he had it buried under more layers of steel-plated emotional armor than a Sherman tank.

And while Tallie was sure he genuinely liked her and certainly enjoyed going to bed with her, the word *love* had never escaped his lips.

"What's he doing about the profits, Tallie?"

"Profits?"

"Oh, for God's sake! Focus, girl. This is two quarters in a row that things have been a little flat. What's going on?"

Tallie mustered her brain cells. She forced her brain to backtrack through her father's words and pick out which things to respond to. "We're making adjustments. Streamlining in some areas, cutting back waste. And we're looking at other options."

"I know, I know. Some marine outfitter," Socrates said impatiently. "I damned well hope so because—"

"Because you have money invested." Which, besides marrying her off, was his other bottom line.

Marrying her off was what he'd tried to do by offering her this job in the first place! He'd *wanted* her to fall in love with Elias. He'd orchestrated the whole thing in hopes that she would get married and be a good Greek wife and stop trying to follow in his footsteps.

She wondered what he would say if she told him it had worked—the falling-in-love part, not the getting-married-and-being-a-good-Greek-wife part. Because if Elias hadn't mentioned *love,* he certainly hadn't mentioned marriage.

"You have some experience with this sort of thing, Thalia," he said. "You should be working with Antonides."

"I am."

"You are? Every day?"

"Of course."

"Then…what the hell's the matter with him? Doesn't he like women?"

"What?" Tallie's brain cells all got together on that!

"You heard me. You're not hard on the eyes, Thalia. You might not be a cover model—"

"Thank you very much," Tallie said drily.

"But—" Socrates steamrollered on, "you are clever and intelligent and you are under his nose from Monday through Friday. Why the hell hasn't he asked you out?"

Because he didn't have to, she wanted to say. *I fell into his bed without him doing a thing. And now we're having an affair and I love him and he's going to dump me and I owe it all to you.*

Instead she said, "Goodbye, Dad, and banged the phone down so hard the battery pack fell out.

She wished she felt the tiniest bit of satisfaction for having done it. In fact, she felt miserable. Elias wanted her in his bed, yes. But for how long? And when he got tired of her, then what?

Clearly she was not a woman cut out for affairs. She stabbed her pen through the papers on her desk and barely noticed. She couldn't work. She couldn't think. She stood up and stuck her crutches under her arms and hobbled out of the office.

"Rosie! I'm going to—" She stopped dead and stared at the back of a black-haired man in faded blue jeans and a loud Hawaiian shirt. "Elias?" She couldn't believe her eyes.

The man had been talking agitatedly to Rosie, but he turned at the sound of her voice and she saw, not surprisingly, that it wasn't Elias at all. He was wiry and leaner than Elias. Younger, too, and darkly tanned, but deeply handsome in the classic Antonides way.

"Thank God, no," he said, and clearly meant it. "I'm Peter. His brother. For my sins." His mouth twisted. But then he turned on his version of the Antonides charm and gave her a warm slow smile. "And you are?"

Tallie hobbled forward and held out a hand to him. "Tallie Savas. It's nice to meet you. What a surprise. You're the surfer dude?"

"Is that what he says?" Peter's smile vanished and sudden anger flashed in his eyes.

"No," Tallie hastened to assure him. "Elias didn't. Cristina did."

The smile returned at once. "You know Cristina? How is she?" he asked eagerly. "I haven't heard from her in ages."

"She's married."

Peter Antonides's jaw dropped. "Married? Crissie? I'll be damned. Who to? Where's she living? When'd this happen?"

"You should ask Elias. He was there."

Peter shook his head. "Big brother doesn't want to talk to me. I waste his time—and his money."

"Oh, I'm sure he didn't mean whatever he said to give you that impression," Tallie said.

"Oh, he damned well did mean it." Peter shoved a hand through his shaggy hair. "And right now I don't want to talk to him, either. I came all the way from Hawaii to make a proposal, to talk to him about this—" he slapped the portfolio under his arm "—and he blew me off."

"A proposal?" So it was business that had brought him here. "What is it?"

"A windsurfer. I designed a better windsurfer." Peter lifted his chin, as if daring her to make something of it.

"Did you?" Tallie's eyes widened. From what she'd heard from both Cristina and Elias, Peter was a surf bum, no more, no less.

But Peter was adamant. "Damned right I did. I ride 'em, but I've got a blinkin' master's in mechanical engineering. I know what I'm talking about. But Mr Fair and Square, Mr Good Business Head couldn't even listen!" He turned toward the door.

Instinctively Tallie caught his arm. "Elias has a lot on his mind right now."

"When doesn't he?"

"Possibly never," Tallie said quite truthfully. "But I'd be happy to listen."

"You?" Peter looked doubtful. "What are you? I don't mean to be disrespectful, but are you Elias's assistant or something?"

"Or something," Tallie said drily.

"Are you sure about this?" Peter persisted. "I don't want to get you in trouble. I know my brother. He's big on loyalty. And he can be a jerk."

"Elias and I have an understanding."

Peter looked speculative. Then his gaze narrowed as he assessed her more closely. "So, what do you do here?"

Tallie grinned. "I boss him around."

"You what?" Peter's eyes grew round.

"There's been a restructuring of the company. And I'm the new president of Antonides Marine."

"You? What happened to Dad? Good God!" The colour washed out of Peter's face. "Did he die and no one told me?"

"No," Tallie reassured him. "He just sold some of his share of the business to, um, my family. And we divided up the jobs." Which was the truth, of a sort. "And I'm president. I'm qualified," she assured him, in case he was wondering.

But he was grinning. "So what's Elias then? Chopped liver?" He looked as if that wouldn't have been a bad idea.

"Elias is still managing director. We work together." *We sleep together. We make love to each other.*

Except Elias didn't believe in love and— She couldn't go there. Not now.

"Come on." She herded Peter and his portfolio into her office. He looked sceptical, but finally allowed himself to be steered through the door. He looked around and whistled. "So you got the window. Heck of a view."

"Isn't it?" Tallie shut the door, then took a page out of Theo's book and rang Rosie's line. "Could you send someone down with coffee and *kolaches*?"

"Kolaches?" Peter stared at her in disbelief. "I guess there has been a restructuring. Elias would never have thought of that."

"A well-fed staff is a harder-working, happier staff," Tallie recited on cue.

"Well, maybe it was his idea, then," Peter muttered, getting annoyed again.

"Sit down." Tallie gestured to a leather armchair. "And tell me about this windsurfer idea of yours."

She didn't have any preconceived notions about Peter Antonides. He wasn't her beach-bum younger brother who had spent years in college while she worked and he surfed to his heart's content. So she had far more patience than Elias apparently had. And a good thing, too, as Peter, encouraged by her attention, drank coffee and ate *kolaches* and went on at length about this new windsurfer he'd designed.

He dragged out technical drawings and explained the aerodynamics and the wind-resistance issues and the best materials to use. He spoke with an urgency that belied the notion that he was a layabout. He was obviously enthused and excited about his project. And the more enthused and excited about it he got, the more he had a look about him very like the one Elias had had when he'd talked about the woodworking he'd done on his apartment.

It was a labor of love for Elias just as this windsurfer was for his brother. Listening to Peter, she wondered what Elias would be like now if he'd been able to follow his own dreams instead of having to take over the running of the family business. Would he be as enthusiastic as Peter seemed to be? Would he smile more and growl less?

"It's going to work. It *does* work," Peter was saying firmly, his dark eyes, so like his brother's, fixed on her own. "I've made countless prototypes myself. I've modified it, tinkered, tuned. And I've got it right. But I don't have the money to go into production. That's why I brought it here. I read in a business mag about some of the changes Elias has made, some of the new stuff AMI is doing. And I thought my windsurfer would fit in, that it might work out well for both me and Antonides Marine. Elias disagreed."

Tallie ran her tongue over her lips and thought about what to say. Elias had already said no. But he'd said no based on his emotions, not based on the potential value of Peter's windsurfer. She didn't know the first thing about windsurfing. So she certainly wasn't going to contradict Elias even though she thought Peter's explanations made sense—at least to her untutored ear.

She also thought that, on a gut level, it was a project more in line with Antonides Marine than Corbett's the marine outfitter was—*if* it was as viable as Peter thought it was.

"It looks interesting," she said at last, because it did. "Can I run it past someone?"

"Not Elias."

"No, not Elias. My brother. Theo's not a professional windsurfer, but he knows a lot about wind. He races sailboats," she explained.

"Theo Savas? *Theo Savas* is your brother?" Peter looked almost awestruck. Then a grin dawned on his face. "Hell, yeah, you can ask him. That'd be fantastic."

"How about if you ask him yourself?"

"Me?" Peter was equal parts eagerness and apprehension. "He doesn't know me from Adam. I can't just burst in and—"

"You won't. I'll get hold of him and set it up. Do you have a number where I can reach you? He's out in Newport now. You'll probably have to catch up to him there."

"No problem. No one was clamoring for me to stay here." Peter flashed her another grin and rattled off his cell phone number. Then he gathered up his drawings, all energy now. "Just tell me when."

"I'll ring you as soon as I talk to him. But listen to me, Peter." She caught his arm. "I am not promising to overrule Elias's decision. I'm simply promising to ask Theo take a look at what you've got. If he thinks it's an idea worth exploring, then I'll talk to Elias about it."

Peter nodded seriously. "Understood. All I want is a fair shot. But if you guys don't do it, someone else will. It's going to work. And it will be good for both of us. I know it." He turned toward the door, then stopped and came back.

"Look," he said, "I know the burden has been on Elias for years. I appreciate that. I appreciate *him*, stubborn jackass that he is. But obviously, if you're here, someone has finally realized that he can't do it all. So thank God for that. All I'm saying is, I'm here now. And I'm just trying to do my part."

Tallie smiled and squeezed his arm. "I'll call my brother."

It had been, conservatively speaking, the day from hell.

First there had been his mother, ranting on about Cristina and missing her wedding—and hatching plots to set him up with a dozen available women.

Then had come Peter and his hare-brained scheme about the windsurfer, which was, Elias was certain, yet another way to extend his beachcomber life in Hawaii and not have to get a real job.

And then he'd tried to put together his notes for Tallie on the Corbett's acquisition, and his computer had crashed.

"You've got a virus," Paul said. He thought it might have come in on an e-mail from Lukas saying he was in Queenstown and he'd broken his arm skiing so if Elias had come up with someone who had a job for him, he hoped he could do it one-handed.

"I'll see if I can clean it up," Paul had disappeared with the processor, leaving Elias with no notes from the Corbett's meeting. So he'd told Rosie to tell Tallie to postpone it because Tallie had someone in her office.

Then his mother called back, having eliminated one of the women on her eligible brides list and added three more.

And Elias found himself shouting, "I don't want any of them!"

He wanted Tallie.

"No need to bellow, darling," his mother said, sounding a little wary now. "I just want what's best for you."

What was best for him was Tallie. She was always there at the back of his mind—her smile, her wit, her laugh, her touch.

He wanted her in ways he'd never even wanted Millicent. He could talk to her about work, about business, about woodworking even. She understood that. She would probably even understand the envy he felt when he'd gone out to see Nikos Costanides's boatyard. She understood him.

And he loved her.

In his ear his mother rabbited on, but Elias wasn't listening. He was waiting for the gut-level rejection of anything to do with love that he'd felt instinctively since Millicent had walked out.

But it didn't come.

Because Tallie was not Millicent.

Tallie was a whole different person. A genuine, loving, caring person. A kind, delightful, funny person. An enthusiastic, energetic person. Not to mention a passionate lover.

Who didn't love him.

That did cause his gut to clench. But he took a deep breath and let it out slowly.

"We'll find you someone, Elias," his mother was saying.

But he didn't want anyone but Tallie.

"Leave it to me."

Elias shuddered at the thought. "I'll talk to you later, Mom," he said. He needed to think.

But before he could even begin, Rosie buzzed him again. "Your father on line two."

He desperately wanted to have her tell the old man he wasn't in. But he knew his father. If Aeolus didn't get what he wanted, he persisted. Better to take the call now and think about what to do about Tallie when Aeolus was back on the golf course.

"Ah, Elias! How are things? I was surprised about your sister getting married." But not annoyed like his wife. Probably Aeolus was glad he missed it. He once said that if he couldn't wear a golf shirt or deck shoes, he never wanted to go. Now he asked questions about the wedding, said he was happy to have Mark in the family because he could always beat his new son-in-law at golf, and then he discussed the weather and his new nine iron.

As usual, Aeolus took his time to get to the point. Hurrying him along did no good at all. So Elias stared out the window and waited.

After the nine iron, they talked about a boat Aeolus had his eye on. They talked about Peter.

"He's in town?" Aeolus sounded surprised. "Haven't seen

him since your mother and I were in Honolulu in March. Haven't seen any of my children in a month of Sundays. Not even Martha. Dumped Julian and took off. You don't know where she went, do you, Elias?"

"No."

"Well, I expect she'll turn up in good time." His father dismissed Martha's absence with the same cavalier attitude with which he dismissed everything—except golf. "Played eighteen holes yesterday with Socrates. Beat him, too," he added with considerable satisfaction.

"I don't suppose you won the house back," Elias said.

"As a matter of fact, I did."

Elias sat up straight. "You're kidding."

"I'm not. But I must admit, I am surprised. I was joking when I said I'd like the house back if I won, and he agreed."

Elias didn't ask what he would have forfeited if he'd lost. He was sure he didn't want to know.

"He's worried about his daughter," Aeolus went on.

"Worried? About Tallie? What do you mean?" Elias was listening now.

"She's consumed by work. All business. Missing out on life. Her fiancé died a few years ago, and since then she's been on her own."

"Fiancé?" She hadn't mentioned any fiancé.

But apparently Socrates had.

"His name was Brian," Aeolus told him. "He was a Navy pilot. Tallie knew him in college. They were going to get married. But he was killed. Training exercise, I think. That's all I know."

But it explained a lot.

"Socrates says she's grieved long enough. She needs to get back out and meet people. Meet men."

She didn't need to meet any more men! She had one.

She had *him!*

"She'll be all right," he said firmly, and vowed it would be so.

"Easy to say. Not so easy when it's your child," Aeolus said. "Parents worry about their children. Like you. We worry about you."

"Dad—"

"You can't shut yourself off from life forever, Elias. You had a bad experience, yes. But you can't refuse to live."

"I'm *not* refusing to live!" How did this suddenly get to be about him?

"You have a bad marriage, you don't run and hide. It's like riding a horse," Aeolus rolled on. "You fall off, you've got to get right back on."

Elias doubted that his father had ever been on a horse in his life. "Who died and made you Roy Rogers?"

Aeolus laughed. "We care about you. You are our son. You work so hard for us. Every day of your life you give to us. It's time we give back."

"By finding me a woman?"

"It's for your own good, Elias."

"Don't do me any favors."

Aeolus sighed. "I'm not sure about these women your mother has found. But if you don't like any of 'em, I can find you a looker. I guarantee it."

"Thanks a lot," Elias said with deliberate sarcasm.

Aeolus was oblivious. "What are fathers for? I can fix you up with a chorus girl if you want. Just say the word."

The word Elias wanted to say wasn't fit for his father's ears. "I don't want a chorus girl, Dad."

There was a moment of disbelieving silence. Then, "You do *like* women, don't you, Eli?" His father sounded slightly aghast at the possibility that just occurred to him. "I mean, I never thought that was why Millicent—"

"Goodbye, Dad." Elias banged the phone down, then banged his head against his desk.

It was nearly six when Tallie finished writing up her final comments on the Corbett's matter. Then she read and signed the letters Rosie had left for her. She could have done them quickly and gone home, but she lingered, waiting, hoping that Elias would come in.

She had barely caught a glimpse of him all day. He'd had a computer crisis, Rosie had reported. He needed to reschedule his meeting with the Corbetts. Then he'd had phone calls, and his brother Peter, and more phone calls.

It was, basically, business as usual.

Her day had been busy, too, with phone calls and letters, reading reports that Paul gave her and finishing up her own on Corbett's. Then she'd spent time with Peter, had arranged a meeting for him with Theo and had rung him to tell him where and when to meet her brother in Newport.

But through it all, she had lived on the memory of Elias's lovemaking—the hunger, the passion and the promise of his last lingering kiss.

What promise?

She sat staring out the window, watching the sun set over Manhattan and not really seeing it at all. She saw Elias in her mind. She held Elias in her heart.

Where did they go from here?

A movement caused her to look around. And there he was, leaning against the doorjamb of her office, his top button open, his tie askew. She didn't know how long he'd been there, just looking at her. But the sight of him sent a surge of joy straight through her.

"Hey!" She smiled at him, but a smile wasn't enough. It broadened into a grin.

Elias straightened. "Hey yourself." He flashed her a quick grin, but as quickly as it came, it vanished. He cracked his knuckles.

"What's up?" Tallie said. He looked uneasy. She frowned. Had he heard about her talk with Peter. Was he about to jump down her throat and accuse her of going behind his back. She didn't want them to fight.

"I want to explain—" she began, but he cut her off.

"I've got a business proposition for you." He came into her office and stood in front of her desk. She thought he might sit down, but he didn't.

He didn't look at her, either. He cracked his knuckles again, then began to pace around the room, jamming his hands into the pockets of his khakis, then yanking them out again.

Tallie, watching him, felt her anxiety level rise. "What sort of business proposition?"

He stopped and turned to face her, meeting her gaze head-on, then took a breath. "Marry me."

Tallie had always heard that hearing was the last sense to go. But even though she could see Elias and, if she reached out, she knew she could touch him, her ears surely had garbled his words. She didn't know what he had really said. But she thought she'd heard the words *Marry me.* But, no. There was no way on earth he could have said that.

Could he?

All of a sudden her heart began to sing. Her fears vanished. Her earlier anguished, *I love him; he loves me not* evaporated.

She loved a man who loved her, too.

A smile began to dawn, but Elias didn't see it. He had turned to stare across the river at the Manhattan skyline. "I know you're not looking for marriage," he said flatly. "I know you don't love me."

"I—"

"But it doesn't matter. This isn't about love. It's just good common sense."

Tallie's heart caught in her throat. It *wasn't* about love?

"You ought to get married," he went on stubbornly, still not looking at her. "You should have a family. You shouldn't just have a job even if you love it. You should have more. A husband. Children. Your father wants you to have a family."

"My *father?* What does my father have to do with this?" Her voice was shrill. She knew it. She couldn't help it. Then she had a further horrifying thought. "He *told* you that?"

She would kill Socrates Savas. She would strangle him with her bare hands.

"No. Not me." Elias rubbed the back of his neck. "He told *my* father. My father told me."

And she would cut him up into little pieces, Tallie thought, mortified to the depths of her being. Thank God Elias had begun pacing again and wasn't even looking at her.

She took one breath and then another, then tried to sound rational when she was only feeling murderous. "And so you'd marry me," she managed to get out with some semblance of calm, "because my father thinks I need a husband?"

"Well, it would free you up to concentrate on business."

"You don't think I'm doing that now?"

"I think it's all you're doing. Well, not all." His gaze flicked to meet hers, and she saw color rise on his neck. She knew what he was remembering. She was remembering, too. But it had meant more to her, obviously, than it meant to him. "I just think it would make things run smoother. And you told me you wanted to focus on business the first day you were here. All I'm trying to do is make it possible."

She didn't answer. She couldn't have answered to save her life.

"I know about Brian," he said when she didn't speak. His voice was quiet, there was a hint of strain in it. But she didn't know what it meant. "I know you loved him," he pressed on. "That's fine. This has nothing to do with that. That was then. This is now. And I thought—I thought if we got married it would make things easier for you. Your father would stop mucking around in your life. You could have your career and, eventually, a family. And—" he shrugged awkwardly "—you have to admit, the sex is good."

Maybe her father wasn't the only one she would kill.

"The sex is good?" Tallie clasped her hands in her lap so she didn't wrap them around his throat—or any other vulnerable parts of his anatomy.

There was a hectic flush across Elias's cheekbones. "It is! You know it is. Better than good. It's fantastic."

"Yes."

"Well then?" He looked at her expectantly.

"Anything else?" she asked after a moment. "In this *business proposition?*"

Like *I love you,* for example.

Elias scowled. He raked his fingers through his hair, chewed his lip, paced some more.

Come on, Elias, she urged him silently. *You can do it. I know she hurt you, but I won't ever hurt you. I love you. You can say those three little words.*

"Fine," he muttered. "It would get my old man off my back, too."

She blinked, her mouth opening and closing like a fish.

"He and my mother are determined to do me a favor and set me up with every damn eligible woman in New York. My mother's got a list as long as my arm of women she thinks would be suitable brides."

"I see."

"No, you don't!" He was almost shouting now. "I don't want them shoving women down my throat. I can't think when they're plotting all these things. And now you're here, they think I've got time and I can spend all of it on these silly women and—"

"What a terrible trial."

"Well, it is. And you know it. It's the same thing your old man wants to do to you. So the way I figure it, marriage would be the smart thing for both of us. Then we can get on with the rest of our lives without them pestering us."

"And the sex is good." Tallie didn't know whether to laugh or cry.

"Exactly." Elias nodded emphatically, obviously relieved that she understood. "So how about it? Will you marry me?"

Tallie swallowed and prayed the tears wouldn't fall as she said the hardest word she'd ever had to say. "No."

CHAPTER ELEVEN

As MUCH as she wanted to say yes, Tallie couldn't.

Marriage, in her mind, was a sacred covenant between two people who loved each other. It was a lifetime commitment that promised faith and love and trust and forever.

It was never just "business."

So all she could do was knot her fingers in her lap and shake her head. "No," she said again, hoarsely. "Thank you, but it wouldn't work."

She couldn't marry him for the wrong reasons. She couldn't love him when he only wanted "good sex" and easy business relations. But she couldn't explain. Not without looking like a fool. Not without admitting she had fallen in love with him— and wished he also loved her.

She chewed her lip and wished the earth would swallow her up, anything to get her out of this office where Elias stood staring at her as if she'd lost her mind.

But then he shrugged casually, almost indifferently.

"Whatever," he said lightly. "Just a thought." As if it didn't matter in the least.

Which should have made her glad she'd refused, Tallie reminded herself. And she would—someday. Really she would. But right now she just wished he would leave.

"So," he said after a moment. "I'll be off then." He started toward the door, then stopped and glanced back. "Afraid I'm not going to have time for any great sex tonight. I've got another commitment."

She felt as if he'd slapped her.

Tallie sucked in a sharp breath and could only nod. Determined not to let him see how much his flippancy hurt, she managed one word. "Whatever."

It actually physically hurt her throat when she said it.

For a long moment they just looked at each other. Elias's expression was stony, nothing at all like the man who had made love to her last night. Then, in what seemed like slow motion, he shrugged, turned and walked out.

Moments later the main office door shut. Not with a bang. Not with any emotion at all. Just a loud click.

In the silence of the empty office, Tallie sat for a long time after Elias left. Everything in her hurt. She felt gutted. As hollow and agonized as when she'd come home from Brian's funeral and realized that her life was stretching out in front of her—vast and empty and alone.

It hurt.

She hurt.

It was better, she thought, swiping away a tear, all those years when she hadn't felt anything at all. Then slowly, like an old woman, she stood up and hobbled out of her office and down the hall into the reception area. She stood by Rosie's desk and turned slowly, taking it all in—the break room where only crumbs and a dab of poppy seed remained of this morning's *kolaches,* the conference room where she had sat and listened to Paul and Dyson and Elias discuss and question and debate, where she herself had offered insights and had learned more than she'd ever thought possible, Elias's tiny office with its wonderful mural, the small library with its volumes of maritime history and shipping manuals and, most of all, its beautifully crafted bookcases that she knew now had been Elias's contribution.

The whole place—the whole business—was all really due to Elias's hard work. The rest of them added bits and pieces, but the company was his. It had started out as his family's, but he was the one who kept it alive, made it thrive.

She'd jumped at the opportunity to take the job when her father had offered it. But she hadn't deserved it. She'd done nothing to earn it. And even though she knew she had made a contribution to the business, she hadn't given anywhere close to what Elias had given to Antonides Marine.

It didn't matter that she was president and he was managing director, in the end it was Elias's company.

And it wasn't big enough for both of them. Not now.

She couldn't work with him every day—couldn't see him across the table in meetings or stand in the office and talk about day-to-day business matters and not ache for wanting him.

And she couldn't just settle for a hollow marriage and good sex. It had nothing to do with grieving for Brian. It had everything to do with wanting it all with the man she now loved. If she couldn't have that, she didn't want any of it.

She rubbed her hand over the smooth oak of the bookcase, and then she sat down at Rosie's desk and wrote Elias a note.

When she finished it, she put it on his desk. Beside it, she left her report detailing the reasons she thought they should pass on the Corbett's acquisition. She said her brother Theo would possibly be contacting him about a better idea. She hoped she hadn't overstepped her bounds.

At the end she wrote, "Everything I've done, I've tried to do for the good of the company. And that is why I quit."

She'd quit.

Elias sat at his desk and stared at the letter in his hand.

He'd found it on his desk just minutes ago when he'd come downstairs. It was brief and professional and to the point. Very polite. Very Tallie.

Very gone.

He sat there, staring at the note that trembled in his fingers, and he felt his throat close and his eyes burn. He clenched his jaw and tried not to feel anything. But he felt shattered. Lost. Empty. And furious.

Damn it all, anyway! How could she just walk out? How irresponsible was that?

Well, the hell with her. If that was the way she felt, it was better that she leave. He didn't need her.

But God, it hurt.

Not that he let on. He made the announcement at a hastily called staff meeting. "Ms Savas has left the company." He paused and looked at the shocked faces in the room. Then he added, "There are some bagels in the break room. Help yourselves."

They looked at him. They looked at each other.

"What happened?" Rosie asked. "Why isn't she here?"

"She just quit? For no reason?" Dyson's brow was furrowed. "I thought she liked us."

"I imagine she got a better offer," Elias lied. If she hadn't already, no doubt she soon would.

"Still seems odd," Paul mused, scratching his head. "Do you think we upset her?"

"No, I don't think you upset her!" Elias's tone was so sharp they all looked at him and blinked. Irritated at showing emotion, he shoved a hand through his hair, then took a steadying breath. "Just forget it, all right?"

He tried to forget, too.

He threw himself into his work. Over the next week he called Corbett and told him they had decided against purchasing his marine outfitter.

"We've decided to move in a different direction," he explained.

"But—" Corbett sounded stunned.

"We had long discussions about the future of the company," Elias told him. "It wasn't a decision made lightly. But while we're developing new avenues, we just felt that we should stick closer to what we know—which is boats—not clothes."

"It's that woman," Corbett muttered. "She didn't like us."

"Ms Savas is no longer with the company," Elias said. "In the end the decision was mine."

But it was true that Tallie's input had counted. She'd been right in her assessment, not of Corbett's worth, but of its worth to Antonides Marine. She understood AMI's focus. She knew its history, its successes, its failures. She had been a good president as long as she'd lasted.

She'd been a good friend. A good lover.

He tried not to remember. He worked day and night. He put up bookcases. He built shelves and cabinets and cupboards. He finished the first floor and went into the basement and knocked down walls.

He was tempted once to knock down Martin who asked what he'd done with Tallie.

"I haven't done anything with her!" he snapped.

Martin shrugged. "Then *to* her."

"Or *to* her!" Elias's fists clenched. His gut twisted.

He expected anyday to hear from his father that she had got some other hotshot job in a bigger company. But his father said nothing.

Even when Elias asked point-blank if she was working for Socrates now, he just shrugged.

"Socrates hasn't mentioned her recently," Aeolus said. "I think he was shocked when she left without telling him. He doesn't know where she is."

No one seemed to know where she was.

Not that Elias looked very hard. But he couldn't help paying attention to what he heard. The trouble was, he didn't hear anything at all.

Tallie might as well have dropped off the face of the earth.

And then one afternoon about two and a half weeks after she left, he got a call from her brother Theo.

"That windsurfer works."

"I beg your pardon?" Elias didn't know what he was talking about.

"Tallie sent your brother out to show me the plans for his windsurfer. It's impressive. You should consider it."

It wasn't the windsurfer or his brother that caught Elias's attention. "Tallie sent him?" he demanded. "When?"

"Couple of weeks ago now. Maybe three." Theo couldn't remember. "I had work to do here. Pete came with me. We sailed up to Boothbay and back. Then we built his windsurfer."

"You built—"

"Yep. Tested it out. Very cool. Like I said, it's worth looking at. If you're expanding, you'll want to talk to him."

"I— Where's Tallie?"

"No clue."

"But—?"

"But I talked to her a couple of days ago. She said when I talked to you to tell you she was sorry."

Elias's heart stopped. "Sorry? About what?"

"Dunno. Quitting, I guess. Women are crazy. Even Tallie, and she's saner than most. Whatever the hell you asked her to do, you must have pissed her off. She just said if you'd asked for the right reasons, she'd have said yes."

She would have said yes?

Yes, she would marry him?

Then why the hell hadn't she?

Elias had wanted her to say yes. Dear God, he had wanted her to say yes!

And what were the right reasons? Well, he knew the answer to that. For himself at least, the right reasons to marry were for love and commitment and a lifetime together.

All the things he hadn't been able to bring himself to say.

He had said them once to Millicent, and she'd thrown them back in his face.

But Tallie wasn't Millicent.

Tallie was as pure and honest and forthright as the day was long. She told the truth. He was the one who'd been afraid.

He bolted out of his office, practically knocking down Rosie. "I'm out," he said. "I don't know when I'll be back."

He broke a speed record getting over to her apartment. He ran up the stairs because the elevator took too long. He hammered on her door and waited and waited and waited, desperate to say his piece.

And then the door opened and all the words he wanted to say dried up. His jaw dropped.

"Peter?"

His brother, wearing nothing but a pair of boxers and some shaving cream, grinned broadly. "Hey, Eli. Fancy meeting you here."

"Where's Tallie?" Elias pushed past his brother into the apartment, looking around wildly.

"She's gone," Peter said unhelpfully.

"What do you mean, gone? Gone where? Theo said he talked to her. When's she coming back?"

"Gone means not here. Not sure where she went. Not sure she knew. Gone walkabout, I think Lukas would say."

"That's ridiculous! She wouldn't do anything of the sort. What are you doing here? And why are you…undressed?"

"Because I just took a shower. And now I'm shaving," Peter said, "because I have a hot date tonight, and I want to impress the lady in question with my smooth skin. And I'm here because I'm living here."

Elias gaped. *"What?"*

Peter shrugged. "As much as I would love to make you think I'm living with Tallie, because I know it would annoy the hell out of you, the truth is I'm cat-sitting."

Elias stared in disbelief.

At that moment, as if on cue, Harvey wandered out of the bedroom, meowing. "Cat-sitting," he echoed. "So she…really isn't here."

"Read my lips," Peter said wearily. "She really isn't here."

"And she hired you to cat-sit? For how long?"

Peter shrugged. "However. She didn't say. She just offered me her place for the time being—while I find a manufacturer for my windsurfer."

The windsurfer he'd tried to interest Elias in. The windsurfer Elias had flat-out rejected because he couldn't believe that Peter was doing any more than wasting time. But Tallie had believed. At least enough to send him to her brother.

That was what her reference to Theo in her note had been

about. It made sense now. One more thing she'd done for the good of the company.

"Let me see it again," he said gruffly.

"Don't do me any favors." Peter's reply was equally brusque.

"I'm not doing you favors, damn it," Elias snapped. "I'm doing business. If it's a good product—and Tallie and Theo apparently think it is—then we might well be interested."

Peter's dark brows lifted. "You're serious?"

"Yes. Bring it by the office tomorrow." Elias paused. "Tell me where she is."

"I don't know. Honest. She called me a couple of days ago. She was in a hurry, she said. Had someplace to go pronto. Wanted to know if I was planning to stick around the city, wondered if I'd be interested in living in her place. I said I'd be more interested if she was here." Peter grinned.

Elias ignored that. "And she didn't say where she had to go?"

"No idea. But I gather she's going to be gone a while. She said if I needed to leave before she got back to take Harvey out to her folks' house."

"I have to find her," he said simply.

Peter gave him a not unsympathetic smile. "Good luck, bro."

It shouldn't have been hard.

A woman with Tallie's talents and business reputation should have been easy to track down. This was the information age, after all. If you knew their habits, discovering anyone's whereabouts was a piece of cake.

Sometimes.

Not this time.

Elias tried asking his father again if Socrates had said anything about Tallie—where she was, how she was doing, if she liked her new job.

Aeolus shook his head. "She called him a few days ago. He offered her a job as his vice president in charge of Pacific Northwest operations. Can you believe she turned it down?"

Elias couldn't. Not at first. He knew she'd always wanted to work for her father. But maybe she didn't want him trying to shove more potential husbands down her throat. With her résumé she could take her pick of job offers.

He'd just have to use a corporate headhunter to track her down.

The headhunter struck out. "I have a lot of people I could send to you for interviews if you want a new president," he told Elias.

But Elias didn't want anyone else. He only wanted Tallie.

So he set about trying to find her himself. He spent a good chunk of every day trying to track down Tallie Savas. He spent more time trying to find Tallie than he did working for Antonides Marine.

To his surprise, Peter took up the slack.

His brother came in with his plans for the windsurfer, stayed for a meeting and after that showed up every morning at eight.

"What?" Peter challenged when Elias looked astonished. "You don't think I can handle this?"

"Just surprised," Elias said. The world seemed full of surprises.

But the biggest one—and the most painful one—was that days went by, weeks went by, and he never found Tallie anywhere.

Helena, who had heard through Peter and Cristina that Elias was consumed with a search for Tallie Savas was delighted. "I knew you would want a nice Greek girl," she said happily. "I can find you a nice Greek girl, Elias."

But Elias was done with subterfuge. "I don't want any other nice Greek girl," he told his mother. "I want Tallie. I love Tallie."

He told everyone else because he couldn't tell her.

Sometimes, it felt as if he'd dreamed the whole thing, as if she wasn't really real. But other people remembered her, talked about her, wished that she was there to tell about a grandchild's piano recital or a baby's first tooth, or to bring in some of her *linzertorte* or *apfelstrudel*.

Even that self-absorbed pompous ass Martin remembered Tallie's *apfelstrudel*.

Elias had brought in some from the local bakery that morning and he had the misfortune to ride up in the elevator with Martin who sniffed appreciatively, then said, "Probably not as good as Tallie's."

"No." He and Martin could agree on that.

"She is a fantastic cook," Martin said. "But it's a bloody waste of talent, her apprenticing herself to a Viennese baker, for God's sake."

Elias, who had been tapping his toe and ready to bolt the moment the door slid open, stopped dead. "What?" he said quietly. "She did *what?*"

With Martin he stood every chance of getting a lecture on the guild system and why apprenticeships were going to be ringing the death knell of Central European crafts—or whatever. And he did. But eventually he also got, "She's got some daft notion of becoming a baker."

"A baker?" Elias stared at him. "Tallie? Where?"

Martin rolled his eyes. "Viennese bakers are generally in Vienna."

"Tallie's in Vienna? How do you know?"

Martin shrugged. "I ran into her last week when I was there doing a story on the UNO."

Her workday started at 4:00 a.m. Tallie was there even before Heinrich, the master baker. She did all the low, tedious jobs that fell to the newest apprentices. Heinrich was a Viennese version of Socrates Savas—and Tallie was having to work her way up.

She cleaned and scoured and scrubbed and then she measured and ground and kneaded and rolled. She worked long, hard hours in the kitchen in the morning and in the shop in the afternoon.

It was a far cry from the fast track of corporate America, but the truth was that she was doing something she loved. It had been her hobby, her stress-reliever, and ultimately it had been her salvation.

She was happy. She was challenged. She was learning German. And she could actually go an hour or two at a time without aching for the loss of Elias.

Of course, she reminded herself as she filled the display cases before the afternoon onslaught of schoolchildren, she'd never really had Elias. They'd had "great sex." The rest had been all in her mind.

The door opened and Frau Steinmetz came in. A regular, she always ordered the same thing. Now she said, *"Grüsse Gott. Zwei strudel, bitte,"* and let Tallie practice her German on her.

Tallie filled her order, took the money, then counted out the change. Frau Steinmetz listened, nodded, corrected her pronunciation, told her that her German was getting better and so was her baking.

The door rattled again and, as Frau Steinmetz said, *"Bitte,"* and departed, two more women came in. Tallie waited on them, then on a group of schoolboys who banged in and milled around.

They were always a challenge, the orders coming thick and fast.

"Pfeffernusse, bitte," a little boy pointed.

"Funf powidlkolatschen," said a bigger one.

"Vanillekipferln, bitte," said a third.

Tallie took all the orders, made all the change, laughed and chatted with them, then looked up to watch them dash out the door with their purchases—and saw Elias standing there.

For a moment she couldn't believe her eyes. She had dreamed of him so often, had let her mind drift over memories of his strong handsome face, his hard jaw, his lean muscular body, his lopsided grin.

Her memories paled against the real man.

Her knees wobbled. Her stomach lurched. She swallowed against a sudden hard lump in her throat. Instinctively she reached for the counter and hung on. He wasn't grinning.

He was looking at her as intently as she was looking at him.

"Elias?" What was he doing here? How had he found her? *Why* had he found her? Or was it just happenstance, one of those odd coincidences like the way she'd run into Martin in the Stephansplatz last week.

Elias closed the door behind him. "Tallie."

She wanted to run to him, to throw her arms around him, to hang on and never let go. But she couldn't. Not when she didn't know why he was here.

"Can I help you?" she asked in English.

His lips quirked. "I don't know. I hope so. I need to show the woman I want to marry that I love her. Any suggestions?"

She couldn't even breathe now. "You...love?"

He nodded. "Always have. Just too stupid to say so. Too afraid," he corrected, meeting her gaze honestly. "After Millicent, I thought I could protect myself if I didn't admit it. I was wrong."

"I'm not Millicent!"

He smiled slightly. "No, thank God. You're not at all like Millicent. You are honest and brave and forthright and gorgeous and—"

Tallie's heart was singing. She almost laughed. "Thrifty, strong and reverent?" she said. "Like a regular Boy Scout."

"Believe me, if you were a Boy Scout, I wouldn't be asking you to marry me," Elias grinned. Then the grin vanished and his expression grew grave. "Will you marry me, Tallie? For the right reasons this time? For love and honor and commitment. Forever?"

"Yes. Oh, Elias, yes!" And then Tallie did her best to fling herself into his arms.

It wasn't easy kissing a man over the top of a bakery counter. There was a lot of cabinet in the way, for one thing. There was a stern Viennese baker lecturing them in fast and furious German for another.

"What's he saying?" Elias wanted to know. He was still kissing her and she was kissing him. It had been so long. She couldn't get enough of him.

"He wants to know if you're buying anything. If not, he wants you to move along," Tallie reported with a grin.

"Ask him how much he wants for the woman behind the counter?"

"She's yours. For your love, you've got her forever," Tallie promised.

Elias hauled her right over the counter and wrapped his arms around her and kissed her with all the love he had in him. "It's a deal."

* * *

Her flat was about the size of Harvey's litter pan. It was on the top floor of an apartment block that looked like something out of *Stalag 17*. But it had a bed, and they fell into it the minute they got there.

Buttons popped, zippers slid. And then they were skin to skin, heart to heart. And for all that Elias wanted to take it slow and show her how much he loved her, Tallie didn't let him.

"We can go slow later," she told him. "We've got forever." She looked him in the eyes. "Don't we?"

"We do," Elias vowed. He kissed her, rocked her, then slid inside her and knew how much more it was than great sex.

"I love you, Tallie Savas," he whispered later. "Don't ever leave me again."

"Never," Tallie promised. She kissed him long and slow and deep. "I didn't want to leave you in the first place. But I couldn't—couldn't marry for less than love."

"Neither could I," Elias said. "I just couldn't admit it." He stroked a hand down her smooth skin, loving the feel of her, wanting her again, even though he'd just had her, but happy to wait, too, because they really did have time—and each other.

"Are you serious about baking?" he asked. "Really?"

"I am. I thought I wanted all the business stuff—and it is exhilarating—but the baking centres me. Like your woodworking," she added, giving him a sideways glance, expecting him to dispute it as he had last time. But he didn't.

"I was thinking about that on the flight over," he said. "Thinking about Pete's windsurfer and Nikos Costanides's boatyard and envying them just a little."

"You saw Peter's windsurfer?"

He nodded. "We're doing it. Theo recommended it. He said you thought it was worth looking at."

"I was leaving it up to you. I just thought maybe—"

"You were right. You were right about Corbett's, too. We didn't buy it. We're doing Pete's windsurfer instead. And he's come onboard as a vice president."

"Peter?"

"Will wonders never cease?" Elias said drily. "He's actually gung-ho about the business now. So I was thinking I might...try my hand at a boat or two. Building, I mean." He seemed almost tentative.

Tallie beamed. "Really? Like Nikos?"

"If you don't mind. Someday I'd like to have what he's got."

"I want you to do what makes you happy," Tallie assured him.

"Boats, then," he decided. "And working with Pete. But mostly—" he looked deep into her eyes "—loving you makes me happy."

"Likewise," Tallie said, nestling against him, laying her head on his chest, listening to the sound of his heart, loving it. Loving him.

Then she lifted her head and looked down at him, still smiling. "We could get to work on it now, you know," she said. "What Nikos has got."

"You want to build a boat?"

"No, darling." Tallie kissed his nose, his chin and then let her lips linger on his lips. "I want to get started on the three stair-stepsons!"

The Greek Boss's Bride

CHANTELLE SHAW

Chantelle Shaw lives on the Kent coast, five minutes from the sea, and does much of her thinking about the characters in her books while walking on the beach. She's been an avid reader from an early age. Her schoolfriends used to hide their books when she visited – but Chantelle would retreat into her own world and still writes stories in her head all the time. Chantelle has been blissfully married to her own tall, dark and very patient hero for over twenty years and has six children. She began to read Mills & Boon® novels as a teenager and throughout the years of being a stay-at-home mum to her brood found romantic fiction helped her to stay sane! She enjoys reading and writing about strong-willed, feisty women and even stronger-willed sexy heroes. Chantelle is at her happiest when writing. She is particularly inspired while cooking dinner, which unfortunately results in a lot of culinary disasters! She also loves gardening, walking and eating chocolate (followed by more walking!).

Chantelle Shaw's new novel,
Untouched Until Marriage, **will be available from Mills & Boon® Modern™ in August 2010.**

PROLOGUE

NIKOS NIARCHOU'S VISIT to the London offices of the Niarchou Leisure Group was the subject of intense excitement among all the staff. All the staff bar one, Kezia thought impatiently, as she crossed the reception area and was assailed by the overpowering smell of furniture polish.

'Anyone would think we were expecting a visit from royalty,' she muttered to Jo Stafford, her colleague from the PR department, as they stepped into the lift.

'A visit from the company chairman is as good as,' Jo replied seriously. 'It's over a year since he last came, and the MD is sweating buckets that we make a good impression. Nik Niarchou demands high standards from every member of staff, from top management down to office junior. You *must* remember him,' she added, when Kezia failed to look suitably overawed.

'I joined the company just after his last visit. I remember there was a lot of talk about it, but I've never met him so I'm afraid I don't know what all the fuss is about.'

'You must have heard about him, though,' Jo protested. 'His reputation in the bedroom is almost as legendary as it is in the boardroom. The gossip columns can't get enough of him—but let's face it: he's a gorgeous Greek multimillionaire who has the added attraction of being single. It's not surprising he grabs the headlines—especially now he's decided to settle permanently in England. Apparently he's bought some fantastic stately home in Hertfordshire called Otterbourne House, and there's a queue a mile long for the position of lady of the manor.'

The lift stopped at Kezia's floor and she stepped out. 'You'd better point this demi-god out to me when he arrives. It could prove embarrassing if I don't recognise him,' she added dryly.

'You'll know him,' Jo assured her with a grin. 'Nik Niarchou is unlike any man you've ever met. Trust me, he's unforgettable.'

Kezia hurried past the front desk of the PR department and shook her head at the sight of the receptionist, who was measuring the length of each tulip stalk before placing the bloom carefully in a vase.

The whole place had gone mad, she thought irritably, and all because of one man. How great could he be? Jo had described Nikos Niarchou as some sort of Greek colossus, but it was amazing how blinding the lure of money could be. In reality he was probably short, balding and middle aged—with a paunch, Kezia added for good measure. However, there was no denying the fact that as company chairman, Mr Niarchou was supremely powerful. It was reputed that he had impossibly high standards and she prayed that her boss, Frank Warner, would actually make it into the office on time and sober this morning.

By ten-thirty Frank hadn't shown up, and she was panicking. She had worked as PA to the head of the Niarchou Group's public relations department for the past year, and had to admit that the job was not quite as she had anticipated. Her boss was struggling to cope with an acrimonious divorce and a drink problem. She wasn't sure which one had triggered the other, but she couldn't go on covering for him for much longer without other members of staff noticing. She was fond of Frank, but right now she could cheerfully boil him in oil, Kezia thought darkly as she walked along to the coffee machine and stared down at the car park, searching for his car. There was no sign of him, and with a groan she headed back along the corridor.

'Damn it, Frank, where are you?' she muttered, halting abruptly in the doorway of her office as a figure swung round from the window.

Her first impression of the man who turned towards her was his exceptional height. He was easily five inches over six feet tall, she estimated, unable to drag her gaze from the formidable width of his shoulders. His black, impeccably tailored suit sheathed a lean, hard body, and she noted the impressive muscle definition of his abdomen visible beneath his silk shirt. As if in slow motion she lifted her eyes to his face—and swallowed as the full impact of his handsome face overwhelmed her. Razor-sharp cheekbones, a square jaw that hinted an implacably determined character, and a mouth that was wide, full-lipped and innately sensual.

Jo had been right, Kezia acceded numbly. Nikos Niarchou was unlike any man she had ever met.

There was no doubt in her mind that the man who was watching her with the silent stillness of a predator *was* the head of the phenomenally successful Niarchou Group. He possessed an air of authority teamed with a barely concealed impatience. But nothing had prepared her for his raw sexual magnetism—or her reaction to it.

'That's a very good question, Miss Trevellyn. Where exactly *is* Frank Warner?'

His voice was deep timbred, with a pronounced Greek accent that was so sexy it made her toes curl. *Get a grip,* she told herself fiercely, irritated by the discovery that she seemed to have lost the power of speech.

His dark eyes travelled over her in a slow appraisal, noting the simplicity of her grey skirt and white blouse, and Kezia crossed her arms instinctively over her chest, longing for the protection of her jacket. Her clothes were smart and practical, but beneath his intense scrutiny she was aware that her blouse gaped fractionally over her breasts and her skirt clung faithfully to her curvaceous hips and rounded bottom. His gaze moved lower and skimmed her legs in their sheer black hose before trawling up again, and she had the feeling that he had mentally stripped her bare, leaving her exposed to his gaze.

With a huge effort she forced herself to relax and moved further into the room. 'You have the advantage of knowing my name, but I'm afraid I don't know yours—Mr…?'

'Niarchou—Nikos Niarchou.'

The gleam in his eyes warned her that he was amused by her pretence that she did not know his identity. He dismantled her air of cool efficiency with humiliating ease, and she blushed as she proffered her hand to formalise their introduction.

'And you are Kezia Trevellyn, Frank's personal assistant.'

His hand closed around hers and instantly engulfed it. She had expected the contact to be brief and impersonal, but incredibly he lifted her hand to his mouth and pressed his lips against her fingers. It was electrifying; she almost literally felt sparks shoot down her arm. Her whole body was on fire, and with a gasp she tore her fingers free from his grasp.

Her legs felt distinctly wobbly as a mixture of embarrassment and fierce sexual heat coursed through her veins. She had never felt anything remotely like it before. It was like being hit by a bulldozer. Jo hadn't lied when she'd said Nik Niarchou was unforgettable. Kezia knew instinctively that his darkly handsome features would be imprinted on her brain for ever. But from somewhere she salvaged a little of her self-possession and glanced at him coolly.

'Yes, I'm Frank Warner's PA, but I'm afraid he's out of the office this morning.' She crossed to her desk and made a show of flicking through the diary. 'His meeting is scheduled to finish around lunchtime. If there's something you need to discuss with him, I'll ask him to call you as soon as he gets back.' She awarded him an impersonal smile and moved towards the door, her body language clearly indicating that she expected him to follow her.

Instead he pulled out the chair from behind the desk and sat down.

'Come and take a seat, Miss Trevellyn—or can I call you Kezia?'

The gleam in his eyes told her he would call her what he liked, with or without her permission. He was patently a man who liked his own way, and she was aware that for Frank's sake she had better curb her hot temper.

Once she was seated opposite him he subjected her to a long, hard stare until she shifted restlessly. His expression was unfathomable, his eyes shaded by long black lashes that matched the colour of his hair. This close she caught the subtle tang of his cologne, and her senses flared. She couldn't think straight, and try as she might she seemed to be physically unable to prevent her gaze from straying to his mouth.

'What's going on, Kezia?' he demanded abruptly, the harshness of his tone making her jump. 'We're both aware that Frank's diary is as empty this week as last. I glanced through it before you came in,' he added blandly, plainly unconcerned by her indignant gasp.

'You had no right to snoop through my desk—' she began, her voice faltering as his brows lifted fractionally. He was the company chairman, he had the right to do what he damn well liked and they both knew it.

'Where is he now? The pub?'

'At eleven o'clock in the morning! Of course not—' She broke off and tucked a stray copper-coloured curl behind her ear. 'It's true Frank has had some difficulties in his private life recently,' she admitted slowly. 'I understand that his divorce from his wife was very bitter.'

'And what part did *you* play in the ending of his marriage?' Nik's hard expression did not flicker as twin spots of colour flared on Kezia's cheeks.

'I'm sorry? Why should Frank's divorce have anything to do with me?'

'It's not unheard of for a man of a certain age to make a fool of himself over his much younger secretary. Especially when that secretary is an attractive woman like yourself,' he added coolly, ignoring the sparks of fury in her eyes. 'Your loyalty to your boss is admirable, Kezia, but I'm curious to understand why you would lie in defence of a man who I understand is out of the office more often that he's in it. Word is, you're carrying Frank. The success of the last ad campaign was solely down to you, although you allowed him to take the credit.'

'And my loyalty to him is proof that I'm sleeping with him?' Kezia snapped, trembling with outrage. 'Frank's a friend and colleague, nothing more, and to imply otherwise is hideous.'

She jumped to her feet and glared at Nik Niarchou across the desk. Sinfully sexy and as arrogant as hell, she surmised darkly. He was also far more aware of the problems within the PR department than she had credited, and she feared there was little she could do to help Frank Warner.

'So, if it's not an affair it must be the drink,' Nik mused. 'You have to appreciate that the situation can't carry on, Kezia.' He rose to his feet, towering over her so that she was forced to crane her neck to look at him.

'What will you do? Frank's a good man...' she muttered as he strolled over to the door. She scurried after him. For a moment she thought he was going to ignore her, but then he turned and glanced down at her anxious face.

'Obviously there will need to be changes,' he told her bluntly.

To her consternation he caught hold of her chin and tilted her face so her eyes locked with his. Instantly her senses quivered. He was a sorcerer, and she was held powerless in his spell. He would be an incredible lover, she acknowledged numbly as liquid heat flooded through her veins. His eyes narrowed, his body suddenly taut, and she was mortified by the horrifying realisation that he must have read her mind.

'Your loyalty to Warner is misjudged but impressive, as is your work record. My PA has inconveniently decided to get married and move to Australia with her husband,' he informed her, and Kezia frowned at the unexpected change of subject. 'After ten years of dedicated service, Donna is deserting me.'

'With good reason, as far as I can see,' Kezia muttered, allowing her unruly tongue get the better of her. But to her surprise Nik flung his head back and laughed.

'Spirited as well as beautiful—a dangerous combination,' he drawled. 'But I like danger. It adds spice, don't you think, Kezia? The post of my PA will become available in the next couple of months. I'll look forward to receiving your application.'

'What makes you so sure I'd be interested?' she demanded crossly, irritated by his arrogance.

'Instinct,' he replied softly, his smile deepening as he noted the hectic colour on her cheeks. 'And I'm rarely wrong.'

CHAPTER ONE

NIK WAS DUE home any minute.

Kezia glanced at the clock on the dashboard and pressed her foot down on the accelerator. At this rate her dynamic and notoriously impatient boss would arrive at his country mansion ahead of her, and all hell would break loose. Nik was bringing a group of Bulgarian businessmen to Otterbourne House, hoping to impress them with his plans for a hotel complex on the Black Sea coast, and he expected his PA to be ready and waiting to greet his guests.

Could the day get any worse? Kezia wondered grimly as she peered through the rain. It was bad enough that the catering company she had booked for tonight's party had pulled out at the last minute. Most of the staff had come down with flu, the harassed administrator had explained. But with a day's notice to try and make alternative arrangements, Kezia had been short on sympathy. Fortunately Nik's housekeeper, Mrs Jessop, had rallied round, and was busy preparing a lavish dinner that was set to impress the guests. It had been left to Kezia to collect a selection of desserts from the patisserie, but the trip into town had taken longer than she had anticipated.

The torrential downpour had caused serious flooding along the narrow country lanes, and now dusk was falling.

She needed to focus all her concentration on the road, but as usual it was a certain sexy Greek who dominated her thoughts. An unbidden image of Nik's handsome face filled her mind as she pictured his classically sculpted features. *Get a grip,* she admonished herself sternly, irritated at the way her heartbeat quickened with every mile that she drew nearer to Otterbourne.

He had been away for the past few weeks, visiting his family in Greece, and she was dismayed at how much she had missed him. It was pathetic for a grown woman of twenty-four to have developed such a ridiculous fixation with a man who was way out of her league, she reminded herself savagely. She felt like a teenager in the throes of her first crush and she would die of shame if he ever guessed how much he affected her.

She reached the outskirts of the village and breathed a sigh of relief. Another five minutes and she would be turning in to the gates leading to Otterbourne House. With any luck she would just beat Nik—although she would have little time to tidy her hair or check her make-up. Not that he would notice, she conceded bleakly. As far as Nik was concerned she was his ultra-efficient PA, whose sole purpose was to ensure that his life ran smoothly.

As he had explained at her interview, three months ago, he didn't want a decorative bimbo running his office; he was looking for someone who was prepared to put in long hours and who would blend unobtrusively into the background. With her unruly curls tamed into a sleek chignon, and her sensible navy blue suit, he had obviously deemed Kezia the ideal choice.

There had been no element of the sexual tension she recalled from their first meeting at the London head office— at least not on his part. He'd given no indication that he even remembered her, and the fact that her tongue had tied itself in knots throughout the interview had added to her embarrassment. It was evident that he was only interested in her organisational skills, and sometimes she wondered whether he would notice if she paraded around the office stark naked.

Without warning something shot out from the shadows and ran in front of the car. Kezia hit the brakes, skidded on the wet road and lost control. She was heading for the trees, and with a frantic cry she jerked the wheel. The engine stalled and she ploughed into the bushes that lined the road. So much for concentrating, she thought shakily. The seat belt had saved her from serious injury, but the force of the impact had caused her to hit her head on the steering wheel, and already she could feel a lump the size of an egg swelling on her temple.

She restarted the engine and cautiously backed up onto the road before climbing out of the car. It was too dark to make a proper inspection for damage, but at least the car was drivable. A wave of sickness swept over her. What was it that had run out? Probably a fox that had now disappeared into the undergrowth, she told herself as she squinted through the rain. She was cold and wet, and running seriously late, but the thought of leaving an animal lying injured on the roadside was abhorrent to her, and with a muttered curse she began to search along the verge.

Ten minutes later she was soaked to the skin and ready to give up when a faint whimper drew her attention to the other side of the ditch. The dog was no more than a bag of bones. Its fur was wet and matted, and in the dark in was impossible to see if it was injured, but when she held out her hand it moved tentatively towards her.

'Come on, boy,' she whispered gently, feeling the animal tremble with a mixture of cold and fright as she lifted it into her arms. 'Let's get out of this rain.'

She waded back across the ditch, but as she scrabbled up the slippery bank she felt the heel of one of her shoes give way and cursed loudly. Her new kitten-heel shoes were ruined, and her skirt was covered in mud. Nik was going to go mad, Kezia acknowledged as she hobbled over to the car and deposited the dog on the front seat. He had spent the past week on the phone, relaying precise instructions for the weekend, and it was safe to assume that he would not be impressed when his PA turned up late, looking as if she'd been dragged through a hedge backwards.

Otterbourne House stood at the end of a long drive, hidden from view by tall conifers. Nikos Niarchou felt his heart lift as the limousine rounded the bend and he absorbed the classical elegance of his English country manor. It was good to be back, he thought with a surge of satisfaction—despite the rain. Much as he had enjoyed his trip to Greece, the past couple of weeks seemed to have lasted a lifetime.

It had been good to spend time with his family, but his parents' unsubtle hints about it being time for him to find a nice Greek girl and settle down had driven him mad. His mother had seized on his visit as an opportunity to nag him to slow his pace, assuring him that he looked tired and accusing him of overdoing things, but it had been the sight of his father, unexpectedly frail and looking every one of his eighty years, that had caused Nik to take a break from his hectic schedule.

Now he was eager to get back to work—starting with the presentation that he hoped would impress the Bulgarians into backing his plans for a hotel complex. He was confident that Kezia had organised tonight's reception with her usual efficiency. As he ushered his guests through the front door, he glanced around the entrance hall expectantly. Kezia was supposed to be here. He had specifically asked her to act as his hostess, and he frowned when his elderly housekeeper stepped forward to greet him.

'Where's Kezia?' he demanded, without preamble.

'Good evening, Mr Niarchou, it's good to have you back.'

'It's good to be back, Mrs Jessop.' His brief smile revealed a flash of white teeth that contrasted with his olive gold skin but failed to add warmth to his dark eyes. 'I was expecting Kezia to be here,' he muttered in an impatient undertone. 'Where the hell is she?'

He had spent a trying day entertaining the Bulgarian businessmen and their wives aboard his private jet, the language barrier having proved an exasperating obstacle to conversation. He needed his PA here, damn it. Corporate entertaining was one of Kezia's duties, and he had planned to leave his guests in her capable hands while he took a break to shower and unwind. He had given specific orders, and he did not expect them to be flouted without a very good reason.

'There were some problems with the caterers. All sorted now,' the housekeeper hastily reassured him, 'but Kezia had to run into town. She'll be here any minute, I'm sure.'

'I hope so.'

Nik's frown deepened in annoyance. He had come to rely on his PA over the past three months. Sensible and efficient, Kezia was an ideal employee, who could be relied upon to get on with

her work without fuss. Beneath her calm demeanour she possessed a sharp wit that made conversations with her interesting—
as he had discovered the first time he had met her at the London
office. He was a man who liked to have his own way, yet he was
secretly amused by Kezia's refusal to let him dominate her. He
had missed her while he was away, he realised with a flicker of
surprise and he was looking forward to renewing their discussions on everything from politics to the arts.

His eyes narrowed as the drawing room door opened and a
familiar figure emerged. 'What is Miss Harvey doing here?' he
muttered under his breath to his housekeeper. Tania Harvey, his
current mistress, was a sinful siren, with a body to die for, but
she had little else to offer other than an encyclopaedic knowledge of celebrity gossip—and he was not in the mood to listen
to hours of tittle-tattle about life on the modelling circuit.

'I understand she's joining you for dinner,' Mrs Jessop
replied brightly.

'At whose invitation?' There was no disguising the irritation in Nik's voice and Mrs Jessop shrugged helplessly.

'I don't know. I assumed you… Perhaps Kezia invited her?'
she murmured. 'That sounds like her car now—you can ask her.'

'I intend to. Believe me.'

Tania was walking towards him, and with a supreme
effort Nik stifled his impatience as she wrapped her arms
around his neck.

'Hello, darling. Welcome home,' she murmured, pouting
prettily in the way he had once found a turn-on but which was
now as annoying as her overtly proprietary air. He had no intention of allowing Tania or any other woman to consider
Otterbourne as *home*—at least not for the foreseeable future.

'Tania, what a charming surprise—I hadn't realised you

would be here,' he greeted her politely, as he disentangled himself from her grasp.

'Your PA invited me—I assumed on your behalf.' The pout deepened. 'You are pleased to see me, aren't you, Nik? Kezia was most insistent that I joined you for dinner.'

'Was she? That was very thoughtful of her,' he murmured dryly. 'Naturally I'm pleased to see you, but I'm afraid I'm going to be busy for most of the weekend.'

'Lucky I'm here, then. I can help you relax,' Tania assured him blithely and Nik's jaw tightened.

Tania Harvey was elegant and blonde, two of the attributes he looked for in a woman, but he freely admitted that he had a low boredom threshold. Her hints that she was hoping for a more permanent place in his life were the last straw. It was time to end the affair—which, if he was honest, had reached its sell-by date even before his trip to Greece.

Close up, Tania wasn't as confident as she appeared. Beneath the glossy façade there were shadows in her eyes, and if he'd had any deep feelings for her he would have felt a tug of compassion. Instead all he felt was irritation with his PA for putting him in an awkward situation. Up until now Kezia Trevellyn had proved to be an excellent assistant, but he didn't need anyone to organise his love-life.

The fleet of limousines lining the drive were evidence that Nik and his guests had already arrived. Kezia parked her Mini and switched on the interior light to inspect her face in the driving mirror. God, she looked a mess, she thought dismally. Her hair had escaped its once neat bun and was tangled around her face; there were streaks of mud on her cheeks and a huge bluish lump on her forehead.

'Prepare for fireworks,' she warned the muddy ball of fur on the seat next to her.

At the sound of her voice the dog cocked one ear and stared at her with soulful eyes. She still wasn't sure if she had actually hit it, or if it had been injured, but to be on the safe side she lifted it into her arms and carried it up the front steps.

'Kezia…my dear.' Mrs Jessop opened the front door and gasped at the sight of Kezia's bedraggled form but Kezia's gaze was drawn to the tall figure whose presence dominated the room.

'*Theos!* What happened to you?' Nik demanded, his face thunderous as he strode towards her.

His expression of utter disbelief would have been comical if Kezia had felt like laughing. Instead, all she could think of was that she had ruined her new shoes and was leaving a trail of mud across the floor. She was so wet that her skirt was plastered to her thighs, and as a final insult there was a huge ladder in her tights.

'I had a slight accident,' she told him briskly, hoping to mask the fact that she felt like bursting into tears. It was delayed shock, she told herself, and had nothing to do with Nik looking as though he would like to strangle her. She hadn't seen him for weeks, and the impact of his exceptional height and broad shoulders encased in a charcoal-grey overcoat made her close her eyes for a second.

He possessed an aura of raw, sexual magnetism—a primal force that was barely concealed beneath the veneer of civilisation his clothes awarded him. Remove the designer suit and the man would still be impressive—probably more so, she acceded faintly as she sought to impose control on her wayward imagination. She had only felt half alive these past few weeks, but now the blood was zinging through her veins.

One look from him could reduce her to jelly, and her face burned as she felt his eyes trawl over her mud-spattered clothes. From the gleam of fury in his gaze it was safe to assume that he was not as impressed by the sight of her.

'What kind of accident? What the hell is going on, Kezia? And what is *that?*' he growled as his gaze settled on the animal nestled in her arms.

'It's a dog. It ran into the road and I had to swerve to avoid hitting it. I'm not sure I was entirely successful,' Kezia added worriedly. 'It could be hurt.' She trailed to a halt beneath Nik's impatient glare.

'Never mind the damn dog. Look at the state of you. I expected you to be here, not traipsing around the countryside collecting waifs and strays.' He loomed over her, his brows drawn into a slashing frown that warned of his annoyance, and Kezia felt her temper flare. She had spent all day trying to organise his wretched dinner party, and she hadn't driven ten miles across the Hertfordshire countryside in the pouring rain for fun. 'Mrs Jessop mentioned a problem with the caterers?' he growled.

'There was, but it's sorted,' she said quickly, remembering that she still had to retrieve the boxes of cakes from her car.

'It had better be. I want this presentation to go without a hitch, and I'm relying on you,' Nik warned darkly, his eyes narrowing as he caught sight of the lump on her head. '*Theos,* you're hurt. Why didn't you tell me?' he demanded, pushing her hair back from her forehead to study the large bruise.

Kezia was suddenly acutely aware of an angry glare from Tania Harvey, who had just walked into the room, and she jerked away from him.

'You didn't give me a chance. Leave it, Nik, I'm fine,' she muttered as he probed the lump with surprisingly gentle fingers.

He was too close for comfort. His coat was unbuttoned and she was aware of the muscles of his abdomen visible beneath his silk shirt. He smelled good—fresh and masculine—and the evocative tang of the aftershave he favoured swamped her senses. Her pulse rate soared and she was aware of the need to put some distance between them before she made a fool of herself. Even more of a fool, she amended wryly as she glanced down at her mud-encrusted shoes. That ditch had been full of stagnant water, and she felt her cheeks burn when Nik wrinkled his nose.

'I'll get cleaned up and call a vet,' she assured him.

'For your head?' He was plainly puzzled.

'For the dog. It may have a broken bone, and it must be shocked, it's barely moved.'

'Blow the damn dog,' Nik exploded in a furious whisper, conscious of the need to keep his voice down so as not to alarm his guests. 'I'm going to ring the doctor. You may be suffering from concussion. Something has certainly addled your brain,' he added sarcastically.

'I'm perfectly all right,' Kezia snapped back, refusing to admit that she had a pounding headache. 'I've arranged for Mrs Jessop's niece Becky and a couple of her friends from the village to help with the party. Becky can show your visitors to their rooms, and we'll meet for cocktails at seven, as planned. Everything's under control, Nik,' she assured him, but he was plainly unconvinced.

'I'm glad you think so. But I'm curious to know what you're going to wear tonight—because you cannot sit through dinner looking and smelling like you do right now.' He let his eyes travel over her disparagingly, unperturbed by her scarlet cheeks. 'You'd better have a bath—you stink—' He broke off as his mistress approached. 'Perhaps Tania can lend you something.'

'I'm not sure Kezia could squeeze into any of *my* clothes; we're very different shapes,' Tania purred, her words drawing attention to her sleek, honed figure compared to Kezia's unfashionable curves.

Kezia gave a bright smile, determined to hide her humiliation and marched towards the stairs leading to the basement kitchen and staff quarters. 'I'll find something,' she promised. 'Trust me, Nik, everything's going to be fine.'

Twenty minutes later the bundle of mud and fur that Kezia had rescued from the ditch emerged from the kitchen sink, transformed into a small, black dog of dubious parentage.

'It looks like a terrier cross,' Mrs Jessop remarked. 'But crossed with what I couldn't say.'

'He doesn't seem to be hurt, just hungry,' Kezia said, and she sneaked a piece of chicken and fed it to the dog. 'He's very friendly. I'll put a notice up in the village tomorrow. Hopefully someone will come and claim him.'

'I wouldn't bank on it,' the housekeeper told her. 'I reckon he's been abandoned. From the look of him, he's not eaten for days—which doesn't mean you can feed him best chicken breast. That's for dinner, Kezia. I don't think Mr Niarchou would be too happy to hear you've fed the main course to a flea ridden stray.'

'He hasn't got fleas. And now I've bathed him I think he looks rather cute.'

Kezia stroked the dog, and her heart melted when it licked her hand. As a child she had longed for something of her own to love, but the boarding school she had attended from the age of eight hadn't allowed pets. The school holidays had been spent with her parents in Malaysia, where her father had worked. She had pleaded with her mother to be allowed to keep a pet, but her parents enjoyed a busy social life and had had little enough time for their daughter, let alone an animal.

'I can't just turn him out in the rain,' she murmured anxiously. 'Would you mind keeping an eye on him, Mrs Jessop?'

'While I prepare a four-course dinner for fourteen, you mean?' the housekeeper teased good-naturedly.

'I'm sorry about the caterers.' Kezia groaned. 'I can't believe they let me down at the last minute. This presentation is important to Nik, and you know how demanding he is. Everything's got to be perfect. If you can manage the cooking, I'll act as hostess for the evening while Becky and the girls serve dinner.'

'You'll be joining them at the table, though, won't you?' the housekeeper queried.

'No. I'll need to organise wine and drinks, and make sure the evening runs as smoothly as possible. I won't have time to sit down and eat.'

'Nik won't like that,' Mrs Jessop warned, and Kezia's heart sank as she envisaged Nik's reaction when she failed to join him for dinner.

'He doesn't have a lot of choice,' she muttered grimly. 'The catering company would have sent a master of ceremonies as well as a team of waiters and without them the evening is in danger of being disastrous. We'll just have to manage. We can't do more than our best. But I don't know what I'm going to do about my skirt.'

'Becky has some spare clothes with her,' Mrs Jessop said. 'I'll ask her if she's got anything you can borrow, you're about the same size. But you'd better get a move on if you're going to join them upstairs for cocktails.'

In the shower, Kezia scrubbed her skin until it tingled and she was sure she no longer smelled of ditchwater. She couldn't forget the expression of distaste on Nik's face, and she was determined that when they next met she would be clean and fragrant.

She discovered Becky waiting for her in Mrs Jessop's bedroom.

'My aunt explained about you falling in the ditch. Luckily I've got a spare skirt with me, and shoes. You're welcome to borrow them if they fit,' the young girl offered.

'You're a lifesaver,' Kezia replied gratefully. 'Thanks, Becky. I'll be ready in five minutes.'

The shoes were black stilettos with three-inch heels. Not the style of footwear she would have chosen, Kezia thought grimly, especially when she was going to be on her feet for most of the evening. Mercifully the skirt was a reasonable length—not one of Becky's mini-skirt numbers—but it fitted Kezia like a second skin, the shiny black satin clinging lovingly to her hips and bottom. Teamed with sheer black tights and the high-heels, she looked very different from her usual image of discreet elegance, and she groaned as she imagined Nik's reaction.

A glance at the clock warned her she was running out of time. Taking a deep breath, she headed for the kitchen to see Mrs Jessop, but stopped abruptly at the unexpected sight of Nik chatting to this housekeeper.

'I thought they'd fit,' Mrs Jessop murmured when she entered the steam-filled kitchen. 'Doesn't Kezia look nice, Mr Niarchou?'

'Very…eye-catching.' Nik was leaning against the Aga, his arms folded across his chest.

His eyes narrowed as he focused on her, and Kezia blushed and nervously smoothed an imaginary crease from the skirt. She felt strangely vulnerable without the protection of her formal work suit, especially when Nik's gaze trawled down to her legs and the killer heels.

'I know what you must be thinking,' she faltered, and his brows shot up.

'I sincerely hope you don't,' he drawled. 'I could be arrested.'

'My skirt and shoes are ruined. Becky kindly lent me these. I appreciate they're not ideal...'

'It depends what you're planning to do in them. Lap dancing, perhaps?' he queried sarcastically. 'That should certainly liven up the evening.'

'Look, if you think for one minute that I'm enjoying wearing these clothes, think again,' she snapped furiously.

The glint of amusement and another, indefinable emotion in Nik's eyes was the final straw, and Kezia glared at him. The frisson of sexual awareness between them existed in her mind only, she was sure. He had made it clear that she was just a member of his staff. She must have imagined the flare of heat in his eyes before his lashes fell, concealing his thoughts.

It didn't help that *he* looked so gorgeous, she thought dismally. He had changed into a superbly tailored black dinner suit and a white shirt that emphasised the golden hue of his skin. A lock of black hair fell forward onto his brow, and flecks of amber warmed his dark eyes. She was acutely conscious of him as he strolled towards her. For a man of well over six feet tall, he moved with the lithe grace of a panther— lean, dark and inherently powerful.

She would be able to detect his presence anywhere. He possessed a charisma that alerted her senses and made the fine hairs on the back of her neck stand up. The house had seemed dead without him these past weeks, but now the atmosphere crackled with a surfeit of static electricity that exacerbated her tension.

'How's the head?' he queried, towering over her so that she took a step backwards and banged into the table.

'It's fine; I told you there was nothing to worry about. Contrary to belief, my brain is in perfect working order,' she added coolly and was awarded a look that did strange things to her insides.

Nik laughed, throwing back his head so that her eyes were drawn to the tanned column of his throat. 'I'm glad to hear it, *pedhaki mou*.'

His earlier anger seemed to have disappeared and she quivered beneath the full onslaught of his charm. In many ways he was easier to deal with when he was angry—at least then she could tell herself that she disliked him.

'I called my doctor about signs of possible concussion. Do you feel dizzy?'

She certainly did—but not because she was concussed, Kezia acknowledged ruefully. Standing this close to Nik was making her head spin.

'No,' she answered firmly.

'Nauseous?'

'No.'

'Do you have a headache?'

She hesitated a fraction too long and his eyes narrowed. 'Do you think you were knocked out? Even for a few seconds? And what about your neck? There's a danger you've suffered whiplash.'

'Nik…for heaven's sake!' Kezia stifled a gasp as he caught

hold of her chin and tilted her face so that she was forced to stare up at him. 'What are you doing?'

'Checking your pupils,' he murmured, in a low, gravelly voice that brought her flesh out in goosebumps.

She felt as though time ceased to exist. The sounds and smells of the kitchen faded as her senses focused on the man in front of her.

'Curious,' he mused softly, after he had spent what seemed like a lifetime staring down at her.

Kezia fidgeted restlessly, wishing she could break free of the spell that seemed to have frozen her muscles. She wanted to turn her head, but found herself transfixed by his eyes that were the colour of rich sherry.

'What is?' she whispered breathlessly. His description of her as curious made her feel as though he was inspecting a specimen in a jar, and brought her hurtling back to earth.

'I can't decide if your eyes are green or grey, they're an unusual mixture of both. Your pupils are slightly dilated. Why is that, do you suppose?' His breath fanned her cheek, and she swallowed and tried to pull free of his grasp, but he merely tightened his hold.

'I really don't know. But I do know that I feel perfectly all right. It's almost seven, Nik,' she said on a note of desperation. 'We should be upstairs, preparing to greet your guests.'

'In a minute—I want a word with you first.'

A sudden nuance in his voice disturbed her, and she felt a flicker of apprehension. What had she done now? 'I'm sorry about the caterers,' she said quickly. 'But it wasn't my fault—and Mrs Jessop has dinner under control.'

'I'm not concerned with domestic arrangements,' he told her coolly. 'My concern is of a personal nature—our relationship, to be specific, and your apparent desire to be involved in my intimate affairs.'

'*What?*' The room swayed so alarmingly that Kezia was forced to grip the edge of the table, and she wondered briefly whether she was suffering the effects of concussion after all. 'I don't know what you mean,' she mumbled, her face flaming.

How had he guessed her feelings for him? Had she inadvertently given some sign that revealed her awareness of his brooding sexuality? She couldn't carry on working for him if that was the case. It would be unbearable. Drowning in humiliation, it took a few seconds for her to realise that he was speaking.

'I mean your decision to invite Tania to dinner tonight. Your role as my PA does *not* give you the right to interfere in my private life.'

The amber flecks had disappeared from his eyes, leaving them dark and dispassionate. His concern of a few moments ago had also gone, and she confronted the sickening realisation that his friendliness had been a callous ploy to make her lower her defences while he prepared his attack.

'I didn't invite her. Well, I suppose I did,' Kezia qualified. 'But she knew about the dinner party, and she gave me the impression that you expected her to attend.'

'Did I specify that she should be included on the guest list?'

'No, but—'

'Then why take matters into your own hands? Your job as my PA does *not* require you to organise my love-life.'

'That's not exactly true,' Kezia snapped, irritated by his arrogance. 'It was left to me to dispatch flowers to your last blonde when you ended the affair. *And* I had to pick out a piece of jewellery,' she added, remembering the demeaning trip to the jewellers Nik had sent her on. 'I thought that keeping your harem happy was very much part of my duties.'

'*Theos,* you forget your position, Kezia,' he growled furiously.

She swallowed, and wondered how he could switch from friend to foe so quickly.

'Naturally there may be times when I need you to deal with private matters, but I assumed I could expect a certain amount of discretion. What do you think I pay you such a generous salary for?'

'My staying power?' Kezia suggested sweetly. 'You can't have it both ways, Nik. If Tania is suddenly off the menu, you should have said so.' Her relief that she had misunderstood him earlier, and that he hadn't guessed she was suffering from a massive case of hero-worship, was giving way to anger at his appallingly chauvinistic attitude. He might have the face and body of a Greek god, but he had a heart of stone. She should count herself lucky that he would never view her as anything other than his boring secretary.

'You should be thankful that I had not invited another…companion for the weekend,' Nik flung at her as he headed for the stairs leading up to the main floor. 'It could have proved highly embarrassing for everyone.'

'But that would have meant two-timing Miss Harvey,' Kezia said slowly, frowning at the implication of his words. His long legs had already propelled him up the stairs, and she raced after him, following him into the drawing room. 'That's a despicable way to behave.'

For a moment she thought he hadn't heard her. He was standing at the bar, his back towards her, but then he turned— and she quailed at the hardness of his expression.

'Let's get one thing straight, Kezia,' he said softly, his tone revealing a degree of cynicism that made her wince. 'How I choose to live my life is my business. In my world, affairs have little to do with the heart, and the women I date know the score. The pursuit of mutual sexual pleasure with no strings,' he elaborated sardonically.

His words made her blush, but inside she felt chilled by his clinical detachment.

His smile was devoid of warmth as his eyes raked over her mercilessly. 'I don't know what Tania has hinted about our relationship, but she's under a delusion if she thinks she is about to become a permanent feature in my life. I suggest you discount any romantic notions she might have put into your head,' he advised. 'In the unlikely event that I should ever need your advice on my private life, I'll ask for it. Until then I expect you to follow my orders and abide by my decisions without question. Is that clear?'

'As crystal,' Kezia replied curtly.

Beneath his charm he possessed a ruthlessness that made her shiver, but even now she was agonisingly aware of him. Since that day when she had discovered him in her office she had been unable to put him out of her mind. He dominated her fantasies and haunted her dreams. She must have been mad to believe she could work for him, she thought grimly. When she'd learned that she had beaten the many other applicants for the job as his PA she had been filled with a mixture of fear and excitement. It was a dream job, and she had spent the past few months travelling to exotic locations aboard Nik's private jet, but all the while she'd had to fight to hide her attraction to a man who barely noticed her while he worked his way through a variety of elegant blondes.

Voices from the hall warned her that his guests would soon

join them, and she struggled for composure. She would rather die than allow him to see her misery—or, even worse, guess the reason for it.

'I think we understand one another perfectly, Nik,' she said coldly, pride giving her the courage to meet his gaze. 'And I can't tell you how glad I am that I'm not part of your world.'

CHAPTER TWO

NIK BIT BACK a retort as his guests filed into the room, but his anger was evident in the rigid tension of his jaw. The words *You're fired* hung in the air and Kezia quickly tore her eyes from his furious face.

She was half tempted to walk out and leave him to it. Let *him* entertain the group of Bulgarian businessmen and their wives—particularly the wives, she thought sourly, noting the way every woman in the room was openly staring at Nik. It wasn't surprising, she conceded bleakly. Despite the fact that all the men present were wealthy and successful—uniform in their formal dinner suits—Nik's height and sheer magnetic presence commanded attention. He teamed sophistication with a raw, masculine sensuality that made him irresistible, and she knew she wasn't the only woman in the room to be fascinated by the idea of taming him.

Another of her fantasies, she reminded herself sharply. Beneath his urbane façade he possessed a wildness that no woman would ever control. Nikos Niarchou answered to no one, and she doubted his glorious arrogance would ever be subdued.

With a sigh, she swung round and came face to face with Tania Harvey, whose late arrival ensured that she was the focal point of attention. In a stunning gold sheath, her blonde hair piled on top of her head, Tania had mastered the art of looking both elegant and sexy, and she smiled confidently as she strolled across the room.

'What on earth has happened to the caterers?' she queried loudly. 'There appears to be a group of teenage girls serving drinks. I would have expected better organisation than this, Kezia.'

'The catering company pulled out at the last minute,' Kezia replied stiffly. 'Becky and her friends kindly offered to help out, and I'm just about to join them in handing round canapés.'

'*You?*' Nik demanded with a frown, and Kezia felt a flash of impatience.

As he had so often pointed out, it was her job to see that his life ran like clockwork, and if that meant playing the role of waitress at his damn dinner party, so be it.

'Yes—unless you have another suggestion? Mrs Jessop is rushed off her feet, and Becky and the girls can't manage by themselves.' She knew she sounded snappy, but she was tired, her head ached, and she was sure Nik was comparing her appearance in the too-tight skirt with Tania's cool beauty.

He was looking at her now as if she had taken leave of her senses. He wasn't used to being spoken to in that tone of voice, and the hardness of his stare warned her to expect the full force of his anger once they were out of earshot of his guests.

Stifling a groan, she marched over to Becky and her friends, praying they hadn't overheard Tania's tactless remarks. Mrs Jessop had prepared canapés with smoked salmon and caviar to accompany the champagne. Smiling encouragingly at the girls, she picked up a tray and moved among the guests, unaware that Nik's dark gaze followed her.

'Darling, we'll really have to think about hiring more permanent staff,' Tania murmured in Nik's ear, and he stiffened, fighting to control his irritation. 'It's silly to have to rely on the housekeeper and a gaggle of spotty teenagers your secretary has dredged up from the village every time we entertain. And God knows where Kezia gets her dress sense from,' she added disparagingly. 'The skirt she's wearing is indecently tight. Perhaps it wouldn't be a *bad* thing if she spent the evening in the kitchen, out of sight.'

'Tread carefully, *agape mou*,' Nik warned softly, his eyes narrowing as he surveyed her. 'I'm quite happy with my domestic arrangements. I'm sure Kezia is doing her best, in a situation that I understand was out of her control, but if you would prefer not to stay I'll have my driver take you home.'

'I didn't mean—' Tania broke off nervously, her composure slipping. 'You can be so brutal sometimes, Nik. Of course I want to stay.'

'Especially after you went to such lengths to engineer an invitation,' he agreed coolly, feeling nothing but indifference at the tremulous wobble of her mouth. 'You know the rules, Tania. Don't overstep the mark.'

Without awarding his soon to be ex-mistress another glance, he moved to mingle with his guests, playing the role of genial host while his eyes scanned the room for Kezia.

She had intrigued him from the start, he acknowledged as he watched her work the room, chatting to the guests while serving flutes of champagne. Her intelligence and unflappable nature had made her the ideal choice as personal assistant. Her willingness to put in long hours and travel at a moment's notice were an additional bonus; he had neither the time nor the patience to deal with staff who led complicated private lives.

Kezia Trevellyn had slipped into her role with seamless ease, but he was aware of the sexual chemistry that hovered like a spectre between them. From the moment they'd met at the London office he had been plagued by a burning desire that was as fierce as it was unexpected. Her lush curves were a distraction he could do without, he conceded derisively as his eyes focused on the delightful sway of her bottom beneath its covering of tight satin. The most sensible course of action would be to forget the increasingly erotic fantasies Kezia evoked and concentrate on her excellent organisational skills. One of his unwritten rules was to keep his work and private lives separate, but the physical attraction he felt for her was proving difficult to ignore.

Sensible had never held much appeal, he accepted honestly. He was a man who liked to live dangerously.

As if alerted by some sixth sense, she looked up at that moment and met his gaze. He noted with interest the flush of colour that stained her cheeks as their eyes clashed, and lifted his glass in salute. It was satisfying to realise that the attraction was mutual.

It had been the evening from hell, Kezia decided several hours later as she glanced at the array of dirty glasses that littered the sitting room. Her calf muscles were throbbing almost as much as her head, and with a sigh she sank down onto the sofa.

Fortunately dinner had been a success, thanks to the excellent meal Mrs Jessop had provided and the hard work of Becky and her friends as they'd waited table. Kezia had been kept busy organising the girls, who had been plainly overawed by the elegant formality of the dining room and the number

of guests seated around the table. She had taken one look at
Nik's glowering expression when he realised she would not
be joining the dinner party, and had kept out of his way as
much as possible. Luckily the wines she had selected to accompany each dish had seemed to meet with his approval.
She'd moved endlessly around the table, refilling glasses, and
by the time the party had moved into the sitting room for
coffee and liqueurs her feet had been aching and she had
longed for her comfortable flat shoes.

Even then there had been no reprieve. Nik had planned a
detailed presentation of his ideas for a hotel and leisure
complex, a short film and a speech, followed by an opportunity
for questions and discussion. There had been no time for Kezia
to relax as she had once more assumed the role of hostess,
serving drinks to the increasingly raucous group of businessmen, and it had been past midnight before the party finally
broke up. Ahead of her loomed a twenty-minute drive through
the dark country lanes to her flat, where she hoped to snatch a
few hours' sleep before returning to Otterbourne tomorrow.

Sighing wearily, she searched through her handbag for her
car keys. They seemed to have disappeared and, muttering an
oath, she tipped the contents of her bag onto the coffee table.

'I take it you're looking for these?'

The familiar drawl brought her head up, and she stiffened,
each of her senses on high alert, as Nik strolled into the room.
He had discarded his tie and exchanged his dinner jacket for
one of black leather. She noted the faint stubble visible on his
jaw and hastily dropped her gaze. He exuded a brooding sexuality that made her nerves tingle, and she swallowed convul-
sively, desperate to hide the effect he had on her.

Taking a deep breath, she scooped her belongings back into

her bag and walked towards him, her hand outstretched.
'There they are. Where did you find them?' she queried,
striving to remain composed when he made no attempt to
return the bunch of keys.

'In your bag,' Nik replied calmly, watching the array of
emotions that crossed her face—surprise, confusion, and
lastly a flash of anger as the implication of his words hit home.

'How dare you? What do you suppose gives you the right
to rummage through my personal belongings?'

'They were on the top,' he informed her hardily. 'And, as
to the question of rights, you're my employee, my responsibility, and I have no intention of allowing you to drive home
alone this late at night—especially as you were injured earlier
this evening.'

'I'm fine.' If she discounted being tired and stressed. She
certainly didn't possess the energy to deal with Nik any more
tonight. 'It's been a long day and I want to go home.' She
glanced pointedly at her watch as she spoke, but Nik continued to study her speculatively while retaining hold of her keys.
'This is ridiculous. You can't hold me here against my will.'

'You should know by now that I can do anything I like,' he
said, with his usual breathtaking arrogance. 'It would be better
if you stayed the night so that I can keep an eye on you. I still
think you should be checked over by a doctor.'

The idea of Nik keeping an eye on her throughout the night
was so mind-boggling that Kezia was temporarily speechless.
'There are no rooms spare,' she said quickly. 'And I don't have
anything to wear tomorrow—unless you want me to spend the
day looking like a lap dancer,' she added tartly, as she recalled
his comments on her appearance at the start of the evening.
'One night of humiliation is enough, surely?'

'There was no reason for you to feel embarrassed tonight,' he told her seriously. 'I was impressed with the way you organised dinner. Especially as I understand you had less than twenty-four hours' notice from the catering company announcing that they were pulling out. The presentation went well, and I'm already putting together a consortium of investors interested in backing the project.'

'I was just doing my job,' Kezia muttered, unable to control a surge of pleasure at Nik's approval.

His earlier bad mood seemed to have disappeared, but as far as she was concerned a friendly Nik posed a serious threat to her equilibrium. He was too close for comfort, and despite her best intentions she was unable to drag her gaze from the sensual curve of his mouth. It was definitely time to leave, she thought frantically as she wetted her dry lips with her tongue. The air was heavy with an unspoken tension that was surely the workings of her imagination—but she noted the way Nik's eyes narrowed as he studied her nervous gesture. Her mind ran riot as she envisaged him lowering his head to brush his lips over hers in a slow exploration, and without conscious thought she swayed towards him.

'Are you ready to go?' His voice shattered the sensual haze, and Kezia stepped back abruptly, her face burning.

'I don't need a chauffeur,' she argued stubbornly. 'I'm perfectly capable of driving myself home. Besides, you can't leave your guests.'

'They've all gone to bed,' he said cheerfully, his eyes gleaming with sudden amusement as he studied her pink cheeks.

Had Tania also retired for the night? Kezia wondered. Was Nik's mistress waiting impatiently in the master bedroom, sprawled across the vast bed that she had once glimpsed when

Mrs Jessop had given her a tour of the house? And, if so, surely he was keen to join her?

'I refuse to allow you to drive your car until I've arranged for a mechanic to check it over,' he told her, in a tone that brooked no argument. 'We'll take the Porsche.'

'What about Max? He'll have to come too.'

'Max?' Nik frowned. 'Who the hell's Max?'

'The dog that I almost ran over. I'm going to take him back to my flat.'

'How do you know that's his name?'

'I don't. But I have to call him something until I can return him to his owners. Mrs Jessop thinks he was abandoned, so maybe no one will claim him,' Kezia added, unaware of the wistful note in her voice. She couldn't bear the idea that the dog had been deliberately left by the roadside. 'I'll just run downstairs and collect him,' she said, hurrying out of the room before Nik could argue.

She knew what it was like to feel unwanted, she acknowledged as she scooped the scruffy terrier into her arms. Her heart leapt with pleasure when he burrowed against her, and she was filled with a fierce determination to take care of him. Her mother had always freely admitted she'd never wanted children, and that Kezia's unexpected arrival had been a shock. It wasn't that her parents didn't love her, she conceded, but they had been a professional couple in their forties when she was born, and had expected her to fit into their busy lifestyle. She had spent her childhood feeling that she needed to apologise for her existence, and her years at boarding school, although not unhappy, had reinforced her belief that she was a nuisance her parents didn't quite know how to deal with.

The entrance hall was empty when she carried Max

upstairs, but she spied her car keys on the table and for a moment contemplated making her escape. Not a good idea, she accepted ruefully, imagining Nik's fury if she disobeyed him. From experience she knew it was pointless arguing with him when he had his mind set on something. He had made it clear that he intended to drive her home.

But as she waited for him she overheard voices from his study.

'Why do you have to take her home?' Tania's petulant tones were clearly audible through the closed door. 'For God's sake, Nik, I haven't seen you for a month. Why this sudden concern for your secretary? If it weren't so laughable I'd almost believe you've got something going with her. I saw the way you kept looking at her tonight, but I can't imagine what you see in her.'

'*Theos!* Don't be so ridiculous,' came the terse reply. 'She's not my type. But Kezia's an excellent assistant, she's worked hard all night, and it's my duty to see she gets home safely.'

Hastily Kezia stepped away from the door, swamped with misery and humiliation. She already knew she was far from Nik's ideal woman, but to hear him state the fact quite so forcefully was agony. Never in a million years would she allow him to guess how she felt about him, she vowed fiercely. Her cheeks flamed as she recalled the stark disbelief in his voice that he could possibly find his PA attractive. It was obvious he regarded her as part of the furniture, as functional and unexciting as his computer. She must have imagined the exigent chemistry between them; it was just an illusion brought on by her wishful thinking.

She couldn't bring herself to look at him when he joined her in the lobby a few minutes later, and she was silent as she followed him down the front steps. The rain stung her face, but she carefully placed Max on the narrow back seat of the sports car before climbing in next to Nik, wondering how he managed to fit his long legs behind the wheel.

In the confines of the small car he was too close. She caught the subtle tang of his aftershave, and suddenly the heater seemed to be working too well. She was burning up, but balked at the thought of fighting her way through her coat and instead stared stiffly out of the window as he turned out of the drive.

'There was really no need for you to leave Miss Harvey,' she muttered. 'I feel awful for putting you to so much trouble.'

'It's not a problem,' Nik assured her. He sounded disinterested. He was probably counting the minutes until he could join his mistress in bed, she thought bleakly, and fell silent for the rest of the journey.

Driving along the pitch-black country lanes required all Nik's attention, but as they reached the outskirts of the busy market town where she lived he glanced briefly at Kezia. 'Do you live alone?'

The query surprised them both. He'd never shown the slightest interest in her private life before. He had picked her up from home a couple of times, usually when they'd had an early flight, but she had always been waiting for him in the car park and had never invited him in. Did she have a boyfriend? he wondered. Was her lover waiting impatiently for her to return? He was irritated to realise how much he disliked the idea.

'No, I share with a flatmate.'

Her ambiguous answer told him nothing, and pride prevented him from pushing the point. His secretary's love-life was none of his business, he reminded himself impatiently. 'I'll pick you up in the morning,' he informed her coolly.

'There's no need.' Kezia's head jerked round, her consternation evident in her wide eyes. 'I don't want you to have to get up early. What would Miss Harvey say?' she muttered, blushing again as she pictured Nik struggling out of bed after a night of passion with his mistress, in order to collect *her*.

He turned into the small courtyard in front of her flat and cut the engine before turning to face her. 'Why don't you let me worry about the finer details of my private life?' he drawled, in a tone that warned her to mind her own business. 'I'll be here at eight-thirty.'

Kezia opened her mouth to argue, caught the glint in his eyes and thought better of it. 'Fine. Have it your own way. You usually do,' she added under her breath as she climbed out of the car. She had only been trying to help, damn it. She certainly didn't want to pry into his sex life. She lifted Max out of the car and smiled politely. 'Thanks for bringing me home,' she said stiffly, assuming that he would drive straight off, but as she ran up the steps to the communal front door he was right beside her, and she had to crane her neck to look up at him.

'I'll see you up,' he said easily, and her temper, born from a mixture of embarrassment and misery, ignited.

'For heaven's sake, I'm perfectly all right. Miss Harvey will be wondering where you are,' she couldn't resist adding, and was mortified when he glanced down at her, his eyes gleaming with undisguised amusement.

'I've already told you. I'll take care of Tania.'

'I'm sure you will.' She opened the door to her flat and closed her mind to images of just how he would take care of his mistress. 'Goodnight, Nik.'

'Aren't you going to offer me coffee before I drive back?' He lolled in the doorway, one arm resting on the frame, so that she was aware of the inherent strength of his muscular chest. He exuded a powerful sensuality so intensely male that she rebelled at the thought of him invading her private bolthole. But a voice from behind her took the matter out of her hands.

'Are you coming in or are you going to stand there all night? Oh—hello!' The voice tailed to a breathless whisper, and Kezia sighed as she turned to find that her flatmate Anna was staring at Nik with wide, appreciative eyes. 'You must be Mr Niarchou. Kezia has told me so much about you.'

'Nik, please,' Nik replied in a voice as thick as syrup. He held out his hand and Kezia's impatience intensified. She had witnessed Anna working her magic countless times before, and doubted there was a man on the planet who would prove immune to her beauty. Slender and willowy, her delicate colouring and ash-blonde hair bore testament to her Scandinavian ancestry, while huge blue eyes and a surprisingly impish smile made her simply stunning. They had been best friends since their first day at boarding school, as close as sisters—although right now she could cheerfully strangle her flatmate, Kezia thought grumpily as she watched Nik fall under her spell.

'Are you stopping, Nik?' the pretty blonde murmured. It was an innocent enough query, but Kezia ground her teeth together as Nik gave one of his sexy smiles that made her toes curl.

'I'm not sure. Kezia's still debating whether or not to invite me in for coffee.' His eyes gleamed wickedly as he took in her furious glare, and Anna chuckled.

'Well, I'll make the decision for her,' she said cheerfully, ushering him into the flat. 'I'm Anneliese Christiansen— Kezia's flatmate,' she explained, her blue eyes sparkling, and with a muttered oath Kezia marched down the hallway.

Let Anna entertain him, she thought darkly. She'd had enough of Nik Niarchou for one day. In the kitchen she filled the kettle while Max sniffed around, looking for somewhere to settle. She dug out an old picnic blanket from the utility cupboard and spread it on the floor. If he was going to be here for any length of time she would have to buy him a basket and a lead, she thought happily. He seemed lively enough, but maybe she would take him to a vet, just to make sure he hadn't suffered any injuries when he had run out into the road.

'What on earth is that?' Anna queried as she preceded Nik into the kitchen.

'A dog, of course. What does it look like?'

'A ball of fur on legs,' Anna replied truthfully. 'I suppose it's another stray you've rescued? You know our tenancy agreement prohibits keeping pets in the flat.'

'It'll only be for a couple of days, while I try to trace his owners,' Kezia muttered. 'I could hardly leave him out in the cold. See how thin he is.'

'Kezia's always been the same,' Anna explained to Nik. 'At school she kept a collection of rescued wildlife in the caretaker's shed. Do you remember the time you cared for that injured fox, Kez?'

'Kezia obviously has hidden depths,' Nik murmured, with a curious expression in his eyes that made her blush self-consciously—although she couldn't imagine what he thought those hidden depths were.

'I'm sure you're not interested in reminiscences about our schooldays,' she said stiffly.

He seemed to dominate the small kitchen, and she wished she didn't find him so unsettling. She couldn't relax, and she envied the way Anna was able to chat so unselfconsciously with him. With a sigh, she left her flatmate to make the coffee and headed for the sanctuary of her bedroom. It was a relief to change out of the borrowed skirt and shoes. Her feet would never be the same again, she thought wryly as she wriggled her toes. Her scalp felt tight with tension, and she freed her hair from its tight knot so that it rippled down her back, all the while trying to ignore the sounds of laughter from the kitchen.

It was ridiculous to feel jealous of Anna, she told herself crossly as she stared at her reflection in the mirror. She was lucky to have good friends, a comfortable flat and a dream job that offered the opportunity to travel the world. It was nobody's fault but her own that she had become fixated with a man who was out of her league. And if she wanted to carry on working for Nik she would have to overcome her fascination for him.

CHAPTER THREE

THE RUMBLE OF NIK'S DEEP VOICE, followed by Anna's laughter, sounded from the kitchen. Listening to them, Kezia was tempted to leave them to it. They appeared to have struck up an instant accord, she noted sourly. But it had been good of Nik to bring her home and, much as she longed to fall into bed, it would be impolite not to join him for coffee.

Wearily she tugged on jeans and a sweatshirt, pulled a comb through her hair and padded barefoot down the hall. The kitchen was empty, and when she pushed open the living room door she found Nik alone, sitting in an armchair with his long legs stretched out in front of him.

'Anna's gone to the flat upstairs,' he explained. 'Apparently your neighbour's suffering some sort of emotional crisis.'

'Vicky must have broken up with her boyfriend—again,' Kezia murmured awkwardly, feeling strangely disconcerted at being alone in her flat with Nik.

It was ridiculous. They spent hours in each other's company—either in his study at Otterbourne or travelling aboard his private jet—but this was her private space, and his presence unsettled her more than she cared to admit. She was aware of his silent scrutiny and hastily reached for her coffee, burying her nose in the mug and inhaling the tantalising aroma. The caffeine boost eased her nerves, but there would be hell to pay later when it prevented her from sleeping, she acknowledged ruefully.

'Run through the agenda for tomorrow.' His voice cut through the silence, and she gave herself a mental shake.

'I've booked us into the Belvedere Hall Health Spa for the day. There's an excellent golf course—if it's not too wet—plus a gymnasium, and sports facilities for those who want them. We'll have lunch at one, and I've arranged for you to use one of the private conference rooms to continue discussions with the business consortium while I remain with the wives.'

The spa offered numerous relaxation therapies and beauty treatments—although to Kezia the idea of spending the day encased in a mud pack held little appeal, and she was dreading having to strip down to her functional black swimsuit to use the pool. She didn't feel comfortable displaying her generous curves at the best of times, and parading semi-naked in front of Nik was something she'd hoped to avoid at all costs.

Tomorrow promised to be a long day. Today, she amended, glancing at her watch and discovering that it was now one-thirty in the morning. 'Would you like more coffee?' she asked politely, stifling a yawn.

'Thanks, but I think I'd better let you get to bed.' He stood up, and Kezia jumped to her feet, her pulse rate accelerating as he strolled towards her. 'You have beautiful hair,' he murmured, taking her by surprise as he reached out to coil a strand of her long hair around his finger. 'Why do you never wear it down?'

'I can hardly swan around the office like Lady Godiva,' she replied stiffly, finding it impossible to drag her gaze from the

chiselled beauty of his face. Nik's puzzled frown cleared as
she explained. 'Legend has it that she was a noblewoman
who, hundreds of years ago, rode naked through the streets
with only her long hair to protect her modesty.'

His brows quirked, and his sudden grin made her heart flip.
'That must have been…chilly,' he drawled. 'But I assure you
I wouldn't object, should you want to follow her example.'

She knew he was teasing her, but the knowledge did
nothing to ease her tension or lessen her fierce awareness of
him. With a determined effort she sidled away from him and
headed towards the door. 'I'm sorry, Nik, but I'm dead on my
feet and we've another busy day ahead tomorrow.'

'I hope I haven't disrupted your weekend too much?' he
murmured as he swung his jacket over his shoulder and
followed her into the hall. 'Am I in danger of being
thumped by an irate boyfriend for encroaching on your
free time?'

'Fortunately I don't have a boyfriend—irate or otherwise,'
Kezia replied dryly.

'Really?' His dark eyes trawled over her speculatively, until
she squirmed. 'I find that surprising. Why would an attractive
woman in her mid-twenties choose to be without a lover?'

Kezia glared at him, twin spots of colour flaring on her
cheeks. She felt hot and flustered and thoroughly confused by
his sudden curiosity about her private life. For the past three
months their relationship had been friendly, but aloof. She
wouldn't dream of prying into his personal affairs, and was
puzzled by his sudden interest in hers.

'I'm not dating at the moment because I…' She tailed to a
halt, unable to reveal that he was the only man who excited her
and that anyone else faded into insignificance compared to him.

His ego would love that, she thought grimly as she searched for a suitable excuse for her lack of love-life.

'I was engaged, but it didn't work out, and at the moment I prefer to concentrate on my career. I imagine you've no objections to that?'

'None at all. Your dedication to your job is exemplary,' he said softly, and once again she had the impression that he was laughing at her.

She followed him down the narrow passageway to the front door, and caught her breath when he turned and slid his hand beneath her chin, tilting her head so that she had no option but to look up at him.

'Whose decision was it to end your engagement? Yours or your fiancé's?'

'Again, I can't see what it has to do with you, but it was a mutual agreement. We just felt that we weren't right for each other. Marriage is a serious commitment that shouldn't be rushed into,' she told him, and Nik threw back his head, the sound of his laughter filling the hall.

'My sentiments exactly, *pedhaki mou*—it's good to see we agree on something. I hope your heart wasn't irreparably broken?' he murmured as he stepped onto the landing. 'All work and no play is not good for the soul.'

'I can't imagine how you would know,' she replied tartly, picturing him with the gorgeous Tania. Nik worked and played with equal fervour, and she doubted he had a soul.

He deciphered the play of emotions that crossed her face and grinned unrepentantly. 'Goodnight, Kezia—and thanks for your hard work this evening. My intention is to have the deal signed and sealed by tomorrow evening, and the party are flying home the following morning. What do you have planned for Sunday?'

Kezia shrugged, her confusion evident. He'd just stated that the Bulgarians were leaving on Sunday morning—why would she have planned anything? She was looking forward to a quiet day at home, a chance to catch up on some housework, and maybe taking Max to explore the local park.

'Nothing much,' she admitted.

'Good. Keep it free. I'm taking you to lunch.' He had already reached the stairs and begun his descent.

'But I might have other plans.' He hadn't issued an invitation, it had sounded more like an order, and she rebelled at the thought of him hijacking her one day off.

'You've already admitted that you don't,' he said easily, ignoring her sharp tone.

'I can think of several things I'd rather do in my free time than spend the day discussing your latest business venture.'

'We won't talk about business, I promise.' He had reached the bottom of the first flight of stairs, and as she hung over the banister he smiled up at her, his teeth flashing white against his dark olive skin. 'I think it's time we got to know each other a little better, Kezia, don't you? It'll be interesting to discover if we have anything else in common, apart from our shared views on matrimony.'

He disappeared before she could formulate a reply, but as she walked back into the flat and closed the door Kezia could not throw off her feeling of unease. She didn't know what Nik was playing at, but she had no intention of getting to know him better. Like a cobra, he was safer held at arm's length.

'So that's Nikos Niarchou!' Anna exclaimed when she burst into the flat a few minutes later. 'No wonder you've been so cagey about him.'

'What do you mean by cagey?' Kezia demanded irritably. 'And what's happened with Vicky and Tim now?'

'Nothing.' Anna's momentary frown cleared. 'I said I was going upstairs as an excuse to give you and Nik some privacy. You've never brought him back to the flat before.'

'I didn't bring him back. He insisted on driving me home and, aided by you, invited himself in for coffee. It's nothing to get excited about. And I am *not* cagey about him,' Kezia added firmly.

Anna shrugged, plainly unconcerned by the flash of fire in Kezia's eyes. 'Every time you mention your boss, you blush. But now I've met the gorgeous Nikos in the flesh, so to speak, I'm not surprised you fancy him.'

'I do not fancy him,' Kezia spluttered indignantly. 'I grant that he's attractive, but...'

'He's the sexiest man on the planet,' Anna stated bluntly. 'You'd have to be blind not to notice those brooding come-to-bed eyes of his.' She grinned irrepressibly at the sight of Kezia's scarlet cheeks. 'Is he aware of your feelings?'

'No, he's not...and I don't have feelings for him.' Kezia gave up and muttered something rude under her breath. 'Anyway, he's got a girlfriend. He's going home to her now,' she finished glumly, unable to disguise the bleakness in her voice.

'With his looks he's hardly likely to live like a monk,' Anna pointed out. 'Why don't you let him know you're interested? While I was making the coffee he was definitely grilling me about your love-life. I think you should try flirting with him,' she advised breezily. 'After all, what have you got to lose?'

'Apart from my pride, my self-respect and my job, you mean?' Kezia queried sarcastically.

'What's the real issue here, Kez?' Anna demanded bluntly.

'It's two years since you and Charlie broke up, and I could count on one hand the number of dates you've been on since. Are you going to allow the fact that you can't have children colour the rest of your life?'

'I'm not,' Kezia denied fiercely.

Anna had supported her every step of the way during the illness she had suffered as a teenager, and the bond of trust between them was unbreakable. But, even so, some things were too painful to talk about. At fifteen she had been devastated when she was diagnosed with leukaemia. She had fought a long and ultimately successful battle against the disease, and it had only been later, when she'd made a full recovery, that she'd learned the treatment necessary to save her life had wrecked her chances of ever conceiving a child.

'It has nothing to do with me not dating, but there's no escaping the fact that my infertility was a factor in my break-up with Charlie. His parents threatened to cut him out of his inheritance if he married me, so don't tell me it's not an issue.'

'And now you're running scared of getting involved with anyone else?'

'I'm not scared. It's just easier this way. The subject of children, and my inability to have them, isn't a subject I can just drop into the conversation on a first date, is it?'

'I'm not suggesting you go looking for your soul mate,' Anna pointed out. 'If such a thing exists at all, which I doubt. You know my feelings on the myth of happy-ever-after,' she added darkly. 'My dysfunctional family has done little to convince me of the joys of marriage. But that doesn't mean you can't have fun, Kez, and Nik Niarchou doesn't strike me as the kind of man who's desperate to settle down. A passionate fling with a sexy millionaire could be just what you need—

as long as you don't do anything stupid like fall in love with him of course.'

Kezia felt her face flame as she sought to avoid her flatmate's intense scrutiny.

'My God! Don't tell me that you've fallen for him?'

'Don't be ridiculous! He's my boss, nothing more. Credit me with some sense, Anna,' Kezia snapped. 'Nik's a notorious playboy. Falling in love with him would be asking for a broken heart, and I intend to keep mine intact, thanks.'

Saturday started badly when Kezia opened her eyes and discovered that her alarm clock had failed to go off. 'Damn and blast,' she muttered as she sped into the shower with less than half an hour to spare before Nik was due to collect her.

She had spent a restless night, due no doubt to the coffee. Her conversation with Anna had reawakened the sadness that continued to haunt her despite her best efforts to concentrate on the future. It was a future that was very different from the life she had dreamed of as a child, she acknowledged bleakly.

Growing up without brothers or sisters, she had decided early on that she wanted a big family. Five or six children at least, she'd confided to Anna. While her friends had planned exciting careers, she'd blithely assumed that marriage and motherhood were her destiny. But her illness had shattered those dreams.

She didn't blame Charlie for ending their engagement, she brooded as she pulled open her wardrobe and searched for something to wear. They had met at university, and from the first she had been honest with him. Charles Pemberton was a future earl, and heir to his family's vast Northumberland estate. Good-looking, and blessed with an easy charm, he'd

proved irresistible to a girl who had spent much of her ado-
lescence at an all-girls boarding school or in hospital. But as
their relationship had deepened so had Kezia's fears that she
would never fit into his aristocratic lifestyle.

Charlie had assured her that her inability to have children
made no difference to his feelings for her, but his family had
been plainly disapproving of the relationship, and had put
pressure on him to end it. Two years ago they had bowed to
the inevitable and parted amicably, but Kezia was determined
not to make the same mistakes again. She refused to waste her
time looking for love and commitment. Fate had dealt her a
massive blow, and it had taken her a long time to come to
terms with the fact that she would never be a mother. When
it had come to the crunch Charlie had realised that he could
not accept a future without children, and it was a sacrifice she
would not expect from anyone else.

The peal of the doorbell dragged her out of her reverie, and
she hastily finished braiding her hair before securing it with
an emerald coloured band that matched her jumper. She might
have guessed that Nik would be on time and, snatching up her
bag, she hurried to greet him.

'Ready?' Nik's gaze skimmed Kezia's appearance, admiring the fluid lines of her cream trousers and the way her
lambswool jumper echoed the colour of her eyes.

He was used to seeing her in the formal suits she favoured
for work, but he definitely preferred casual, he decided, his eyes
narrowing as he noted the way her sweater moulded her full,
rounded breasts. For a few seconds he pictured himself exploring those curves with his hands, taking the weight of her breasts
in his palms and gently moulding them. To his chagrin heat
surged through his body, and he felt an uncomfortable prick-

ling sensation in his groin. Stunned by his reaction, he stepped abruptly away from her, his nostrils flaring.

It didn't help that she was staring at him with those stunning eyes, he thought irritably. He'd never noticed before that her eyelashes were tipped with gold and her creamy skin was flawless. Her only concession to make-up was the touch of pink gloss that emphasised the fullness of her lips, and he was tempted to discover if they lived up to their promise of sensual delight.

'I'll just fetch Max,' Kezia murmured, her pulse leaping at the sight of Nik in designer jeans, a soft grey shirt and leather jacket.

'You're surely not intending to take a dog into a health spa?'

'Of course not. But I can't leave him here alone all day. Anna is flying to the US for several modelling assignments. It's fine, Nik,' she assured him as Max obediently followed her onto the landing. 'Mrs Jessop is going to look after him while we're out. He's very well behaved,' she insisted, when Nik failed to look impressed. 'I can guarantee he won't chew the carpets.'

'He'd better not,' he muttered as he eyed the scruffy terrier suspiciously. 'What are you going to do if no one claims him? I understand you're not allowed to keep pets in these flats—and he's not living permanently at Otterbourne, so don't even think about it,' he added hardily.

'If it comes to it, I'll just have to move,' Kezia said cheerfully when they reached the car park.

Nik opened the door of his top-of-the-range Porsche and watched in faint disbelief as the dog scrambled over the leather seats and settled comfortably on the back shelf.

'I told you I should have driven my car home last night,' Kezia remarked tartly, correctly interpreting the look of horror in his eyes. The car was Nik's latest toy, his pride and joy, but she refused to leave Max alone in the flat all day; he might feel lonely. 'I'm not going anywhere without him,' she said stubbornly, folding her arms across her chest and wincing as Nik cursed beneath his breath.

'Fine, but if he makes one mark on the upholstery I'll dock it from your wages.'

Fortunately the journey to Otterbourne passed without incident, and Max bounded up the steps of the grand house as if he owned the place.

'He seems to know his way around already,' Kezia commented admiringly. 'He's so clever. See—he's headed straight for the kitchen. He must feel at home here.'

'Forget it, Kezia,' Nik warned silkily. 'I don't want a dog, and if I did I'd choose an animal that at least *looked* like a dog, rather than a floor mop. Max is your problem, not mine.'

'Your heart really is made of stone, isn't it, Nik?' she said caustically, and was rewarded with a sardonic smile.

'What heart, *pedhaki mou?*'

'I assumed Miss Harvey would be joining us for the day,' Kezia commented an hour later, when the last of their guests finally emerged from the house and climbed into the waiting limousines.

There had been no sight of Tania all morning. Perhaps she was worn out from an energetic night in Nik's bed? Kezia thought cattily, blushing beneath his narrow-eyed scrutiny.

'Tania won't be joining us today, or at any other time in the future,' he informed her coolly. 'And, to satisfy your curiosity, she didn't stay last night either.'

'I'm not curious. It's no business of mine who you spend

your nights with,' she snapped, the colour of her cheeks deepening from pink to scarlet. 'I can't imagine why you think I might be interested,' she added indignantly. 'I'm just your humble secretary.'

'Humble!' Nik gave a shout of laughter as he slid onto the back seat of the limousine next to her and tapped on the glass for the chauffeur to drive on. 'That's not a word I would use to describe you.' His eyes gleamed with amusement as he studied her flushed face, and Kezia pursed her lips.

'I know I'm going to regret asking, but how *would* you describe me?'

'Spirited, strong-willed—a green-eyed wild cat,' he replied instantly, lifting her neat plait into his hand. 'Now that I've seen your hair in all its glory, I'm not surprised. You're a true redhead.'

'And you think the colour of my hair denotes a hot temper?' she queried scathingly. Common sense warned her to drop this conversation now, before it got any more personal, but the imp in her head had scant regard for common sense.

'Actually I find the colour of your hair incredibly sexy.'

Dear God! He was teasing her—wasn't he? She tore her gaze from the indefinable expression in his and stared out of the window, aware that her heart was performing somersaults in her chest. 'You shouldn't say things like that,' she muttered stiffly. 'It's…inappropriate.'

'You would prefer for me to lie?' he queried, his lazy smile doing nothing to settle her nerves.

'I would prefer you to keep your opinions to yourself.' She was intensely aware of his thigh, pressing lightly against hers, and carefully edged along the seat, ignoring his low chuckle that warned he knew exactly how much he unsettled her.

The first time they'd met, in the London office, she had rec-

ognised the undercurrent of sexual chemistry that sizzled
between them. Her awareness of him had been agonising.
She'd felt as though she had been hit by a thunderbolt, and
even more unnerving had been the realisation that the attraction was mutual.

It had been with a mixture of excitement and trepidation
that she had accepted the post as his PA, but in the three
months she'd worked for him she had been secretly disappointed by his purely professional attitude. Obviously she'd
been mistaken, she had told herself. Nik wasn't interested in
her for any other reason than her secretarial skills, and she
must have imagined the flare of desire in his eyes that day.
Now, suddenly, she wasn't so sure. She wished she knew
what he was thinking—but then again, perhaps it was better
that she did not, she acknowledged as she threw him a
sideways glance and met his bland smile. Where Nik was concerned, ignorance was definitely the safest option.

The car swung through the gates of Belvedere Hall, and
Kezia took a deep breath before turning to face Nik. He was
her boss, nothing more, she reminded herself briskly. It was
obvious he had finished with Tania, but if he believed she
would fill the role of his lover for the day, he was in for a big
disappointment.

In fact, she did not see him for most of the day. The rain
of the previous night had cleared, to leave a cool but sunny
spring day, and he took advantage of the weather to continue
his business discussions on the golf course. They met up
briefly for lunch, and afterwards the men settled in one of the
conference rooms while Kezia and the businessmen's wives
made use of the steam room and aromatherapy cave.

She had never felt so pampered in her life, she thought

later, as she joined the others by the pool. After a day of such indulgence she should be feeling completely relaxed, but the full massage with a range of essential oils had served only to heighten her tension as she'd fantasised that it was Nik's hands stroking her body. A swim was the only answer, she decided grimly.

The water was cool on her heated skin, and she struck out, completing lap after lap as she sought to ease the fierce tension that her erotic daydreams had evoked. She could not carry on like this. Somehow she was going to have to get to grips with the overwhelming attraction she felt for Nik before he realised the effect he had on her.

Exhaustion finally overtook her, before she could complete her final lap, and with an effort she hauled herself up the steps at the opposite end of the pool to where she had left her towel.

'Hey, Kezia, are you training for the Olympics?' One of the Bulgarian businessmen sitting at a poolside table smiled as he rose and strolled towards her. He was younger than most of his contemporaries, and good-looking, she supposed—he certainly seemed to think so. She forced a smile as he stepped in front of her.

'I'm just trying to keep in shape,' she replied easily, and then wished she'd kept quiet as his eyes trailed over her.

'You look in pretty good shape to me,' he noted, his insolent grin widening as he studied her pink cheeks.

She'd felt his eyes following her the previous evening, and now stifled a groan when he moved closer and wrapped his towel around her shoulders.

'Here—let me help you dry off. You're freezing,' he said solicitously, and he began to pat her with the towel in a way that was far too personal for her liking.

She was tempted to tell him to get lost, but he was one of Nik's most important clients and she could hardly be rude.

'Thanks, that's very kind of you.'

'You're welcome,' he murmured as he slipped his arm around her waist and drew her over to his table. 'Come and have a drink.'

'Actually, I really must go and get changed. Nik's probably wondering where I am,' she muttered hastily as she wriggled free of his grip.

'Stop fretting. Your boss is sitting at a table at the far end of the pool. He was watching you while you were swimming. I think he doesn't like you out of his sight for too long,' he added softly, and Kezia followed his gaze, her heart sinking as, even from this distance, she saw Nik's dark frown.

Taking a deep breath, she forced herself to walk around the pool—but as she neared the table where she had left her robe, her steps slowed. Nik was fully dressed, one leg crossed over his thigh in a position of indolent ease, but his watchful stillness warned that he was not as relaxed as he appeared.

For a second she was tempted to turn tail and flee. She felt acutely vulnerable, with her wet swimming costume clinging to her like a second skin. She was so cold that her nipples had hardened to tight buds that strained against the black Lycra, and she longed for the protection of her robe. Steeling herself, she closed the gap between them, daring Nik to comment.

He dared. 'You looked like you were having fun—although I'm not sure that flirting outrageously with the male guests really comes under the spec of corporate entertaining,' he drawled, the sardonic amusement in his tone instantly making her want to slap him.

'I was not flirting; I was merely being polite. *He* was the one flirting—with *me*,' she snapped. 'You're sitting on my robe. Can I have it, please? I'm cold.'

'So I see.' His gaze settled unforgivably on her breasts, and to her chagrin she felt them tighten until they ached unbearably. 'Would you like me to help you get dry? You seem happy to allow every other Tom, Dick and Harry the privilege of rubbing you down.'

Kezia took her time, burying her face in her towel and making a show of drying herself while she assembled the correct order of words to tell him exactly what she thought of him.

'That's a vile thing to say. If I'd followed my first instinct I would have pushed him into the damned pool. I wish I had now, and to hell with your precious business deal,' she added furiously.

'I never asked you to prostitute yourself on my behalf,' Nik retorted, the fierce glitter in his eyes warning of the tenuous control he had on his temper.

The unexpected force of his anger surprised her, particularly as she could not understand the reason for it, and tears stung her eyes as she pushed her arms into her robe and tied the belt securely around her waist before replying. 'I didn't think for one minute that you would expect me to prostitute myself. I have more respect for you than that, Nik. It's a pity you don't feel the same about me, instead of jumping to the conclusion that I was leading that man on. How dare you think I was enjoying myself?'

Snatching up her bag, she swept past him. But he was instantly beside her, and caught hold of her wrist to pull her into a quiet corner where they were shielded from view by tall potted ferns.

'Don't walk away from me,' he growled furiously. 'And don't you dare *cry*. How is it that a woman can always resort to tears?'

His impatience was palpable, but Kezia was beyond caring as she fought to free herself from his hold.

Nik stared at her downbent head and inhaled sharply. He was surprised to find his anger draining away. Perhaps it was because Kezia's distress was genuine, rather than a calculated display of emotion, he brooded. All he knew was that the sight of her stunning green eyes glistening with tears was tearing at his insides, and with a muttered imprecation he pulled her into his arms.

'I'm sorry, all right. I'm sorry,' he muttered, struggling with the unfamiliar words of apology. 'I didn't mean to hurt you.'

'Well, you have,' she told him fiercely, scrubbing her face with the back of her hand.

The gesture was strangely child-like, revealing the true extent of her vulnerability and increasing his feeling that he had behaved like an utter bastard.

'I honestly don't know what I've done to make you so angry,' she whispered huskily.

She was staring up at him through her wet lashes and Nik found that he could not drag his gaze from her tremulous mouth.

'I didn't like seeing you with another man,' he admitted slowly, staring down at her with an intensity that made Kezia tremble. 'I didn't like watching you smile at him, and I certainly didn't enjoy the image I had in my head of him kissing you as I know he wanted to do.'

His voice was so low, his accent suddenly so pronounced, that she had to concentrate on his words. His breath was warm on her cold cheek, but as his arms tightened round her she shivered violently. In the background she could hear the sound of voices echoing around the pool, but she was barely aware of them. All she knew was that Nik was holding her, looking at her in a way that sent heat coursing through her veins, and instinct told her it was no longer anger that made his eyes glitter so fiercely.

'Why not?' she whispered, her eyes wide and unblinking as his head lowered.

'Because I wanted to kiss you myself,' he replied with stark honesty.

His lips brushed lightly over hers, warming her. He hesitated fractionally, before increasing the pressure slightly, stifling her low murmur of protest as he initiated a slow exploration. Her resistance was minimal. She had wanted this since the moment she'd first seen him, and heat unfurled in the pit of her stomach. Her lashes drifted down and she parted her lips, the sweep of his tongue so sweetly erotic that she ached to feel him even closer. Her arms crept up to his shoulders, all her senses attuned to the taste of him, the seductive warmth that emanated from his body.

It was heaven, and she would happily spend the rest of her life in his arms, but it couldn't last. This was Nik—a man who only moments before had accused her of making a play for one of his business associates. Her eyes flew open and clashed with his dark gaze. She could see the hint of regret in their depths as he eased back fractionally, grazing his lips gently over hers in one last, lingering caress.

Abruptly Kezia jerked out of his arms and covered her mouth with her hand. 'You shouldn't have done that,' she whispered fiercely, trembling with shock as reaction set in. 'I wasn't leading *anyone* on, and I'm not an easy lay.'

There was genuine amusement in his eyes as he released her and stepped back. 'I'm relieved to hear it, *pedhaki mou,*' he replied softly. 'I prefer a challenge!'

CHAPTER FOUR

KEZIA SPENT THE return journey to Otterbourne House in a state of shock and simmering temper. She couldn't fathom why Nik had kissed her, but it was unlikely that he had been overcome with passion for her, she thought cynically. She remembered all too clearly his categorical denial to Tania that he was attracted to his PA. It was more likely that his sudden interest had resulted from his fiercely competitive streak.

But she had been unable to control her response to him. The feel of his lips on hers had sparked the passion she'd tried so hard to deny for the past few months, and she had kissed him with a fervour bordering on desperation. He must have wondered what had hit him, she thought grimly. Maybe that was the reason he had avoided her for the rest of the afternoon. The knowledge increased her humiliation, and she longed for the day to be over so that she and Max could go home.

She couldn't bring herself to look at Nik, let alone speak to him, and was grateful that they were sharing the car with some of his guests. When they reached the house she scrambled out of the limousine with more speed than dignity but he caught up with her as she raced up the front steps, his eyes narrowing as she gave a violent shiver.

'Stop running away from me,' he demanded bluntly. 'What's the matter with you anyway? You're as white as a ghost.'

'Nothing. I just don't seem to be able to get warm, that's all.' And if he suggested sharing bodily heat she would hit him, she vowed, dragging her gaze from the sudden gleam of amusement in his.

The guests had disappeared, either upstairs or into the sitting room, and she was painfully conscious that she and Nik were alone for the first time since he had kissed her. She wanted to ask him why he had done it, or perhaps make some flippant remark to prove it had meant nothing to her.

'I'll go and see if Mrs Jessop needs a hand,' she muttered instead, her nerve failing beneath his dark-eyed scrutiny.

'There's nothing more for you to do here. If you're ready to go home, I'll take you.'

'No,' she replied quickly. 'There's no need. The mechanic said my car's fine.' She was aware of the note of near panic in her voice, but she needed some time out, away from him. She certainly couldn't handle the thought of inviting him up to her flat again. 'I'm not going straight home anyway. I have to go to the store for a few essentials.'

It was only a small lie; she would really go shopping in the morning. All she wanted to do right now was have some time alone. Her head was pounding, and she was aware of a prick-ling sensation at the back of her throat. The prospect of spending the rest of the weekend suffering from a cold was the last straw she thought dismally as she ran down to the kitchen to collect Max.

By the time she reached home Kezia felt as though someone was driving a pickaxe into her skull. The central heating had been running for a couple of hours, but the flat still felt cold and she turned up the thermostat. Bed was the only remedy if she was coming down with a virus, she decided, as she inspected the empty fridge and gave up on the idea of supper. Tomorrow she would take advantage of the Sunday opening hours to stock up on food for the week—but first, and most importantly, she would phone Nik and tell him she was unavailable for lunch.

Max had settled quite happily on his blanket in the kitchen. Mrs Jessop had allowed him the run of the garden at Otterbourne, and now he curled up into a ball and gave a blissful sigh when Kezia stroked him. Perhaps his owners would see the notices in the village and come to claim before she became too attached to him, she thought. But deep down she had to admit it was already too late. The scruffy mongrel was fast taking up residence in her heart.

She slept through the whole night and woke feeling like death. Sunlight was streaming in through a chink in the curtains, and she could hear Max whining. Gingerly Kezia swung her legs over the side of the bed, and groaned as the room swayed alarmingly. She had definitely picked up a virus and could only hope it would be short-lived; Nik had a punishing schedule booked for the coming week and she didn't have time to be ill.

Somehow she forced herself to pull on jeans and a sweatshirt, and struggled down to the communal gardens to give Max a run. There was something vital she had to do this morning, her brain registered foggily, but by the time she had managed to stagger back upstairs all she could do was collapse on the sofa and fall back to sleep.

Her dreams were fractured and disturbed when from somewhere came an insistent ringing sound that hurt her head, and the distant sound of a dog barking. In her dream she was looking into Nik's eyes, and he was laughing at her as she pleaded with him to kiss her.

'Kezia…wake up!'

Slowly she opened her eyes. Nik was staring down at her, his face grim and unsmiling. He was part of her dream, wasn't he? She shook her head, wincing at the pain that the slightest movement evoked.

'Nik?' She was in her flat, huddled on the sofa and wrapped in the folds of her duvet. Though before she had been frozen, she was now burning up, and with a muttered cry she fought her way out of the heavy cover. 'What…what are you doing here?' she croaked. Her throat felt as though she had swallowed shards of glass, and she tried to moisten her dry lips with her tongue.

'Your neighbour let me in,' he explained quietly. 'I've been ringing the doorbell for the past ten minutes, and almost gave up, but I could hear Max and I was sure you wouldn't have gone out without him.'

Lunch, Kezia remembered. Nik was here to take her to lunch. She had planned to phone him and cancel, but she had forgotten and now it was too late. He was here, looking so devastatingly sexy that, despite feeling so awful, she felt her heart lurch.

He held his palm against her forehead, his touch light and blessedly cool on her heated skin. 'You're running a high temperature. Tell me what feels wrong, exactly?'

'Everything,' she admitted with a faint attempt at humour. 'But it's just a cold, Nik. I'll spend the day sleeping it off and I'll be fine tomorrow, you'll see.'

'Aha.' His tone was plainly disbelieving. 'Drink this.'

The ice-cold water soothed her throat, but could do nothing to ease the aching of every muscle in her body. Weakly she closed her eyes and wished Nik would go. From past experience she knew she must look a mess. Her skin was probably sickly white and her eyes red-rimmed—not an attractive combination. She was sure he meant well, but the sounds he was making as he moved around her flat went straight through her head.

She had drifted into a light sleep when he materialised by her side again, but instead of leaving her in peace he slipped his arms beneath her shoulders and knees and lifted her up.

'What on earth…? Nik? Put me down, please. I'm ill.'

'I'd never have guessed,' came the dry retort. 'Why didn't you say something last night? I would never have let you drive home if I'd known how you felt. I'm taking you back to Otterbourne,' he told her, as he was forced to walk sideways down the narrow hall to prevent her from banging her head on the wall. 'You can't stay here on your own; you look terrible. And before you start arguing, I already know that your flatmate is away.'

'You can't carry me down two flights of stairs,' Kezia muttered feebly, as she fought the urge to give in and lay her head on his shoulder. He was so big, so solid, and already she could feel her muscles relax as she absorbed his warmth. 'You'll break your back,' she mumbled, but he ignored her and carried her down to the car park with impressive ease.

Kezia was vaguely aware of him placing her in the passenger seat of the Porsche, and her senses leapt as she breathed in the scent of his aftershave when he leaned over her to adjust her seatbelt.

'You don't need to go to all this fuss. I can take care of myself,' she whispered, her eyes filling with silly tears at the unexpected tenderness of his smile.

'Humour me, hmm, *pedhaki mou?* I want you where I can keep an eye on you.'

He stowed the bag of essentials he had hastily packed in the boot, and moved round to slide behind the wheel. She was deathly pale, her eyelashes glinting gold on her white cheeks. His mouth tightened at the knowledge that she had spent the night alone and ill in her flat. She could barely stand, let alone take care of herself, he noted grimly, and with a muttered oath he fired the engine and drove off.

Kezia opened her eyes and stared in confusion at her unfamiliar surroundings. She was lying in bed, but it was not her bed, she realised with a frown as her mind creaked into life. The elegant cream walls and rich green velvet curtains were vaguely recognisable. She had been here before—but where was here?

'So, you've finally decided to join the land of the living— about time,' a deeply sensuous voice murmured softly.

'Nik!' She licked her parched lips as she slowly turned her head and found him sitting in an armchair close to the bed.

His long legs were encased in faded denim, his shirt loosely buttoned so that his dark chest hair was clearly visible. With his ruffled hair and the dark stubble shading his jaw he looked markedly different from the urbane business executive she knew, but no less gorgeous.

'At the risk of sounding ridiculous—where am I?' she croaked.

'Otterbourne, in the bedroom adjoining mine.'

'Oh…yes.' Snatches of memory resurfaced—of Nik bundling her into his car, and of feeling so cold that her body had been racked with agonising shivers. She felt masses better, she realised. Her head no longer hurt, and her muscles had stopped aching. 'I told you it was just a cold and that I'd sleep it off. You needn't have brought me here this morning.'

'This morning? You've been here for the last four days— and asleep for most of the time. So it's not surprising you don't remember.'

Feeling slightly stunned, Kezia stared up at the ceiling as she absorbed Nik's words. How could she have been in bed for four days and not realised? Her eyes flew open, and she sat bolt upright as a horrifying thought struck her.

'Max!' If he had been trapped in her flat for four days without food or water, he would surely be dead. 'Nik, I have to go home right now.' She swung her legs out of bed, only to have them placed firmly beneath the covers again. 'Max is all alone…' She slapped ineffectually against Nik's chest, her eyes brimming with tears.

'Calm down. You'll make yourself ill again. The damn dog's here,' he informed her impatiently. 'You don't really think I'd have left him behind, do you? At this moment Max is in the kitchen, waiting for Mrs Jessop to finish cooking his dinner. I believe he's having steak today,' he added sardonically, brushing a tear from her cheek in a surprisingly gentle gesture.

'Thank God,' Kezia breathed fervently as she collapsed back against the pillows. 'Are you sure he's all right?'

'He looks a lot better than you,' Nik told her, with an honesty that made her wince.

She felt hot and sticky, and in desperate need of a shower. Her memory was returning: vague images of strong arms supporting her while a glass of water was held to her lips, and she recalled a soothing voice bidding her to drink, a hand gently stroking her hair from her hot brow. But there were vital gaps in her memory. She couldn't remember changing out of her jeans into her nightdress, and she stared at Nik suspiciously.

'I suppose Mrs Jessop helped to look after me?' She laughed self-consciously. 'I must admit, I don't remember a thing about changing out of my clothes.'

'No, you were pretty well out of it,' he replied blandly. The gleam in his eyes told her he knew exactly what was bothering her, and she glared at him.

'Are you telling me you took my clothes off?'

'Several times,' he said cheerfully. 'You were running such a high temperature that I've used all the nightclothes I packed for you. But don't worry; they've all been laundered.'

Don't worry! She glared at him, scandalised by the notion that he had stripped her without her even being aware of it.

'I was a perfect gentleman,' he assured her, his grin widening as he took in her scarlet cheeks. 'I left your under-wear in place—although I have to admit that those enticing scraps of lace you're wearing sent my temperature soaring almost as high as yours.'

'You're despicable,' she snapped furiously, more unsettled than she cared to admit by the wicked glint in his dark gaze. She was sure he was teasing her, but the knowledge did nothing to quell her quiver of awareness at his potent sexuality.

'I didn't have much choice,' he said, more seriously. 'Mrs Jessop had to take care of her elderly mother for a couple of days. From the sound of it, half the village is ill.'

He leaned back in the chair and stretched his arms above his head, the action lifting his shirt from the waistband of his jeans to reveal the whorls of dark hair that arrowed down over his abdomen. Suddenly the atmosphere in the bedroom seemed way too intimate, and she tore her gaze from him to stare down at the bedcover. Overcome with a weakness that she suspected had little to do with her illness, she closed her eyes and feigned a yawn.

'Sleep now, *pedhaki mou,* and when you wake Mrs Jessop will bring you something to eat. The doctor said you were struck by a particularly virulent virus,' Nik explained as he strolled over to the door. 'It'll be a few days yet until you recover your strength.'

'But what about work?' Kezia murmured anxiously. 'You had meetings in Paris and Cologne this week. How have you managed?'

'I cancelled them,' he said unconcernedly. 'There's nothing so vital that it can't wait until you're better.'

'Right,' she murmured faintly as she absorbed this startling announcement from a man who possessed the dynamism of a tornado. 'Thank you for taking care of me.' She carefully avoided his gaze as an unbidden image of him undressing her filled her mind. 'I'm sure I'll be back to normal in no time.' She paused fractionally, fearful of sounding ungrateful. 'I'd like to go back to my flat tonight.'

'Not a chance,' he said cheerfully, no trace of regret in his voice. 'You'll stay here until I decide you're well enough to go home. And, just to make sure you're not tempted to disobey me, I'll hang on to these.' He dangled her car keys in the air before slipping them safely in his pocket, and smiled unrepentantly before disappearing out of the door while she was still searching for the words to tell him just what she thought of him.

'I must say you're looking a lot better than you did twenty-four hours ago,' Nik's housekeeper remarked when she entered Kezia's bedroom an hour later. 'I've brought you something to eat. A nice omelette—nothing too heavy.' She placed a tray on Kezia's lap and propped up the pillows.

Kezia murmured her thanks, and her face lit up as a familiar figure trotted through the door. 'Max! There you are. I've been so worried about you.'

'I can't imagine why—that dog lives the life of Riley,' Mrs Jessop said with a laugh. 'Mr Niarchou has bought him a collar and new basket, but he's spent every night curled up at the end of your bed.'

'No one's come to claim him, then?' Kezia said, unable to disguise her satisfaction that she would have to hang on to Max for a while longer.

Mrs Jessop shook her head and busied herself with adjusting the bedcovers. Mr Niarchou had instructed her not to say anything about the bullish farmer, Stan Todd, who had turned up at the house demanding the return of his dog. Max had taken one look at him and shot down to the kitchen, where he had later been found cowering beneath the table. He was quite safe now, she had assured the dog. Mr Niarchou had bought him—paid a small fortune for him too. She had overheard the sharp exchange of words between the two men. Stan Todd had a reputation around the village for mistreating his animals, but he wasn't daft. He'd insisted Max was his pride and joy, despite the fact that the dog had been plainly underfed. Mr Niarchou had countered his demands for money with a blistering retort, and had only paid up in return for Stan's assurance that he would make no further claim on Max.

It was funny, Mrs Jessop mused, she'd never thought of Mr Niarchou as a dog lover. But maybe there were other reasons for his change of heart, she realized, as she studied

Kezia's delicate features and the riot of red-gold curls spread over the pillows.

'How are you feeling now?' she asked, when Kezia had managed to eat half the omelette. 'That was quite a scare you gave us. Mr Niarchou had the doctor out twice, and he's spent most of the last few days up here with you. He brought his laptop up so that he could carry on working while you were asleep.'

'Did he?' Kezia murmured faintly as she digested this piece of information.

She felt uncomfortable with the idea that Nik had watched her while she slept. It made her feel vulnerable—especially when he featured in so many of her dreams. She just prayed she hadn't called out his name. She was surprised by how tired she still felt, and when Mrs Jessop left she snuggled beneath the duvet and fell back to sleep.

It was dark when she awoke. Someone had switched on the bedside lamp, and when she rolled onto her side she discovered that Nik was back in the armchair, his laptop balanced on his knee.

'You're looking a little better,' he commented when he glanced up and caught her staring at him. 'You've lost that sickly pallor.'

'Thanks!' Kezia grimaced, and wished she could hide beneath the bedcovers, certain that she must look a sight. Nik, on the other hand, looked as though he had stepped from the pages of a male pin-up magazine. His jeans moulded his thighs, leaving little to the imagination, and she sighed and shut her eyes, as if by doing so she could lessen his impact.

'You're bound to feel weak; you've been very unwell,' he said gently.

The virus had hit her hard, he brooded as he switched off

his computer. The delicate flush on her cheeks looked a lot
healthier than her hectic colour of two nights ago, but she still
looked fragile. He had been seriously worried about her—to
the point that he had contacted her parents in Malaysia to
explain her condition. But, although Jean Trevellyn had expressed both concern and sympathy, he had gained the impression that Kezia was not close to either of her parents. He
knew she had no siblings, and it seemed that there were no
other relatives in England he could contact—apart from an
elderly aunt who lived in a nursing home in Kent.

No wonder she was so fiercely independent, he thought.
He couldn't imagine being so alone. His large, noisy, intrusive family back in Greece drove him to distraction, but he
had grown up secure in the knowledge that he was adored.
Somehow he doubted that Kezia had enjoyed that same
feeling of unconditional love, and he was surprised at how
protective of her that made him feel. Beneath her prickly
exterior he had glimpsed her soft heart and innately generous
nature. Her concern for a scruffy stray dog was proof of that.
She was a woman who deserved to be loved, and instinct told
him she would give her love unselfishly in return.

Where had that disturbing thought come from? he
wondered derisively as he uncurled his legs and walked over
to the bed. His interest in Kezia—and he couldn't deny that
he *was* interested—was purely physical. The sexual awareness
that had simmered since the first time he'd seen her had not
lessened in the three months that they had worked closely
together. Rather, it had developed to such an extent that he
seemed to spend an annoying amount of his time thinking
about her. With her fiery hair and lush curves, Kezia Trevellyn
was nothing like his usual choice of sophisticated blondes.

And he had a feeling that her flashing green eyes spelt trouble. They were witch's eyes, and he was fast falling under her spell.

'So, who's Charlie?' he asked, as he settled comfortably on the edge of the bed—far too close for comfort as far as Kezia was concerned.

'He was my fiancé,' she replied, looking puzzled. 'Why do you ask?'

'You were calling out his name in your sleep. You seemed upset,' he added softly. 'It's said that our dreams reveal our innermost hopes and desires. Perhaps deep down you regret ending your engagement more than you realize?'

'I don't. Of course I don't,' Kezia replied quickly. She had no idea why she had called for Charlie, and she shuddered to think of the hopes and desires she might have inadvertently revealed to Nik while she was asleep. 'Er...did I mention anyone else?'

'You didn't give a list of past lovers,' he said dryly.

'That's because there isn't a list. Only Charlie.'

'Do you mean that he was your first long-term relationship?'

'First and last,' she quipped flippantly. 'When we broke up I decided that I don't want to be tied down. I'm not looking for love and commitment. I enjoy my independence too much.'

'And yet you still dream of him? Perhaps you were more affected by the split than you care to admit?' Nik suggested. 'Did you love him?'

'Yes,' she said honestly. 'But there were reasons why our marriage would never have worked.'

Reasons that were far too painful to reveal, she thought bleakly. Her infertility was a secret sadness she had only shared with her closest friends. There was no reason for Nik to know.

'I can't believe how much better I feel,' she said brightly, desperate to alter the course of this conversation, which was becoming too personal.

She didn't understand Nik's sudden interest in her private life, and found it unsettling. Maybe he was bored with being cooped up in the house with her for days—or possibly he was regretting ending his relationship with Tania. She couldn't forget the way he had kissed her at the spa, but now she wondered if she had imagined it. Perhaps it had been a figment of her fevered dreams while she was ill. Yet the feel of his lips on hers, the taste of him, lingered in her mind.

'I'd like to have a shower,' she said firmly, hoping he would take the hint and go away.

He studied her speculatively for several minutes, his eyes hooded beneath heavy lids so that she had no idea of his thoughts. 'If you're sure you feel up to it, you can use my bathroom—but I'll be waiting outside, and you're not to lock the door. I want you to promise you'll call me if you feel dizzy or faint.'

Some chance! 'Of course,' she assured him innocently. The thought of him storming into the bathroom while she was taking a shower was enough to make her head spin, and she was grateful for the arm he slipped around her waist as he supported her.

She had been sleeping in the small dressing room adjoining the master bedroom, and as he led her through to the *en-suite* bathroom she quickly averted her gaze from the magnificent four-poster bed that dominated his room.

It was a room designed for seduction, she thought weakly as her heart-rate accelerated. The pale, neutral coloured walls provided a backdrop for rich burgundy velvet curtains that matched the drapes around the bed. The satin bedspread had been thrown back to reveal cream silk sheets, and the pillows still bore the indentation of his head. Her imagination went into overdrive as she pictured his naked body stretched out on the silk, his handsome face relaxed in sleep while impossibly long black lashes feathered his cheeks.

'Excuse the mess. I'm not the world's tidiest man,' he confessed with a complete lack of contrition as she stepped over a black silk robe that was lying in a heap in the middle of the floor. 'My mother insists that I need to find a wife—God forbid!' His mouth curved into a smile that pierced her soul. 'Like you, I value my independence.'

His eyes skimmed the silvery grey chemise that he had helped her into some time during the previous night. She had been so hot that he'd had no option but to change her nightclothes yet again. It was lucky that when he had gone to her flat and found her ill he had simply scooped up the contents of her underwear drawer and flung them in a bag. True, the tiny grey wisp of satin could hardly be described as practical, he conceded, but it was the only clean thing she'd had left. He found himself wondering what she'd had in mind when she'd bought it—or, more pertinently—who. It certainly hadn't been designed to sleep in, he thought cynically as his gaze settled on the delectable fullness of her breasts revealed by the low-cut neckline.

Had she bought it to please her fiancé? Had Charlie once unfastened those ribbon straps and drawn the gossamer silk down so that her breasts spilled in creamy abundance into his hands? His displeasure at the thought was intense, and his mouth tightened. He had never experienced jealousy in his life, and had no reason to suppose that the burning feeling in the pit of his stomach now was anything other than indigestion. But that didn't explain why he was filled with such a violent dislike of a man he had never even met.

Kezia was fast becoming a complication in his life that he could no longer ignore, he mused, as his gaze settled on the red-gold curls that tumbled over her shoulders. She'd barely eaten a thing for the past few days, and her cheeks looked hollow, but fortunately she still retained her gorgeous sexy curves, he noted as his eyes trailed over her hips. She had a body that would tempt a saint—as he had discovered when he'd cared for her during her illness. While she had been unwell he had steeled himself to ignore the temptation her semi-naked body posed, but now she was better and his good intentions were slipping.

Experience warned him of the dangers of mixing work with pleasure. Ordinarily he would not have contemplated an affair with a member of his staff who had proved herself to be such an excellent PA. But these were no ordinary circumstances, he acceded derisively. He had never wanted anyone as fiercely as he wanted Kezia. Not since he was a teenager, when he had been fixated with a glamorous thirty-something Greek actress had he been held at the mercy of his hormones. He couldn't look at Kezia without remembering how it had felt to kiss her and wanting to do it again. And what was to stop him? he asked himself as he ushered her into the bathroom. She wasn't immune to him. Her response when he had kissed her had been unexpectedly passionate. And even now he was aware of her tension, of the slight tremor of her hand as she pushed her hair out of her eyes, telling him she was not as self-assured as she would have had him believe.

'There's fresh towels in the cupboard. Call me if you need anything,' he bade with a smile, as she stared at him with her stunning eyes. 'Unless you'd like me to stay and help?' he added, enjoying the way her cheeks flooded with colour.

'I can manage, thanks,' she said stiffly.

Definitely not immune, he noted with a surge of satisfaction. Her pupils were dilated, her lips slightly parted, and he knew she was as aware of the exigent chemistry that simmered between them as he. What harm could there be in allowing their mutual attraction to develop into a full-blown sexual relationship? Kezia had already stated that she enjoyed her independence. She wasn't looking for commitment any more than he was. They could indulge in an affair, confident that neither had expectations of it leading to anything more permanent.

It really was an ideal situation, Nik decided as he closed the bathroom door and stretched out on his bed while he waited for her to finish her shower. It made perfect sense for Kezia to fill the dual roles of his PA and mistress. There would be no annoying separations while he was away on business, because as his assistant she'd always travel with him, and as his lover they would spend their nights together as well as the days.

And when they decided, some time in the future, that the relationship had run its course, she could return to being his PA. She was good at her job, and he didn't want to lose her— but he wouldn't need to. She had told him she wasn't looking for love. When their affair ended she would presumably be happy to continue with her career, and there would be no bad feelings or messy recriminations.

All he had to do was convince her that an affair was the logical solution to the fierce attraction that burned between them. And, without wanting to be over-confident, he didn't anticipate too many difficulties on that score. Persuading his

numerous lovers into his bed had never proved a problem—
his wealth had helped with that, he conceded with a degree
of self-derision. And, in addition to the Niarchou fortune, he
had been blessed with a face and body that acted like a magnet
to women of all ages.

But Kezia was different from the usual brittle sophisticates
he dated. She might not be looking for love, but he doubted
she was the type to participate in a string of casual sexual encounters. She had admitted that her fiancé had been her only
serious boyfriend, and although he was certain that she was
attracted to him, she seemed determined to fight her feelings.

If he wanted Kezia, he would have to woo her, Nik
brooded. He would have to take his time, persuade her with
all the subtle means at his disposal of the benefits of having
an affair with him. He had gained the distinct impression
from his conversation with her mother that there had been
little fun in her life. He would wine her and dine her. He
would lavish his attention on her until he broke her resistance.

The bathroom door opened and she stepped hesitantly into
his bedroom. Her hair fell in damp tendrils around her face
so that she looked young and infinitely vulnerable, and Nik
felt something tug at his heart. He was impatient to make love
to her—every instinct told him that sex with her would be
mind-blowing—but first he would have to win her trust. It was
a long time since he'd had to try at anything, and as he smiled
at her he was filled with a sense of anticipation. She would
be worth the wait.

CHAPTER FIVE

IT WAS LATE when Kezia followed Nik out of the restaurant and over to his car. Dinner at an exclusive London hotel had been out of this world, she mused, remembering the rich chocolate mousse that she had been unable to resist. She would regret the extra calories tomorrow—along with the two glasses of champagne Nik had tempted her to. As the evening had progressed she had begun to feel relaxed, and the tiniest bit light-headed—which presumably had been his intention. He had been buttering her up before he dropped his bombshell.

'I don't want to go on a cruise,' she argued now, for the twentieth time, as he negotiated the busy London traffic. 'I don't like boats and I get seasick on a pedalo.'

'You won't feel sick on the *Atlanta,*' Nik assured her calmly. 'She's the pride of the Niarchou fleet—a luxury liner that has just undergone a multimillion-pound refit.'

'Well, I still don't like the idea of spending three weeks at sea.'

Any more than she relished the thought of spending three weeks cooped up on a boat with Nik, with no chance of escape, she thought dismally. It was two weeks since he had taken care of her while she was ill, and in that time she had detected a subtle shift in their relationship. The sexual awareness that had simmered beneath the surface was more intense, and she could no longer blame the fierce tension between them on her imagination.

Nik wanted her. She was aware of the barely concealed hunger in his eyes when they trailed slowly over her, hovered longer than they should on her breasts, before moving up to stare at her broodingly, as if he was looking for an answer to the unspoken question that hung over them. The question that occupied her mind to the exclusion of virtually everything else. What, if anything, was she going to do about their undeniable attraction for each other? Ignore it, seemed the most sensible option. She understood now why ostriches stuck their heads in the sand. Part of her wished she could hide away until Nik's interest in her had cooled—as it surely would. He freely admitted he had a low boredom threshold, and she knew that any kind of relationship between them would be brief and designated almost exclusively to the bedroom.

The thought should have shocked her, but far more shocking were the explicit images that filled her mind of Nik's naked body entwined with hers as he made love to her on his huge four-poster bed. Common sense warned that he only wanted her for one thing, and that when their affair ended it would also probably spell the end of her job. She couldn't blithely carry on working as his PA while he moved on to his next mistress; it would tear her apart. And therein lay her problem, she acknowledged heavily. She had sympathised with Charlie's reasons for ending their engagement, but it had still hurt, and she'd vowed never to make herself so vulnerable again. She had no intention of falling in love with Nik, but some deeply buried instinct for self-preservation warned against surrendering to the desire that burned between them. It would be playing with fire, and she was afraid of getting burned.

Twenty minutes later he swung the Porsche into the parking area outside her flat and cut the engine. Would he expect her to invite him up for coffee? She glanced at him, and felt her heart lurch as her gaze clashed with his in the dim interior of the car. The evening had been wonderful, despite the fact that she had felt on tenterhooks most of the time.

They had attended a show at the London Palladium before dinner. The musical had won rave reviews, and tickets had been sold out months in advance, but Nik had seemingly had no problem in booking a private box. Helping him to entertain clients was one of her duties, he had pointed out when she had initially declined his invitation. And so it had been with a mixture of reluctance and feverish anticipation that she had slipped into an elegant black evening dress and paced her flat until it was time for him to collect her.

He had waited until they'd arrived at the theatre before revealing that his clients had been forced to cancel at the last minute. But there was no reason why *they* should not enjoy the show, he'd murmured persuasively, awarding her one of his sexy smiles that made her go weak at the knees.

Sitting with him in the intimacy of the private box, she had been acutely aware of the formidable width of his shoulders, the slight pressure of his thigh pressed against hers, and she had barely been able to concentrate on the stage below. Her senses had been finely tuned to every breath he took, every slight movement he made, until she had felt suffocated by his presence. For one mad moment she'd wondered how he would react if she turned her head and pressed her mouth against the tanned column of his throat visible above the collar of his shirt…

Get a grip, she told herself crossly, as she dragged her mind back to the present and released her seatbelt. She was a twenty-four-year-old professional career woman, not a teenager at the mercy of rampaging hormones. She could handle Nik's presence in her flat for half an hour—and besides, there was still the subject of the cruise to discuss. And, more pertinently, her determination not to accompany him on it.

'Would you like to come up for coffee?' she murmured as she opened the car door.

'I thought you'd never ask,' he drawled sardonically, and she blushed as she belatedly realised how long they had been sitting in the car.

Max greeted her joyously, wagging his tail ferociously—although fortunately he seemed to understand her pleas not to bark. It was growing increasingly difficult to smuggle him in and out of the flat, past the prying eyes of the caretaker who lived on the ground floor, and Max's future was another problem looming on Kezia's horizon.

Nik had told her he'd managed to trace the dog's owners and discovered that they were no longer able to care for him. Max was her responsibility. She refused to countenance the idea of taking him to a dog pound, and he was another very good reason why she couldn't spend the next three weeks cruising around the Mediterranean.

'He can stay at Otterbourne. I've already checked with Mrs Jessop and she's quite happy to take care of him,' Nik assured her blandly when she brought up the subject of Max.

'But I don't want to leave him for all that time,' she muttered, unable to disguise her disgruntled tone as her fool-proof excuse for staying on dry land disappeared. 'He might forget me.'

'I doubt it. You're not easily forgettable,' Nik told her silkily, the sudden gleam in his eyes setting her nerves on high alert.

He had followed her into the kitchen and dominated the room as she moved between the worktop and the fridge to collect milk for the coffee. She wished he would go and sit down in the living room, she thought as she was forced to squeeze past him.

His trip aboard the *Atlanta* had been scheduled in his diary for weeks. The first voyage of the Niarchou Group's newly refitted cruise liner was being promoted as the trip of a lifetime, offering unequalled luxury for those fortunate enough to be able to afford it. As company chairman, it was not surprising that Nik had decided to join the ship for its first sailing—but it hadn't occurred to her that he would expect her to accompany him. She had viewed the three weeks that he would be away as a much-needed breathing space, a chance to get a grip on her wayward emotions and she was dismayed by her secret thrill of anticipation at the thought of travelling with him

'Surely it would be better if I stayed behind to run your office?' she argued valiantly. 'You don't need me with you while you're sunning yourself around the pool—unless my duties now include applying sunscreen to your back, of course.'

'I'll have it written into your contract,' he said, with a wicked grin that made her blush. 'I need you with me because this is a working trip. Not a holiday.'

'I see.' Kezia sniffed.

Work was safe; she could handle him if they stuck to their roles of employer and assistant. Her fear had been that since he hadn't yet replaced Tania in his bed he might expect her to fill in as his mistress. But of course there would be a queue of nubile blondes on board only too eager to offer their services in that department, she acknowledged grimly.

'I suppose I'd better get myself organized, then,' she said grudgingly. 'The ship sails next week. That doesn't leave me much time to pack.' Especially as she would need to fit in a couple of shopping trips before they left. The weather in England was unseasonably cold for late spring, and she was still wearing her winter boots and coat, but the temperatures in the Med would require a variety of summer outfits. 'I may need to take a day's leave during the week,' she murmured.

'No problem. You'll have to rearrange my diary anyway. I'm returning to Greece for a few days, but I'll be back in time to join you on the ship when it sets sail from Southampton.'

His smile faded, and she had the impression that his thoughts were suddenly miles away. She turned her attention to the task in hand and added a spoonful of sugar to his coffee, but no milk. In many ways he was a stranger to her, and yet she knew so many intimate details about him—how he took his coffee, the fact that he liked his steak rare and preferred red wine over white. She had become adept at reading his moods too, and although the expression in his eyes was unfathomable, she knew something was troubling him.

'Is something wrong at home?' she queried softly, aware that, wherever he settled in the world, the small Greek island in the Aegean Sea where he had spent his childhood was where his heart lay.

'My father's in hospital.' He took a gulp of his coffee and stared down at the cup, as if debating whether to elaborate further. 'He fell and broke his hip a couple of months ago, and it's not healing as well as it should. Now he has an infection and may need surgery.'

'I'm sorry. You must be worried about him,' Kezia murmured gently, instinctively reaching out to put her hand on Nik's arm. Although he frequently bemoaned the fact that his large family drove him crazy, he plainly adored his parents, as well as his four sisters and a multitude of nieces and nephews, but she guessed that he was especially close to his father. 'This must be a difficult time for all of you.'

Nik shrugged and carefully avoided her gaze. It was a telling gesture from a man who was perceived by most to be invulnerable, and her heart ached for him. 'He's eighty, his bones are brittle, and he has a weak heart,' he admitted gruffly. 'But he insists he's sticking around until I've settled down and produced the next Niarchou heir—so no pressure,' he quipped dryly.

'You're their only son, so I suppose your parents are keen for you to have children one day,' Kezia said quietly, wondering why her heart felt as though it was splintering.

'My mother in particular is obsessed with the idea that I must continue the Niarchou line,' he agreed ruefully. 'Every time I go home I'm presented with a selection of nice Greek girls who she's deemed suitable wife material.'

'Poor you!' Her sarcasm disguised the ridiculous urge to burst into tears and she lifted her hand from his arm, but as she did so he captured her fingers and entwined them with his.

'As I've already mentioned, I've no desire to investigate the joys of matrimony. Certainly not at the moment,' he drawled, the glimmer of amusement in his eyes fading as he studied the delicate beauty of her upturned face. 'I like my life the way it is: uncluttered, uncomplicated, and full of interesting possibilities.'

Without her being aware of it, he had moved closer so that she was trapped against the worktop, her fingers still caught in his grasp. A gentle tug was all that was necessary to draw her up against his chest, and as her lashes flew open she felt her heart lurch at the burning heat of his gaze. The sudden tension in her small kitchen was tangible, and a shiver of excitement ran the length of her spine.

'Nik…don't,' she pleaded, watching with wide-eyed fascination as his dark head slowly lowered. His mouth was millimetres from hers, a sensual temptation she knew she should resist, but her will-power had deserted her and only a fierce, elemental hunger remained. Nervously she moistened her lips with the tip of her tongue, and his eyes narrowed on the frantic movement.

'Don't what? Don't do this?' He brushed his lips lightly over hers, tasting her with delicate precision that left her aching for more. 'I can't help it, *pedhaki mou*. I wanted to kiss you senseless the first time I saw you. We'd met barely five minutes before, yet that day in the London office I wanted to rip your blouse from your shoulders and ravish you. And you wanted it too,' he added softly, capturing her gasp of denial with his mouth.

This time his lips were firmer, demanding her response as he deepened the kiss to a level that was unashamedly erotic. With a sigh she opened her mouth, so that his tongue could make an intimate exploration that left her trembling with need. She could no longer deny him or herself, and her arms crept up around his neck to hold him to his task. The movement brought her body up hard against his, and she revelled in the feel of every muscle and sinew pushing into her soft curves.

'I don't know how I've kept my hands off you for so long,' he admitted thickly. 'Especially since I cared for you during your illness and discovered the gorgeous sexy curves that you keep hidden beneath your prim suits. The temptation of your near naked body drove me almost to distraction, but you were unwell and I could do nothing to assuage my desperate need to make love to you.'

As he spoke he slid one hand into her hair to hold her still while the other roamed down to her bottom, back over her hip and up, to discover the dip of her waist and above it the generous fullness of her breasts.

'You have a body to *die* for, Kezia,' he groaned, his voice velvet-soft as he rolled each syllable of her name on his tongue.

He trailed a line of kisses down her neck and then lower still, following the neckline of her dress to the valley between her breasts. Kezia held her breath as he cupped one soft mound in his hand, took the weight of it and gently kneaded her flesh through the barrier of her dress. She wanted more, wanted to feel his hands on her skin, and she released her breath on a low moan of pleasure when he eased his fingers beneath the material to caress her. Her nipple had hardened to a tight bud that throbbed unbearably when he brushed his thumb pad across it. Heat coursed through her so that she strained closer to him, no thought in her mind but her desperate need for him to continue his sensual magic.

She felt bereft when he released her breast, and muttered her disapproval against his mouth. But he smiled and slid his hand down to caress her bottom with slow circular movements that forced her thighs into close contact with the hard proof of his arousal. It should have shocked her, but instead she felt a surge of triumph that he wanted her so badly, and clung to him as he rocked his hips against her.

'Desperate as I am to make love to you, I'm not sure that your kitchen table is big enough for what I have in mind—or sturdy enough,' he murmured in her ear, his voice tinged with a hint of amusement that brought her skidding to a halt. 'I'm sure we'll be a lot more comfortable in your bedroom.'

What in heaven's name was she doing? Her lashes flew

upwards, and she stared at him in a mixture of bewilderment and growing shame. His eyes were hooded, but nothing could hide the gleam of fierce desire in their depths. Nik was hungry for her, and for a few scandalous seconds she was tempted to blank out the whispered warning in her head and lead the way to her bedroom. She wanted to feel him skin on skin, to glory in the touch of his hands on her naked body and enjoy the exquisite pleasure of his mouth caressing every inch of her.

So much for her vow to ignore her overwhelming attraction for him, she thought derisively. She had melted at the first touch of his lips on hers, and even now her body was trembling with the urgent desire to remain in his arms. Fortunately her brain outvoted her body as it struggled to make sense of her uninhibited response to him, and she jerked clumsily out of his grasp, dismayed to see how eagerly her breasts were straining against the silky material of her dress.

He was watching her silently, like a predator waiting for the right moment to strike, but he made no move to prevent her from stepping away from him. Kezia gripped the edge of the worktop and forced oxygen into her lungs.

'Nik, we can't…this was…'

'A mistake?' he suggested softly. 'The result of too much champagne?' You can do better than that, *pedhaki mou*. We both know this has been brewing since the first time we met. But—' he shrugged indolently, his mouth curving into a smile that was wickedly sensual '—I agree. It's too much, too soon. We have plenty of time.' He seemed wholly satisfied at the thought, and his confidence shook her.

Plenty of time for what, exactly? she wondered as panic swamped her. Nik plainly assumed that she was his for the taking, and her response to him tonight had surely added fuel to that belief, she acknowledged grimly. How could she convince him that she had no intention of ever sharing his bed? How could she convince herself?

She sensed rather than saw him move, and her muscles tensed as she prepared to reject him. But he made no attempt to touch her, and instead reached into his jacket.

'This is for you,' he said, as he took a plastic card from the selection in his wallet. 'I've taken it out in your name so that you can go on a shopping spree in preparation for the cruise.'

Kezia stared at him blankly while her brain assimilated his words. 'I can afford to buy my own clothes, thank you,' she replied stiffly.

'Of course.' He gave a careless shrug. 'But the trip will require more than your usual choice of workwear, and I don't expect you to have to foot the bill for designer evening dresses.' He held out the card and frowned when she made no move to take it from his fingers. 'Enjoy it, Kezia,' he murmured indolently. 'It's not every day that you're given the opportunity to shop in Bond Street. I'm looking forward to seeing you in clothes that show off your gorgeous figure. Choose outfits to please me…hmm, *agape mou?*'

'I am not your lover,' she choked, outrage and blinding fury filling her in equal measures.

Her grasp of Greek was limited, but there was no mistaking the meaning of his words. His eyes slid over her in insolent appraisal, as if he was mentally stripping her, and she felt sick with shame. Her role in his life was purely on a professional level, and she would *not* allow him to treat her as a sultan would his favourite concubine, clothing her in fine silks for his delectation.

'I'm your personal assistant, Nik. Not your whore,' she

snapped icily. 'I'm afraid you're mistaken if you think that what happened tonight was a prelude to three weeks of sun, sea and sex while we're stuck on your damn ship. You said it was a working trip,' she reminded him, when he said nothing, just stared at her in stunned silence—although the glitter in his eyes warned of his anger. 'I'll be accompanying you as your PA, nothing more. My working hours are nine to five, and just because we'll happen to be in the middle of the Mediterranean, I see no reason why that should change. I certainly won't be swanning around in designer gowns, playing the role of your mistress.'

For a moment she thought he would explode. His face was a taut mask, the skin stretched tight over his sharp cheekbones, his jaw rigid as he fought to control his temper. 'Perhaps I should remind you that your working hours are entirely at my discretion?' he said in a clipped tone. 'I expect you to be at my beck and call whenever I require your…services,' he added silkily, his mouth curling into a contemptuous smile as he studied her scarlet cheeks. 'I also expect you to be suitably dressed to dine with the exclusive clientele who have chosen to travel aboard a Niarchou ship. See to it that you don't disappoint me, Kezia.'

He flung the credit card onto the table and stalked out of the kitchen without awarding her another glance. Kezia had never seen him so angry, and her heart was thumping as she followed him down the passage to the front door.

Maybe she had misjudged him? As a representative of the Niarchou Group, it *was* her duty to look and act the part of the chairman's PA, she conceded with a groan. Nik's offer for her to charge the clothes that would be a necessary part of her job to the company account had not been a ploy to persuade her into his bed. It had been an act of kindness that she had flung in his face—and now he was going, storming out of her flat in a furious temper to race to the bedside of his ill father.

'Nik, I'm so sorry.'

He had already flung open the door, but halted and spun round to face her, flicking her a glance of such disdain that she shrivelled.

'I think I may have been mistaken about the reasons behind your offer. I didn't mean to be insulting.'

'God forbid that you should ever try,' he snapped sarcastically, reining in his impatience at the look of misery in her eyes. 'I see nothing wrong with admitting to feelings of sexual desire, Kezia. It's not a crime. You're an incredibly beautiful woman, and I'm quite honest about the fact that I'm attracted to you—as I suspect you are to me. We're two consenting, uncommitted adults,' he pointed out coolly. 'Why shouldn't we spend the night together?

'I can think of at least a dozen reasons,' she said tightly. 'Number one being that I don't do casual sex.'

'And yet you've already told me that since your engagement ended you've not been looking for a long-term relationship? So, what do you do to appease the natural physical desires of a healthy young woman, Kezia?' His eyes moved over her flushed face, and she detected a hint of amusement in his dark gaze.

'I don't have any desires. Physical or otherwise,' she muttered icily, her temper flaring when he threw back his head and laughed.

'Now I know you're lying, *pedhaki mou*. The way you come alive in my arms is proof of that. You are the most sensually responsive woman I've ever met, and I'm genuinely interested to know why you're so desperate to deny yourself the joy of sexual pleasure. Perhaps your parents indoctrinated you with strong morals?' he murmured, almost to himself. 'Did you learn somewhere in your upbringing that sex is a sin?'

Oh, God! She couldn't be having this conversation, Kezia thought frantically as anger and embarrassment fought against the insidious voice in her head that whispered Nik had a point. Why couldn't she be more relaxed and simply go with the flow? She wanted Nik, it would be a lie to deny it, and he'd made it clear that he found her attractive. There was no reason for her to turn down a night of passion with him other than fear—not of him, but of herself. She simply did not have the courage to give her body and still retain control of her heart when, for her, the two were inextricably linked.

'Leave my parents out of this,' she demanded angrily. 'Is it beyond your comprehension to understand that I simply don't *want* to go to bed with you?'

'When you respond to me the way you do—yes.'

She knew him well enough to realise the folly of challenging him, but was still unprepared for the speed of his actions as he jerked her against his chest. One hand slid to her nape, his fingers tangling in her curls as he lowered his head and found her mouth with unerring accuracy. His kiss was brief and hard, stinging her lips and leaving her wanting more, but as she melted into him he pulled back and stared down at her, making no attempt to hide his derision.

'I know exactly what you want, Kezia, but I can't force you to be honest with yourself. And one other thing,' he added, as he released her and it became obvious that his scathing comments had rendered her speechless. 'I don't remember asking you to be my mistress. Perhaps you should wait until you're invited before you rush to turn me down.'

His exit line left her seething, and as she prepared for bed she came up with a dozen clever retorts that she could have flung at him if only she'd had her wits about her.

Her anger kept her awake until the early hours as she tossed restlessly beneath the sheets. It didn't help that her body still throbbed with unfulfilled longing for his possession. She'd never suffered sexual frustration before, or such a desperate, clawing hunger that obliterated common sense and made her behave like a wanton creature in Nik's arms.

If nothing else, it was proof that marriage to Charlie Pemberton would have been disastrous, she acknowledged ruefully. He had been her first lover, but their relationship had been a gentle romance and he had never aroused in her one tenth of the fiery passion she felt for Nik.

With a sigh she sat up and thumped her pillows, needing to expend some of her pent-up physical energy. She wasn't looking for love, she reminded herself as she rolled onto her side, away from the digital clock that flashed three a.m. on the screen. But did she possess the nerve to take her desire for Nik to its logical conclusion? And could she trust herself to remain emotionally uninvolved?

CHAPTER SIX

NIK HAD CALLED the *Atlanta* the pride of the Niarchou fleet, and the description was certainly justified Kezia thought as she glanced around her stateroom. The ship was spectacular, offering luxurious accommodation for three thousand passengers. The brochure she'd found in her room detailed the four swimming pools, dining rooms and show lounges. There was even a gymnasium and golf course.

It was astounding to think that Nik owned this ship, along with her three sister vessels and numerous hotels around the world. The Niarchou Lesiure Group had originated from humble beginnings three generations before, and although it had grown to become a global company it was still very much a family business, with Nik at the helm.

Curiously, she had never thought of Nik in terms of his wealth before. It was the man who intrigued her, not his money. Now, for the first time, she realised the true extent of the Niarchou fortune and her heart sank. They came from different worlds, she acknowledged bleakly, and she had no place in his life.

Slowly she wandered through from her room into the adjoining sitting room, with its wide sweep of windows that overlooked a private balcony. An interconnecting door on the opposite wall led to Nik's stateroom, but the door was closed and she'd learned from the cabin maid, Maria, that Mr Niarchou had not yet arrived on board.

He was cutting it fine, Kezia thought concernedly. The ship was due to leave Southampton dock in less than an hour, and her heart fluttered at the prospect of seeing him again. They had spoken on the phone a few times during the week, but their conversations had been brief and strictly about work issues.

From the coolness of his tone she'd gathered that he was still furious with her, and she hadn't found the courage to enquire about his father. For all kinds of reasons it would be better if their relationship reverted to that of employer and staff. Common sense dictated that she should take no more than a polite interest in his private life, but she couldn't forget the shadows in his eyes when he'd revealed his concern for his father. She cared about him more than she should, she conceded heavily. But for her own good it was imperative that she harden her heart against him.

A tap on the door made a mockery of that resolve, and her pulse-rate accelerated as she crossed the room—only to plummet once more when she discovered Maria in the corridor.

'Mr Niarchou has sent a message to say he regrets that he is unable to join the ship today,' the friendly maid explained. 'He has been unavoidably detained, but will meet you in Lisbon in two days' time.'

'I see. Thank you, Maria.' Kezia forced a smile that disguised her disappointment. Two more days seemed like a lifetime, and it was frightening to acknowledge how much she longed to see him again. So much for hardening her heart, she thought dismally. Where Nik was concerned hers had the consistency of a marshmallow.

'He also requested that I give you these,' Maria added, as she presented Kezia with an enormous bouquet of roses. 'Enjoy your trip.'

The blooms were exquisite, with their tightly furled petals of dark red velvet and a perfume that was innately sensual. Kezia buried her face in them and inhaled the heady fragrance before fumbling to open the attached envelope. The note was brief and to the point, in Nik's inimitable style.

Roses remind me of you—beautiful to look at but prickly to hold. Don't jump ship. Nik.

Her lips twitched, and at the same time her eyes filled with tears. Dear God, how was she going to handle three weeks at sea with him? And how could she ever contemplate a life without him?

Two days later her stateroom was filled with the scent of roses, providing a powerful reminder of the man who had sent them. Not that she needed reminding of him, Kezia thought as she changed for dinner. She'd spent the whole day in a state of nervous tension, expecting him to arrive on the ship at any moment, but now, as evening fell, there was still no sign of him.

The *Atlanta* had left behind the grey shores of England and was now in the Atlantic Ocean, having stopped first at Vigo, on the coast of Portugal, and now at Lisbon, where Nik had said he would join her. Tomorrow the ship would head for Gibraltar, where the itinerary promised an excursion ashore to explore the great rock. But she was more concerned with Nik's whereabouts than riding the cable car to visit the famous ape

With a sigh of frustration she opened her wardrobe and selected one of her new evening dresses—a floor-length sea-green sheath with narrow shoulder straps and a daringly low-cut bodice. It had seriously dented her bank balance, but she'd refused point-blank to charge it to the credit card Nik had given her.

The dress was worth every penny, she decided as she studied the graceful folds of the skirt in the mirror. She had left her hair loose, so that it fell halfway down her back in a mass of curls, making her look softer and undeniably sexy she noted with a groan. Much as she wanted to deny it, she had chosen the dress with Nik in mind. She'd wanted to please him, to catch the flare of desire in his gaze when he looked at her, But Nik wasn't here, and she faced going to dinner alone.

She was seriously tempted to forgo her place at the Captain's table in favour of cabin service, but reminded herself that as Nik's PA it was her duty to represent him in his absence. After completing her make-up, she applied perfume to her pulse-points, snatched up her purse and opened the door to the sitting room—only to stop dead in her tracks as a familiar figure swung round from the window.

'Nik! I had no idea… When did you arrive?'

'An hour or so ago. But I went straight to meet the Captain,' he replied smoothly, his lashes falling to hide the flare of leasure her appearance had evoked.

He strolled over to the bar, lifted a bottle of champagne n the ice bucket and filled two glasses. She was not as self- ed as she would like him to believe, he noted, catching nt tremor of her hand as she reached to take the glass red. He felt a surge of satisfaction at the evidence that isturbed her. She had been in his thoughts constantly this last week, but nothing compared with seeing her in the flesh. And what exquisite flesh, he mused, feeling his body stir. The soft folds of her dress clung to her curves and moulded her breasts, offering them up like ripe peaches that begged for his attention. For a moment he envisaged sliding the diamanté shoulder straps down her arms, so that the creamy globes spilled into his hands, imagined lowering his head and taking first one and then the other dusky pink nipple into his mouth and hearing her soft cries of pleasure as he suckled her.

Enough, he ordered himself firmly, moving away from her while he sought to bring his raging hormones under control. He had made the mistake of rushing her before, and was determined not to do so again. Kezia was a volatile mix of emotions and she needed careful handling. He knew from the soft flush of colour on her cheeks and the tremulous curve of her mouth that she was not immune to him, but for some reason she was fighting her own private battle, and he would have to pursue her with a degree of patience that did not come easily to him.

'How is your father?' she queried huskily.

'Weak, but determined not to show it. He has indomitable will-power,' Nik told her proudly, his voice filled with affection for the man he respected above all others.

'I wondered where you'd got it from,' Kezia murmured dryly, her heart kicking in her chest as he stepped closer. 'I' glad he's okay; staying in hospital isn't much fun...I gue she added awkwardly, aware of the sudden curiosity in gl

She wasn't about to detail the year she'd spent battli just leukaemia, but also the effects of the treatment. Th no reason to tell him of the illness that had nearly cos

life, or of its devastating legacy. She was unaware of the
sudden shadows in her eyes as he slid his hand beneath her
chin and gently tilted her face to his.

'Don't look so sad, *pedhaki mou*. My father's a fighter, and
he isn't ready to give up yet. You have an unexpectedly soft
heart,' he murmured, as he noted the glimmer of tears in her eyes.

She swallowed at the latent warmth of his gaze. 'Beneath
my prickly exterior, you mean?' Her mouth curved into a
smile as she remembered his note. 'Thank you for the roses.
They're beautiful.'

'My pleasure.'

He towered over her, heart-stoppingly handsome in his
black dinner suit and snowy white shirt. His eyes were dark
enough to drown in, and, trapped in his gaze, she swayed
towards him, forgetting everything but the need to feel his
mouth on hers. She couldn't think straight when he was near,
and all her carefully constructed barriers tumbled as she
breathed in the exotic musk of his aftershave. He must have
come straight from the shower. The hair at his nape was still
damp, and she longed to slide her fingers into it, guide his head
down to hers and lose herself in the glory of his kiss. Uttering
a soft sigh, she parted her lips in unwitting invitation.

'I understand Captain Panos has invited us to join him for
dinner? It wouldn't do to be late,' Nik murmured gently, and
roke the fierce sexual tension that shimmered between them.

Kezia inhaled sharply and instantly stepped away from
ı, her face burning. As rejections went, it had been sensi-
y done—but she still felt as though he had slapped her.
had she expected? she thought miserably as she
ed him along the rabbit warren of narrow corridors to

the dining room. He was probably sick to death of her blowing hot and cold, and it was entirely her fault that she had no control over her emotions where he was concerned.

Captain Panos was a Greek sailor of thirty years' experience—fifteen of which he had spent working aboard Niarchou cruise liners. He stood as they approached the top table, and greeted Nik as if he was his long-lost son before turning to Kezia.

'Miss Trevellyn—I'm delighted to have the pleasure of your company once again. It's good that your escort has finally shown up, hmm?' he joked in his heavily accented English. 'I'm surprised at you, Nik, for leaving this beautiful young lady alone for even one day. It's not like you to be so careless, my friend,' he added, his eyes gleaming with humour.

'It's a situation I intend to remedy for the rest of the trip,' Nik murmured, the warmth of his gaze causing Kezia to blush self-consciously as she slid into her seat.

She had met several of the guests who were seated around the table the previous evening—notably the brash American billionaire Des Norris.

'So you're Nikos Niarchou?' Des said loudly, extending a podgy hand towards Nik. 'Damn fine ship you've got here, sir. And that's quite a compliment coming from me. I demand the best for my money—don't I, Marlene? This is my wi' Marlene,' he continued, without giving the woman at his s' time to speak, 'and my daughter Sammy-Jo.'

Des introduced a strikingly pretty girl whose face se to be set in a permanently bored expression. At the si

Nik the young girl's eyes lit up, and she directed her smile at him whilst managing to completely ignore Kezia.

'Hi—it's great to meet you, Nik. You don't mind if I call you Nik do you?'

She shook her platinum blonde hair over her shoulder in a plainly provocative gesture that Kezia found irritating. She guessed the girl to be no more than seventeen or eighteen, but youth obviously presented no handicap for Sammy-Jo. She was openly flirting with Nik—who didn't appear too troubled by the attention Kezia noted dourly. Of course with his looks and charisma, not to mention a handy multimillion-pound fortune, he was bound to be the most sought-after catch on the trip. The fact was unlikely to have escaped him, but he didn't have to look as though he was enjoying the American girl's eager advances quite so much, she thought, as she forced herself to take a forkful of a seafood cocktail that suddenly tasted as interesting as sawdust.

'You're very quiet. Is something wrong?' Nik murmured towards the end of the meal, when she was trying to summon up enthusiasm for her *crème brulée*.

The cuisine was out of this world, with sumptuous menus offering an extensive choice of superbly prepared dishes. Kezia had been panicking as she'd envisaged piling on the pounds, and had even contemplated trying out one of the aerobics classes, but it seemed that jealousy was an excellent appetite suppressant.

'I'm fine. What could possibly be wrong?' she replied jolly. 'The food is wonderful.'

'But you don't view the company with quite such enthu- m?' he guessed, his eyes gleaming with amusement as he 'ed her frown. 'Despite her couture gown, and the rather 'ng array of diamonds at her throat, I imagine Sammy-Jo is younger than she looks, and I have no interest in spoilt little girls.'

'It's really none of my business.' Kezia tore her gaze from his and smiled politely at Des Norris as he addressed her in the booming voice that drew the attention of everyone at the table.

'So, what made you decide to come on this cruise, Kezia?' he demanded as he leaned across the table and leered at her cleavage. 'An attractive, single young woman travelling alone— maybe you're hoping for a little on-board romance, eh?'

'Actually, I'm Mr Niarchou's personal assistant. And romance is the last thing on my agenda,' she replied sweetly, refusing to glance at Nik, although she was aware of his soft chuckle.

Sammy-Jo was patently delighted. 'I thought you two were an item. But I guess there's no reason why you can't dance with me, Nik.' She grinned unrepentantly as she tugged him to his feet and flicked an uninterested glance at Kezia. 'You don't mind, do you?'

'Be my guest.' Kezia knew Nik was far too much of a gentleman to publicly embarrass Sammy-Jo by refusing to dance with her, but she couldn't control the sick feeling in the pit of her stomach as the young girl dragged him onto the dance floor and slotted into his arms as if she belonged there.

Murmuring her excuses to the remaining guests seated at the table, she headed purposefully towards the doors leading out onto the deck. Perhaps a dose of fresh air would cool her temper? she thought as she drew her stole around her shoulders and stared out across the moonlit sea. From the admiring glances Nik had received as he'd walked onto the dance floor she guessed he would have no shortage of willing partners not least the excitable Sammy-Jo. She didn't care wh danced with, Kezia reminded herself fiercely. She was his secretary, nothing more.

With a heavy sigh she began to wander back across the deck, intent on returning to her cabin, when a familiar figure from the past stepped out of the shadows.

'Hello, Kezia.'

'Charlie!' For a few seconds she was almost speechless with shock. 'What are *you* doing here?'

'Working, believe it or not.' Charles Pemberton's face broke into a wide grin as he strolled towards her. 'I run my own travel agency business—catering for the top end of the holiday market, of course,' he added unashamedly.

'I wouldn't have expected anything else,' Kezia replied, her lips twitching. Charlie possessed an easy charm, and his good humour was hard to resist.

'I'm here to report on the *Atlanta*'s new refit. I like to give my clients a first hand account of the trips I'm trying to sell them. And the Niarchou Group has really surpassed itself this time; the facilities on board the ship are superb,' he said admiringly. 'But enough of me. What about you, Kezia? I noticed your name on the passenger list, and I was determined to find you, but I admit I was surprised to see you at the Captain's table with Nikos Niachou tonight. Don't tell me you're his latest flame?' he joked, unable to disguise his curiosity.

'Certainly not. I'm his PA, and this is a working trip for me too.'

'In that case I can safely offer to buy you a drink without fear of reprisal from a six-foot-plus Greek,' Charlie said with satisfied smile.

Kezia hesitated; Charlie represented the past, and although no longer had the power to affect her she still viewed the ending of their engagement with sadness. 'I'm not sure...sometimes Nik likes to work late.'

'He looked pretty cosy with the energetic blonde from your table when I walked past the dance floor,' Charlie assured her cheerfully. 'He can't make demands on every minute of your time, surely?'

No, but he filled her mind exclusively every waking minute, Kezia acknowledged silently. Her fascination with Nik was bordering on the obsessive and for the sake of her sanity it had to stop.

'I'd love to have a drink with you, Charlie,' she said firmly. 'We've a lot of catching up to do.'

Forcing a bright smile, she followed the young Englishman into the bar, where a pianist was playing a medley of popular tunes.

'I understand you're a married man now?' she murmured as Charlie assisted her onto a tall bar stool. The cocktail he had ordered her tasted deliciously fruity, but she detected the kick of vodka and sipped it cautiously. 'I saw a photo of you and Amanda in the newspaper.' His marriage to Amanda Heatherington, daughter of a peer, had gained extensive coverage in the British press.

Charlie looked embarrassed. 'Yes, the parents were pleased. They've been friends with Amanda's family for years—' He broke off, his face suddenly serious. 'I'm sorry things didn't work out for us, Kezia. We had some good times together, didn't we?'

'Yes, we did,' Kezia agreed gently. 'But I think we always knew we weren't right for each other, and your family were never happy about us—especially when they found out th I'm unable to have children. I'm glad you're with Amand she told him honestly. 'But I can't believe you didn't bring her on the cruise with you.'

'I'm only going as far as Rome, and then I'm flying home. Amanda didn't want to travel with the baby...' He paused uncertainly before admitting, 'We have a three-month-old son.'

'Charlie, that's fantastic!' Kezia was genuinely pleased.

'Yeah, he's the greatest,' he grinned, unable to hide his paternal pride. 'I've got some photos...but maybe you'd rather not see them.' His cheeks reddened and he dropped his gaze, aware that it was a sensitive issue for her.

'I'd love to see them,' she reassured him softly.

Charlie's frown cleared and he pulled several pictures out of his wallet and handed them to her. The sight of the tiny face peeping from the folds of a shawl hurt more than she had expected, and Kezia felt a sharp pang in her chest. She dealt with it, and smiled, her eyes clear as she glanced up at him. 'He's beautiful; congratulations.'

She took a long sip of her drink, suddenly grateful for the heady feeling it induced. The tears that burned her eyelids were an unwelcome surprise. There was no point in crying. It wouldn't change anything and would probably embarrass Charlie. She was pleased for him—especially when she remembered the pressure he'd been under from his family to produce an heir.

She drained her glass, and had gathered up her purse, ready to return to her cabin, when a deep, husky voice sounded from behind her, sending a quiver the length of her spine.

'So this is where you're hiding. I've been looking for you,' Nik murmured silkily, although she was aware of the note of censure in his voice. 'Won't you introduce me to your friend, *edhaki mou?*'

He had used the endearment deliberately, Kezia was sure, and she stiffened as his hand settled heavily on her shoulder in a blatantly proprietorial gesture. 'This is Mr Pemberton. We were at university together,' she explained stiffly. 'And this is Nikos Niarchou.'

'Nice to meet you, Mr Niarchou,' Charlie said a shade nervously as Nik surveyed him with a cool, hard stare. 'Fantastic ship. I'll certainly be recommending it through my agency.'

'I'm glad to hear it,' Nik drawled. 'Goodnight, Mr Pemberton.'

'Right—well, I'll be off, then. Maybe we can meet up tomorrow for a game of tennis, Kezia?' He kissed her awkwardly on the cheek, and disappeared with rather more haste than dignity.

'Do you mind?' Kezia turned on Nik as soon as Charlie was out of earshot. 'He's an old friend, and you were incredibly rude.'

'You can hardly lecture *me* on manners when you left our table without a word,' he retorted, unfazed by the storm brewing in her eyes. 'I've been scouring the ship for you.'

'There was no need; I'm perfectly capable of looking after myself. I couldn't tell you I was leaving because you had your hands full—literally—with Sammy-Jo,' she added coldly.

'And now I'm here, to escort you back to your cabin. Do you have any idea how much attention you're attracting in that dress?' he demanded harshly. 'Your *friend*'s eyes were on stalks.'

With her lush curves exposed by the dipping neckline of her dress, and her silky curls tumbling over her bare shoulders, she could have been one of the legendary sirens who lured men to their death on the rocks. She was a temptation that was testing his will-power to the limit, and he would b damned if he would sit back and allow some floppy-haired Englishman to drool over her, Nik vowed savagely.

'Rubbish,' Kezia snapped, stung by his tone. 'Anyway, I'm not ready to go back yet. I'd like another drink.' She had the beginnings of a headache, and wanted nothing more than to seek the peace and quiet of her cabin, but some imp of mischief in her head was intent on challenging Nik. 'Don't let me keep you,' she murmured sweetly, as she beckoned to the barman.

'You are trying my patience, *pedhaki mou,*' he warned softly. 'I think you've consumed enough alcohol for one night. Particularly as you rarely drink.'

'I feel like living dangerously.' She met his dark gaze and shivered at the unfathomable expression in their depths. She knew she was playing with fire but, hell, she was bored with always taking the safe options in life.

Seeing Charlie and, more importantly, the photos of his baby son had brought home to her how much she had lost. She would never cradle her own child in her arms and the life she had planned—a home filled with children—was a shattered dream that she hadn't completely come to terms with.

Why *shouldn't* she have some fun? she demanded silently as she sipped her cocktail. Life was for living; she knew that better than most. Why not seize whatever Nik was offering, even if it was only a brief fling? What harm could it do?

'So you and Pemberton met at university?' Nik murmured. 'Were you friends, or lovers?'

'We were engaged. Charlie was my fiancé—I've mentioned him before,' Kezia replied steadily. 'But his family made no secret of the fact that they were against the match.

For several reasons.' The most pertinent of which she had no intention of revealing.

'Did Pemberton end the engagement?' Nik was studying her intently, as if determined to prise the truth out of her, and she sighed.

'I've told you—ultimately it was a mutual decision, but I understood the pressure he was under. His family hoped he would marry someone with suitably blue blood, and now he has,' she added, unaware of the shadows in her eyes as she met Nik's gaze. She took another sip of her drink, grimacing slightly at the cloying sweetness of pineapple and mango juice which masked the taste of spirits. The second drink hadn't been a good idea, she conceded as the room swayed alarmingly.

'I think you've had enough of that,' Nik drawled in a faintly amused tone that inflamed her temper. She drained the glass and glared at him belligerently.

'You're not my keeper,' she told him crossly.

'No, I'm your incredibly patient boss, who's just about to escort you to your cabin—if I don't have to carry you,' he added dulcetly.

Kezia would have liked to march out of the bar without giving him a backward glance, but instead found herself grateful for his supporting arm around her waist. The deck seemed to be slanted at a peculiar angle, and the blast of fresh air made her head spin.

'I warned you I get seasick,' she told him when they finally reached their suite. He glanced at her, not bothering to conceal his impatience. 'If you feel ill, it's entirely self-induced, so don't look to me for sympathy. Can you manage to get into bed, or do you need my help?'

There was no polite answer to that, and she stormed over to her room in dignified silence that was ruined when she caught her heel in the hem of her dress and tripped.

'*Theos!* You would drive a saint to distraction,' he muttered as he caught her and swung her into his arms.

The sudden contact with the hard wall of his chest was too much for her senses to cope with. She could feel the warmth of his skin emanating through his fine silk shirt, and glimpsed dark chest hair at his throat, where he had unfastened the top couple of buttons.

'Put me down. I can manage,' she told him as she wriggled furiously in his grasp. This was dangerous territory. Already she could feel her muscles relax as liquid heat coursed through her veins.

'I noticed,' he answered dryly, ignoring her request and carrying her into her cabin, where he deposited her on the bed. 'Let's get shot of those heels. That way you may have some chance of standing upright.'

He dealt with the buckles of her strappy sandals with deft movements but the brush of his hands on her ankles was enough to make her shiver with pent-up need. He was kneeling by the side of the bed, his hair gleaming like polished jet in the lamplight, and she longed to run her fingers through it.

'Nik…' Her soft whisper brought his head up, and she heard him sigh.

'You've had too much to drink, *pedhaki mou.* You'll feel better in the morning.'

'I'm not drunk,' she assured him solemnly. 'I know what I want.'

'And what is that?'

'I want you to kiss me,' she said simply. It was the truth, and there was no point in denying it.

For a second heat blazed in his eyes, before his lashes fell, concealing his emotions. His face was a taut mask, his bone structure so perfect, that she raised her hand and traced the sharp line of his cheekbone with her finger.

'You're so beautiful, Nik.' Saying what was in her heart suddenly seemed so simple, and she watched, transfixed, as his mouth curved into a rueful smile.

'It's debatable who you're going to hate most in the morning. Yourself or me,' he said gently. 'But unfortunately my will-power to resist you is almost non-existent.'

He moved to sit beside her on the bed, his eyes never leaving hers as he tilted her chin and slowly lowered his head. As his mouth fastened on hers she uttered a low murmur of approval and parted her lips, shuddering with pleasure at the first sweep of his tongue. He took it slow and sensual, tasting her with a level of enjoyment that was evident from his low groan as she responded with uninhibited passion.

This was where she was meant to be, she accepted. When she was in Nik's arms she forgot the past and was uncaring of the future. Here and now was all that mattered, and she urged her body closer to his, desperate for him to remove the barrier of their clothes so that she could feel his skin against hers. A tremor of excitement ran through her when she felt him slide the zip of her dress down her spine. She was aware of him easing the straps over her shoulders, but then he stopped, his mouth gentle on hers as he ended the kiss and turned her away from him.

'Here, put this on.' He thrust her lacy nightdress into her hands and she stared at it in confusion.

'But I thought—' She broke off, her eyes the colour of the sea on a stormy day as she swung her head round to stare at him. 'I want you to stay,' she whispered, her heart thudding painfully in her chest as he stepped away from the bed.

He seemed very big and tall, but it was not just his size that overwhelmed her—it was the man himself. His eyes still glittered with desire, but incredibly it seemed that he had decided against taking up her offer. Had she misunderstood the heat in his gaze? Had her eager capitulation aroused his contempt rather than his lust? Scalding colour flooded her cheeks, and she was unaware of the utter misery evident in the droop of her mouth that almost saw him denounce chivalry and pull her into his arms once more.

'I've obviously made a huge mistake,' she said stiffly, wishing that he would stop staring at her with an expression that looked horribly like sympathy. She didn't need him to feel *sorry* for her, damn it!

'No, you're not mistaken about my desire for you, Kezia. But your timing is appalling. When I make love to you it will be because you really want it, not because your judgement is clouded with alcohol,' he told her bluntly, smiling softly, as if to lessen the sting of his rejection. 'I fear I have too much pride to make a good consolation prize,' he added quietly.

'You're not. A consolation prize for *what?*' she demanded through an agony of embarrassment.

'For your English lover, Charles Pemberton. I saw the sadness in your eyes tonight, *pedhaki mou,* the regrets for what might have been. But your fiancé chose to marry another woman, and until you can come to terms with the past I can't ee that we have a future. Try to sleep now,' he bade her, when she sat unmoving on the bed, clutching her nightgown to her chest as if it was a life raft.

He wondered if she had any idea how vulnerable she looked, with the shimmer of tears making her stunning eyes seem too big for her pale face. Not just vulnerable but innately sensual, he admitted grimly as he stepped out of her cabin and closed the door. His body throbbed uncomfortably with unfulfilled desire, but he refused to take advantage of her in her alcohol-induced, highly emotive state. With a muttered oath he poured himself a large brandy before heading for the shower.

CHAPTER SEVEN

MORNING BROUGHT GLORIOUS sunshine streaming into Kezia's cabin. For a few seconds after she woke she lay still, watching the sunbeams dancing on the ceiling, but almost instantly her memory returned, and she groaned as she buried her head beneath her pillow. Perhaps the events of the previous evening had been a bad dream? she wondered. But she knew it was the faint hope of a drowning man—or in this case woman.

The sight of her dress, lying in a pool of green silk on the floor where she had dropped it, was evidence, if any were necessary, that last night's fiasco had taken place. Her gaze settled on her sandals, neatly stacked beneath a chair, and a shudder went through her as she remembered the feel of Nik's hands on her ankles as he'd eased the shoes from her feet.

What had she done? The answer was almost too unbearable to contemplate. She had made an utter fool of herself. And although it was tempting to blame her behaviour on the exotic cocktails, she accepted with searing honesty that she had been fully aware of her actions. She had made a play for Nik, had practically begged him to kiss her, and when he had done so she had responded with such wild abandon that he had been left in no doubt that she wanted him to take her to bed.

So why hadn't he? she wondered painfully. His rejection had been gentle, and he'd spouted some nonsense about her still having feelings for Charlie, but it had been a rejection nonetheless, and she didn't think she could ever face him again. The plain truth was that he didn't want her, she acknowledged miserably. She'd probably embarrassed him, and had certainly embarrassed herself but even if she handed in her resignation immediately she would still have to work a month's notice—three weeks of which would be spent trapped here on the *Atlanta* with him.

The ship had to be the most luxurious prison in the world, she though wryly as she headed for the shower. But right now she would give anything to escape back to her flat, where she could bask in Max's devotion and kid herself that she had never even heard of a man called Nikos Niarchou.

He rapped on her door while she was combing her wet hair and she stiffened, every muscle in her body clenched in fear that he would walk in.

'Rise and shine—it's almost nine o'clock,' he called through the closed door. 'There's a mass of work to catch up on today.'

He sounded his usual whirlwind self, and for once she was glad of his impatience. She dressed swiftly in a simple navy skirt and white blouse, swept her hair into a businesslike knot on top of her head, and took a deep breath before going out to meet him.

'I ordered the continental breakfast,' he said, barely lifting his head from his laptop as she joined him at the table. 'The coffee's hot, help yourself.'

He had opened the patio door, so that a warm sea breeze lightly tugged the corner of the tablecloth. The ocean was an intense blue, the sky a shade lighter, dotted with tiny wisps of cotton wool clouds, and Kezia inhaled the fresh air as she slid into her seat. Only then did he look up, and she felt herself blush as she met his speculative gaze.

'Sleep well?'

'Yes, thank you.'

It was a blatant lie, and Nik studied the bruises beneath her eyes for several minutes before returning his attention to his computer screen.

She looked as fragile as fine porcelain this morning, the tremor of her hand as she poured herself a cup of coffee evidence that she was not as self-assured as her neat appearance suggested. He wondered what she would do if he strode round the table, swept her into his arms and kissed her with all the pent-up frustration that had kept him awake until the early hours. She would probably throw the coffee at his head he acknowledged wryly, and forced himself to concentrate on the complicated report in front of him.

The next few hours were devoted entirely to work. Kezia was grateful to be back on familiar territory, where conversation with Nik related only to business, and gradually she relaxed to the point where she no longer felt as though she wanted to die of embarrassment whenever she caught his gaze.

When she eventually took a break she was surprised to find that it was past lunchtime, and she left him deeply involved in a conference call while she stepped out onto the private balcony. The ship was sailing down the Spanish coast to Gibraltar, and all around the huge expanse of sea sparkled in the brilliant sunshine. It was a far cry from the cold air and gloomy skies of England, she thought as she lifted her face to the sun. Working for Nik was a dream job, if only she could control her feelings for him.

'How do you fancy pizza for lunch?'

He suddenly materialised at her side, looking urbane and utterly gorgeous in beige chinos and a black polo shirt, his eyes shaded by designer sunglasses. She felt the tenuous hold on her control instantly crumble, and tore her eyes from him to stare at the horizon.

'There's a pizzeria overlooking the pool, if you'd like to eat outside.'

'Sounds good.' She managed just the right amount of cool enthusiasm in her voice as she awarded him a brief smile.

'Do I detect a thaw in the big freeze?' he queried, the gentle amusement in his voice bringing her head round.

'What did you expect?' she muttered awkwardly. 'I made a complete fool of myself last night.'

'Don't be so hard on yourself, *pedhaki mou*. Everyone drinks more than they should at least once in their lifetime.'

Innate honesty made her confess, 'I wasn't drunk. I knew what I was doing.'

He had moved closer without her being aware of it, and she turned to find him caging her against the railings, his muscular brown arms forming a barrier on either side of her. 'I'm glad to hear it,' he murmured softly, seconds before his head blotted out the sunlight.

His lips claimed hers in an evocative caress that broke through her reserve. Her senses flared as she inhaled the clean, seductive scent of him, and she lost the will to resist him as his tongue explored the contours of her lips before dipping between them to initiate an intimate exploration. She was losing her grip on reality as she slid into a place dominated by sensation, but even as her arms crept up around his neck her brain was urgently reminding her that she could no bear another rejection. Somehow she found the strength to break the kiss, and stared up at him in confusion.

'But I thought... You don't want...'

'Of course I want you, Kezia. I don't think my hunger for you can be in any doubt, do you?' he added, his voice suddenly harsh as he relaxed the savage control he'd imposed on his muscles and leaned into her.

The rigid proof of his arousal pushing against her belly should have shocked her, but instead she was filled with a mixture of tenderness and fierce exultation. He was not as in control as he would like her to believe and the knowledge gave her a heady feeling of feminine power.

'Then why did you walk away last night?' she whispered. 'I've spent the past twelve hours despising myself for my weakness where you're concerned,' she added indignantly, her temper triggered by the memory of the hours of mental torture she had suffered.

She frowned as she recalled his words from the previous night, when he'd told her there was no future for them while she still cared for Charlie. She'd never envisaged a future with Nik that lasted longer than a couple of months anyway, she thought bleakly, unaware that he could read the emotions that chased across her face.

'My engagement to Charlie ended two years ago. I'm not in love with him. We're friends, that's all.'

'Then why did you look so sad last night?' Nik demanded fiercely. 'Do you think I didn't notice the longing in your eyes when you looked at him? I notice everything about you,' he muttered, seeming as taken aback as she was by this last statement.

'It wasn't because of Charlie. I was just remembering the

good times we'd had at university—' She broke off help-lessly, unable to reveal the real reason for the ache in her heart. 'Life seemed simpler then,' she admitted quietly.

Seeing the pictures of Charlie's baby son had evoked a powerful maternal instinct within her that would never be fulfilled. Last night the future had beckoned, lonely and loveless. It was little wonder that she had wanted to lose herself in the passion Nik's burning gaze seemed to promise.

'I'm not in love with him,' she insisted, her heart flipping in her chest at the sudden warmth of Nik's smile.

'Then I'll try to restrain myself from rearranging Mr Pemberton's features when I next see him,' Nik murmured lightly. 'I'm starving. Let's go and find that pizza.'

Kezia stretched out on her sunbed and wriggled her shoulders blissfully. The beach at Nice in the South of France was busy, but not unpleasantly so. The sand was dotted with brightly coloured parasols and the air rang with the sound of children's laughter and the gentle lap of the waves on the shore. It wasn't a bad way to make a living, she thought wryly as she stared up at the azure blue sky. She couldn't help but feel a fraud—especially when she remembered her various friends who were toiling away in London office blocks.

To be fair, she had done *some* work during the past week, while the *Atlanta* had cruised the Mediterranean, stopping at Valencia, Barcelona and Marseille, before arriving at the bustling resort of Nice. Each morning she joined Nik on their private patio for breakfast before settling down to several hours at her laptop whilst he ran his global empire from the ship. But after lunch they invariably relaxed around the pool— or, if the ship was in port, went ashore to explore the sights.

It was a lifestyle she could easily grow accustomed to, Kezia decided as she rolled onto her stomach and peeped at the man stretched out beside her. Nik in swimming shorts was a sight to behold, and she felt the familiar squirmy feeling in the pit of her stomach as her eyes travelled over his broad chest, with its covering of dark hairs, his flat stomach and strong thighs. At that point her gaze skidded to a halt, and she hastily buried her head in her arms. The molten heat that surged through her had nothing to do with the warmth of the sun, and she sighed as she felt her breasts swell and tighten.

'Are you too hot, *pedhaki mou?*' Nik's deep-timbred tones sent a quiver through her.

Oh, my—how was she to answer that? She was burning up.

'Your skin is so fair, you must take care not to burn,' he said seriously as he rolled onto one hip and studied her flushed face. 'Shall I put some more sun cream on your back?'

'No! I'm fine,' she replied quickly. No way could she cope with his hands sliding over her body, smoothing oil onto her skin with frankly sensuous movements. It had been purgatory when she'd agreed to it an hour ago and her hormones were in such a stew she would probably self-combust.

'It's no trouble,' he assured her gravely.

She was sure the devil was laughing at her, but his eyes were hidden behind his shades and as usual his thoughts were a mystery to her. This past week had seen a new era in their relationship. She could no longer kid herself that he was simply her boss now that he took advantage of every opportunity to kiss her. Not that she was complaining, she acknowledged, her nerve endings tingling as she remembered the touch of his mouth on hers, the evocative caresses that hinted at his barely leashed passion. When Nik turned on the charm he was impossible to resist. She had revelled in his attention as they discussed every topic under the sun and yet carefully steered clear of the subject of the fierce sexual awareness that simmered between them like volcanic lava ready to explode.

'I'm going to cool off in the sea,' she told him as she tore her gaze from his face and jumped to her feet.

Jumping had not been a good move, she conceded silently, as her breasts fought to escape the tiny triangles of emerald Lycra that purported to be a bikini.

On their first trip to the pool Nik had taken one look at her functional black one-piece and hauled her off to the on-board boutiques.

'You can't sit on the beaches of the Côte D'Azur looking like you're a Victorian governess. Most women go topless, you know.'

'I'm not most women,' Kezia had pointed out firmly, as she'd watched him select half a dozen bikinis in rainbow shades.

In the ensuing argument over who would pay for them, which he had eventually won, she hadn't bothered to try them on—something that she deeply regretted now, she decided grimly, as his eyes travelled down to her hips and the equally minuscule bikini pants.

'You have a gorgeous body, Kezia. Why do you insist on covering it up?' he murmured, his indolent tone at variance with his heated gaze as he watched her wrap a sarong tightly round her. 'You should enjoy having such a fabulous figure. I know *I'd* like to enjoy it,' he added dulcetly, his lips twitching as she threw him a scandalised glare.

'I don't want to burn,' she muttered stiffly before running down to the sea.

He was the bitter end, she thought as she dropped her

sarong at the water's edge and plunged into the waves. The level of sexual tension between them was white hot. They were both aware of it. And yet he had made no move to take their relationship further. Despite treating her to wonderful romantic dinners at the *Atlanta*'s various restaurants, and dancing in the nightclub, their bodies closely entwined, he seemed curiously reluctant to take her to his bed.

Perhaps he was waiting for a sign from her—a clear indication that she wanted him to make love to her? she brooded as she struck out into deeper water. It was impossible to believe he really thought she harboured feelings for her ex-fiancé, as he had once accused. She had met up with Charlie a couple of times, and enjoyed his easy company, but Nik could not possibly imagine she felt anything deeper for the younger man than friendship.

Incredibly, she had detected definite signs of jealousy from Nik, and the light-hearted tennis match she'd played with Charlie had been followed by a far more hostile battle between the two men. The fifth set had been played with the serious-ness of a Wimbledon final beneath the blazing Mediterranean sun, and unsurprisingly, considering Nik's stronger physique and fierce determination, he had emerged the victor.

She knew Nik desired her—his urgent kisses every night were proof of his hunger—so why couldn't she link her arms around his neck when he escorted her to her cabin and suggest that they fulfil their mutual desperation for each other rather than spend another frustrating night apart? She was scared, she acknowledged as she flipped onto her back and floated the gentle swell. Not of Nik—her every instinct told her would couple passion with sensitivity and consideration he made love to her. It was herself she was afraid of.

She had once told him she wasn't looking for love, but dared she risk her emotional security for a few weeks, months at most, of physical pleasure and then walk away when it was over with her pride intact?

Her silent reverie was rudely shattered when she felt something tug at her legs, dragging her beneath the surface. Almost instantly she bobbed back up, spluttering and thrashing her arms wildly as she recalled the old movie about a killer shark. The predator swimming next to her bared his white teeth as he grinned at her unrepentantly.

'You look like a mermaid,' Nik told her as he threaded his fingers through the long strands of her hair that were floating on the water.

'Scaly and with a tail, you mean?' she snapped, as she snatched air into her lungs.

His smile deepened, and he caught hold of her around the waist to pull her up against his chest. 'Definitely no tail,' he assured her, after sliding his hands over her hips to make a thorough investigation of her legs. 'Or scales. Your skin is like satin.'

His shoulders gleamed like burnished bronze in the sunlight, the whorls of dark hair on his chest slightly abrasive against her palms as she was forced to cling to him. She was out of her depth in more ways than one, she thought frantically. She'd never met a man like him and would probably never do so again.

The sea's current was causing them to bob up and down so that his near naked body rubbed sensuously against her creating havoc with her hormones. *Live dangerously, just once,* the voice in her head whispered, and with a low murmur of capitulation she slid her fingers into his hair and drew mouth down to hers to initiate a kiss that stirred his sou

Nik waited a heartbeat before taking control and deepening the kiss, cupping her nape so that he could angle her head to his satisfaction. What was it about this woman that made him ache to possess her? he wondered. In his thirty-six years he'd had countless lovers, particularly when he'd been younger and driven by his hormones to follow up every flirtatious glance that came his way. In recent years he had become more selective, but he made no denial that he enjoyed women. He had a high sex drive and a low boredom threshold. There had even been occasions when he'd had a mistress on three continents—elegant socialites who understood that their influence over him ended at the bedroom door. He valued his independence, yet in the past few days he'd found himself wondering if he would ever tire of Kezia's smile, or the way her eyes darkened to the colour of the sea when he kissed her.

A rogue wave took them both by surprise as it lifted them up and propelled them inland. Kezia reluctantly broke the kiss, gasping as she was sucked beneath the surface, but Nik tightened his grip and hauled her up.

'Not so much a mermaid as a drowned rat now,' he teased, and she retaliated by splashing him, before tugging out of his arms and racing up the beach, squealing for mercy when he pulled her down in the shallows.

'Nik, this is a family beach,' she reminded him urgently as ̧e lowered his body onto hers, supporting his weight on his ̀bows. He was tantalisingly close, and she loved the sound ̄is laughter as he threw back his head.

̄o it is, *pedhaki mou*. I guess I'll have to wait until later ̧ my retribution.'

̧gleam in his eyes caused a tremor of excitement to run ̧her, but instead of shying away she calmly met his gaze. 'I guess you will,' she whispered, and heard him mutter a fierce imprecation beneath his breath as he dropped a brief, hard kiss on her lips before he stood and tugged her to her feet.

'Would you like to eat on board tonight? Or shall we go back to the ship to shower and change and then return to explore the Old Town? I know of a particularly good seafood restaurant.'

'That sounds nice,' Kezia replied. 'But if I carry on eating the way I have been, I'm going to put on weight.'

'You need to regain the pounds you lost when you were ill,' he told her unconcernedly. 'And I love your curves. Like all Greek men, I prefer real, voluptuous women—not some unhealthy-looking stick insect. I love your bottom,' he said, with stark frankness, 'and the fact that your breasts are doing their best to fall out of your bikini.'

'Whose fault is that?' she demanded, her cheeks scarlet as she struggled to hide the offending bosom beneath her sarong. 'You chose it.'

'True, but I've paid the penalty by spending most of the day in the sea, desperately trying to hide my body's reaction to you,' he said, his unabashed confession rendering her speechless for the whole of the journey back to the ship.

The night sky was studded with stars—like diamonds on a huge velvet pincushion, Kezia thought as she studied the beautiful canopy above her. The bright lights that marked o the coast were growing fainter as the motor launch sped acr the bay back to the *Atlanta*, whose outline was clearly de by colourful twinkling bulbs.

'Are you cold?' Nik's husky tones sounded close to ' and she smiled as he draped her stole over her should air was cooler now than during the day, but her shiver had been born of excitement, and a sense of feverish anticipation that could no longer be denied.

They had spent a magical evening exploring the Old Town of Nice, with its wonderful architecture and pretty pastel-coloured buildings, before dining in an exclusive restaurant tucked away down one of the narrow side streets. Nik had been charmingly attentive, their conversation easy, but it had been the unspoken words and shared intimate glances as their gazes met across the table that had left Kezia longing to return to the ship.

'I understand there's a disco tonight, out on deck. Would you like to visit for a while, maybe have a drink?' he murmured once they were safely on board the *Atlanta*. 'Or are you tired, *pedhaki mou?*' There was a wealth of subtle suggestion in his query, causing a quiver to run through her as his breath stirred the tendrils of hair at the nape of her neck.

Definitely not tired, she acknowledged silently. She'd never felt more *alive* in her life. Her senses were heightened to such a degree that she was conscious of the salt tang of the sea carried on the breeze, mingling with the evocative scent of Nik's aftershave. Neither did she want a drink. After the events of a week ago she had stuck religiously to iced water, and tonight it was imperative that she keep a clear head. She didn't want there to be any more misunderstandings between them.

'We could watch the dancing for a while, if you like,' she ⸺ huskily, her nerve failing her. She was not some inexperi-⸺ virgin, for heaven's sake she reminded herself irritably. ⸺ as a grown woman who had made the conscious ⸺ to make love with the man who was slowly driving ⸺ e with need. Why couldn't she smile at him, award him one of the flirtatious glances she'd seen other women send his way, and coolly suggest that they return to the suite?

At the bar, her good intentions dissolved, and she sipped the crisp white wine Nik handed her with a grateful sigh as warmth stole through her veins.

'Dance with me?' he asked softly, a mixture of sympathy and gentle amusement in his dark gaze as he recognised the silent battle raging within her.

It was frightening how well he knew her, she brooded as the music changed to a slow ballad and she slipped into his arms. She had the feeling that he could read her mind, but in many ways he remained a stranger to her—and she had no idea what was in his head.

'Relax,' he murmured, his arm tightening around her waist as she stumbled. He threaded his hand through her hair, and with a sigh she sagged against his chest, closing her mind to everything but the music, the moment, and the man who had stolen her heart.

How long they danced together she did not know. She lost all concept of time, content to stand in the circle of his arms as they swayed with the slow tempo, hips and thighs brushing together as mutual arousal built to a level where there could only be one outcome.

'Ready to go?' His lips feathered her lobe before trailing down her throat to the pulse that jerked frantically at its base.

Wordlessly Kezia nodded, unaware of the stark vulnerability in her eyes that made Nik's gut clench. Someh without him understanding the how or the when, she become infinitely precious to him. How had she s beneath his guard to the extent that his own desir second place to his need to do what was right for

was a complicated mixture of emotions—fiercely independent and yet acutely sensitive. He would never knowingly hurt
her, he vowed as he brushed his lips over hers and felt his body
harden at her instant response.

Already he could not envisage a time without her. He would
miss the sound of her laughter, her acidic comments when she
dared to answer him back—which she frequently did. He had
never met a woman like her, and he accepted that he would want
her in his life for a long time—months, years, even, he brooded.

The sobering thought saw him escort her back to the suite
in silence, his mind reeling at the possibility that he wanted
more than a brief affair with Kezia. Once inside, he strode
across to the bar and poured himself a large brandy.

'Can I get you a drink?'

'No, thank you.'

She had followed him into the room and was hovering by
the patio doors, seemingly fascinated by the far-off lights that
delineated the coast. In her black lace evening dress and high-
heeled sandals she looked elegant and sophisticated, but the
rigid set of her shoulders, the way she fiddled restively with
her purse, spoke volumes about her nervous tension.

Silently cursing himself, Nik swallowed the contents of his
glass in one gulp. He had never needed Dutch courage before
in his life—but he'd never pursued a woman with such
patience before either, he conceded ruefully; usually he had
fight them off. He had always treated his lovers with
ect, and he'd certainly received no complaints, but getting
ht had never mattered so much before. He wanted the first
e made love to Kezia to be perfect.

ng down his glass, he strolled towards her, noting the
stiffened as he approached.

'Are you interested in the stars?' he asked gently, when she remained staring resolutely at the heavens.

'I know nothing about astronomy,' she replied with a faint smile. 'But on a night like this space seems so infinite and so beautiful, don't you think?'

'Exquisite, he murmured, his gaze fixed on her delicate features as he turned her in his arms. He glimpsed the faint shimmer of tears, the agonising uncertainty in her gaze, and was flooded with tenderness as well as passion. 'Stay with me?' he whispered, before claiming her mouth, his fingers sliding into her hair to cup her nape.

With every other woman he had taken to bed he'd always felt the need to qualify that statement, to specify that the invitation was for the night only, but with Kezia he was certain that one night would not be enough to satiate the hunger he felt for her.

'I want to make love to you,' he told her as he eased the pressure of his kiss and traced the outline of her lips with his tongue. He needed to spell it out, wanted her to be absolutely sure, and he felt his heart kick painfully in his chest when she nodded wordlessly before she wrapped her arms around his neck and clung tightly, as if she would never let go.

CHAPTER EIGHT

NIK'S STATEROOM WAS slightly bigger than Kezia's, but equally sumptuously appointed, with soft blue velvet carpet, discreet lighting, and a double bed that was the immediate focus of her attention.

She was not here to admire the décor, she thought, her heart pounding as he entwined his fingers through hers and led her through the door. It would have been easier if he had lifted her into his arms and carried her, she acknowledged as her steps slowed. At least then she could convince herself that she had been swept away on a tide of passion. Instead, the decision of whether to stay, or flee to her own cabin, was entirely in her hands.

Was he aware of her apprehension, mixed with an undeniable sense of anticipation? She shivered, and felt every nerve-ending prickle unbearably in a sensation that was closer to ain than pleasure.

'Are you afraid of me, *pedhaki mou?*'

he tenderness inherent in his tone touched a nerve, but she her head fiercely. 'Of course not.' She was not afraid . But his expectations terrified her.

as used to worldly-wise, sophisticated women, whose

level of expertise between the sheets matched his skilful love-making. Self-doubt rocked her. She couldn't possibly compete when her only experience of sex was with Charlie. One lover in twenty-four years hardly made her an expert in the art of seduction, she brooded, unaware that he could read the play of emotions in her eyes.

'You have no idea how often I wish I'd followed my first instincts the day we met in the London office,' he said suddenly, his voice breaking the tense silence. At her look of puzzlement he elaborated. 'I took one look at you and was overwhelmed by the urge to fling you down on your desk, remove your clothes and lose myself inside you—take us both to the heights of sexual ecstasy,' he added steadily when she gaped at him.

'You felt like that *then?*' she whispered incredulously, casting her mind back all those months.

All the days and weeks that she had been beating herself up over her inappropriate feelings for him, and *he* had been feeling them too! Her nervousness dissolved in a flash, aided by the unconcealed hunger in his gaze. Nik wanted her, had always wanted her, and the chemistry she'd felt between them that day had been real, not some figment of her imagination or wishful thinking.

'So what stopped you?' she queried lightly as she laid her palms flat against his chest and felt the erratic thud of his heart beneath her fingertips.

'It would have broken every rule of political correctne and possibly landed me in court on charges of sexual har ment,' he replied with a smile, as his arms came round h pull her close, so that she was made achingly aware power of his arousal. 'And you were not ready, *agap*

She acknowledged the truth of that with a soft smile, her eyes wide and clear as she murmured, 'I am now. I want you to make love to me, Nik.' Whatever else she might have said was lost beneath the force of his kiss, that plundered her soul and drove every thought from her mind other than her desperate need for him to love her. His tie was quickly discarded, his jacket flung carelessly to the floor, and she scrabbled with his shirt buttons, parting the material to run her hands over the bunched muscles of his abdomen. His skin was like satin, overlaid with a fine covering of dark hairs that arrowed down and disappeared beneath the waistband of his trousers. As he trailed his lips down her neck and traced the line of her collarbone she fumbled with his zip, her inhibitions blown away with the force of her longing to feel him deep inside her.

'We have plenty of time,' he said softly, his mouth curving into a sensuous smile at her eagerness to undress him.

He dealt with his zip and then hers, sliding it the length of her spine so that he could tug her dress from her shoulders. In a black lace bra and matching briefs she was unutterably beautiful, and he inhaled sharply as he reached behind to unfasten the clip so that her bounteous breasts spilled into his hands. He couldn't repress a groan as he took the weight of them in his hands, firm yet deliciously soft. He shaped their rounded fullness before lowering his head to take one nipple into his mouth.

Kezia whimpered as sensation pierced her. It was exqui-
, and she slid her hands into his hair to hold him to his task.
ands roamed her body, cupped her bottom and pulled her
gainst his thighs while he transferred his mouth to her
ipple and metred out the same punishment, until she
n his arms and cried out, begging him never to stop.

With a low groan he lifted her up, deftly pulled back the bedspread and laid her on sheets that felt blessedly cool on her heated skin. She felt boneless, her limbs heavy and languid, as she opened slumberous eyes to watch him strip down to his boxers. In the lamplight his skin gleamed like copper, and she held her breath as with one swift movement his underwear joined his trousers on the floor and he stood, legs slightly apart, gloriously and unashamedly naked. The full strength of his arousal brought a moment's panic, and she caught her bottom lip with her teeth as she viewed him, imagined him driving into her with firm, hard thrusts. Liquid heat pooled between her thighs, and her fear disappeared as she caught the gentle emotion in his eyes.

'There's no rush, *pedhaki mou.* I want this to be good for you,' he told her as he joined her on the bed and drew her into his arms.

Being held against the warmth of his broad chest was akin to reaching heaven, Kezia thought with a sigh as she burrowed closer. The scent of his cologne mixed with the more subtle drift of male pheromones stirred her senses, and with great daring she nipped one flat nipple with her teeth.

'You know I'll have to repay that in kind,' he teased, as he rolled her flat on her back and took her mouth in a fierce kiss, his tongue probing between her lips to initiate an intimate exploration that left her trembling. He then proceeded to administer the same attention to each of her breasts, taking first one and then the other fully into his mouth and suckling hard, s that heat unfurled in the pit of her stomach and she twis her hips restlessly.

Her knickers formed a barrier he deftly removed, ar held her breath when he trailed his hands across her st and thighs to rest lightly on the tight red curls at the

She arched her hips as his fingers gently eased a path, parted her with infinite care and dipped into her to discover her moist inner heat.

'Nik,' she cried out as he probed deeper, stroking her with one finger and then two, forcing her legs to widen so that he could continue the skilful caress.

It was too much. She could feel the waves of sensation building and twisted frantically on the mattress.

'Please—I want you,' she whispered, sure she would die if she did not feel the full length of him inside her.

For a heart-stopping moment he withdrew, and she tensed, terrified that he had for some reason changed his mind. Perhaps she wasn't doing enough to pleasure him, she thought desperately, but as she reached for him he gave a husky laugh.

'Not this time, my sweet Kezia. Not unless you want this to be over before it's begun.'

At the sound of his voice she opened her eyes, her fear that he was about to reject her fading when she realised the reason for his brief hesitation. Now was not the time to explain that there was no need for him to use protection, she thought painfully. The one thing she could be utterly certain of was that she would never conceive his child.

He mistook the sudden shadows in her eyes and hovered above her, the harsh planes of his face thrown into stark relief as he fought to hold himself back.

'If you've changed your mind, you need to say so in the next ten seconds,' he grated.

She could see the frustration mirrored in his gaze, and with absolute respect for her. It was her decision, he wouldn't her and as she stroked the rigid line of his jaw she felt rt melt.

'I want you. More than I've ever wanted a man in my life. Make love to me, Nik,' she pleaded, and she drew his head down and kissed him.

He muttered something in Greek as he slid his hands beneath her bottom and angled her hips, moving over her so that his throbbing shaft pushed against her. She clung to his shoulders, her eyes locked with the burning heat of his as she parted her legs and felt him ease forward. He took it slow, penetrating her with infinite care, then drawing back a little to enable her muscles to stretch around him.

'Nik!' She wanted more, and moved her hips so that he thrust forward again, deeper this time, filling her so that every atom of her being was focused on the feel of him as he made them one.

He set a rhythm that was as old as time and she matched him, welcomed each stroke by arching her hips and drawing him ever deeper. It was indescribably good, she acknowledged with the tiny part of her brain capable of thought, but as he increased his pace she lost all grip on reality and gave herself up entirely to sensation. Pleasure began to build, in little ripples at first, that grew stronger and more urgent. She dug her fingers into his back, held on tight as the first waves of her climax sent spasms ripping through her body.

Still he drove into her, with strong, steady strokes that were taking her inexorably higher and higher, until she reached the pinnacle and cried out, her breath coming in harsh sobs as she shuddered with the force of her release. Only then did he falter, his face rigid as he fought for control, but as her muscles contracted around him he groaned and sur into her with one last, powerful thrust, before collapsin top of her.

She should move, Kezia thought. She should slip

Nik's arms, gather up her clothes and make some teasing remark about needing to return to her own cabin to get some sleep. She did none of those things. Her body seemed to be held in a state of lassitude that kept her firmly pinned to the mattress, and she could feel her eyelids drift closed.

'Sleep, *pedhaki mou*,' Nik's voice was as soft as velvet, and as he brushed his lips over hers she was powerless to prevent her response.

His breath was warm on her neck, stirring the tendrils of hair, and she sighed as he settled her comfortably against his chest. She must not cling, the voice in her head sharply reminded her. She must be cool and composed, as if making love with him had been a brief few moments of pleasure rather than the most earth shattering experience of her life.

'I must go back to my room,' she muttered, finding speech difficult when her face was pressed against his chest.

She felt rather than saw his smile. 'But then I'll have to come and find you when I want to make love to you again,' he murmured huskily, sending a quiver through her as she imagined going through the whole process once more. 'And that could be very soon,' he added, his voice laced with sensual promise. 'Stay here with me, Kezia *mou*. I don't want you to go.'

The thought was sufficiently disturbing to keep him awake until dawn, and it was only after she had stirred in his arms and he had taken her again, with tenderness as well as passion, that he finally slept.

Kezia opened her eyes and winced—previously little-used es were making themselves known. Not that she was ining, she thought with a smile as she turned her head on the pillow and found Nik watching her, the softness of his gaze making her heart leap.

'Good morning, *pedhaki mou,*' he greeted her gently, as he had each of the past four mornings that she had woken in his bed.

Did he ever sleep? she wondered as she lifted her hand and ran her fingers over the dark stubble on his jaw. She always fell asleep in his arms, utterly satiated by the passion they'd shared each night, and no matter what time she woke he was lying quietly beside her, watching her.

'Good morning.' She returned his greeting gravely, her senses flaring as he brushed his lips across her fingertips.

Even that fleeting gesture was enough to stir her body into urgent life, she thought despairingly. She felt her breasts swell and quickly pulled the sheet around her, desperately trying to hide the fact that her nipples had hardened to tight, throbbing peaks. Of course he knew the effect he had on her, and his mouth curved into a slow, sensual smile as he studied her flushed cheeks. It was so unfair, she thought bitterly. One look was all it took to reduce her to a mass of quivering emotions, and the moment he touched her she went up in flames.

For the sake of her pride she needed to take control of the situation and bestow a brief kiss on his cheek before collecting her robe and sauntering into the *en-suite* bathroom. The sudden flare of heat in his eyes trapped her to the bed. He was not wholly unaffected by the sizzling chemistry between them, she noted, her satisfaction increasing when she trailed her other hand over his hip and met the rigid proof of his arous

'We really should get up and do some work,' murmured, the token protest lost beneath the pressure o mouth as he initiated a kiss that swiftly dispensed wit idea she might have had of trying to resist him. She wa cause, she acknowledged, with a sigh that became a moan of pure pleasure as he tugged the sheet away and shaped her breasts with his hands.

'The only urgent business you need to worry about is pleasuring your master,' he growled playfully, and he took her by surprise and flipped her over so that she was lying on top of him. He gently pushed her so that she was straddling him, in a position that gave him perfect access to her breasts. 'Beautiful,' he muttered, his voice slurred with satisfaction and he stroked her, his dark, tanned hands making an erotic contrast with her milky white skin.

Knowing how easily she burned, she had slathered on the sunscreen and was suddenly glad that she hadn't had the nerve to sunbathe topless. She shook her head so that her red curls tumbled over her shoulders, and felt a thrill of feminine pleasure at the way Nik's eyes narrowed. With his hands cupping her ribcage he drew her forward and took one nipple in his mouth, suckling gently before turning his attention to its twin, his tongue flicking across the sensitive peak until she cried out and ground her hips against him. His penis pushed into her belly, and she felt the flood of warmth between her thighs that indicated her readiness to take him inside her.

She had assumed he would roll her onto her back but instead he lifted her and guided her down onto him, his eyes locked with hers as he watched her look of shock slowly change to pleasure. It was the first time he'd allowed her to take control, but her uncertainty quickly disappeared as instinct took over and she set a pace that had him gritting his teeth as he fought to hold back. It was only when he felt her muscles contract around him and heard her sob his name as the waves of her orgasm hit that his control snapped. With a groan he rolled her over, crushing her beneath him as he drove in, hard and fast, until he could bear it no more and tumbled them both over the edge.

'What would you like to do today?' he queried lazily as he brushed his lips across hers in a lingering caress before rolling onto the mattress beside her. 'I have a meeting scheduled with Captain Panos later this morning, but we could meet up for lunch.'

'Don't you have any work for me to be getting on with?' she said seriously. 'I've hardly done a thing for the last few days.'

Since leaving Nice, the *Atlanta* had made a leisurely journey down the coast of Italy. They had stopped for two nights at Pisa, and had travelled inland to spend a glorious day exploring the beautiful city of Florence, birthplace of the Renaissance. The rich culture of the city had been almost too much to take in as they'd visited art galleries to view originals by Rubens, Botticelli and Michaelangelo, and Kezia had quietly determined that she would one day return, to spend more time in the place she had instantly loved.

Yesterday the ship had docked again, and Nik had given her a guided tour of Rome, which boasted some of the most incredible architecture she had ever seen. The cruise on the *Atlanta* was turning out to be the experience of a lifetime in more ways than one, she acknowledged ruefully as she admired Nik's naked form when he stood and strolled towards the bathroom.

'There's nothing vital on the agenda,' he assured her with a smile as he saw her sudden frown. 'You're free to do as you like today, *agape mou*.'

'In that case I might go ashore again and do shopping. I promised Anna I'd bring her a souvenir every place we stopped.'

'Good—you can choose some baby clothes while you're there.'

Nik had disappeared into the bathroom and so did not see the look of acute shock on her face. What on earth was he talking about? He had used protection every time they'd made love, and she hadn't yet steeled herself to explain that it was impossible for her to fall pregnant.

'I think it's a bit premature to be worrying about that,' she muttered, her voice sticking in her throat as a wave of desolation swept over her. Even if by some miracle he fell in love with her and begged her to be the mother of his child, she would never cradle Nik's baby in her arms.

'For my sister's new baby.' He reappeared through the doorway, his handsome features split by a wide grin. 'Silviana is my youngest sister. She gave birth to her first child—a little girl—a month ago. What's the matter?' he demanded, his voice suddenly sharp with concern. 'You're as white as a ghost.'

'I'm fine. I sat up too quickly, that's all,' she lied. 'I'm used to spending most of my time horizontal just lately,' she added, forcing a smile. 'But I don't know much about baby clothes— or babies, come to that.'

'They're not aliens from another planet,' he told her, his expression suddenly speculative as he stared at her. 'Most women would enjoy the chance to browse in a babywear shop. I know your career is important to you, Kezia, but if you're anything like my sisters you'll start to feel broody in a couple of years or so.' His tone was lightly teasing, but she stared at him levelly.

'No I won't,' she said fiercely. 'Motherhood is not for me, Nik. I can assure you of that.' She left him then, and hurried across the sitting room to her own cabin before he could see her tears.

Nik stared after her, his brows drawn into a frown. He couldn't comprehend why her words disturbed him so much, and his temper was not improved when he cut his chin on his razor, his hand strangely unsteady as he shaved.

Nik was not in their suite when Kezia returned to the ship a few hours later. He must still be talking to Captain Panos, she guessed as she took a bottle of cold water from the fridge and stepped onto the balcony. It was only a little past lunchtime, and with all the wonderful food she'd indulged in lately she was hardly hungry—not for food anyway, she amended, her cheeks growing even warmer as she recalled her hunger for the man who dominated her every waking thought.

Nik's lovemaking was becoming an addiction she would have to break some time soon. Possibly at the end of this trip. The way her heart lurched painfully in her chest at the thought was proof that she dared not allow the affair to continue. Her confidence that she could enjoy a brief fling and walk away unscathed had been sadly misplaced, she acknowledged dismally. The idea of leaving Nik tore her to shreds, but pride dictated that she should end their relationship, both as lover and employee, when they returned to England.

She could not bear to wait until he grew tired of her, always looking over her shoulder and wondering if the next attractive blonde would be her replacement in the bedroom. As his PA, would he expect her to buy her own flowers and a suitably expensive trinket? she wondered cynically. No, Nik had more respect for her than that, she reminded herself impatiently. And she couldn't blame him; he'd made it clear from the beginning that he was not in the market for long-term commitment—a sentiment she'd assured him she shared. Unfortunately her stupid heart seemed to have a will of its own and it had given itself completely and irrevocably to a man whose family were desperate for him to one day produce an heir.

It was a case of history repeating itself, she thought sadly, remembering her engagement to Charlie and the reason they had ended their relationship. She had promised herself she would never put herself in such a position again, which was why, as soon as the *Atlanta* docked at Southampton, she would tell Nik it was over.

A knock on the door dragged her from her pit of dark thoughts, and she quickly crossed the sitting room to answer it.

'Charlie! I thought you were flying home today,' she murmured distractedly to the fair-haired young Englishman standing in the doorway. Her mind was still clinging to memories of the past, but inherent good manners made her add, 'Won't you come in?'

'My flight's not until this evening, but I'm going to spend the afternoon in Rome. I didn't want to leave without saying goodbye, Kezia,' he said gently as he studied the shadows in her eyes. 'Are you okay? You look upset.' He hesitated fractionally, and then continued, 'Is it Niarchou? I couldn't help but notice that he's obviously more than your boss, but I'm afraid he's not in your league, Kez.'

'What would *you* know, Charlie? It's two years since we split up, and I've changed a lot in that time. I'm tougher than you think,' she told him sharply. 'I can handle Nik.'

'I hope so, because to me you appear the same sweet girl I knew—and I'd hate to see you get hurt.'

'For the second time, you mean?' she queried, instantly regretting her sarcasm when Charlie blushed.

'I'm sorry. I shouldn't have come here,' he muttered awkwardly. 'And, as you've so rightly pointed out, I'm the last person to give you advice on your love-life.'

He turned to go, his shoulders slumped in a way that reminded her of a small boy who'd been caught misbehaving. Charlie hadn't changed, she thought with a smile as she put her hand on his arm.

'I'm the one who should apologise. I've got a few things on my mind at the moment,' she admitted ruefully. 'I'm glad you're here, because I bought a present for your little boy.' She crossed to the table and picked up a smart little sailor suit. 'It looks a bit big, but I suppose he'll grow into it,' she said doubtfully. 'I don't spend a lot of time in baby shops.'

'Kez! I don't know what to say.' Charlie smiled warmly as he held up the suit. 'This is great—thank you. I'm sorry about…everything.' He shrugged helplessly. 'I wish things could be different for you.'

'They're not. I can't have children. But there are plenty of people a lot worse off than me.' She gave a determinedly bright smile and he slipped his arm around her shoulders.

'You're a beautiful person, Kezia—inside and out,' Charlie told her softly. 'Take care.' His kiss was a fleeting caress to seal their friendship, but a slight noise from the doorway caught Kezia's attention, and she jerked out of his arms as she met Nik's furious gaze.

'Charlie was just saying goodbye. He's leaving today,' she explained falteringly, her temper flickering into life as Nik continued to stare at her as if she was something unpleasant swimming about at the bottom of a pond. 'I bought a present for his new baby,' she added pointedly.

'And now it must be time for you to leave, Mr Pemberton Nik ignored her and addressed Charlie in a tone that cause the younger man to edge hastily towards the door. 'You don't want to miss your flight.'

'You seem to be making a habit of being rude to my friends,' Kezia snapped as soon as Charlie had gone.

'Just the one friend. And on each occasion I have caught you in his arms. I think that qualifies as an excuse for any rudeness, don't you?' he queried mildly as he crossed to the fridge and extracted a beer.

'No, I don't. I could have been rolling around stark naked on the carpet with him and it still wouldn't have given you an excuse to speak to him like you did.' She glared at him, hands on her hips, while her hair flew around her shoulders like a halo of fire. 'You wanted a no-strings relationship— remember? You can't go and move the goal-posts when it suits you.'

The intrinsic truth of her statement did nothing to improve Nik's temper, he acknowledged grimly as violent anger coursed through him. And the fact that he was not supposed to feel jealous of Pemberton only added to his irritation.

'Have you always had such a hang-up about commitment? Or is it a result of the split with your ex-fiancé?' he growled as he stalked through to his stateroom.

'*Me* have a hang-up? That's rich, coming from a man whose most successful relationships can be counted in weeks rather than months!' Kezia followed him into his cabin, her anger melting away as she watched him unbutton his shirt. 've told you; Charlie's just a friend now. I admit I was upset quite a while after our relationship ended, but I understood reasons, and I was over him a long time ago.'

What *were* the reasons?' Nik queried as he shrugged out shirt and released the button at the waistband of his trousers. 'Do you have some horrible habit that I haven't yet discovered?'

'No—!' She broke off, her cheeks scarlet. Now was an ideal time to reveal her secret, to tell him about the illness that had struck her as a teenager, and the devastating consequences of the treatment. 'I've told you already—his parents didn't approve of me,' she muttered as her nerve failed her.

She searched frantically for a way to change the subject, her eyes widening as he stepped out of his trousers. His skin had darkened to the colour of bronze, and she felt the familiar weakness flood through her as she imagined running her hands over his chest, following the path of dark hairs over his abdomen to the edge of his silk boxers.

'We can't solve every argument we have with sex,' she said breathlessly, some external force propelling her towards the bed.

'I hadn't intended to,' he replied smoothly, his eyes narrowing on the hectic colour of her cheeks. 'I was just getting changed.'

Too late she noticed the pair of khaki shorts on the bed, and felt sick with mortification. 'Of course. My mistake,' she muttered, wishing a hole would appear in the floor and swallow her up.

He let her suffer for thirty seconds, before strolling round the bed and snaking an arm around her waist as she made to escape. 'I'm intrigued by the idea of you rolling around on the carpet stark naked. Would you care to give a demonstration?'

She bit her lip, torn between the desire to run away and hide, and the more basic urge to lay her head on his chest and absorb his masculine strength.

'I only do it on special occasions. It's hell for friction but' she told him gravely, and caught the answering glint of an ment in his eyes before he captured her mouth and initiated a slow, thorough exploration that left her boneless in his arms.

'It'll have to be the bed, then,' he said a shade regretfully, and he tumbled her backwards and instantly covered her body with his own, his boxers doing nothing to disguise the proof of his arousal.

This could not continue, Kezia thought faintly as she assisted in the removal of her clothes and tugged the offending boxers over his hips. She could not spend her life as a mindless sex slave, unable and unwilling to resist him. But the alternative—to live without him—would be unbearable.

There was still another week until they returned to England, and she could only pray that it would be enough time to free her heart from the silken web he had spun around it.

CHAPTER NINE

THE BAY OF NAPLES, with its sparkling blue waters and Mount Vesuvius looming in the distance, was a breathtaking sight. The city was a vibrant, colourful place, brimming with history, and renowned among other things for being the home of pizza.

Kezia found it a magical place, and was determined to do as much sightseeing as possible. But although the sunshine was glorious, the heat sapped her energy, and she was glad when Nik led the way back to the harbour.

'Do you want to go back to the ship? Or shall we have lunch here?' he asked as he tucked a stray curl beneath the brim of the straw hat he'd insisted she wear at all times. 'You look warm, *pedhaki mou.*'

'Be honest—I look like a boiled lobster,' she replied dryly.

Her face was hot, her feet ached, and she'd managed to drip ice cream down her skirt. Nik, on the other hand, looked cool and eye-catchingly gorgeous in cream chinos and a pale blue shirt that contrasted with the golden hue of his skin. With his glossy dark hair and designer shades, he drew admiring glances from women of all ages, and Kezia was tempted to stick a sign on his forehead saying—*Hands off!* It wasn' easy for a mere mortal to partner a demi-god, she acknow

:dged ruefully, although to be fair Nik had been faultlessly
ittentive.

'We could try that little restaurant by the water's edge,' she
,uggested. 'It's so lovely here, and cooler than in the town.'

The sea breeze tugged at her hat and played with the hem
>f her skirt, lifting it to reveal a length of slim leg that was
he immediate focus of Nik's attention.

'Perhaps we should return to the *Atlanta* and have a lie-
lown?' he murmured, the frankly sensual quality of his tone
ind the familiar gleam in his eyes sending a quiver of excite-
nent through her.

'Later,' she told him firmly, fighting the urge to head back
o the ship by the fastest route possible, even if it meant
wimming across the harbour. She could *not* give in to her
iunger for him at every opportunity, she reminded herself,
gnoring the voice in her head that was counting down the
lays they had left before they returned to England.

'Spoilsport,' he teased as he threaded his fingers through
iers and led the way across the harbour.

He was a tactile, affectionate lover, and she relished the
asy familiarity of their relationship. He slowed his pace in
ime with hers, walking so close to her that their thighs
rushed. He was so tall, the width of his shoulders so for-
nidable, that other men kept a respectful distance, and she
>ved the feeling that she was utterly protected. She loved *him,*
he accepted, and felt her heart miss a beat at the hopeless-
ess of it all.

There was no future for them. To Nik, she was just one in
long line of sexual encounters, and although she believed
cared for her in his way, he would never love her. It was
iculous to wish for the moon.

The moped speeding through the bustling harbour was no different from the dozens of others she had noticed weaving manically through the narrow streets of Naples. Kezia took scant notice of it until it screeched to a halt a few feet from her, and only then did she feel a jolt of apprehension as she stared at the two figures whose features were concealed behind their helmets.

'*Signorina!*'

She half turned, and blinked as a flashbulb momentarily blinded her.

'What…? Nik, what was all that about?' she queried faintly as the moped sped away, narrowly missing running over her toes.

'Damn paparazzi! Although they won't live long if they continue to drive like that,' he said grimly, as the pillion passenger swung round and pointed a camera at them. 'Are you all right, *pedhaki mou?*'

'I'm fine. But why were they taking pictures of us?'

Nik's face had hardened, and he seemed suddenly remote when he glanced down at her. 'The Niarchou Group's new ship has attracted a lot of attention in the press,' he said, failing to add that he, the chairman of the company, was also of considerable fascination to certain elements of the media. 'Forget it,' he urged as he noticed her obvious concern. 'They were probably taking pictures of the *Atlanta* and wanted a couple of shots of tourists on the voyage.'

'I suppose so,' Kezia murmured, but throughout lunch she could not throw off a feeling of unease.

She was certain she had noticed the distinctive pattern on the helmets of the moped rider and his companion in the town earlier that day. She was probably imagining things, she told herself impatiently. There were literally hundreds of mopeds whizzing around Naples, and the idea that she and Nik were being stalked was fanciful nonsense.

By the time they returned to the ship, to spend a leisurely evening watching a show, she had almost forgotten the incident in the harbour. Nik seemed distracted, but he made love to her that night with such skilful dedication that nothing else mattered but assuaging her desperate need for him.

He could very easily become her reason for living, she thought sleepily as the last ripples of her orgasm left her limp beneath him. When he moved to ease away from her she wrapped her arms around his neck, revelling in the weight of him. She felt him smile against her skin, and he captured her mouth in a slow, sweet kiss that drugged her senses.

'I'm too heavy for you, *agape mou*. You'll have to let me go before I hurt you.'

The truth of his last statement made her heart ache, and she kissed him with a fervour that shook them both. Murmuring something in Greek, he rolled onto his back and instantly scooped her against his chest, his lips gentle on her brow before exhaustion claimed them.

They spent the next two days at sea as the *Atlanta* journeyed to Athens. Kezia was looking forward to visiting Nik's homeland, eager to learn as much as she could about the country he was so proud of. He had promised to take her to the Acropolis, she remembered as she stirred and opened her eyes before rolling onto her side to wish him good morning.

The bed was empty, and she sat up, instantly awake. It was the first time since she had shared his room that she had woken alone, and she was shocked by her reaction. She felt though a black cloud had covered the sun and all joy had

been drained from the day because she was denied the
pleasure of his first kiss.

Voices sounded from the sitting room, and she paused to
snatch up her robe before heading for the door. She could
make out a torrent of voluble Greek. Nik sounded in a furious
mood, and she wondered who he was yelling at down the
phone. She was unprepared for the sight of him fully dressed
in an impeccably tailored grey suit. With him was an older
man—also Greek, she guessed—who surveyed her curiously
as she stepped out of the bedroom. A tide of colour flooded
her cheeks as she fumbled to fasten the belt of her robe, and
her eyes were wide with confusion and growing apprehension
as she stared at Nik's grim expression.

'What is it? What's wrong?' she demanded, and heard
him sigh heavily as he swung away from her to stare
moodily out to sea.

'You'll have to see them some time, so I suppose it may as
well be now,' he said obliquely, before swinging back and
thrusting a newspaper into her hands.

With a feeling of dread Kezia took it from him, her face
turning ashen when she glanced at the photograph on the
front page.

'My God!'

Her first thought was that she looked enormous. The
picture was a close up—so close up, in fact, that the camera
lens was practically inside her bikini top—and she groaned
at the sight of her breasts spilling out of the tiny triangles of
material. She wasn't sure where the photo had been taken—
possibly Nice, she guessed, as she stared at the shot of her and
Nik frolicking in the waves. It could have been worse, she
conceded, remembering another occasion when he had pul

er into the sea and untied her bikini top. At least she retained ome iota of modesty in this photo.

But as she glanced at Nik's furious face her heart sank. 'What does the caption say?' she asked, recognising the Greek alphabet, but unable to read the words.

'That particular one reads—*"On the job! Niarchou boss gets personal with his assistant!"*' he translated, no glimmer of amusement in his voice. 'There are others.'

'So I see.' She sifted through the pile of newspapers on the table with shaking hands. There was some consolation that they had only made the front pages of the Greek papers, but the photo and others like it appeared inside all the British tabloids, as well as most of the other European papers. 'The men on the motorbike,' she whispered, her memory of the faceless individuals hiding beneath their helmets returning to haunt her. 'But why—?'

She broke off and swung her gaze from the photos to Nik. She knew why—he was the chairman of a multimillion-pound empire and the subject of intense interest both in Britain and abroad. Pictures of him cavorting in the surf with his secretary would have been a great scoop for the photographer, who had no doubt sold them for a small fortune.

'It's not the end of the world,' she ventured at last, when she could stand the tense silence no more. 'It's just a few pictures.'

'Several million pounds have been wiped off the company's share value since trading began this morning,' he told her coolly. 'Shareholders don't react kindly to the sight of their chairman flaunting his mistress on the company's flagship—especially when that mistress is also a representative of the company.'

'I see.' Kezia paled at the harshness of his tone. 'But what

can we do now that the pictures have been published?' She
knew he was angry but the idea that he somehow blamed *her*
was unbearable.

'The most important thing is to initiate a damage limita-
tion exercise. This is Christos Dimitriou, one of the Niarchou
Group's top lawyers.' Nik briefly introduced her to the older
man, who had so far remained silent.

Feeling acutely embarrassed, Kezia gripped the lapels of
her robe together and shook hands with the unsmiling Greek

'Christos is seeking an injunction to prevent the publica-
tion of any more photographs. Meanwhile, we'll leave the ship
as soon as possible,' Nik continued, in the same clipped tone

'I'll go and pack,' she said quickly, glad of the excuse to
return to her cabin as her heart splintered. It was over, she acknowledged bleakly. Nik was a typically proud Greek and he
would hate feeling a fool. The pictures of the two of them
spread across every newspaper spelled the end of the brief
happiness they had shared.

'The maid is already packing for you,' he informed her. 'Go
and get dressed. The helicopter will be here in twenty minutes.

'Are we flying straight back to England?' The thought of
leaving the secure cocoon of the ship terrified her. For more
than two weeks the *Atlanta* had provided a haven away from
the rest of the world—a place where she had found her private
nirvana in Nik's arms. How would she survive without him
she wondered despairingly. He was the love of her life, but
she could not return to Otterbourne House as his full-time secretary and some time mistress.

Nik's jaw tightened as he noted the mixture of shame and
misery in her eyes. She had no reason to feel ashamed, he
brooded furiously. He was thankful she could not understan

most of the scurrilous newspaper articles that suggested she was little more than a common tart, enjoying a freebie holiday and getting paid for sleeping with her boss. It was a foul insinuation, and he clenched his fists in impotent rage before quickly hiding the English paper at the bottom of the pile, until he could safely destroy it.

The whole mess was *his* fault, he acknowledged bleakly. He should have guessed that the paparazzi would be curious about the Niarchou heir's new companion. It would be impossible to protect Kezia from the press once they left the ship; he knew only too well of the lengths journalists would go to in their bid for more pictures. There was only one place he could take her until the furore died down, but he had a feeling she wasn't going to like it.

'We're not going to England,' he informed her briskly. 'My family own a private Aegean island. The helicopter will fly us to Zathos, where we'll be out of reach of the media.'

'But what about your family? Will they be there?' Kezia queried cautiously as she struggled to keep up with a situation that was fast running out of her control.

'Of course—they're looking forward to meeting you.'

'Oh, come on!' She laughed bitterly. 'How will you introduce me—secretary or strumpet? Perhaps you'll explain that currently fill both roles in your life? Although the second is on a strictly temporary basis,' she added fiercely.

'My parents are as appalled as I am that our relationship has been vilified in the press,' he snapped. But she ignored the warning glitter in his eyes and glared at him. Pride was all she had left, and she was determined to hang on to it.

'We don't have a relationship,' she reminded him. 'You're always telling me your parents long for you to meet a nice

Greek girl. You can't turn up with your PA, whom you just happen to be sleeping with at the moment.'

'If it's not a relationship, how would you describe what we share, Kezia *mou?*' he queried silkily, his anger all the more unnerving because of the tight control he imposed on it. 'If you believe it's just sex...' he paused and flicked a glance at his watch '...we may as well make the most of the fifteen minutes before the helicopter arrives and enjoy one last session.'

'Nik!' His crudeness was almost as shocking as his implication that they shared something deeper than sexual compatibility, and her confusion was tangible as she stared at him.

She couldn't be having this conversation—especially with the grim-faced Greek lawyer as a spectator she thought wildly. She didn't know how much English Mr Dimitriou understood, but she was acutely aware of his presence.

'Think very carefully about your answer, *pedhaki mou,*' Nik bade her softly, his sudden movement catching her off guard as he jerked her against his chest.

'I don't know what you want from me,' she whispered, afraid to blink in case he should see her tears. 'It wasn't meant to be like this.'

When they'd first become lovers she had accepted that all he was offering was a casual fling, and had steeled herself for their inevitable parting. Incredibly, it now seemed that Nik hoped to further their relationship—but to what end? she wondered as her heart lurched in her chest. There could be no real future for them—not least because he was the last Niarchou and he needed an heir.

The sheen of tears turned her eyes the colour of aquamarine. Nik felt his gut twist as his anger drained away and was replaced with compassion. The emotional attachment h felt to her had taken him by surprise too. He understood the puzzled despair in her voice when she'd cried that it wasn't meant to be like this. At first he'd also assumed that he would be content with a brief affair, but with every passing day that he spent with her he'd found she was becoming increasingly important to him. They had something special, something he'd never experienced before, and if he was honest he wasn't sure what he wanted to do about it.

He stared at the tremulous curve of her mouth, glimpsed the uncertainty in her eyes, and recognised with stark clarity that he could not let her go.

'Go and get dressed,' he ordered, the sudden tenderness in his voice causing a solitary tear to roll down her cheek. 'We'll talk about this later.' He caught the tear with his thumb-pad before cupping her face in his hands, but as his head lowered she caught sight of the stack of newspapers and gave a low moan.

The media had turned something beautiful into a grubby scandal, and she couldn't bear for him to kiss her. She felt sullied, her privacy exposed in the most repugnant way, and with a strength born of desperation she tore out of his arms and fled to her cabin.

The helicopter flew above the brilliant blue waters of the Aegean towards an island that formed the only land mass as far as the eye could see. Zathos appeared on the horizon like an emerald set in a crystalline sea, and as they came in low over the coast Kezia held her breath and prayed they did not clip the treetops.

Her nerves fluttered as they dipped down over a hilltop, and she spied a tiny village of white flat-roofed houses that glinted in the sunshine like sugar cubes. At any other time she would have enjoyed the flight, and the wonderful views afforded by the glass bubble of the helicopter cockpit, but as they started to descend apprehension choked her.

She turned to Nik, who was sitting grim-faced beside her, and reached into her handbag. 'I think I should give you this,' she said quietly.

'What is it?' He sounded faintly bored, and made no move to take the handwritten document from her fingers.

'My resignation; I'll look for another position as soon as we get back to England.'

His eyes glinted with mocking amusement as he took the letter and ripped in two. 'If you're bored with the missionary position, I'm more than happy to spice up our love-life, *pedhaki mou.* You should have said,' he drawled sardonically.

'Damn you, Nik, I'm being serious,' she hissed furiously. 'It's over between us, and the sooner you explain to your parents that the newspaper articles were a misunderstanding the better.'

'The hell it's over.'

He sprang before she had time to react, his hand gripping her nape as he captured her mouth in a devastating assault. She knew the futility of fighting him when his strength easily outmatched hers, and instead forced herself to remain passive. His tongue probed the mutinous line of her lips before forcing entry, and she swallowed a sob of frustration as heat flooded through her veins. Sensing her capitulation, he deepened the kiss to a level that was provocatively sensual until she melted against him, any idea of resistance forgotten as she responded with a desperation she could not disguise.

Only when she was utterly pliant in his arms did he ease the pressure, his tongue tracing the swollen contours of he mouth before he lifted his head. The fierce gleam in his eyes warned of his implacable determination to bend her to his will.

'Look at me and tell me this means nothing to you,' he demanded, his expression softening slightly when she stared at him in stunned silence. 'During the past few weeks you've come to mean more to me than any women I've ever met. Who knows where this might lead?' he murmured thickly, as he stroked an errant curl from her cheek.

'It won't lead anywhere. It can't,' she replied on a note of pure panic. Nik was offering her a glimpse of heaven but she was agonisingly aware of the hell that would surely follow once he knew the truth about her. He wasn't suggesting that their relationship could lead to marriage, she reassured herself. But what if he fell in love with her? His confession that she meant something to him had shaken her to the core. This was Nik, the man with a heart of stone, who changed his women as regularly as most men changed their socks. She'd never meant for him to love her, and for one glorious second she imagined what it would be like to hear him say those words, to give her love freely and without fear of rejection in return.

Reality intruded, and she tore her gaze from the heartbreaking tenderness in his. She had been through this once with Charlie—had allowed her hopes to build, only to have them cruelly shattered when he had decided that having a family was more important to him than marrying her. She couldn't bear that level of pain again, she thought bleakly, not with Nik.

'What are you so afraid of, *agape mou?*' he queried gently. Do you think I'll hurt you like your fiancé once did?'

'I think it's very likely,' she replied bluntly, her voice sounding over-loud in her ears as the helicopter fell silent and he realised that they had landed.

Nik cupped her chin and stared into her eyes, as if determined to make her believe him. 'I'm not Charlie. You can trust me, Kezia *mou*. All I'm asking is for a chance to prove it.'

'I forgot to mention it's my sister's birthday,' he said ten minutes later, as the car transporting them from the helicopter landing pad swept through the gates of a huge white-walled villa. 'Everyone will be here.'

'Everyone?' Kezia queried faintly, staring in wonder at the profusion of vibrant pink flowers that covered the walls of the house. Bougainvillea, she guessed, and growing alongside it jasmine, with delicate creamy blooms and a heady fragrance that filled the air.

She followed Nik across the gravel driveway that led around the side of the house, her steps slowing as he pushed open a gate leading to an enormous, immaculately kept garden. The entire population of Zathos seemed to be assembled on the lawn, but her eyes were drawn to the gazebo and the frail looking man seated in a wheelchair in the shade. Even from a distance she noted his resemblance to Nik, and her heart thudded in her chest. She was about to meet Nik's parents, something she had never in her wildest dreams imagined would happen, and she was terrified.

What would they make of her when they must have seen the photographs of her over-exposed body in the pages of the newspapers? Did they blame her for bringing shame on Nik and on the Niarchou name? she wondered nervously.

She wiped her damp palms on her dress, and then prayed she hadn't left a mark. The dress was of cool linen, belted at the waist, with a narrow skirt and a gently scooped neckline and she wondered if she had subconsciously chosen white for its virginal connotations—hoping to impress Nik's parents. Some hope, she thought ruefully as she stared at the reception committee who had gathered beneath the gazebo.

'There seems to be a lot of children. They're not all your nieces and nephews, surely?' she murmured when Nik turned to her.

'I'm afraid they are. Come and meet them—they don't bite, you know,' he added gently, when she appeared rooted to the spot. He took her hand and lifted it to his mouth, his lips grazing her knuckles in a gesture that took her back to the first time she had met him at the Niarchou head office. Just as then a spark of electricity shot down her arm, and she stared at him helplessly, her heart in her eyes. 'Trust me, *pedhaki mou,* they'll love you,' he insisted, and he slid his arm around her waist and led her across the grass.

'Will they?' She could not disguise the doubt in her voice. 'Do you often bring your...' she faltered slightly '...girl-friends to meet your family?'

'I've never brought any woman to Zathos before,' he replied seriously, the velvet softness of his gaze causing her heart to perform a somersault, but as she absorbed his words they reached the group, and he tugged her forward.

'Kezia—you have a beautiful name,' Nik's father murmured in his heavily accented English, once formal introductions had been made. 'We've heard much about you—and seen quite a bit too,' he added, so softly that for a second she thought she must have misheard him.

Her startled gaze took in the glimmering amusement in his eyes, and her lips twitched. Yannis Niarchou obviously shared the same wicked sense of humour as his son, she thought wryly.

'I'm so sorry—' she began, but the old man held up his hand.

'There's no reason for you to apologise. The paparazzi are...' he shrugged his bony shoulders '...unforgivably intrusive. But my son will deal with the matter,' he said, with unwavering confidence. 'Nikos has explained everything.'

Had he? Kezia seriously doubted that Nik had explained the true nature of their relationship, and she blushed beneath his father's speculative gaze.

'You are in love with Nikos. This I see in your eyes,' Yannis explained gently as her cheeks turned scarlet. 'I am old, and stuck in this thing,' he said with a disparaging glance at his wheelchair, 'but I see plenty. I see what is in your heart, Kezia Trevellyn.'

Kezia was unable to forget Nik's father's words, and spent the rest of the day in a state of shock. Was she really so transparent? she wondered dismally. And, God forbid, was Nik also aware of her feelings for him?

Her eyes were drawn across the garden, and a dull ache formed around her heart as she watched him swing one of his little nieces onto his shoulders. The children flocked around him like bees to a honey pot, and he seemed equally fond of them, the sound of his laughter filling the air as he chased them across the lawn.

'My brother will make a wonderful father some day,' a voice murmured in her ear, and she turned to offer a tentative smile to his sister Athoula, who had joined her on the garden bench.

'He's very good with children,' Kezia replied quietly. 'I had no idea.'

'Well, he's had plenty of practice. Between us, my sisters and I have twelve little ones—although the others sensibly had theirs one at a time,' Athoula said with a grimace.

'It must have been a shock to discover you were carrying

triplets,' Kezia remarked, as she picked out the three identical little boys who were dressed in matching red shirts.

'My husband still hasn't got over it,' Athoula laughed. 'They're a handful, but I wouldn't be without them.'

Nik's sisters were nice, Kezia mused a few hours later, as she strolled down to the far end of the garden, away from the party. Indeed, every member of his family had treated her with quiet courtesy that did not fully hide their curiosity, but although they were friendly she sensed their reserve. It was to be expected, she reminded herself when she turned to watch them, her expression unconsciously wistful as she tried to imagine being part of such a close-knit family. Nik had done his best to ensure that she was included in conversation, but many of his older relatives in particular did not speak English, and in her heart she knew she was an outsider.

She suddenly longed to be back in England, where her life had been far less complicated and emotionally draining than in the weeks she'd spent with Nik. It was time to go home, but even the thought of seeing Max, the scruffy terrier she had rescued, did nothing to ease her heartache.

She watched Nik stride down the garden, her eyes focused on the chiselled beauty of his face and the inherent power of his wide shoulders. She would never love anyone the way she loved him. But for her pride's sake she had to act cool, she told herself.

'I've been looking for you,' he said a shade reproachfully as he drew her into his arms and lowered his head to initiate a slow, evocative kiss that shredded her fragile emotions. 'Stop hiding down here. Some more of my cousins have arrived and want to meet you.'

'I can't believe you have so many relatives,' she

murmured when he threaded his fingers through hers and led her across the lawn.

Two little boys in red shirts suddenly ran past, from the far end of the garden, and she watched them, unaware of the shadows Nik glimpsed in her eyes, or his frown as he tried to guess the reason for her sadness.

They carried on walking towards the gazebo, but something was niggling in her mind. Two red shirts when there should have been three? she puzzled, and she glanced around the grounds of the villa in search of the third triplet.

'That gate in the far corner of the garden—where does it lead?' she asked Nik.

'To the ponds,' he replied. 'My father keeps fish, but the gate's kept locked while the children are here—for obvious reasons.'

To his astonishment he found that he was talking to thin air as Kezia tore back down the garden. She knew where she had seen the third red shirt, she remembered, a premonition of dread filling her as she reached the gate and pushed it open.

The surface of the main pond was covered with water lilies, but their beauty left her unmoved as she searched frantically for a flash of red among the reeds. She spied the infant on the opposite bank, his dark curls gleaming in the sunshine as he leaned forward to watch the fish. The second that he toppled into the water she literally flew around the edge of the pond, adrenalin coursing through her as she grabbed a handful of shirt and hauled him to safety.

'*Theos!* That was close.' Nik had followed her through the gate and was staring at her from the opposite side of the pond, admiration and another indefinable emotion in his dark gaze.

The air in the enclosed garden was curiously still, and so

silent that Kezia could hear her heart pounding as reaction set in. Fortunately the child was too young to comprehend the danger he had been in, and he grinned at her happily as she lifted him into her arms and began to walk back to the gate. He was dripping wet, but she didn't care when he squirmed closer and wrapped his chubby arms around her neck. The instinct to nurture tugged at her heart, and for a second she hugged him close and rubbed her cheek on his satiny curls. Nik would one day have a son who looked just like this adorable little one, she thought, and the pain in her chest was so sharp it felt as if a knife had pierced her.

'You're an amazing woman, you know that?' he murmured softly as he lifted the child onto his shoulders and slipped his arm around her waist. 'You put on this act that you're not interested in children and then spend the entire day acting as mother hen, watching over the brood. My family have much to thank you for—and I've a feeling they're about to do so right now,' he added dryly, as the entire Niarchou clan raced across the lawn towards them.

Athoula was in tears, and there seemed to be a furious row going on between various relatives over who had unlocked the gate, but as Kezia stood, looking dazed, Nik's mother pushed to the fore and enveloped her in a suffocating embrace.

'You saved my grandson's life, Kezia, and now you will always have a place in my heart,' she announced in her broken English. 'She's a good girl, huh?' she demanded, as she turned to the rest of her family, and then, as an aside to Nik, 'She'll make a wonderful mother; she's got good hips.'

For Kezia it was the last straw, and with a cry she ran towards the villa. She had no idea where to go. All she knew was that she had to get away from Nik before her heart cracked open.

CHAPTER TEN

TODAY SHE WOULD TELL NIK she wanted to go home Kezia vowed, the minute she opened her eyes. Pale rays of sunlight filtered between the blinds as dawn heralded another glorious day on Zathos, but she couldn't stay here any longer. A week had passed since they had arrived at his parents' villa. Seven long nights spent tossing and turning in her lonely bed while he slept in his own room at the far end of the corridor.

Separate rooms was not his choice, he'd told her, his frustration evident in the fierce hunger of his kiss when he escorted her to her room each night. But his mother was old-fashioned, and out of respect for her he could not make love to Kezia under his parents' roof.

She understood his reasons, and loved him all the more for his sensitivity, she acknowledged with a sigh. But if she'd hoped that a week without the exquisite pleasure of his love-making would lessen his grip on her emotions she was disappointed. Since that first day, when he had followed her into the villa and demanded to know why she was crying, they had spent every waking moment in each other's company. It had been relatively easy to convince him that her tears had been a reaction to dragging his little nephew out of the pond, but impossible to prevent herself from falling ever more deeply in love with him.

Somehow, the fact that they could not fulfil their physical desire by leaping into bed at every opportunity had intensified the emotional awareness that simmered between them. Nik cared for her; she knew it from the tenderness of his smile, the way that whenever she looked at him she found his dark gaze focused on her, sending her a message that she was afraid to decipher. And with every day that passed it was becoming harder and harder to reveal that there was no future for them because she could never give him an heir.

A light tap on her bedroom door saw her scramble out of bed, her breath catching in her throat at the sight of him leaning indolently against the wall.

'Nik! What are you doing? Do you know what the time is?' she babbled, as she sought to control the familiar pain around her heart.

His sun-bleached denims were stretched taut over his hips, his black shirt open at the throat. She would never tire of looking at him, she thought as her pulse-rate accelerated. He was so indecently good-looking that she felt weak with longing, and stepped back from the door, unconsciously hoping that he would follow her into her room.

'It's a little before six,' he replied easily, as he caught her chin and tilted her face to his. 'I thought we'd watch the sunrise together.' He covered her mouth with his own in a kiss that stirred her senses, but instead of deepening it he eased back, and smiled at her undisguised disappointment.

'I'm not dressed,' she mumbled, pink-cheeked.

'I can see that, *pedhaki mou.*' His voice was dry as his eyes skimmed her, noting the silky disarray of copper curls before focusing on the firm swell of her breasts visible beneath her thin nightdress.

Did she have any idea what a temptation she presented? he wondered, as his body reacted with its usual eagerness to the sight of her. One week without her in his bed and he was climbing the walls. Life without her sparkling, joyous presence would be no life at all, he conceded and a gentle smile tugged his lips as he glimpsed the mixture of emotions in her eyes. He would do whatever it took to persuade her they had a future together.

'Go,' he bade her, as he swung her round and tapped her smartly on the derrière. 'You've got five minutes before I come in and get you.'

'Couldn't we have watched the sunrise just as easily from the terrace?' she asked twenty minutes later, as she followed him up a steep, rocky path that seemed more suitable for goats.

'This is the best place on Zathos,' he assured her, when she finally joined him on a vast, grassy ledge that afforded an incredible view of the sea. 'That's why I'm going to build my house here.' He had spread a blanket on the ground, and grinned as she collapsed beside him, her breath coming in sharp gasps. 'You need to work out more,' he teased, rolling onto his back and drawing her down on top of him.

'Are you really going to have a house here?' she asked, desperately trying to ignore the throbbing proof of his arousal that was pushing against her belly. Liquid heat pooled between her thighs, and she wriggled—until she realised how much he was enjoying it and glared at him.

'I certainly am. The builders start laying the foundations next week. I'll show you the plans once we've had breakfast.' His hands eased beneath the hem of her tee-shirt, and he gave a growl of approval at the discovery that she wasn't wearing a bra.

'I can't see a picnic basket,' she said thickly. 'What did you bring for breakfast?'

'You,' he replied simply, before he tugged her down and claimed her mouth in a kiss that drove everything but her over-whelming need for him from her mind.

She had been starved of him for a week, and responded to his touch with a fervour that bordered on desperation as she wrenched open his shirt buttons and ran her hands over his chest. He pushed her so that she was sitting astride him, and whipped her tee-shirt over her head, his hands skimming her chest before cupping her breasts.

'Someone might come,' she whispered fearfully, torn between her desire and the need for propriety.

'There's nobody here. Only the goats,' he told her, watching the way her eyes became glazed when he stroked his thumb-pads across her nipples until they tightened to hard peaks that begged provocatively for him to repeat the action with his tongue. He drew her forward and captured one dis-tended peak between his lips, loving the way she ground her hips against him when he suckled her.

'You don't know how desperately I've longed to do this,' he muttered, his voice muffled against her throat. 'It's been the longest week of my life, *agape mou,* and if I don't have you right now I think I'll explode.'

'Don't explode just yet,' she urged, as she obligingly wiggled her hips so that he could tug her shorts down her legs. With a muffled oath he flipped her onto her back, shrugged out of his jeans and boxers and dispensed with her briefs with a deftness that left her trembling and exposed to his gaze.

'You are so very lovely, Kezia *mou.*'

He trailed his hand over her stomach and gently eased her legs apart, so that he could dip between them, his fingers parting her with delicate precision to discover her moist inner heat. Kezia half closed her eyes and gave herself up to pure sensation as he explored her with a thoroughness that drove her to the brink. She could smell the sweetness of the grass mingled with the faint tang of the sea, the air cool and clear as the sun streaked the sky with streaks of pink. There was something elemental, almost pagan about lying naked beneath the heavens, and as Nik moved over her she stared at him, her emotions stripped bare.

'I want you, Nik,' she whispered, and he needed no second bidding as he nudged her thighs apart and entered her with one powerful thrust.

Instantly her muscles closed around him, drawing him deeper as she matched his rhythm with an eagerness that had him gritting his teeth and fighting to hang on to his control. Their bodies moved with total accord in a primal dance as old as man. Above them the sky lost its first rosy blush as the sun rose and filtered through the leaves of the olive trees, dappling their entwined limbs with gentle warmth.

Kezia clung to Nik's shoulders as he increased his pace and drove into her, faster, deeper, until her breath burst from her body in painful gasps, her whole being focused on reaching that magical place she had only experienced with him. Suddenly she arched beneath him, trembling on the brink of ecstasy, and as she tumbled over he caught her cries with his mouth, his tongue mimicking the fierce thrusts of his body with a degree of eroticism that stunned her.

Wave after wave of pleasure engulfed her, but still he kep

his steady rhythm, so that he took her up once more, her second orgasm so intense that it seemed almost impossible to withstand. Only then, when she sobbed his name over and over, did his control splinter, with spectacular results, and a feral groan was ripped from his throat to be carried away on the breeze.

Her first conscious thought as she drifted back down to reality was that she had given herself away this time. She had made love to him with her heart as well as her body, and as she held him close and listened to his ragged breathing gradually return to normal, she was filled with tenderness. The moments after a man had experienced sexual release were said to be his most vulnerable, and she crossed her hands over his back in a gesture of protection. She would willingly give her life for him, she acknowledged, as the tears that had gathered behind her eyelids overspilled.

He caught them with the finger he trailed down her cheek, his eyes darkening with emotion.

'Will you marry me?'

Her shock was so great that she could have sworn the earth actually tilted on its axis. She wondered if she had misheard him, wondered if he was making some sort of cruel joke, but the intentness of his expression warned her he was deadly serious.

'Why?' she croaked, sounding as though she had swallowed glass.

His smile stole the breath from her body, and for a few seconds she allowed herself to believe the impossible—that fairytales did exist and there could be a happy ending for them.

'Because I love you, *pedhaki mou*,' he murmured, his lips grazing her collarbone before trailing a path to her earlobe. 'Sometimes I think I've loved you for ever, but for a long time I fought it,' he admitted ruefully. 'From the day I first met you, valiantly trying to make excuses for your alcoholic boss, I was hooked.'

He rolled onto his side and scooped her up against his chest, his fingers threading through her hair as if he could not bear to be apart from her.

'At first I assumed it was simply physical,' he continued with frank honesty. 'I couldn't wait to get my hands on your lush body, and I told myself I would be content with a brief affair. But you crept under my guard, Kezia. I found that I wanted to be with you every minute of the day, as well as the night, and the passion we shared was only part of the joy I felt in your company. Why are you crying?' he asked softly as the tears slid unchecked down her face. 'I want you to be my wife, to live here with me in the house that we'll build…'

'To be the mother of your children?' Kezia finished for him, and she tore out of his arms and forced her stiff limbs into her clothes.

'At some point in the future I would hope we would consider starting a family,' he said, his voice cooler now, his expression no longer gentle, but tinged with suspicion and a degree of hurt that shredded her emotions. 'But not straight away, *agape mou*—I know how much you value your independence, and there's no reason why you shouldn't continue with your career for a few more years.'

'Nik, I can't,' she burst out, needing to say the words now, before her will-power deserted her. She pulled on her shoes and stood, staring down at his naked form. He looked like a Greek god, his skin gleaming like bronze, and already she could feel herself weakening.

'You can't what?' he demanded harshly, reaching for his clothes.

She had assumed he would start to dress, but instead he pulled a small velvet box from the pocket of his jeans and held it out to her.

'Before you say any more, this is for you. It's proof, if you need it, that I'm serious. I want to marry you, Kezia, despite the fact that you seem to view the idea as a fate worse than death,' he added sardonically.

With shaking fingers she flicked open the box to reveal a brilliant sapphire surrounded by diamonds that reflected the fire of the sun. Its beauty pierced her soul, and she bit back a sob of utter despair. 'I can't marry you,' she whispered as she snapped the box shut and thrust it at him. 'I'm sorry.'

He jumped to his feet then, and dragged his jeans over his hips before rounding on her. 'Why the hell not?' he growled savagely. '*Theos,* Kezia, I've spent most of my adult life determined to avoid matrimony. The irony of your rejection isn't lost on me,' he added darkly. 'It's Pemberton, isn't it?' he muttered, a nerve working in his cheek. 'You've never got over the fact that he married another woman. Are you still in love with him? Is that it? Or did he hurt you so badly that you're afraid to give your trust again?' His expression softened as he moved towards her, his hand outstretched, as if he was approaching a particularly nervous colt. 'I swear I'll never hurt you, *pedhaki mou.* I love you, and I know you feel something for me too. You just have to find the courage to look into your heart.'

Her heart was about to splinter into a thousand pieces, Kezia thought wildly as she jerked away from him and began to scramble down the steep path. He was right behind her, and she knew that if he caught her in his arms she would be lost. For his sake she had to deny her feelings for him.

'You're wrong, Nik,' she cried over her shoulder, slipping

and sliding down the dusty path. 'I don't love you and I never will. I don't want to marry you—do you hear?'

His blistering reply burned a hole in her heart that she knew would never heal, but a desperate glance revealed he had given up the chase and had stopped dead on the brow of the hill, as if he had been hewn from marble.

Later, Kezia could recollect little of her wild flight back to the villa, of throwing a few basic essentials into her case and changing into loose cotton trousers and a shirt that were comfortable to travel in.

In the sanctuary of her room a little of her sanity returned, bringing with it the temptation to tell Nik the real reason she had turned down his proposal. He had told her he loved her— not just with words but with his body, she realized, as she remembered the way he had made love to her with such reverence that her eyes had filled with tears. In return she had cruelly rejected him by denying that she loved him.

Surely she owed him the truth about her feelings for him? All she needed was courage, he'd told her. But where he was concerned she had none. She could not bear to see his face when she revealed that she would never be able to give him a child. Shock would turn to dismay, followed by undisguised relief that she had refused to become his wife. Even worse, he might feel a mixture of guilt and pity that she would find unbearable. He had nothing to feel guilty about. He'd made no secret of the fact that he was under considerable pressure to produce the next Niarchou heir, and her infertility was a problem that would eventually destroy their relationship.

In a torment of indecision she finally poured out the reason she had turned him down in a letter, giving details of the illness she had suffered as a teenager and the devastating consequences of her treatment. She kept it brief and unemotional.

hoping that he would simply accept that there was no future for them and move on with his life. She did not reveal that hers would be empty and utterly joyless without him.

For once the villa was quiet. Nik's parents had travelled to Athens, so that Yannis could attend the hospital, and they planned to stay overnight in the capital. Of Nik there was no sign. None of the staff had seen him that morning, one of the maids explained, unable to disguise her surprise when Kezia asked how she could get to the mainland. The boatman, Stavros took some persuading and only agreed to ferry her across the water when she assured him that Nik knew she was leaving.

As the boat chugged across the waves she turned and stared at Zathos until it disappeared from view, her eyes burning with tears that she finally let fall.

Otterbourne House basked in the early summer sunshine, its sandstone walls glowing mellow and warmly inviting. Kezia parked her Mini on the driveway and glanced up at the graceful pillars that stood on either side of the front door. She had fallen in love with the house with almost the same intensity with which she'd lost her heart to its owner, and the knowledge that this was her last visit tore at her already fragile emotions. At least she had Max, she consoled herself, her spirits lifting slightly at the thought of seeing the scruffy little terrier again.

She had arrived back at her flat the previous afternoon, after a nightmare journey from Greece, during which she had been forced to spend twelve hours at Athens airport, waiting for a cancellation. By the time she'd reached home she'd been mentally and physically drained, and had worked her way through a box of tissues as she poured out her heart to her sympathetic flatmate, Anna. And now she faced the pressing problem of searching for a new flat as well as another job. Anna had decided to move to the US for six months, to fulfil several lucrative modelling contracts.

There was no real reason for her to stay in the London area, Kezia brooded. She loved the countryside, although the exclusive area of Hertfordshire where Otterbourne was situated was out of her price bracket. And for the sake of her sanity she needed to live as far away from Nik as possible—Scotland seemed tempting, and maybe she would find a place with a garden for Max.

'I'm sure he sensed you were coming.' Nik's housekeeper, Mrs Jessop laughed when she opened the front door, and Max shot down the steps, barking excitedly as he leapt into Kezia's arms. 'He's been restless since you phoned this morning.'

'Oh, Max—did you miss me?' Kezia murmured as she hugged his wiry little body. 'I'll never leave you again, I promise.' The dog wagged its tail and bounded back into the hall, pausing in the doorway as if waiting for her to follow him.

'Why don't you wait in the study while I go and get his basket and lead?' Mrs Jessop invited.

It was a perfectly reasonable request, and Kezia forced herself to walk up the front steps, unable to explain her reluctance to enter the house that held so many memories of Nik.

'Would you like a cup of tea?'

'No, I have to leave as soon as possible. I'm flat-hunting,' she said apologetically as she pushed open the door of the study.

Max ran off after the housekeeper, leaving her alone in the sun-filled room that Nik had chosen as his office. Coming here had not been a good idea, she acknowledged as she fumbled in her bag for the letter she'd written to him and placed it on the desk. If she closed her eyes she could almost imagine he was here, his dark gaze glinting with the mixture of amusement and simmering sexual awareness she remembered so well, his voice deep and sensual to her ears.

'You seem to be making a habit of leaving letters for me.' The familiar drawl sounded from behind her and she whirled round, her eyes huge and shocked in her white face. 'Perhaps you should consider a career in the postal service?' Nik added sardonically, his expression unfathomable as he surveyed her.

'What are you doing here?' she whispered, sounding so indignant that his fury lessened a degree.

'I live here,' he reminded her laconically. 'I flew back on my private jet the minute I'd read the note you left for me on Zathos. Why are *you* here?' he demanded harshly.

'I came to deliver my resignation letter. You tore up the last one,' she reminded him huskily, unable to tear her eyes from him. In black tailored trousers and matching silk shirt he was so breathtaking that the pain in her chest intensified.

'I won't make the same mistake again,' he assured her coolly, and he strolled over to his desk and picked up the letter. 'In the circumstances, I think we can dispense with the formality of a month's notice, don't you? You're free to go whenever you like, *pedhaki mou.*'

The careless endearment, coupled with the faintly bored expression on his face, tore her apart. She had expected anger, but his indifference made her want to weep. So much for his declaration that he loved her, she thought bleakly. He certainly didn't appear to be heartbroken that they would never see one another again. But of course now he knew the secret she had kept from him throughout their relationship, he was no doubt relieved to be shot of her.

'I'll just collect Max and I'll be off,' she mumbled, dragging her eyes from him to stare at the carpet while she blinked back her tears.

Nik studied the dejected slump of her shoulders and fought the urge to drag her into his arms. She was fiercely proud, and would reject him out of hand if she thought he pitied her. Right now he was torn between the desire to shake some sense into her stubborn, obstinate body and kissing her senseless, but neither action would guarantee him the prize he was utterly determined to win.

'You can't take Max, I'm afraid,' he told her briskly. 'He's my dog and he belongs at Otterbourne.'

'But…you don't even like dogs,' Kezia said shakily. 'You once said Max looks like a floor mop, and he *isn't* yours—I found him.'

'And *I* paid a ridiculous price for him to that rogue farmer who realised I'd give him whatever he demanded.'

'You did that…for me?' A warm feeling crept around her heart at the realisation that even back then he must have cared for her. 'Then let me take him, Nik?' she pleaded. 'I love Max.'

'Lucky Max,' Nik snapped, his patience close to breaking point. 'There's only one way you can have him. If you marry me you can lay claim to all my worldly goods—including my dog.'

The flare of emotion in his eyes was too much, and she wrapped her arms around her body, as if she could somehow prevent herself from falling apart. 'You know why I can't,' she whispered. 'You're the last Niarchou; your family are depending on you to provide an heir.

'To hell with my family,' he swore savagely. 'They're important to me, yes,' he continued, when she stared at him in stunned silence, 'but not as important as the way I feel about you, Kezia *mou*. Between them my sisters have provided my parents with a dozen grandchildren. There's a whole future generation who will grow up and one day help run the company.'

'But I saw the way you were with your nieces and nephews, Nik,' she said brokenly. 'You love children, and nothing will convince me that you hadn't hoped to have a family of your own one day.'

'I won't lie to you,' he said gently, moving closer, so that she found herself backed up against his desk with nowhere to run. 'I'd blithely assumed that the gift of children would be granted to me in the same way that I've been blessed with so much else in my life. But a child isn't a foregone right. I didn't fall in love with you because I viewed you as a brood mare. I love you for your bravery and honesty, for the fact that you are utterly loyal and so generous that I feel humbled when I'm with you.' His voice cracked with emotion, his face working as he laid his heart bare, but it was the tremor of his hand as he gently smoothed her hair from her face that brought fresh tears to Kezia's eyes. 'You ended your engagement when your fiancé learned that you couldn't have children, didn't you?' he murmured softly.

She nodded. 'I wanted to tell you, but at first it didn't seem necessary. I assumed we would have a brief fling—sex without the complication of emotional involvement—but I was lost from the start,' she admitted sadly. 'I love you so much it scares me,' she whispered, one solitary tear sliding down her cheek. 'That's why I won't marry you, Nik. My infertility isn't something that can be cured, and I won't allow you to sacrifice your chance to have a family just because you feel sorry for me— What are you doing?' she cried fearfully, when he suddenly swung her into his arms and strode towards the door.

'I'd wondered if that was the reason you'd turned down my proposal,' he said, his tender smile taking her breath away. 'Or rather, I hoped,' he added huskily, as he relived the agony of her rejection and the pain he'd felt for her when he had read her letter.

It had taken less than a minute for him to accept that her inability to have children made no difference to his love for her. If anything he loved her more, he acknowledged silently as he glimpsed the uncertainty in her eyes, the vulnerability that made him ache with the need to protect and care for her for the rest of his life.

'You are my life, *pedhaki mou,*' he told her as he took the stairs at a steady pace and headed with implacable determination for his bedroom. 'You are the only woman I will ever marry, so you'd better get used to the idea.'

He dropped a tantalisingly brief kiss on her lips, shouldered the door and dropped her unceremoniously in the centre of the bed, his body instantly covering hers before she could escape. This time his kiss lasted longer, so sweetly evocative that her defences crumbled and she clung to him, unable to stem her tears.

'Who knows what the future holds?' he whispered as he trailed his lips over her damp cheeks. 'All I care is that we share it, side by side, the joys and the disappointments. We may even be blessed with a family.' He laid a finger against her lips as she shook her head. 'There are thousands of children in the world who need parents to love them.'

'You mean we could adopt?' The little flame of hope inside her blazed into life, and her smile was filled with the emotions she could no longer deny. 'I love you so much, Nik.'

Simple words that meant the world to him, he acknowledged, and he closed his eyes briefly and felt an unfamiliar stinging sensation behind his eyelids. He shrugged out of his clothes and dispensed with hers with hands that shook slightly, his body instantly hardening as he studied her voluptuous curves. His woman—for eternity, he vowed, as he reached for the small box on the bedside table, opened it, and took out the sapphire that glowed with the intense blue of the Aegean.

'Nik, are you sure?' Kezia whispered, the shadows not quite banished from her eyes as she stared down at the ring he had slipped onto her finger.

'I've never been more sure of anything in my life.'

The fierce intensity of his response dealt with the last of her fears, and she inhaled sharply as he trailed a sensuous path from her mouth to her breasts. They swelled in his hands, aching for his possession, and as he anointed one tight bud and then the other with his lips she rubbed her hips urgently against his and pleaded for him to make love to her.

'Nik!' She groaned her frustration when he moved over her, but held back from pushing the hard length of his arousal deep inside her.

'Not yet, *agape mou*,' he muttered hoarsely. 'Not until you've said the words I need to hear.'

'I love you,' she cried, moved to tears by the edge of uncertainty in his voice.

'And you'll marry me?' His control was slipping, and sweat beaded his brow as he stared down at her, his love for her blazing in his dark eyes.

'Yes.' She sighed her pleasure as he entered her, slow and deep, filling her. 'But only if you promise never to stop doing that.'

'You have my word, *agape mou*,' he vowed, and then there was nothing but sensation, soft murmurs of pleasure that built inexorably to a crescendo, and finally the whispered pledges of everlasting love.

EPILOGUE

'NIKOS ALWAYS SAID he'd build a house here.' Yannis laughed as he stared out over the sweeping gardens of the recently completed villa on Zathos to the sparkling sea beyond. 'Even as a small boy he knew what he wanted, and he was determined to get it.'

Kezia smiled at her father-in-law as she tucked a blanket around his knees. 'Are you warm enough?' she fussed, aware that the old man had grown frailer in the past year. 'The sun's not very hot this early in the spring.'

'He wanted you for his wife. I saw it in his eyes the first time he brought you here,' Yannis confided, his expression filled with genuine affection as he glanced at her, and then across the garden to his son.

Kezia followed his gaze, and felt the familiar softening of her heart as Nik strolled across the lawn. The child in his arms was eighteen months old, with the same glossy black hair and dark eyes as his father. The resemblance between them was uncanny, she thought, as she smiled at her son, but perhaps not entirely unexpected, when most Greek men shared similar characteristics.

The adoption agency had no details about little Theo's biological parents. He had been found, wrapped in a shawl, in the entrance of a hospital on the mainland, and her heart ached for the woman who had been driven by unknown circumstances to abandon her baby. Theo had spent the first nine months of his life with foster parents, but the moment she had cradled him in her arms Kezia had been overwhelmed with love for him. With the documentation finally complete, Theo was now officially a member of the Niarchou family, and she was looking forward to taking him to Otterbourne to meet Max, later in the summer.

'He's utterly fearless on that swing, you know,' Nik said proudly as he handed her their son and leaned down to kiss her with barely concealed desire. 'With any luck he'll have a nap this afternoon—like his grandfather,' he added when Yannis emitted a snore.

'We'll have an hour to ourselves,' Kezia murmured lightly. 'What would you like to do?'

'I'll give you three guesses,' he replied, the gleam in his eyes sending a quiver of excitement through her as she rocked her son to sleep.

Life couldn't get any more joyous than this, she thought dreamily. But a short while later Nik proved that it could!

A collection of three powerful, intense romances featuring sexy, wealthy Greek heroes

The Greek Millionaires' Seduction
Available 16th April 2010

The Greek Tycoons' Takeover
Available 21st May 2010

The Greeks' Bought Brides
Available 18th June 2010